DRIVE LIKE HELL

A NOVEL

Dallas Hudgens

SCRIBNER

New York   London   Toronto   Sydney

SCRIBNER
1230 Avenue of the Americas
New York, NY 10020

SCRIBNER and design are trademarks of
Macmillan Library Reference USA, Inc., used under license
by Simon & Schuster, the publisher of this work.

For information about special discounts for bulk purchases,
please contact Simon & Schuster Special Sales:
1-800-456-6798 or business@simonandschuster.com

Designed by Kyoko Watanabe
Text set in Life

Manufactured in the United States of America

1   3   5   7   9   10   8   6   4   2

Library of Congress Cataloging-in-Publication Data
Hudgens, Dallas, [date]
Drive like hell: a novel/Dallas Hudgens.
p. cm.
1. Young men—Fiction. 2. Georgia—Fiction. I. Title.
PS3608.U325D75 2005
813'.6—dc22
2004056576

ISBN 0-7432-5163-6

To Deborah

ACKNOWLEDGMENTS

With thanks to Joe Regal for his insight and unwavering belief, and to Brant Rumble for supporting this book and providing his editorial skill. I'm especially grateful for my friends Wendi Kaufman, Robyn Kirby Wright, Scott W. Berg, and Corrine Gormont, who provided help and encouragement from start to finish. Special thanks to Casey McKinney, Tom Jenks, and the Museum of Television and Radio's Jane Klain. I also want to acknowledge Paul Hemphill's *Wheels* as a resource on the history of stock car racing.

DRIVE LIKE HELL

I may not have spent much time with Lyndell Fulmer, or have known him the way that some people think a son ought to know a father, but I understood him.

"If you remember anything," he said, "let it be this. A real man eats pussy and drives a stick shift."

He told me this when I was ten years old. He was drinking Lem Motlow as we skimmed along a blacktop outside of town in his '66 Chevelle Super Sport. Three in the morning.

I was the one behind the wheel, perched up at the edge of the seat so I could reach the gas and the clutch, edging up to 50 in a 45. Lyndell was riding shotgun and doing his talking, most of it about driving, like how to downshift and work your heel and toe on the brakes and the accelerator at the same time.

He was lean and dark, with kick-ass sideburns and a junior Porter Wagoner pompadour. A Kool snagged in his teeth and the pint of Motlow between his legs, he fiddled with the radio dial, trying to find something worth listening to, all the while letting me drive as if I were Cale Yarborough.

He pointed to an oak tree up ahead of us, sitting off a bend in the road. "That's your entry point, right there," he said. "When you get to that tree, squeeze the brakes and cut the wheel. Don't jump on the gas again until you start to unwind."

"Unwind what?"

"The steering wheel," he said. "What else?"

"Well, what if I start spinning?"

"You ain't gonna spin. Jesus Christ, don't be so goddamn negative."

He leaned back and mulled over the situation. "Of course, if you do spin, remember to turn into it, not against it."

"Got it."

"All right. Good."

He dialed in a Charlie Rich song on the radio and turned it up nice and loud, so he could hear it over the screaming engine. The Silver Fox was singing about what goes on behind closed doors. Lyndell closed his eyes and started playing the dashboard like it was a baby grand. He didn't appear concerned in the least that I might wreck his car. I pointed the high beams right at the oak tree and prepared myself to brake and downshift.

> *My baby makes me proud, Lord don't she make me*
> *   proud.*
> *She never makes a scene by hanging all over me in a*
> *   crowd.*

Claudia, my mother, was disappointed in Charlie Rich. She thought he'd sold out and forsaken the hard-core, gut-bucket country shit that she really loved. Claudia stood firmly in the corner of folks like Hank and Lefty and Lester Flatt, Faron Young, Webb Pierce, and Hank Thompson. She liked the twang and the heartbreak and people talking about killing their lovers. Sounding too smooth never sat well with her. She never had much good to say about "Gentleman" Jim Reeves or Eddie Arnold. "There's no place more boring than the middle of the road," she'd say.

She and Lyndell had the radio playing in the kitchen one night. They were smoking and fretting over my older brother, Nick, who was in the midst of a twelve-month prison term on account of marijuana trafficking. They'd been to see him that afternoon, and they were talking about his lawyer and his upcoming parole hearing. That's when Charlie Rich came on the radio. He was singing about the most beautiful girl in the world, prompting Claudia to forget all about Nick.

"He used to be good," she said, "back when he sang real country music."

I was eating a bowl of Pet vanilla ice cream, and Lyndell was tapping out the beat to the music with his Zippo. He shrugged and frowned. "It's only a song, Claudia. Why can't you just relax and enjoy it?"

"Because," she said, "the more you listen to that stuff, the more of it they're gonna make."

She looked down at me. "Do you like this song?"

I shook my head. "I don't like any of that country stuff. They all sound like a bunch of hicks."

Claudia could always get sidetracked by music. It might have even meant more to her than cars meant to Lyndell. They each had their Saturday-night destinations. Lyndell's was the dirt track, where he'd change the tires on the Chevelle, slap a pair of magnetized number 7's to the doors, and race in the hobby stock class. Meanwhile, Claudia would be working over at the fish camp, dishing out hush puppies and slaw in the serving line until the house band called her onstage to sing her two songs: "I Can't Help It If I'm Still in Love With You" and "Just Someone I Used to Know."

She'd be wearing her Wranglers and straw cowboy hat, her thin, blonde hair pouring out the sides of it. She always waited for some fellow from the dance floor to give her a boost onto the stage, and then she'd drop her apron and take her spot behind the mike, calling out "one, two, three" in an unsure voice, like she wasn't going to pull it off. Then the Green Lake Gang would start up with their playing, and her voice would suddenly grow strong and run like cool water atop all of their twanging and banging. The men standing down front would stare up at her until their partners grabbed their shoulders and turned them back around to dance.

Claudia and Lyndell could have been one of those couples in a country duet, maybe something by Dolly and Porter, or Conway and Loretta. Verse one would have covered the early years, Claudia sixteen and living with a second cousin, just a quiet girl who'd been abandoned by her mother. Then Lyndell comes along, a good bit older, already been through one marriage and a stint in Korea, nursing a constant hangover while he fixes transmissions at a garage. He's got a glow that's not all whiskey, and Claudia falls for him. She turns up pregnant, they get married, and Nick is born. Life's sunnier than July.

Verse two would have to introduce the heartbreak; Lyndell drifting and drinking and fighting his demons, finally leaving and getting married to another woman. Claudia's all alone again, except for the kid. It ain't July anymore.

Verse three would provide the reconciliation, with Dolly doing the singing:

> *And then, eight years later, he called me out of the blue.*
> *He said, "Honey, I'm with this other woman, but I've*
>   *been thinking of you."*
> *He said, "I'm the water and you're the moon, and if I*
>   *can't see you soon,*
> *then I do believe my heart will turn to dust."*

That would have been a good ending right there, Dolly taking him back and then fading things out with a nice refrain about lovers under the moon. But Lyndell and Claudia's story still had a few more verses to go, and they really weren't all that song-worthy. Of course, I still had to be born. And then Lyndell would run back to his wife, who'd eventually find out about the fling that produced me. She'd shit a brick, divorce Lyndell, settle up for possession of his GTO, and then burn it right in front of his eyes for spite. Lyndell would drift for several years, until he heard about Nick being locked up. And that would bring him back again. He was no longer the dashingly drunk paramour. He was just a man who needed a place to stay. And so Claudia offered him the sofa.

I met Lyndell at two o'clock in the morning, when he slipped into my bedroom smelling of sweet liquor and cigarette smoke. I didn't know who he was. I only heard the floorboards creaking in the darkness, so I reached under the bed for my Rico Carty baseball bat. As soon as the tall, dark figure stepped into the strike zone, I took his ass to right field.

All the air rushed out of his body. He groaned, dropped to his knees, and fell onto his side. He looked like a wrestler who'd just been thrown from the ring. "My kidney," he whimpered. "Oh, God. I think my kidney's ruptured."

The hallway light came on and Claudia swept into the room, still tying her blue bathrobe. I was standing on the bed with the bat cocked behind my ear, and Lyndell was lying on his back with his hands covering the top of his head.

Claudia rushed over and grabbed the barrel of the bat. "Holy shit, Luke. Don't kill him. That's Lyndell. That's your father."

My heart slowed to a trot. I pulled the bat off my shoulder and tilted my head to get a better look. My body felt warm and tight all of the sudden, like someone had rolled me up inside a big, heavy rug.

Ever so slowly, Lyndell's hands parted. When he realized I had no intention of smacking him again, he swiped his hand across his chest. "That's the take sign," he said.

I dropped the bat on the bed. "You oughta try knocking. I thought somebody was breaking in."

Claudia helped him sit up. He groaned and touched his fingers to his side.

"Jesus, boy. You swing like Willie McCovey."

I hopped off the bed, dressed in my skivvies and socks. That's what Nick slept in, at least before he went to prison. He'd told me the socks were more important than pants—they took longer to put on in case you had to make a fast getaway.

"You're lucky I was choking up," I said.

Lyndell pushed himself to his feet. He was wearing his Wranglers, a blue T-shirt, and a gray Amoco jacket with his name stitched over the heart.

Claudia couldn't help but smile a little as Lyndell leaned against the wall, still hurting and doubled over from the blow. "So what's the word?" she asked. "Are you gonna live?"

"I think so." He laid his hand on his side again. "I might be pissing blood for a few days, but otherwise . . ."

"Well, what were you thinking, sneaking in here like that?" she asked.

He pointed my way. "I was gonna see if he wanted to take a ride."

"At this time of night?"

"Well, yeah. It's the best time. No cops. No traffic."

"Oh, Lord." She was smiling, though, and Lyndell was looking over her shoulder. He was smiling, too. He even gave me a wink.

The next night, I was ready to make a fast getaway, wearing my

Keds and my Toughskins under the covers. Lyndell was careful to knock. He stuck his head in the door and waved his hand for me to follow him.

We padded out of the house and climbed into the white Chevelle. It was long and low-slung, with a twin-bulge hood, a Muncie four-speed, and mag wheels. The front fenders were embossed with crossed flags and the words "Turbo Jet." I'd never been impressed much with cars before then, but this one got my attention. It was the smell as much as anything else, the cigarette smoke and the leather and the gasoline. It smelled like the place to be at two o'clock in the morning.

Lyndell coasted down the driveway so the engine wouldn't wake Claudia. He rolled halfway down the street and fired up the motor on the fly. *BA-WOOM, WOOM, WOOM, WOOM.* The big V-8 scared me. It felt like that engine was over us, under us, in front and behind us. I grabbed hold of the dashboard with both hands. Lyndell glanced over and smiled. I let go and tried to sit back like I wasn't all that impressed.

We didn't talk much at first. Lyndell drove toward town, playing with the radio as he steered us along the crooked roads, braking and downshifting and romping on the gas when it was needed. He drove faster than anybody I'd ever seen, and it took a while for me to relax and start to feel like the engine wasn't so much surrounding me as a part of me. It made me feel fast, strong, loud, and hard to break.

We lived forty miles north of Atlanta in a town called Green Lake. It hadn't even been a town before World War II, just an empty river valley. The Army Engineers drove in after the war and decided the valley would be the perfect spot for a huge dam to help water and electrify all the people in Atlanta. The result was Green Lake, a forty-thousand-acre pond, which had become, as I'd learned in social studies class, a "valuable water, power, and recreation resource." Or as Claudia used to say, "Take away the lake, and there goes the Dairy Queen and the Holiday Inn."

Lyndell wheeled the Chevelle past the Holiday Inn. It was a fairly impressive structure for Green Lake in 1973—a two-story job, all lit up, the parking lot filled with automobiles. Tom T. Hall was on the car radio, singing about heaven and how the water there tasted an awful lot like beer.

"Hmm." Lyndell slowed the car and eyed the hotel's lighted swimming pool. It shone like a bright, blue gem out in the middle of the parking lot. "I think me, you, and Claudia might need to come over here one night and take a dip in that thing."

We passed the Krystal, the Big Star, and the Dairy Queen. The buildings glowed under the spring moon, their neon signs still flickering long after closing. The bank's time-and-temp sign said it was 2:46 A.M. and 65 degrees.

Lyndell drove down to the end of the commercial strip and pulled into Wilson's Auto Supply, an old cinder-block eyesore. He pulled around back, cut the lights, and stepped out onto the gravel. He motioned for me to follow him.

"You ever seen one of these?"

We were standing in the shadows at the back door of Wilson's. Lyndell was holding up a greasy piece of metal.

I shook my head. "Uh-uh."

"It's a distributor cap," he said. "I need a new one for the car. You think you could get in under that door and get me one?" He pointed to the dog door that was cut into the bottom of the door frame. It was small, barely the size of a dachshund. I knew it would be a tight fit.

"I thought you worked at a garage. Can't you get one of those for free?"

"Well, I don't exactly have a job yet. I mean, hell, I just moved in with y'all yesterday." He crossed his arms and scratched at his chin. "I've got a line of credit here. Me and the owner go way back. We used to race together and everything, so he doesn't really mind me coming in and taking what I need."

"Wouldn't he give you some keys if he didn't mind you coming in?"

Lyndell scratched at his head and looked back over his shoulder. My questions were making him awfully itchy, but I kept asking them.

"You really raced together?"

Lyndell shrugged in a dodgy sort of way. "More like against each other. We don't get along too well."

"How come? Did you beat him?" I imagined Lyndell standing in the winner's circle with a big trophy.

"Sort of," Lyndell said. "He ran me into the wall one night when I was leading. Two laps to go in the feature race. Came up underneath me and hit my rear axle."

"And you still beat him?"

"Well, no. Not in the race, anyway. Hell, I couldn't even finish because my car was so busted up. But after it was over, I wrapped a tire iron in newspaper and went after him down in the pits. I got in a good head shot before they pulled me off him. Split his scalp wide open."

"That'd be a better story if you'd come back and won the race."

"Yeah, I know. Funny thing is, I met his wife a couple years later in this bar." He smiled and wolf whistled, remembering the occasion. "I got him back real good then."

We stood there staring at each other. "You mean you hit his wife in the head with a tire iron, too?"

He shook his head and scratched his shoulder. He wasn't used to telling his stories to kids.

He pointed to the dog door again. "So what do you think? Will you do it?"

I'd stolen some stuff before: candy bars and cinnamon toothpicks from Elmore's Five and Dime, and a Hot Wheels car from a kid's desk at school. I'd actually felt bad when the kid started crying about his toy car. Nevertheless, I wanted to impress Lyndell.

"You need anything else while I'm in there?"

Lyndell smiled. "Now that you mention it, I could use a new oil filter. But that's all. There's no need to get greedy."

I had to wiggle my ass a little to get my hips through the dog door. Lyndell helped me along with a shove. "In you go," he said.

The stockroom was windowless and pitch black. It smelled like mildew and grape soda. I switched on the flashlight Lyndell had given me and made my way up front. The caps and the filters were exactly where he'd said they would be. I pocketed the goods and scrambled back to the dog door. I felt like Colonel Hogan on one of his nighttime scouting missions outside the stalag.

Lyndell had said he would time me on his watch to see how fast I could get in and out. I slid the distributor cap, oil filter, and flashlight through the door and wormed my head and shoulders out into the cool night air. I looked up from the ground, still half in and half out of the store. "How long?" I asked.

Lyndell had already retrieved the goods. He was reading something off the back of the oil filter box. He glanced at his watch and shrugged. "About two minutes, eighteen."

"That's bullshit," I said.

His mouth dropped open in a gesture of mild shock. "Does Claudia know you talk like that?"

"She doesn't care. As long as it's not at school." Of course, that was a lie. But I figured if he was going to ask me to steal things, I might as well get something in return.

He nodded like the deal made sense. "All right. I was just checking. But don't go overboard. If you cuss all the time, people won't take you serious." He went back to reading the package.

"I counted in my head," I told him. "There's no way I was in there two minutes."

He didn't say anything, so I craned my neck and tried to look him straight in the eye. "You didn't really time me, did you?"

He sighed and jerked his thumb back over his shoulder in the direction of the empty road. "Well, I had to keep a look out." He walked over to the car and tossed the stuff into the open window. He turned my way again and waved his hand through the air. "Come on out of there."

I tried to slide the rest of the way through the door, but my ass was stuck again. This time I couldn't work it free.

"I can't."

"What do you mean, you can't?"

"I mean I'm stuck."

Lyndell grabbed my arms and started pulling. He pulled, and I wiggled. I tried holding my breath, blowing it all out, sucking in my stomach, tightening my butt, the whole nine yards.

"I can't move either way, now. I think my legs are falling asleep."

Lyndell stepped back and observed the situation. "Well, what the hell did you do, eat a T-bone steak while you were in there?"

He stood above me for a moment, thinking. He took a look at me and then the Chevelle. His eyes lingered on the car.

"If you leave me, I'll tell on you."

He pulled his Kools out of his jacket pocket and smiled. "You wouldn't rat out your old man, would you?"

"Does a hobby horse have a hickory dick?"

Lyndell laughed. "Hey, where'd you hear that one?"

"From Nick."

He shook his head, still smiling. "I bet you didn't know he heard it from me. Ain't that a kick in the ass?"

"It'd be a bigger kick if I wasn't stuck in this door."

"All right, then. Just hold your damn horses."

He went to the car and grabbed his tire iron from the trunk, then he walked back over and sized up the problem. The tire iron dangled at his side.

"I guess this guy, Wilson, hates to see you with one of those."

Lyndell gazed down and chuckled, then he squatted and went to work. By the time he'd finished hacking up the door, a good-size hunting dog could have scampered through the hole. I crawled right out, stood up, and brushed off my jeans.

Lyndell held the tire iron up in the air and grinned. "Now that's what you call an all-purpose tool."

We ended up on Green Lake Road that night. It was a crooked two-lane running along the banks of the lake. There were no other cars out, so Lyndell took it upon himself to double the speed limit. We were doing 90, the pine trees streaming past us like fence posts. Every now and then there'd be a break in the trees, and I'd catch a glimpse of the lake.

Lyndell plucked the cigarette lighter out of the ashtray and held the orange tip to a fresh stick. He glanced my way, smoke filling the air.

"You like cars?" he asked.

"They're all right."

"Well, you don't sound too committed."

"It's not like I can drive."

"Says who?"

"You ever heard of the police?"

Lyndell waved his hand through the air. "You don't need a damn license to be able to drive. I know plenty of drivers who don't have a license. Most of them can drive better than the people who do have one. Even when they're drunk."

He flung us around the curve, pressing me up against the door. He caught a little bit of the shoulder coming out. The tires thumped like we'd run over a squirrel. Lyndell dropped the Muncie into fourth and jumped on the gas again.

"Well, what else?" he asked. "What do you like to do?"

"I don't know."

"Well, you gotta like something."

"I don't like school, if that's what you're getting at."

"Shit, no," he said, "that's not what I'm getting at. I just mean for fun. If you've got a day to kill, what would you do with it?"

Only one thing came to mind. "I'd probably watch TV."

Lyndell smiled, nodded. "You get that from Claudia. I remember when we bought our first Emerson. Hell, I couldn't get her out from in front of it. She'd sit there all day with Nick in her arms, watching those soaps."

"She's still like that," I said.

"*General Hospital*?" he asked.

"Every day at three, watching those Quartermaines."

He laughed. "I never cared much for the soaps. I do like that *Love, American Style* show. That's a good one. That, and *Flip Wilson.*"

He asked what shows I liked best. I took him down the list, starting with the eight o'clock programs. *Gunsmoke, Bonanza, Mod Squad, Emergency!* I also made sure I mentioned *Georgia Championship Wrestling,* which conflicted with one of Claudia's favorites, *Hee Haw.* Sometimes, she'd blackmail me and force me to sing that "Gloom, Despair and Agony" song from *Hee Haw* just for the privilege of watching wrestling. For some reason, she got a kick out of hearing me sing it. I thought the whole thing bordered on psychological abuse.

"Who's your favorite wrestler?" Lyndell asked.

"I like Buddy Colt. Him and Mr. Wrestling Number Two."

"What about the Funk Brothers?"

"They're all right. They can do some damage."

Lyndell nodded. "That stuff's fake, you know."

"Yeah, I know. Claudia met one of those guys at the fish camp."

"Who? A wrestler?"

"Yeah. His name's Rowland, but he wrestles as Big Boy Brown. He's not on TV, though, so you wouldn't know him."

Lyndell frowned. He didn't speak for a moment, but he kept glancing over at me like he was hoping I'd say something.

"So is that her boyfriend?"

"Who, Rowland?"

"Rowland. Big Boy. Whatever the hell he goes by."

"Nah, Claudia only went out with him twice. She said he'd landed on his head one too many times."

Lyndell nodded. He was staring out over the hood again. "So I guess she meets a lot of men at the fish camp."

My heart gave my rib cage a little *tap-tap-tap,* just to let me know this might be a good time to play dumb.

"Not many," I lied.

He cast a suspicious glance in my direction. "Claudia's an awfully pretty woman," he said. "You might not have noticed that, seeing how she's your mother. But other men notice."

"Lee Gordon said she reminded him of a young Angie Dickinson."

"Who's that?"

"She was in that John Wayne picture, *Rio Bravo,* and the one with Burt Reynolds, *Sam Whiskey.*"

Lyndell shook his head. "Hell, I know who Angie Dickinson is. I mean, who the hell is Lee Gordon?"

"Oh, he's the manager at the Big Star. He plays that stand-up bass in the Green Lake Gang."

Lyndell was getting all puffed up, like he wanted to fight somebody. He was squeezing the steering wheel extra tight.

"I don't know him, but he's a damn idiot. She don't look a thing like Angie Dickinson, I can tell you that. She's got prettier hair than Angie Dickinson."

"You jealous or something?"

He snorted, but without a whole lot of conviction. "Hell, no, I'm not jealous. Me and Claudia have an understanding about these things. I just wanna make sure she doesn't get mixed up with the wrong guy."

"She said there's a lot of men who are lucky she's not a big singing star."

"Why's that?"

"Because she could sing some real mean songs about them."

Lyndell got quiet for a moment. He switched off the radio in an agitated way. Roger Miller, one of his all-time favorites, had been singing. Even Claudia liked Roger Miller. Hell, even I liked Roger Miller.

"Well, I sure hope she wasn't including me on that list," Lyndell said. "I might not be perfect, but I've always had her best interests at heart."

We never got around to swimming in the Holiday Inn's pool. Lyndell and Claudia were hardly ever together. Lyndell eventually found work at a garage. He had a habit of going in late and coming home even later. I don't believe Claudia ever saw much money from him, but she was always friendly enough toward him. They played gin sometimes in the evenings, Claudia whipping Lyndell's ass time and again while the radio played.

"Goddammit, this game ain't nothing but luck." Lyndell fired his hand down on the table after another futile effort. He turned in his chair, crossed his legs, and lit a cigarette.

Claudia smiled and winked at me. I'd been sitting there pretending to read one of my schoolbooks.

"Poor Lyndell," she said, "he's lost his touch."

Lyndell had his arms crossed. He was sulking and drawing the life out of his Kool.

"The thing is," she said to me, "he's the one who taught me to play this game. Taught me years ago, and now that I'm better than him, he doesn't like it much."

Claudia never stopped seeing other men while Lyndell was staying with us. Sometimes, on fish camp nights, she wouldn't come home until five in the morning. Lyndell would have stumbled in long before her, a quart of Schlitz in his hand, his face and clothes caked in the red powder from the dirt track. We'd fall asleep together on the sofa, watching the TV in the dark, James Brown's *Future Shock* and then the monster movies on channel 17. Lyndell was a big James Brown fan.

One Sunday, I woke up to Lyndell and Claudia arguing. It was the only time I ever heard them raise their voices at each other. Lyndell was back in Claudia's bedroom.

"You're just doing this to get back at me," he said. "It's nothing but spite."

I tiptoed down the hall and gazed through the crack in the doorway. Claudia was standing there wrapped in a towel, still wet from the shower. Lyndell stood in front of her, dressed in his racing clothes from the night before. Claudia flicked the towel with her thumb and let it fall to her feet. She stood there in front of him naked. I turned away as fast as I could.

"It's not spite," she said, her voice cool and measured. "It's called blowing your chance. And you blew it twice. So, take a look, Lyndell. Get your eyes full. Because all you're gonna have is a memory."

Lyndell didn't have anything else to say.

We kept up the late-night car rides. Lyndell would come in and wake me a couple times a week. At school, I would daydream about the Chevelle, the smell and the feel of the engine when it threw my head back against the seat. I drew pictures of it in my notebook. I pictured myself on the dirt track, behind the wheel, banging fenders on the last lap. Lyndell had taken me to the Green Lake Speedway to watch him race a couple of times. He'd set me up in the stands with a funnel cake and a Coke. He hadn't made the feature race on either occasion, but he hadn't wrecked, either. It was about the most fun I'd ever had. I realized that the only thing better than one loud, fast car was a whole bunch of them driving in circles together.

One of the best things about our car rides was hearing Lyndell tell stories about his own father, C.W. It was C.W. who had taught Lyndell to drive in his '39 Ford Coupe, the same car that C.W. used to run liquor down from north Georgia to Atlanta. Lyndell was barely twelve when he started driving that car.

"It's best to learn young," he said.

"Why's that?" I asked.

He thought for a moment, then shrugged. "Hell, I don't know. It just is."

Lyndell had all sorts of C.W. stories. C.W. winning illegal stock car races in cow pastures, outrunning the law, sharking people at pool and then fighting his way out of the bar with a cue stick. My favorite tale involved the time he was hauling ass through Buford after dropping off a load of whiskey. The deputy pulled him over and walked up to the window, whereupon C.W. presented him with a twenty-dollar bill. The deputy gave C.W. a puzzled look and said, "Goddamn, C.W. After all the times we've done this, you should know a speeding ticket only costs ten dollars." C.W. just nodded his head, one foot still riding the clutch and the other revving the motor. "I am fully aware," he said. "But seeing how I plan to be in a big hurry when I come back through here tonight, I'd like to go ahead and pay the other fine up front."

Lyndell had promised to let me drive the Chevelle before he moved out. When that time came, he drove us out to Green Lake Road this particular night, pulled onto the shoulder, and slid the stick into neutral. The moon was high and full and white as a marble. George Jones was singing "The Race Is On."

"I'm probably rushing things here a little," Lyndell said, "but it's now or fucking never."

I knew what he was getting at. "I'm ready."

He considered my face and my hands. "Are you scared?"

For some reason, I decided to be truthful. "A little bit."

He smiled and nodded. "That's good. A little fear is a good thing. It'll keep you alert. I guarantee you Richard Petty gets a little nervous before races."

He pressed in the cigarette lighter and waited for it to catch fire. He already had the Kool dangling from his lips.

"Are you planning to leave or something?" I asked.

He turned down the radio a little and pulled the cigarette out of his mouth. "It's kind of looking that way," he said. "Nick'll be out in a few months, and the racing season's almost over. Plus, I got an offer to work at this race shop up in Bristol."

"Does Claudia know?"

"Yeah, she knows. I think she'll be glad to have me gone."

He got a concerned look on his face. "Are you okay with it?"

I thought about my room, empty and dark, and how I didn't want to be there, how I could have spent every night like this. We sat there a moment longer. I kept waiting for him to open the door so we could switch sides, but he never made a move in that direction. He still had his hand draped over the wheel, staring out the windshield like he was trying to spot something up ahead of the high beams.

I asked him what he saw. He grunted and shook his head like he was trying to clear some things out of his mind. He pulled the Lem Motlow out from under the seat, unscrewed the cap, and took a pop.

"I was just thinking," he said. "You know, Claudia thought that maybe having me around would be good for you. She thought that maybe the reason Nick got into trouble was because I hadn't been around when he was growing up."

The lighter finally clicked, and he whipped it out and sparked his Kool with it.

"I don't think that's why Nick got into trouble," I said. "He told me it was because some guy turned state's evidence on him."

Lyndell smiled. "Yeah, I know all about that. I'm just talking about something different. What Claudia was hoping is that maybe I could teach you some things, maybe give you an idea of how a man should act, so you wouldn't get into any trouble yourself. She thought it might be a way for me to sort of make amends."

He studied my face. Something about it seemed to frighten him. He pulled back a little. "I didn't teach you a damn thing, did I?"

I dug really deep, hoping I could bail him out. I could tell it was important to him.

"A tire iron comes in pretty handy," I said. "That's one thing."

He laughed, but soon he was frowning. I started to worry he might change his mind about letting me drive.

"Don't worry," I said, "I'm not gonna get thrown in jail when I grow up. I only had detention seven times last year. This kid, Marty Atkins, got it twenty-three times. I heard Mr. Rogers, the principal, say that Marty was gonna make a good convict one day."

Lyndell sat there a while longer, squeezing the steering wheel. "There's something I want to tell you," he said.

"What's that?"

He had a real serious look on his face, like he was about to pass along some grave news. I couldn't imagine what it might be.

"It's about C.W.," he said. "It's about those stories I told you."

"What about them?"

"Well, they're all a bunch of shit, basically. I stole them from other people." He turned and blew his smoke out the side window. "Truth is, C.W. wasn't no character. He was just a drunk, an outlaw, a womanizer. Pretty much a sonuvabitch, really."

He looked at me and draped his arm across the back of the seat. His eyes were wide and remorseful.

"You know, he sent me out one time to set fire to a man's sugar sacks. It was another moonshiner, a mean-ass sonuvabitch who'd have just as soon gutted you as look at you. He'd short-changed C.W. on a run, and C.W. wanted to get back at him. I wasn't much older than you at the time, but I knew that sugar was something a moonshiner would kill over, especially this sonuvabitch. We were parked out in the middle of the woods, and it was late at night. I told C.W. I was scared. I told him I didn't want to do it. But he just looked at his car. He said, 'It's a long walk home, boy. A long walk.'"

I felt bad for Lyndell. At least he hadn't left me behind at the auto supply store.

He took another drink out of the bottle. He was getting near the bottom. "You know, I used to take Nick out like this. That was back before you were born." He squinted his eyes, thinking hard, trying to keep the history straight. "Actually, I guess we were in the process of making you. That's when me and Claudia had our second go-round. That's before she'd had enough of me."

"Did you ever let Nick drive?"

"Oh, yeah. Sure, I did. I had me a Plymouth back then. Nick must have been about your age." Lyndell whistled and shook his head. "Good Lord, he scared the shit out of me. Took this turn too fast and spun us around. We ended up in the front yard of this old shack with some sonuvabitch's mailbox lying on the hood of the car. The lights come on in the house, and then this man and woman step out onto the porch. I look over at Nick, and I'm expecting him to be scared to death. But that little rascal was already trying to get the car started. He fired up that sonuvabitch and lit off down the road with the mailbox still on the hood. He finally looked over at me, and he said, 'Lyndell, the mail service sure ain't what it used to be.'"

We both laughed. All I could see was Nick with his grown-up head and long hair, but a kid's body and a little leather motorcycle jacket.

"Now that story is the truth," Lyndell said. "That's the God's honest truth."

"It's a good one," I said.

He drank the last of the bourbon, reached out the side window and hooked the bottle over the top of the car. It bounced down the hill, finally clanking against some rocks near the lake's edge.

"I never did get around to telling Nick the truth about C.W.," he said. "I've been wondering if that might have done some good."

He gave me this aching look. A few years would have to pass before I could recognize someone casting out for a reassuring word. All I knew then was that he seemed to be waiting for me to say something. So I asked a question that I'd always wanted answered. It felt like as good a time as any to ask.

"Do you and Claudia love each other?"

He took a hard pull on his Kool and blew out the smoke. He watched the cloud rise as if it might hold the answer. "We do," he said. "It's just a complicated thing. It's not as simple as those songs Claudia likes, where somebody's always to blame for things going wrong."

He let out a sigh. The music was barely trickling from the dashboard, Glen Campbell singing "Wichita Lineman."

"You meet somebody," he said, "and then you fall in love with them because they give you something you ain't ever had before. But the mean part of love is that, after a while, you find yourself needing other things. So you go out looking for it from somebody else. Hell, everybody does it. They might say they don't, but they're full of shit. And the church folk, they're the worst of all about it."

He flicked his cigarette onto the road and rolled up the window.

"So, why do you keep coming back?"

It was almost like I'd pulled a gun on him. He drew back from me, and his face turned white as the moon. He stared off into the distance, searching for words.

"I don't know," he said. "It's like I was her first, and I can't help thinking I should have been the only one."

He looked at me again. "But I suppose I already had my chance at that. At least that's what Claudia says."

He left after that night. He went up to Bristol, Tennessee, and took the job working on engines at the race shop. Several years later, he married the daughter of the man who owned the racing team. They even had a baby girl together.

I was fifteen when Claudia told me all of this. She said she'd gotten the news from Carl Bettis, one of Lyndell's old racing buddies who worked at the Amoco.

"Can you even picture that?" she asked. "Lyndell Fulmer working a full-time job and keeping up a family? They say he's even quit drinking."

Truth is, I hadn't even thought about Lyndell for a couple of years. I meant no offense by it. He'd just become like an old, broken piece of furniture that you move out to the garage with every good intention of reclaiming one day. Problem is you end up setting something else in front of it, and then another thing, and another, and pretty soon you've forgotten all about that one chair.

Besides, I had other things on my mind just then, namely selling a nickel bag of pot at the 7-Eleven and getting my driver's license when the official date rolled around the coming spring. I was doing a little dealing of my own with Marty Atkins, trying to save money for a car that I could fix up to race at the speedway. Not that I was exactly on the fast track to ownership. My pot operation was small stakes, most of the inventory consisting of weed that I stole from Nick's house. Nick was on parole at the time, following a second round of incarceration over a measurable quantity of contraband. He was one misstep away from a twenty-year sentence.

"Are you mad at Lyndell?" I asked.

"Of course not," Claudia said. "You should never begrudge someone their happiness."

She looked like the saddest person in the world when she spoke those words.

I pushed my chair away from the kitchen table. I stood and watched Claudia. She was leaning against the door, looking down, fingering the frayed edges of her hat brim.

"All right," she said. "I'll probably be late tonight." And then she left.

The house was awfully quiet. I walked over to the sink and switched on the radio. It was already tuned to the country station. I didn't recognize the song that was playing, but it sounded sad, a pedal steel guitar driving slowly and plaintively across a bridge. I switched the radio back off, stopping the lyrics before they ever caught up to me. I can't say if it was about a man or a woman, happiness or despair, people leaving, returning, drinking, or dying. For all I know it might have been about love itself, how it can be a complicated and mean companion.

1

I turned sixteen on a Saturday, March of 1979. I woke early to a cool spring morning, the air bristling with the sharp smells of the season: the mulch and the fescue and the fig bush that always reminded me of spice cake. A hopeful gown of yellow light had settled over everything.

Claudia chauffeured me down to the DMV. The two of us were standing there when they unlocked and opened the doors. After a perfect score on the written portion, just as I'd expected, I was well on my way to duplicating that feat on the driving test. That's when the patrolman dicked me out of five points in the parallel parking trial, claiming I'd touched the rear pylon.

"You must be high," I said. "I wasn't even close to that thing."

He looked up from his little clipboard. "You wanna run that by me again," he said.

"Yeah, there's no way I hit that pylon."

He angled his flattop at me and started pointing with his fat little index finger. "For your information," he said, "I can fail your ass just for having a bad attitude."

"Well, why don't you have Ponch and Jon come out here and watch me do it again 'cause you just screwed me out of five points."

He nodded, really pleased with himself. "You keep talking like that," he said, "and you won't be driving for a long damn time."

We were standing at the rear bumper of Claudia's Mazda GLC. Claudia and I referred to it as the "Gross Little Car." Claudia coughed from where she was standing on the sidewalk. I got the message and backed down.

The next step was waiting in line to have my picture taken. I'd grown my hair out extra long for the occasion, had even practiced different types of scowls in front of the mirror. The act must have been working. The woman in line ahead of me turned and handed me a flyer for a Campus Crusade barbecue.

Once I'd had my picture snapped, I stepped into another line. This one moved so slow you'd have thought the people up front were getting haircuts. After all the waiting, I was severely underwhelmed when the patrolwoman sitting behind the desk handed me a flimsy piece of paper instead of a laminated license with my menacing mug on it.

"Is this all I get?"

The woman took a sip of her coffee and rolled her eyes like every idiot who came through the line asked the same question. "Permanent license is sent through the mail. Two weeks."

She looked over my shoulder while I was still standing there. "Next!"

Claudia tossed me the keys for the two-mile journey back to the house. That was my big reward. I tried to pass a cement truck on the main road into town, but the Mazda wasn't up to the task. I had to drop back in line and let the truck fart diesel fumes all over us while three other cars filed past us.

"We oughta drop your sewing machine into this thing. It'd probably run faster."

Claudia laughed. "What's the matter, did that little patrolman get under your skin?"

"He was a peckerhead. You give a guy like that a badge and a gun, it's bad news."

"Well, you're lucky he even gave you a license. You show up looking like Charles Manson and acting a smart-ass. What'd you expect?"

"I should've gotten a hundred on that test."

"Just relax," she said. "It's not like you get to drive faster or anything."

She switched on the radio and started fishing for music.

"Speaking of law enforcement," I said, "have you called the cops about the TV yet?"

She shook her head and held up her hand to shush me. She'd come across Willie singing "Red Headed Stranger."

"You know who stole it," I said. "Just call Wade Briggs and tell him to go pick up Reggie. You don't even have to press charges. Just tell Reggie to give back the TV."

She was pulling her hair into a ponytail, gazing into the vanity mirror at her eyes. "I'll be seeing Wade tonight at the fish camp. Maybe I'll say something."

Wade Briggs was Green Lake's newest deputy, as well as the latest lead picker and singer for the Green Lake Gang. Claudia had gotten to know him at the fish camp, where they traded verses on "Slipping Around" and "One by One." I saw no harm in asking the singing deputy to roust Claudia's deadbeat ex.

"Are you really gonna ask him?"

She let her hair fall and looked at me. "I just said I would, didn't I?"

"Yeah, but I can tell you don't mean it. You might feel bad about cutting Reggie loose, but that doesn't give him the right to come in and take our RCA. That's like stealing a cowboy's horse."

Willie was still singing.

> *Don't cross him, don't boss him*
> *He's wild in his sorrow.*

"I could get it back, you know."

Claudia batted her eyes nervously. "What are you talking about?"

"I mean, I know where Reggie's staying. I called that guy he knows at ABC Pawn. Reggie's been camped out over at the Fisherman's Cove Motel ever since you broke up with him. Seems he's back in the breaking-and-entering business again. He's been giving ABC a lot of business."

"Why'd he tell you that?"

"I put on my Robert Mitchum voice and told him I was GBI. I told him Reggie was in some deep shit, and if he didn't start singing, we were gonna shut his ass down and send him to Reidsville."

Claudia sighed and closed her eyes. "Oh, Lord."

I turned onto our street and drove past the little houses until I reached the chalky, white face of our own two-bedroom rambler. The house was starting to get that beat-down and gloomy look, like an old relative who sits around all day drinking and talking about his ailments; not a relative you want to spend a lot of time with, especially without a TV to drown out the complaining.

I climbed out of the car, and Claudia took the wheel. She had to get to her day job at the fabric store. She rolled down the window, and I leaned over to hear what she had to say.

"Now you listen to me," she said. "I don't want you taking this little investigation of yours any farther. Just let me talk to Wade tonight, and I'll see if he has any ideas."

"You won't do it."

"Quit saying that."

"I mean, damn, we missed *Rockford* and *Dallas* last night. That's no way to live."

She just shook her head, rolled up the window, and backed down the driveway. I stood there alone, under the gold sun, with my limp piece of paper blowing in the wind. I knew what I had to do.

Our landlady, Mrs. Dees, lived directly across the street from us. She was an elderly woman just shy of being a shut-in. She owned a white Ford Maverick and stowed the keys above the sun visor. I'd sort of borrowed her car a few times before, just to make runs to the 7-Eleven so I could sell weed and pick up frozen pizzas. I'd always returned the Maverick before she had noticed it was missing. On one occasion, I'd even topped off the tank for her—and that's when high-test was pushing a buck sixty a gallon.

I peeked through Mrs. Dees's living room window to make sure that she was watching her Saturday-morning wrestling, and then I climbed in the Maverick, coasted down the street, and started the engine on the fly. The block inside was almost as feeble as the GLCs. We were in the dark age of economy cars and oil embargoes. It was not a great time to get your driver's license or steal a car. And, sadly, this had all come about while our former governor, Mr. Jimmy Carter, was occupying the White House.

The Maverick had a slush box, so there was no stick to slide around. It didn't really feel like driving at all. It was just going somewhere, getting from *A* to *B*. I kept it slow and steady, right at the speed limit, steering through town, across the railroad tracks, and beyond the city limits toward Nick's place.

Nick was renting an old tenant's house in those days, a two-bedroom nest that had once been part of the Van Earl chicken farm. He shared the place with a fellow named Dewey, who worked mainte- nance down at the hydroelectric plant. Dewey played drums in Nick's band and also bummed lots of rides from Nick, since he'd lost his driver's license for three months due to excessive DUI arrests. Dewey was a funny guy who loved watching TV almost as much as I did. As a tribute to his favorite show, he stowed his weed in the sleeve of a *Hawaii Five-O* record album.

Nobody was home when I got there, which was fine with me, as it only served to make the task at hand that much easier. I lifted a win- dow and climbed inside.

The living room smelled like stale beer and cigarettes. The furniture was on the spartan side, just a tattered green sofa, a busted recliner, some Coca-Cola TV trays, and Dewey's white-pearl Ludwig Classic drum kit. Nick's gold Les Paul stood propped in a corner, right beside his Sun amp. Posters and album covers cluttered the walls, mostly Nick's blues heroes: Son House and Robert Johnson, a Honeyboy and two Sonny Boys and a pair of Blind Willies. Their expressions were solemn, faces gaunt, guitars held close to their sides as if they were next of kin.

Jimi Hendrix had his own wall, set apart from the bluesmen, right above the TV and the tinfoil vines climbing out of the rabbit ears. Gaz- ing at Jimi, I noticed a recent addition to the decor: a pair of blue panties draped over a corner of the TV set. I couldn't help standing there for a moment to take it all in. The place always gave me this big, happy rush of recognition, like I was seeing my own future.

I found Nick's golf bag tilted against the wall in his bedroom. The fat leather holster was his office. He kept most of the pot in there, along with his cash, a ski mask, and his "shooting wedge," which is what he called his Daisy .22 BB pistol. It looked enough like a genuine damage- imparting weapon. I stuffed it along with the ski mask into the front of my jeans, grabbed a couple of nickel bags I didn't think Nick would miss, and headed out the way I'd come in.

Reggie was the youngest guy I'd seen Claudia date. He was probably in his late twenties, whip thin with long, dark hair, a scraggly beard, and cowboy boots. Claudia was big into the Outlaws in those days: Willie, Waylon, Kris, and that bunch. She liked Willie best, though she thought that Kristofferson held his own in the songwriting department. Reggie was no musician, but he had the outlaw look going for him. Plus, he could dance a little. That was enough to land him three months in Claudia's life.

Reggie proved to be quite the delicate outlaw, though. He suffered from vertigo, which rendered him a first-story operator. Trying to stretch himself, he'd taken a couple of nasty tumbles, one from a second-story window with a pillowcase full of loot tucked under his arm. That one left him with a severe concussion. The doctors thought it had impaired his memory, but they hadn't known Reggie before the accident. After some jail time, he tried to go legit as a short-order cook at Waffle House, but he couldn't keep the orders straight. *Scattered, smothered, covered*— the poor sonuvabitch would nearly have a nervous breakdown if you said one of those words around him.

Claudia had given Reggie his walking papers soon after hearing the news about Lyndell. Reggie was despondent. He'd just lost another cooking job, this one at the Ham 'n Egg Kitchen, a step down from the Waffle House to begin with. He showed up at our place one night at 2 A.M., crying on the front stoop and asking Claudia to take him back. She woke me up and asked me what she should do.

"Jesus Christ, call the cops. He's out of his fucking gourd."

"I don't think I've ever made anyone cry in my whole life," she said.

Reggie finally left. But he returned the next day when we were gone. He busted a window, climbed in, and took our nineteen-inch RCA ColorTrak. True to form, he left behind his Levi's jacket, probably after he'd wrapped it around his hand to break the window.

I tried to talk Claudia into calling the cops as soon as she came in from work, but she just sat there at the kitchen table wringing her hands.

I held out the phone receiver, but she wouldn't take it from me.

"Why won't you call?" I asked.

She shrugged. "I don't know. I just keep thinking about him crying."

She averaged about 3.2 boyfriends a year, and she was usually the one who applied the brakes, so I couldn't understand what had gotten into her all of the sudden.

*   *   *

The pawnshop owner had passed along Reggie's room number at the Fisherman's Cove. I slid Nick's ski mask over my face and knocked hard on the door of 212. I could hear the TV playing the Saturday-morning wrestling on channel 17. The announcer, Gordon Solie, was breathless: *"And here come the Freebirds! They've jumped Kevin Sullivan for the thousandth time!"*

The TV died. The only sound in the air was the birds chirping in the trees down near the lake. I banged on the door again, this time with the butt of Nick's BB pistol.

"Open the fuck up! It's the GBI!"

My voice had a whiskey-and-cigarettes edge to it. James Coburn with a hangover. I'd tried to get it that way smoking a fat one on the drive over. Now my head felt light as a balloon. I almost started laughing.

The chain rattled from the other side, and the door opened a crack. Reggie peeked out through the narrow shaft of darkness.

"Did you say GBI?"

I didn't wait for his brain to click into gear. I kicked the shit out of the door and went in after him. I threw my forearm into his chest, knocking him back onto the bed. I whipped out the pistol and aimed it right at his melon.

Reggie was shaking. He held his hands up in front of his face and started pleading with me. "Oh, Jesus. Don't kill me. Please, don't kill me. I don't wanna die." His legs were quaking like he was having a seizure.

"Shut up and be still!"

I reached back and slammed the door. The room smelled like fried chicken and wet carpet. It was littered with pilfered goods: three TVs in one corner, a pile of car stereos in another. He even had a stack of toasters on the dresser.

"You planning on making some toast?"

Reggie gazed over at the dresser. "I could, if you'd like." His voice was high and sincere, just like a choirboy's.

Suddenly, he looked down in shame. "Of course, I don't have any bread right now."

"Shut the fuck up!" I swung the gun back in his direction. He covered his face again and hiked up his legs like a dog playing dead.

"You're lucky I don't stick your goddamn hand in one of these things." I held up one of the toasters in a sinister way. Now, I was just showing off. I couldn't help myself.

I checked out the TVs. None of them was ours, but I did spot a nice Sony Trinitron: a twenty-three-inch model with a remote. It was a major step up from the RCA. I walked back over to Reggie. He was still splayed across the bed in his jeans and tank top, too scared to move.

"I'm looking for a nineteen-inch RCA."

He lowered his hands just a little. "I had one," he said, "but not anymore." He pointed to the stash in the corner. "You're welcome to one of those, if you'd like."

I considered the Trinitron again. A remote control was not to be taken lightly in those days. When I turned back to Reggie, he appeared to be studying me.

"Do I know you?" he asked.

I pressed the gun right up to his forehead. Reggie bunched up the muscles in his face until it looked like he was trying to pass a kidney stone.

"You don't wanna know me, motherfucker. I'm bad fucking news."

"Are you really GBI?" he asked.

"I told you I was, didn't I?"

"Well, why are you wearing a mask?"

"Because I like to wear a goddamn mask! You got a problem with that?" I burrowed the gun into his skull.

"No, sir. It's a pretty mask."

"All right, then." I stepped back and plotted my escape. There was no way I could carry the Sony without using both arms. So I wanted to make sure that Reggie was too scared to try anything once I'd slipped the shooting wedge back into my jeans.

"Let me ask you something," I said.

"Okay."

"Do you believe in Jesus?"

Reggie nodded. All of the color had run out of his face. A faint, animal whimper slipped from between his lips.

"You ready to meet him?"

A sob burst out of him, but he caught himself as best he could. He clamped his hand over his mouth and tried to get his shit together.

"Not right now," he said. "Oh, Lord, I'm not ready."

"Why's that?"

He thought long and hard on the matter. His legs began to shake again. When he finally answered, he sounded unsure of himself.

"Because I wanna do better?"

"You're goddamn right, you do. And does that mean no more stealing TVs?"

"It sure does."

"What about those car stereos?"

"I'll put them all back, if you'd like."

"And the toasters?"

"I don't even like toast." He wiped the tears from his eyes and smiled.

"Then I think we've got this settled. Now what I want you to do is turn over and lie facedown. Once you've done that, I want you to start singing 'Blessed Assurance,' and don't get up until you've finished all three verses. Do you think you can handle that?"

"I sure can."

"Roll on over, then." I waggled the pistol like I was giving a command to a retriever, and Reggie eagerly complied. He started singing with conviction. I could tell he meant every word of it. I stuffed the pistol in the back of my jeans, grabbed the Trinitron, and made haste for the Maverick. Blessed assurance, the Sony was mine.

I couldn't see Mrs. Dees missing her car right away. Plus, Claudia wouldn't be back from working until late in the afternoon. So I decided to take a little drive around the lake. It made sense at the time. I'd just smoked my second joint of the morning. I had a license, flimsy though it might have been. The ink was dry, and the sun climbed ever higher. I didn't need any more excuses than that.

I drove over to my and Lyndell's old stomping grounds on Green Lake Road. It just felt like the natural thing to do, like a dog returning to his favorite pissing spot. I'd been on that road hundreds of times since Lyndell had let me drive it, riding shotgun with Claudia, Nick, or one of my friends. It was still familiar to me: the curves and dips and potholes and the one long, quarter-mile run. I could have driven that road with my eyes closed.

Of course, the Maverick felt nothing like the Chevelle. It was slug-gish on the straights and squirrely in the curves. But I soon found myself in a groove, just driving and thinking and listening to the radio in case something good came on. The day was rebounding. The sun was still high, casting its net over the sailboats on the lake.

I braked for a curve, then stepped on the gas, unwinding, heading into a straight patch, my thoughts wandering ever farther down the road, to the day when I'd be driving my own car and heading for the track on a Saturday night. I could even see a new address for myself. It just hit me, all of the sudden—a trailer near the water, like Rockford's. I'd never thought about it before, but he had the perfect setup, living there in the restaurant parking lot with surf-fishing out his back door. It was everything you needed, and all within a few steps. Food. Fishing. A place to park your wheels. Those television writers were brilliant. All I had to do was figure out how I might swing that sort of arrangement. Selling weed, like Nick, maybe. People coming and going from my place, always having a party. There'd be music playing and a pair of blue panties hanging on the corner of the television.

I don't think I could have been much happier, just driving and day-dreaming and considering the notion of another joint. The only thing wrong at the moment was the music. WPND, the Green Lake rock sta-tion, was in the midst of a Foghat superset. But there was hope on that front as well, seeing how the DJ had promised to play the Stones next. I had this feeling it was going to be something good, maybe from *Exile on Main Street*.

And then I saw the blue light in the rearview mirror. My heart snapped like a big rubber band. I looked for somewhere to go, a street to turn down, or a cave to drive into, but the road wasn't offering any of those options. The wide, sparkling lake sat off to my right side and a thick strand of pines to my left.

Even in my panic, there was no mistaking the long face behind the police car's windshield. It belonged to the singing deputy, Wade Briggs.

I was practically standing on the gas when Wade pulled alongside me in his Crown Vic. I checked the speedometer and observed the needle to be just under the 70-mile-per-hour line. It was a sad com-mentary on the state of automobiles in those days.

The sun shone across Wade's rake-shell face. His hair was dark and wavy, and his blue eyes gazed solemnly from cavelike sockets. He waved for me to pull over, doing a double-take in the process. His face lit up with recognition, and then he mouthed my name as if it were a question.

I tried not to look at him. I just kept on driving, hoping that some sort of plan might take root in my skull. That wasn't happening, though, thanks to my overindulgence in Nick's product line. And the situation quickly took a turn for the worse. Panicked, stoned, and distracted, I was a little slow reacting to a bend in the road. The tires caught the shoulder. Before I could correct the car's path, it was *rat-tat-tat*ting its way down the bank of the lake, headed straight for the drink. I slammed on the brakes, but they were fighting a losing battle against momentum, mud, and pine straw. I was bracing for splashdown when the fat trunk of a water oak intervened. Next thing I knew, my head was hurting real bad.

"Luke Fulmer? Is that you?"

Wade had opened the car door. His big head floated above me, his eyes studying my forehead with some measure of concern.

I was sprawled across the front seat, trying to pull Wade's face into sharper focus. My eyes were swimming in murky water, and I couldn't break the surface. The car was quiet, except for the radio. Of course, it wasn't the Stones. The Eagles were singing "Life in the Fast Lane." I hated that song. Those fucking lying DJs. I reached over and turned it off.

Suddenly, I could hear the water lapping at the shore, and I knew I had better start explaining some things to Wade.

"Mrs. Dees asked me to put some gas in the car for her."

That was the best I could come up with under the circumstances.

"Mrs. Dees reported her car stolen about an hour ago, Luke."

I stared down at the wheel.

Wade patted me on the shoulder in a kind way, just before something on the floorboard caught his eye. He reached down and grabbed the two nickel bags, one of which had been severely depleted. He held them up in the air and considered me as though he were expecting some sort of explanation.

I dug as deep as I could. "Mrs. Dees doesn't look like the type, does she?"

Wade sighed and stuffed the bags in his pants pocket. "Is there anything else you need to tell me?"

"There's a TV in the trunk," I said. "It might be stolen."

Wade nodded and gazed out the rear window. He had his arm draped across the steering wheel, and he seemed to be considering his options for handling the matter. I was still lying there, staring at the car's ceiling.

"Luke, do you know how serious this is?"

"I'm guessing it's pretty serious."

"You're damn right it is." He'd only raised his voice a little, but it felt like an ice pick stabbing my brain. I grabbed my temples, but that only made things worse.

"You've got auto theft, possession of contraband, possession of stolen property, not to mention evading an officer." He ticked off the offenses on the fingers of his hand. The only thing left was a thumb.

That's when I remembered the pistol. I slid it out of my jeans and handed it to him.

"Good Lord, Luke. What were you thinking?"

My mouth had gone dry. I licked my lips and tried to explain. "It's just a BB gun. I was trying to get our TV back."

I blinked hard, but Wade's head just wouldn't be still. It was hovering over me, bobbing and weaving like a bumblebee. All of that motion kept launching these big waves of nausea across my stomach.

"I don't know what to do," he said. "Claudia's gonna be broken up about this. She just doesn't deserve to be put through such an ordeal."

I held up my hand and laid it on Wade's cool forehead. "Could you be still?" I asked. "You're moving all over the damn place."

Wade leaned in close and looked right into my eyes. "I think you might have a concussion," he said. "I better call an ambulance."

I finally gave up on trying to look at anything. I shut my eyes and let myself drift, the water from the lake sweeping over me, luring me down into the dark where the big catfish swam, slapping their whiskers against my arms and my face. I was sinking, clutching my TV, trying to forget what went wrong.

2

Mrs. Dees's daughter wanted to press full charges against me for taking the Maverick. She even threatened to have us evicted from the house. But Claudia took a walk across the street and spoke to Mrs. Dees herself. The old lady said she understood, that she'd had a couple boys of her own who'd caused her some trouble, though nothing as bad as stealing a car. That comment sort of pissed Claudia off, but she bit her tongue and worked out a deal. Mrs. Dees agreed not to press charges if I would pay for the $600 worth of repair work to "Millie," which is what she called the Maverick.

Wade Briggs had been kind enough to take care of the marijuana and the BB pistol while I was passed out on the front seat of the Maverick. That left me facing one count each of possessing stolen property, evading an officer, and driving in a reckless manner. Wade told Claudia that I needed to face some consequences. Naturally, she agreed with him. Despite the trouble I'd caused her, I think she enjoyed having an excuse to get to know Wade a little better.

The charges bought me a date with one Judge Dot Knox at the Green Lake County Justice and Administration Building. I never expected the judge would be a woman, and it eased my fears when I first laid eyes on her. She was slight, middle-aged, with short, graying hair and spectacles. At first glance, it would have been easy to picture her baking cookies in a TV commercial.

Claudia and I met Knox in her office. She sat behind a huge desk with her nose stuck in a file that had my name on it. She didn't even bother to say "hello" or "eat shit" when we walked in.

"When did you turn sixteen, Luke Fulmer?" She clipped off her words in a sharp manner that belied her gracious appearance, and she refused to look up at me.

"March seventeenth," I answered.

"And you just couldn't wait to get out on the road and endanger the lives of others?"

I knew better than to touch that one.

"Do you think you're special, Mr. Fulmer? Do you think you deserve privileges others are not afforded?"

"No, ma'am."

"Well, based on your record, I'd say that you pretty much believe you can do whatever you want. Steal a car. Steal a TV. Drive like hell."

"Actually, ma'am, I didn't know the TV was stolen."

She peered over the tops of her reading specs, allowing me a glimpse of her eyes. Slate gray, like the bars on prison cells. I knew right then and there that the woman was not planning to bake me any cookies.

She wagged a bony finger at me. "Don't you *ma'am* me, Mr. Fulmer. If you think you can win me over by saying *ma'am,* you are dead wrong. When was the last time you even said *ma'am*? I bet you can't remember."

I shook my head and gazed down at my work boots. They looked stupid with the baggy suit that I was wearing. It was a gray pinstripe number, a hand-me-down from Nick. He'd worn it during his first drug-trafficking trial. So far, it was 0-and-1 against the criminal justice system.

"I bet you never even say it to your mother, do you?"

Claudia was standing beside me. She shook her head, hanging me out to dry.

"Mrs. Fulmer," the judge said, "will you allow me to be blunt with your son?"

Claudia nodded firmly, the way that people nod during a hard-preached church sermon. She was wearing a navy suit, tailored close to her body. She looked smart in it, maybe a little too smart, as I saw it. She was starting to act like one of Knox's prosecutors.

"I'm going to tell it to him like it is," Knox said. "He's not going to like it much, and you might not like it either."

"That's okay, Judge. You say whatever you feel is necessary."

Knox cast her gaze my way. She'd taken off her glasses and was holding them up like they were an important piece of evidence.

"Do you know what recidivism is?"

I shook my head again. I'd just about decided she wasn't going to ask me any questions that I could answer in the affirmative.

"It's when I get to know somebody on a first-name basis. Because they keep committing crimes, usually the same ones, over and over again. It used to surprise me. Somebody would come in here, say a young man like yourself, first offense, something that was forgivable. So I'd pop his hand and send him on his merry way, thinking he'd learned his lesson. And then, not two months later, he'd be back in this room again. Now, I'm not against giving second, or even third, chances. But let me tell you something, friend. If I ever see you in here again, then you better bring your damn toothbrush and a clean pair of underwear. Because your little fanny's going straight to the youth correctional institute in Alto, Georgia. And if you think I'm bluffing, just try me."

Her voice had gotten loud by the end. I was still having headaches from the concussion. Plus, I hadn't smoked any dope that morning. My heart was flapping around like a bream in a bucket. She'd succeded in getting my attention.

I tried to appear chastised. Gazing downward, my eyes landed on the nameplate atop the judge's desk. I suddenly realized the similarity between the name Dot Knox and Don Knotts.

Knox turned to Claudia again. "Mrs. Fulmer, seventy-five percent of the kids in juvenile hall are repeat offenders. And that's my main concern. Stopping this kind of behavior before a pattern develops. That's what I mean by recidivism."

Claudia frowned. "Well, I'm afraid that might run in our family, Judge."

"I've heard about your other son," Knox said. "But that doesn't mean we can't nip it in the bud with this one. And from what I've seen, the best way to do that is with some hard-nosed discipline. That's why I'd have no qualms whatsoever about sending him to Alto for twelve months. I'd start him off in the ninety-day boot camp program. I think it'd do him a world of good."

I looked at Claudia, hoping she'd protest on my behalf. But she appeared to be about as scared as I was. I don't believe she blinked a single time while I was staring at her.

"Tell me, Mrs. Fulmer. Does your son have a job? Any chores or duties around the house?"

"No, ma'am," Claudia said.

"Well, that would be a good start," Knox said. "And then I'd take away the TV. It's a drug, just like the marijuana, cocaine, and heroin."

"He does watch too much of it," Claudia said. "First thing he does when he gets home from school is turn it on. He'd stare at a test pattern if there was nothing else on."

I began to wonder if Claudia was trying to make everything worse. I tried to protest, but Knox cut me off.

"Then get that idiot box out of the house," she said.

"It's already gone," Claudia said, "and I don't plan on replacing it."

I felt like a wrestler who'd been double-crossed by his tag team partner. She might as well have picked up a chair and laid it across the back of my head. I wanted to remind Claudia that she was the one who'd gotten me hooked on the "idiot box" in the first place. And she needed it as much as me. She had a rock-bottom habit of her own with those soaps. While I'd gone cold turkey, she'd been watching *General Hospital* on the back-room TV at the fabric store.

Knox finally dealt the punishment: one-year probation and a five-thousand-word essay on the importance of traffic laws.

"You might want to buy a dictionary, Mr. Fulmer."

She offered a final warning. There would be no more chances to prove myself both willing and able to abide by the laws of Green Lake County.

"I can assure you of one thing," she said. "The correctional youth facility is not an enjoyable place."

She closed my file and set it on her desk. No mention of traffic school, or picking up trash along the highway. I thought I'd slipped the noose.

Then she brought down the big hammer of injustice.

"Six months suspended license."

She'd spun a masterful web, crippling me with the threat of prison time and then finishing me off with the license maneuver. My knees buckled like she'd just tossed me a nasty slider. I almost doubled over.

I had to reach out with my hand and brace myself on the front edge of the desk.

Claudia and Knox considered me with narrowed eyes. Knox held out her hand and waited for me to turn over the license. I just stood there, paralyzed. I'd only received the laminated copy the day before. The photo had turned out even better than I'd imagined: long hair, eyes ablaze.

Claudia tapped me on the shoulder. Her expression was urgent. "Well, go on," she said. "Hand it over."

With shaky hands I fished the license out of my wallet, took one last admiring look at my bad-ass head of hair (I'd had to get it cut short for the court date), and laid the plastic into the clutches of Judge Knox. It was like having to pluck my own heart out of my chest, a frigid wave of sorrow rushing in to fill up the empty space.

And Knox wasn't even finished. She reached into her drawer and pulled out the largest pair of scissors I'd ever seen. She could have cut off my dick with those things. Instead, she applied them to my license. She halved and quartered it like a bell pepper. She sprinkled the remains in her wastebasket. The pieces fluttered down into the dark canister like a sad little bale of confetti.

As soon as we'd stepped out into the sunlight, I loosened the knot on my tie and fell back against the rough, unforgiving walls of the courthouse. Claudia immediately slapped me upside the head. It was way out of character for her to be upset like that.

"You fix that tie right now," she said.

"Why?"

"Because I'm mad at you, that's why."

I tightened the noose again. It was navy blue with little red profiles of Chief Noc-A-Homa, the Atlanta Braves' mascot, on it. Evidently, Lyndell had bought it years ago when he needed a tie for a funeral. Between the tie, the boots, and the masking-taped pants, I figured my haberdashery had done little to swell Knox's opinion of me.

"What the hell are you so mad about?" I asked. "You stabbed me in the back in there. I'm lucky she didn't just go ahead and send me to Alto."

Claudia snorted. "You have got to be kidding me. I was trying to save your ass in there."

"How? By telling her I'm lazy, that all I do is watch TV and act disrespectful? Jesus, you were eating right out of her hands."

She eased up a little. "Well, I didn't know what to say."

"Didn't you notice me? I wasn't saying anything at all. That's what Nick told me to do. He said, 'Never incriminate yourself.'"

Claudia leaned back against the wall beside me. A breeze kicked up and beat a long wave of hair across her face. An older man in a gray jacket was climbing the stairs in front of us. He let his eyes walk up and down her body, not even trying to hide it.

All of the sudden, I felt sorry for her. She looked tired, defeated, and confused, like she was bobbing around waterlogged in the same boat as me. She fumbled in her purse for a Virginia Slims Menthol and fired it up with her Bic lighter.

"I'm sorry you lost your license, Luke. I truly am." She pulled her hair off her face and blew out a mouthful of smoke. "I wish I could have thought of something to say."

I reached out and patted her shoulder. This was no small gesture, seeing how neither of us was much for grand displays of affection. Hugs and kisses had never been Claudia's thing, at least not the mothering kind. But I had never doubted that she loved me.

"It wasn't your fault," I told her. "And I hope that judge crashes her fucking broom on the way home."

Claudia smiled a little. "She really was a witch, wasn't she?"

I imagined myself dragging a key along the judge's car. I had her figured for a LeBaron owner. Either that, or an AMC Pacer. Something boxy and slow, that's for sure. I hated the woman. But then, at the same time, I had this swelling desire to make her think highly of me. I wanted to run back into her office and tell her that she had gotten me all wrong. Hell, I wasn't a recidivist. I wasn't a criminal at all. And I sure wasn't coming back to her office with my toothbrush and underwear.

The sky was just as bright and glorious as it had been on the day I'd wrecked the Maverick. I tried to focus my thoughts elsewhere, but there was no ignoring the obvious.

"Six whole months without a license," I said.

Claudia sighed. "It'll go by fast. You're getting older, anyway. Six months shouldn't seem that long to you anymore."

She made it sound like both of us were over the hill. It was hard to figure, seeing how, at forty-two, she could still pass for half her age. The way that she wore her hair long and went around dressed in her old jeans, snap shirts, and worn hat, people were always mistaking her for my big sister.

She finished the cigarette, dropped the butt and ground it out with the toe of her pump. "Besides, it'll give you some time to think about what you did. Maybe you'll get your shit together before you turn fifty years old, unlike someone else we know."

She gazed down the steps, out at the parking lot and the rows of cars. The automobiles taunted me with their smiling grills.

"I know you were out there driving where he used to go."

I shrugged. "It's just a good place to drive, that's all."

"Lyndell was always fun in a car," she said. "That's what we used to do when we first started dating. He'd drive around like a madman, making me laugh, saying all these crazy things."

"Yeah, he could say some crazy stuff."

"Like what?" she said. "What'd he tell you?"

She looked at me, her face bright and expectant.

There were plenty of things to tell her. I don't know why I made the choice that I did.

"He said he thought you'd had enough of him."

She stood there, considering Lyndell's words while the morning sun rose higher above the trees, striking her eyes with its gauzy light and finally forcing her to look downward.

"I guess I was a little mad at the time," she said. "I guess I wanted to teach him a lesson. Of course, I didn't understand a lot of things back then, especially about people leaving."

Leaving went back a long way with Claudia, back to her own mother dumping her at the cousin's house when she was just a baby. Her cousin already had a husband and two boys, but she took Claudia in. She fed her, gave her a bed and not much else. It was the woman's husband who spent the most time with Claudia. He was a voice teacher, and he was the one who taught her so much about music. When he died, he left her an old gut-string guitar and his entire record collection.

The cousin and the sons weren't too pleased, but they turned them over to Claudia anyway. When I was a kid, she spent hours listening to those country records and playing along on the guitar. She even took music lessons through the mail. After Nick's second brush with the law, when it looked like he might go away for a long time, she had to hock the records and guitar. Claudia had to get rid of a car, too, and some decent furniture in order to pay for a good lawyer. She never did get any of it back. That was the first time I'd ever really seen her do any amount of drinking. Not wild drinking with other people, but the quiet kind, at home, out of a tall bottle, just to go to sleep at night.

People were streaming out of the courthouse, headed off to get their lunches. The smell of fried steak was drifting over from the cafeteria across the street.

Claudia and I climbed inside the GLC and headed off to get a bite of our own. She drove and smoked, with the window rolled halfway down and the radio playing low.

"I didn't mean to upset you."

She glanced over as if she didn't have any idea what I was talking about.

"About Lyndell," I said. "What he told me. He was lit up pretty good when he said that."

She waved her hand like it hadn't been such a big deal. "Wade Briggs says that ninety percent of the people in the world aren't with the person they want to be with. He says that's why there's so many sad songs."

Claudia thought the world of Wade Briggs, even before he'd saved me some trouble by making the pot and the pistol disappear. He'd been through a lot of shit over the years, a broken marriage and a big-time drinking problem for starters. Green Lake was where he'd come for a new start, getting remarried and organizing the AA meetings at the local Baptist church. There was no ignoring some of the similarities between his comeback story and Lyndell's.

I asked Claudia if singing sad songs made her feel better.

"Feeling better isn't really the point."

We sat at a traffic light, waiting among the herd, neither of us speaking. I could tell that she was distracted. Kenny Rogers was singing

"Lucille" on the radio. She hated Kenny and usually pounced on the dial before he could sing the opening verse.

The light turned green, and she threw the stick back into first. She worked her way through the gears, looking like an old pro on the straight shift.

I decided to change the subject. I asked if she really thought she could do without the TV.

She snorted. "Of course I could. There's nothing good on, anyway."

"Is that right?" I asked. "Then I don't guess you'd know what's been happening at the Campus Disco."

Her eyes darted in my direction. "No, I wouldn't, as a matter of fact."

"Or how about Luke Spencer? I hear he's on some sort of mob hit list."

"Haven't heard anything about that," she said.

"Oh, come on," I said, "anybody can see you're lying. I tried to call you at the fabric store last week. Colleen up front said you'd been in the back room half the day watching that little black-and-white of hers."

Claudia frowned. "That bitch. Why couldn't she just call me to the phone?"

"So you're admitting it?"

"Yes, I'm admitting it. I'm full of shit. There's no way I'm going without a TV set. I don't care what that stupid judge thinks. But let me tell you something . . ."

She took her eyes off the traffic and stared me down.

"There are going to be some changes," she said. "And I mean big ones. I'm not going to spend all my time worrying about you the way I have with Nick and Lyndell. You're gonna get your little shit together. Do you hear me?"

She finally realized Kenny was crooning on the radio. She snapped it off in an irritated sort of way, like me and the Gambler had been in cahoots together.

"What kind of changes?" I asked.

We'd rolled into the heart of the commercial strip, past the Holiday Inn and the KFC. The midday traffic was streaming in both directions. Claudia put on her blinker and eased into the turning lane. She was lined up for touchdown with the T-Bone King parking lot. The big red-roofed restaurant had taken the place of Wilson's Auto Shop a couple years back.

"Big changes," she said. "I'm tired of floating through life without a plan."

I sat there, both expectant and a little apprehensive. I wanted to hear what a genuine plan sounded like. The closest I'd come to something along those lines was my decision to live in a trailer by the ocean.

"So, what is it?" I asked her.

She popped the clutch and toed the gas pedal, peeling across the opposite two lanes. The horn blared on a truck coming from the other direction. The driver shook his head like he couldn't believe what he was seeing. The grill of the truck dipped, and smoke billowed off its back tires. The bearded driver swerved and barely missed clipping us.

Once we were safe in the parking lot, Claudia slowed down. She swung into a parking space, killed the pitiful motor, and smiled. "You'll see," she said.

3

The T-Bone King was a favorite of ours, a steak-house chain that served up corn-fed beef and stuffed Idahos. It also featured the landmark (and trademarked) all-you-could-eat Mega Food Bar, a buffet board so long you could have landed a Cessna on it. Four ninety-nine pretty much bought squatters' rights to the ribs, fried chicken, vegetables, and roast beef that spilled over the edges of the barrel-size chafing dishes. Unlimited trips to the make-your-own-sundae bar were also included in the fee. Needless to say, it was a hungry man's wet dream.

The clock hands pointed straight up to noon, and the restaurant hummed with conversation and the clatter of stainless steel cutlery. I could barely make out the song playing on the PA system, which was fine with me, seeing how it was Andy Williams singing "Una Paloma Blanca." That line about how "no one can take my freedom away" struck a nerve, since I'd just been in the office of the very person who was capable of it.

Claudia told the hostess we were meeting people, which was news to me. The woman led us over to a long table by the window, where Charlie Papp sat all by his lonesome. Charlie had recently taken the reins that had been yanked from Reggie's hands, becoming Claudia's interim boyfriend. Edging past sixty and sporting a gut and gray hair, he looked nothing like an outlaw, which is why I had him pegged as short-term material. I thought it was kind of a shame, too, seeing how Charlie had at least two things going for him that Claudia's other boyfriends had always lacked. First off, he was a successful businessman, founder and owner of the liquor-store chain Six Pack City. Second, and most important, he was actually a decent guy, always eager to please Claudia, sometimes even a little too eager.

Charlie stood to greet us. He had this nervous head-bobbing energy about him, like a big-footed dog. He also drank a lot, mostly scotch with a splash. He took my hand in both of his, squeezed it, and offered me a truly grave and sincere look, as though he were expressing condolences at a funeral.

"Are you hanging in there, buddy?"

"Yeah, I'm all right." I had to look down at my hand so he'd let go of it.

Charlie tried to hug Claudia, but she raised her hands and stopped him from getting too close. She turned her head and made a face like his breath smelled bad, only allowing him a little peck on the cheek.

"I need a drink first, Charlie. Just give me some space."

After we'd taken our seats, she called to the waitress and asked for a Tom Collins. Charlie raised his own glass and jiggled the ice for a backup.

Charlie's outfit was a somber one, at least for him: burgundy sport coat with brass buttons and a white golf shirt underneath. Claudia had taken to calling him Sport Coat Charlie behind his back, on account of the loud Hickey Freemans that he often wore. Sometimes, when he was walking up the driveway to the house, she'd look out the window and shake her head. "Good Lord," she'd say. "Charlie's done killed another sofa and put it on his back."

Charlie slid his chair back a little and reached over to massage Claudia's shoulders. She rolled her neck around like it actually felt good, then pushed him away. She opened up her purse and rifled through it until she found her pill bottle.

"It's been a long day already," she said.

I'd just reached for a menu when I felt a hand touch my own shoulder. I turned around to find Nick standing over me with his girlfriend, Bev, beside him. Nick was squinting and puffing a Winston, looking like a guy who had been cool from day one, like he'd probably sawed his way out of his baby crib with a cigarette dangling from his mouth and a chain swinging from his diaper.

"I've never been so damn disappointed in my life," he said. "Stealing a fucking Maverick. What's the matter, you couldn't find a Pinto?"

Bev laughed right away, then Charlie and Claudia. Nick grabbed me in a playful headlock and pulled me into his creaky leather jacket. All I could manage at the time was a halfhearted smile. Bev and Nick took the chairs on either side of me. Bev reached out and rubbed at the stubble on the side of my chin. "Damn," she said, "you're starting to look like a man."

"That's my twelve o'clock shadow," I told her.

I had to take pride in what little hair I had left, even though the stubble had actually been the result of having not shaven for at least four days.

Bev giggled. "Well, don't shave it. I like that rough look in a man."

Bev was a tiny thing, stick-thin in her jeans and Allman Brothers T-shirt, long ringlets of strawberry blonde hair spilling onto her shoulders. She wasn't exactly pretty, but she had a talent for sticking out in a crowd. I think it was this way of standing that she had, cocking her hip out to the side and smirking as though she'd seen everything at least once and was just daring you to impress her. She and Nick had been going together, off and on, ever since high school. It was the longest-running man-woman relationship I'd ever been around.

Naturally, everyone wanted to hear about my encounter with Judge Knox. I laid it on the table, and they all shook their heads and commiserated with me. Nick blew out a cloud of smoke and studied it as though it were the scales of justice.

"Six months is rough," he said. "They only took away Dewey's license for three months, and he had eight DUIs and a hit-and-run."

"Next time around," Claudia said, "she told him he was going to the youth detention facility."

Nick shook his head in a wistful sort of way. "They've got some real hard asses riding the benches around here."

Mercifully, there was no need to spend all our time dwelling on my legal troubles. Claudia asked Nick how things were going with his parole officer.

"Not bad. He keeps bugging me about getting into Lakeside Community College."

Claudia's expression turned hopeful. "For what?"

"Ah, I don't know. We've talked about some different stuff."

Bev was sipping her Coke through a straw, eyeing Nick in an

unhappy way. "You're already twenty-six," she said. "Don't you think that's a little old for college?"

Nick glared at her but then chose not to say anything back. It was probably for the best. From what I'd witnessed, their arguments had a tinderbox quality about them. Bev had been known to throw pieces of furniture around the house. She'd even given Nick a couple of stitches over his eye once, courtesy of an ashtray.

"What about the landscaping job?" Claudia asked. "Is that still working out?"

"Yeah, pretty much." Nick smiled. "Keeping it green."

The job in question consisted of supplying high-grade pot to the owner of Turfari Landscaping. The owner, in turn, vouched for Nick as a reliable employee and kept him on the payroll. I knew about the setup but Claudia was still in the dark.

I started to scan the menu, even though I knew it by heart. The T-Bone King chain was started by Lance Hillin, a former All-American defensive tackle at the University of Georgia who went on to play for the Packers, Lions, and Rams. Hence, the restaurant's walls were covered with photos from Hillin's playing days. Even the menu bore a gridiron theme. The smallest T-bone (a twelve-ouncer) was called "the scatback," while the middle cut (eighteen ounces) was known as "the quarterback." The large steak (twenty-four ounces) drew "the linebacker" label. And the biggest of all, a gargantuan, thirty-eight-ounce slab of flesh, was, of course, known as "the lineman," in honor of Lance Hillin. Most people chose to share that one. The menu advised: "Double-team this bad boy, just as opposing offenses double-teamed the great Lance Hillin."

My appetite had been on vacation the last few days, but it was starting to return with a vengeance. Charlie must have heard my stomach growling, seeing how he reached across the table and patted my arm.

"Get whatever you want," he said. "It's on me."

I took down a linebacker, medium rare, and a stuffed potato. Charlie couldn't finish his quarterback, so he shoved his plate my way. "Go on and sack his ass," he said. And I did just that.

Nick and Claudia spent a lot of time catching up. They hadn't spoken all that often in the year and a half since Nick's last prison stay. I could tell that she resented Nick for what he'd put her through. There was no other way to explain why she hardly ever returned his calls anymore, or never asked him over to the house, even at Christmas. She'd replaced a few of the records she'd sold and bought a fairly nice guitar. But it didn't have "that same, lonesome sound," she told me.

Nick never flat-out admitted it, but the cold shoulder bothered him. Whenever I'd ride my bike over to hang out at his place, he'd always ask if she'd said anything about him, or if she was mad at him. When I told him his name hadn't come up, I think it hurt worse than if she'd been putting the poor mouth on him.

So, I think Nick was happy to be at the T-Bone King with all of us. He was smiling and telling Claudia and Charlie about his cover band. He played guitar, of course, and Bev sang. Dewey banged the skins and this new guy, Carlton, attempted to play bass.

"We played at Smokey the Bar and Whatchamacallit's last month," Nick said. "Then we did a couple of fraternity parties up in Athens."

"We've got a gig over in Augusta tonight," Bev said. "We're playing a wedding party for a guy Nick met in the can."

"Well, what's the name of your band?" Charlie asked.

Nick and Bev considered each other and smiled. Nick had a Winston dangling from his mouth.

"We used to be called Whiskey Dick," Bev said. "But we just changed our name to Puss 'n Booze. I thought it sounded classier for a wedding."

Charlie appeared confused. "Did this fellow Dick quit the band?"

Nick and Bev burst out laughing. I laughed, too, though I felt kind of sorry for Charlie. Claudia was sitting there looking embarrassed to even know him.

After we'd had our way with the sundae bar, everyone sat around the table looking drowsy. Nick and Claudia fired up a couple of sticks, exchanged glances, and nodded in a conspiratorial manner.

Nick leaned my way and draped his arm around my shoulder. "You think you might want to come to Augusta with us? Maybe be our roadie?"

The invite caught me by surprise.

"Me and Nick had a little talk last night," Claudia said. She looked down and tamped some ashes from her Virginia Slim into the already full ashtray and waited for Nick to finish her thought.

"How'd you like to come live with me for a while?" he asked. "Maybe move into the hacienda for an extended stay. You've seen the layout. Twelve acres. Swimming pool. Jacuzzi. Petting zoo."

Bev snorted. "You mean that filthy rat who sneaks in and eats your damn food?"

Nick turned and wagged a finger in Bev's face. "Don't you be talking about my goddamn rat, woman. His name's Roberto. And that's Mr. Roberto to you."

While he and Bev were laughing, I gazed in Claudia's direction and asked if this was for real. She shrugged as though she hadn't completely sold herself on the idea.

"Charlie's getting ready to open a couple of liquor stores down in Jacksonville," she said. "He just bought a condo on the beach in Ponte Vedra, and he asked me to come down and spend the summer with him. I told him no at first. But then, after all of this stuff with Mrs. Dees, I started thinking that maybe a change of scenery might do us all some good right now. It just feels like the two of us are smothering in that little house."

I had to agree with her on that. Besides, I liked the plan. As I said before, Nick's house felt like destiny. There was always something happening, people coming and going, playing music and telling jokes and having contests to see who could roll the fastest joint. I rode my bicycle over there every chance I got.

"We're gonna shake things up a little," Nick said. "Besides, we're brothers. We need to spend more time together."

"Of course, there's going to be rules," Claudia said. "And discipline, just like Judge Knox talked about."

I knew there had to be a catch somewhere. "Here we go," I groaned.

Nick slapped me on the back of the head, but he was grinning.

"Charlie knows the beverage manager at the Holiday Inn," Claudia said, "and he got you a busboy job working in the restaurant. You'll be doing it in the evenings. That's how you're gonna pay back Mrs. Dees for the car."

"Which nights?" I was already thinking about my TV schedule.

"Sunday through Thursday," Charlie said. "You can pretend Saturday's the Sabbath."

I loosened my necktie again. Friday and Saturday would leave me with *Rockford* and *Dallas*. Slim pickings, but quality pickings. Plus, I could always watch the Braves replays at one in the morning. This setup would certainly inflict some pain, but I figured I could live with it.

"Don't worry," Nick said, "it ain't gonna be *Stalag 17*. But I am gonna whip your sorry ass into shape. We'll go into training together. Get up early. Lift weights. Drink beer and eat barbecue potato chips for breakfast."

Claudia frowned. "Nick, that's not what—"

Nick waved his hand through the air. "I'm just kidding about the beer."

He made a point then of turning in his chair and looking me squarely in the eyes. He even set his hand on the back of my chair. I could sense that a challenge was about to be issued. I felt like one of those *Scared Straight* kids, only Nick wasn't scary at all.

"Seriously, bro, you need a little discipline. Hell, everybody does. Now I know I'm not the best example, but I've learned a lot from my many, and ongoing, stumbles. And I bet I know what that judge made you feel like in there today: like a rotten, dirty, low-down piece of shit. Am I right?"

He was on the money, and I nodded accordingly.

"I bet she even made you feel like you didn't deserve to breathe the same air as other people. She made you feel like you'd never amount to nothing, like you were just taking up space. Am I right?"

Now my throat was starting to swell. I hadn't expected anybody to know how I felt, not even Nick. Hell, even I wasn't sure how I'd felt.

"She's gonna find a way to lock me up," I croaked.

Nick lit another Winston, waved out the spark on his matchstick, and shook his head.

"Ain't gonna happen," he said. "The thing is, this ain't about being locked up. It's about you getting some damn respect—earning it, really. You see, all they wanna do in that courthouse is beat your ass down. They don't wanna help you succeed. Hell, it's easier for them to just lock you up and forget about you. But I got a plan for you, something that's gonna make you feel like a good citizen of the world."

I liked the sound of that a whole lot better than "contributing member of society." Hell, that one had always sounded about as important as "utility infielder."

I stared intently at Nick, like a killer seeking God on execution day.

"First off," he said, "any money you make goes to fixing that old lady's car. That's your debt for fucking up and you can't walk away from it. But . . ."

Here, he paused to dot the air with the tip of his cigarette. It looked like something a millionaire might do.

". . . I'll match half of everything you make on your paycheck, just so you have some walking-around money. And the other half of your stub, I'll hold that for you until you get your license back. Then you can use it to help buy yourself a car."

Charlie was smiling now, too. "Hell, I'll pay the rest." He gazed across the table at Nick and nodded in an approving way. "I like your brand of justice. Firm, but fair."

Nick leaned back in his chair and took a satisfied toke off his Winston. "They don't call me the Velvet Hammer for nothing."

I suppose Nick's greatest talent in all of this was how well he managed to wear his own transgressions. For someone who'd served more than seven hundred combined days in prison by the age of twenty-six, he sure did a helluva job selling me on the rewards of hard work and discipline. After he'd finished talking to me, I felt like I could have taken on the young Lance Hillin, whose agile, flattopped, All-American self was crouched low in a photo on the wall in front of me.

Nick and Bev tore out of the T-Bone King parking lot on Nick's motorcycle, a loud silver 400CC Triumph. Charlie was still inside paying at the register, while Claudia and I waited outside by the newspaper boxes.

The front of the *Atlanta Constitution* featured a picture of the Three Mile Island nuclear reactor. I'd watched a report about the reactor's meltdown on the *Today* show that morning. Tom Brokaw had said the radiation was the kind of trouble you couldn't see, smell, or hear, at least not until it was too late.

"Well," Claudia said, "I sure hope I'm doing the right thing leaving you with Nick."

I gazed up from the smoking reactor. "It'll be okay. What could go wrong?"

Claudia smiled. "You got a legal pad and a sharp pencil?"

We laughed, and then she told me it would be all right if I said no. She was having second thoughts. "I don't mind staying here with you," she said. "But you're still taking that job and cutting down on the TV."

"I'll be fine," I said.

Claudia had been lucky to meet Charlie, someone who had the means to support her in a venture like this. They'd hooked up at the fish camp a couple of days after she'd gotten the news about Lyndell's marriage and sobriety. Charlie was still grieving over a daughter who'd died a year earlier in an auto accident, thrown from her drunk boyfriend's pickup truck during a rollover. He went over and talked to Claudia after she'd sung a Kitty Wells song. He told her she made the hair stand up on his neck.

Charlie walked out of the restaurant, toothpick in his mouth and credit card receipt in hand. He buttoned his sport coat over his gut and smiled at Claudia. "You look young enough to be your own son's girl-friend," he said.

Claudia made a face and shook her head. "That's disgusting, Charlie. You should think before you say stuff like that."

"Well, I meant it as a compliment."

He slid the toothpick out of his mouth and puckered up to kiss her, so she gave him a quick peck, then reached out and straightened the lapels on his sport coat.

"I haven't seen this one before," she said. "That is one sharp jacket."

She gazed over Charlie's shoulder and winked at me as we started toward the car. Charlie looked as proud as could be. "Pierre Cardin," he said. "Forty-eight long."

4

Dewey was the first to greet me at Nick's house, stepping off the porch and squeezing my shoulder. He shook his head in a mournful way.

"I heard about the license," he said. "Damn, that's some cold-ass shit."

Dewey and I now possessed a close bond, seeing how we were members of the suspended-license brigade.

"How long have you got left?" I asked.

Dewey didn't bat an eye. "Fifty-three days."

He gazed off into the woods behind the house, full of a longing that I immediately recognized.

"Well, I'm looking at the big one-eight-three. Plus twelve months in Alto if I don't shake twice every time I piss."

Dewey clucked his tongue and shook his head, standing there in his usual outfit of faded jeans and Atlanta Flames hockey jersey. He was built like a pulling guard, at least six-four and about two and a half bills on the scales, with a short, brambly beard and long black hair.

I could hear Nick and Bev arguing inside. It sounded like a stage-one confrontation, meaning all screaming and no projectiles. Dewey steered me away from the dustup.

"She's having one of her spells," he said. "She gets a little temperamental before a show."

He grabbed a can of PBR off the porch steps and led me out to a van that was parked in the dirt driveway beside Nick's old Plymouth Fury. The side of the van read *AAA-Action TV Repair.* Carlton, the new bass player, was standing by the back door loading Dewey's drum kit.

"Careful, now," Dewey said. "Don't bruise my skins."

I had yet to meet Carlton. He was crouched over Dewey's bass drum, looking irritated and sweating. He was wearing a fire-engine-red silk shirt unbuttoned to his navel. The sleeves were rolled up to reveal a pair of red-white-and-blue wristbands.

Carlton shot Dewey a nasty look. "You think it might kill you to give me a little help?"

Dewey flexed his hand, wincing as though the slightest movement caused a measure of pain. "I got a little tendinitis in the wrist. I'm thinking I better save myself for the show."

"That's what you get for beating off all the time," Carlton said.

"Hey, hey," Dewey said. "That's no way for a bassman to talk to his drummer. I'm like your left nut, junior."

Carlton went back to loading equipment. Dewey nudged my shoulder and pointed at Carlton's head. I had a feeling he was going to say something about Carlton's hair. It was a sight to behold, blond and curled into a clownish explosion of follicles. I could smell the scorched perm solution five feet downwind.

"So what do you think about Bev's handiwork?" Dewey asked.

I wasn't all that eager to jump into their pissing contest, so I deferred with a mere shrug.

Carlton tugged at the ends of his corkscrews. "She said it'd loosen up in a week or so. I hope she's right."

Dewey chuckled. "Yeah, I guess she learned that when she was studying at MIT."

He winked at me. "That's Middle Indiana Tonsorial, in case you were wondering."

Carlton seemed like an okay guy, if only a little too eager to mention his part-time DJ job at WPND. The first question he asked was where I went to school. When I told him Green Lake High, he brushed his hands together and squinted in a gesture of deep thought.

"I think we're doing one of our Friday school-spirit remotes from there in a couple of weeks."

Dewey rolled his eyes. "Oh, Lord. Here we go."

Naturally, I had to ask what Carlton was talking about, and that's when he told me about his once-a-week gig at the station. "I'm on from two to five, on Sundays."

I was somewhat impressed. "I bet you have a lot of listeners that time of the afternoon. People out on their boats and stuff."

He looked away from me like a bashful, bushy-haired toddler. He picked up Nick's amp and set it in the back of the van.

"Actually, I'm on from two to five in the mornings. But you'd be surprised who listens."

"Yeah, he's got a varied fan base," Dewey said. "Four crank addicts and a guy who works at the morgue."

Carlton picked up one of Dewey's cymbals and flung it into the van like a Frisbee.

"You goddamn sonuvabitch," Dewey said, "that's a Classic drum kit you're fucking with."

He handed me his beer and told me to hold it for him while he kicked Carlton's ass. By that time, Carlton had already scooted to the other side of the van. They played cat-and-mouse like that, hurling threats but making no real moves on each other, until Nick came out of the house and told them to get in the van.

"I can't take all this damn yelling," he said.

Bev stood on the porch with her arms crossed, seething.

"This ain't the creative tension I've been talking about."

We rattled down I-20, headed for Augusta in the big van. Carlton worked for AAA-Action TV Repair, thus explaining our use of the company vehicle. (Not that Carlton's boss actually knew anything about the van's after-hours duties.) I was bouncing along on the floor, wedged between a nineteen-inch Emerson and Nick's amplifier. Carlton drove, and Nick rode shotgun. Bev and Dewey were in the back with me.

Between the TVs and music equipment, there was hardly any room to move, but Nick had still managed to find space for a cooler. Dewey was crawling around on his hands and knees passing out cans of Pabst.

"That's pretty good service," Nick said. "Maybe you oughta try to get on with Delta. Shake that tight little ass of yours up and down the aisle."

"I got your bag of nuts right here," Dewey said, grabbing the crotch of his jeans.

Carlton was steering with one hand and digging through a shoe box full of cassettes with the other. He veered into the emergency lane three times before he found what he wanted: *Are You Experienced?*

Once the Hendrix had started up, Dewey asked Carlton if he knew the name of Jimi's bass player. Carlton failed to produce an answer.

"It's Noel Redding," Dewey hollered. "Of course I wouldn't have expected you to know that. He's good, and you suck."

Carlton fired back with his middle finger.

"Hang it in the air, or stick it up your ass," Dewey said, "but you still can't play the guitar with that thing."

Pretty soon, a hefty joint was being passed around. Nick lowered the music and turned to address those of us sitting in coach. He held up his hands as though an announcement was forthcoming.

"I hate to be the hard ass," he said. "It goes against my very nature. But I'm gonna have to ask that my younger sibling abstain from the herbal remedy currently in use. I promised his mother that I'd keep him on a law-abiding track for the next few months."

Bev and Dewey eyed me with a fair amount of pity.

"Well, what about you?" Bev hollered. "You're not setting a very good example."

Nick merely smiled at her. "Bev, honey, I've already talked to young Luke about this. It's a matter of do as I say, not as I do."

He turned back to face the windshield and jacked up the music again. But then he seemed to remember something. He killed the Hendrix and looked toward the back again. This time, he pointed right at me. "And by the way, I know you've been stealing from my stash, you little shit."

Bev and Dewey started laughing. After Nick had turned around again, Dewey passed me the daddy and nodded for me to partake. I didn't let him down.

"Look at that," Dewey said. "Puffin' like a pro."

I passed the joint to Bev. She was sitting on the other side of the Emerson, already wearing her stage outfit: low-riding jeans and a clingy chamois halter top. It would have surprised me to learn that she actually owned a bra.

Nick was dressed for the stage as well, sticking with the tried-and-true bad-ass look: jeans, scuffed motorcycle boots, and a faded red BSA Motorcycles T-shirt with the sleeves cut out. His long black hair was pulled back into a ponytail.

Carlton was the only one who didn't appear to belong. Between the silk shirt and the fuzzy do, his look wasn't working on any level. Nevertheless, he and Nick were in deep conversation up front, sharing their own joint and waving their hands animatedly. Dewey was watching them with a disgusted look on his face. Once, while Carlton was talking, Dewey looked at Bev and started flapping his fingers and thumb together like they were a set of lips.

"What the hell is he yapping about?" Dewey asked.

Bev pointed to her ears. The music was loud, but not inappropriately so. "You think I can hear?" she shouted.

Dewey slid over to mine and Bev's side of the van. He leaned into Bev until their heads were almost touching. "Let's me and you tell Nick that we want Carlton's ass gone after tonight."

Bev narrowed her eyes like she was irritated with him. "Who are we going to get to take his place, dumbass?"

"I don't know. Does it even matter? We could kidnap a monkey from the zoo and teach him to play better."

"We already turn his volume way down," she said. "What else do you want to do to the poor guy? He knows he sucks."

"Well, he's a fucking embarrassment. Look at that shirt. He oughta be working the pirate ride at Six Flags."

Bev couldn't help but laugh.

"And you fucked up his hair but good," Dewey said. "He looks like goddamn Curly from the Three Stooges."

"Fuck you," Bev said.

She jabbed the heel of her boot into Dewey's gut and doubled him over. Then she glanced my way and smiled. "This is what you call creative differences."

I figured it probably was not a great time to correct Dewey; he meant Larry instead of Curly.

"So what's the problem with Carlton?" I asked Bev. "Outside of the hair."

"There's no problem," Bev said. "Dewey's just being a horse's ass."

Dewey was holding his hand to his stomach like he'd just been gut shot by one of the Cartwrights.

"He can't play his instrument is the problem," Dewey said.

"Yeah, well, I don't see any bands knocking down your door, Mr.

Keith Moonface. Besides, you know what your problem is? You're a know-it-all jackass."

The words were harsh, but she had a point. If someone mentioned a band in Dewey's presence, he would typically call them sell-outs and then refer to the most obscure cut on their most obscure album. "Now that's when they were good," he'd say. He was also given to grand declarations, such as: "Anybody who doesn't think John Bonham is the greatest drummer alive today can lick my left nut." Nick was the only person who could pull him down off his high horse. He'd say, "Shut the hell up, Dewey. It's only rock and roll."

Dewey argued that Nick only let Carlton play in the band because of his DJ job at WPND.

"That's not why," Bev said.

"The hell it's not. I saw Nick reading one of those Georgia School of Broadcasting brochures. He said if he got a degree, Carlton would hook him up with the station manager. Until then, he's gotta be assy kissy with Goldilocks up there."

Bev took a long, angry drag off her cigarette and glared at the back of Nick's head. "Broadcasting school?" she asked.

"That's what he told me," Dewey said.

"Well, he hasn't said a fucking word to me about it."

Dewey bunched up his meaty shoulders like he was expecting another boot to the midsection. "Oh, shit. You didn't hear that from me."

"The hell I didn't," she said. "Now spill the beans, fat ass."

"That's all I heard," Dewey said. "I swear."

"Well, that's the problem," she said. "You heard it, not me."

She looked over at me. "It's just like that community college shit he was talking to Claudia about. You think I'd heard anything about it before today? Hell, no."

I tried to picture Nick walking around a campus with a stack of books under his arms. It was practically inconceivable, though I could have envisioned him sitting behind a DJ's mike. Nick was like Claudia when it came to music. He knew his shit.

I asked Bev if she thought he was serious about going to school.

"Who the hell knows," she said. "He doesn't tell me anything, anymore."

She sat there for a long time, sucking the life out of her cigarette, glaring up toward the front of the van. Dewey didn't say another word.

A blue, dusky light had settled over Augusta by the time we pulled into the Best Western's parking lot. The big sign out front said CONGRATS WALTER AND BRITNEY. It might have been a classy touch if the *E* in Britney had not been a backward 3. Apparently, the hotel needed to buy some more vowels.

The wedding party was taking place in the hotel's banquet hall. Not that we were in any hurry to get there. Nick had some business to take care of first. He turned off the radio and pointed to a white Seville parked in the back of the hotel lot.

"Those are the guys," he told Carlton. "Pull over beside that Caddy."

He spun around and looked at Bev. "You still got the tickets in your backpack?"

Bev unzipped her dusty red bag and pulled out a short stack of green tickets and badges.

"Oh, hell," Dewey said. "Must be Masters time again."

Nick smiled. "Starts next week. I figured while we were over here . . ."

"Are those the counterfeits?" Dewey asked.

"Why don't you buy 'em and find out," Nick said.

Dewey patted his jeans pockets. "Damn, I must have left my wallet back home in my green jacket."

Carlton pulled up beside the Caddy. Nick hopped out and walked around to the trunk of the white car. I scooted to the back of the van and watched through the window while he shook hands with two men. They looked to be in their thirties, and I took them for brothers. Both were plump in a well fed sort of way, like they'd downed their share of hot dogs and Snickers through the years before making the turn for the back nine.

Nick had been into golf ever since his last stay in prison. He'd read a book from the prison library about Lee Trevino and decided he wanted to learn the game. These days he did most of his dealing at the driving range just so he could work on his swing between transactions.

Nick said something to the brothers and made a swinging motion with an invisible club. Both of the men laughed in a friendly way. They were dressed alike—khaki pants and bright golf shirts: one pink, the other mint green. The brother in the green shirt also wore his pant cuffs a little too high. I could see that he wasn't wearing any socks with his loafers. The tops of his swollen feet were sunburned.

Nick handed the tickets to the sockless fellow, and the other one handed Nick a white envelope.

Dewey slid over beside me and took a peek out the window.

"Are those tickets real?" I asked him.

Dewey scratched at his chin. He looked like he was trying to figure his yardage on an approach shot. "It's highly unlikely," he said. "At least based on what I saw last year."

"You mean he's done this before?"

"Yeah, he knows a guy up in Hiawassee who stole some plates from the ticket company. He does the printing, and Nick handles the distribution for him. They made about three grand last year selling these things. That's a nice spike in the yearly income."

"Well, what about the pot? Doesn't he make enough on that?"

Dewey groaned and shook his head. "It's getting harder these days, bud. Between the cops, the cocaine, and the competition, Nick has to work his ass off. I tell you, I worry about him sometimes. I'm afraid he's spreading himself too thin."

This wasn't the sort of news I'd wanted to hear about the profession I was considering. While I was aware of the incarceration risks, I didn't know about the competition and the shitty hours. Nick's "good citizen of the world" speech was looking better all the time.

Dewey glanced over at Bev to make sure that she wasn't listening, then he leaned in close to me. "I hear him talking more and more about getting out. Going fucking legit. That's what this whole broadcasting thing's about."

"Well, what about Bev? She doesn't sound too high on the prospects."

"She could be a problem," he said. "She likes to pull the damn strings. She ain't gonna like it if he does."

5

While Puss 'n Booze might not have been a traditional sort of wedding band, Britney and Walter were not exactly your traditional bride and groom. Like the rest of their wedding party, they were dressed as if they'd just arrived from Sturgis, all denim and leather and Sailor Jerry tattoos. The only thing setting the bride and groom apart from their fellow revelers was headwear. Britney had chosen to don a black veil for the occasion while Walter wore a houndstooth fedora, or as he called it, "my Bear Bryant lid."

According to Nick, their marriage might not have even been legal, seeing how the ceremony was performed earlier in the day by another of Nick's and Walter's former prison mates. The minister in question was currently wanted in Alabama on charges of mail fraud stemming from a phony evangelical association for which he'd been collecting donations. To make things even stickier, Britney's divorce from her first husband hadn't yet been finalized. In fact, Nick wasn't even sure if any papers had been filed.

"It is one goddamn tangled web," Nick said as we lugged his amp in from the van.

Whatever troubles might lay in their future—and it was hard to imagine their future being without its share of problems—I don't think Walter and Britney ever regretted hiring Puss 'n Booze to play their wedding party. Nick and the band performed two sets—really loud ones—and Bev nearly tumbled out of her halter top a half dozen times while she strutted and stomped around the little bandstand that was tucked into a corner of the hotel's banquet hall.

The band played pretty much whatever they wanted to play and ignored all requests. That meant plenty of Stones tunes ("before Mick went disco," as Dewey liked to say) as well as some blues numbers, like "Stormy Monday," so that Nick could show off his slide skills. They played "Calling Dr. Love" and "Gimme Three Steps" and "Hair of the Dog" just so Bev could change the lyrics from *sonuvabitch* to *motherfucking sonuvabitch*. I can honestly say that I have never met anyone who derived such pure pleasure out of profanity as Bev.

I think that most people kept their eyes on Bev, even when she wasn't singing in that raspy snarl of hers. She'd be standing there at the mike while Nick played a solo, shucking her shoulders and slithering to Carlton's unsure groove, making kissy faces to the biker guys down front and basically winning over everyone in the room.

It turned out Carlton wasn't half bad with his volume down low. He'd scattered cheat sheets atop his amp to help steer him through certain bridges and solos. Nevertheless, he struggled on a few songs, most notably "Heartbreaker." After he took a wrong turn during the guitar solo, Dewey flung a drumstick through the air and hit him upside the head. Some of the guys down front laughed, but Carlton looked like he wanted to cry.

I stood in the back of the banquet hall near the cash bar. Nick had supplied me with a Nikon camera of unknown origin and instructed me to shoot two rolls of the band.

"You might wanna get me leaping off the stage during 'Stranglehold.' I always do that right before my solo. But wait until I kick my leg in the air."

Since the bandstand was only two feet high, I lay on the floor and shot upward as Nick took flight. When we got the pictures back from the photo shop, he looked like he had some serious hop in his boots.

My other job was to keep everyone backed up in the beverage department. Bev downed four screwdrivers over the course of two sets, and Nick drank five Heinekens, using one of the empties to play slide. Carlton must have realized he had no business drinking and playing bass, seeing how he stuck with Sprite and grenadine. As for Dewey, I quickly lost count of his Jack-and-Coke tally. Finally, during the second set, the bartender sent me to the stage with a fifth of Jack, a six-pack of Cokes, and an ice bucket. Dewey casually saluted the guy with one of his drumsticks.

The band closed the evening with a slow song, giving Walter and Brit a chance to nuzzle amid their sea of well-wishers. Nick pulled his acoustic off its stand and started strumming softly. Bev introduced the number in her best whiskey-glass voice.

"We wanna congratulate you motherfuckers on getting married."

A cheer went up. A guy at a back table squealed, "Owwww!" He was bleary-eyed and disheveled, teetering back and forth in his boots, trying his damndest to flick the cigarette lighter held above his head.

"We just want Walter to promise us one thing," Bev said.

A lone voice down front called back to her: "What is it, sugar?"

"When the time comes to give that first taste of loving," she said. "When the time is nigh and poor old Brit has to lay there and take one for the team, we want you to remember this, Walter. Because if you don't, I'm gonna come back down here and put my boot halfway up your sorry ass."

The crowd went nuts. The best man even bent over and offered his backside to Bev. And with that, she started singing the opening verse of "Try a Little Tenderness." It might not have qualified as a touching moment, but it certainly proved that Puss 'n Booze had some versatility. Walter pulled Britney into his chest and held her tight, standing in place, swaying to the music. Brit was crying, dabbing her eyes with a cocktail napkin while Walter rubbed his hand across her ass and chewed on her shoulder.

The parking lot was shiny and wet, the van sitting right where we'd left it, draped in a salty, artificial light. I loaded all of the equipment by myself while Nick and the band carried the party up to a hotel room with some of the wedding group. By the time I finished packing the van, my head started to ache again from the concussion.

I slid the keys into the ignition and turned on the radio. For some reason I left it on a country station. Johnny Cash was singing "Sunday Morning Coming Down," and it made me think of Claudia cruising down I-95 with Charlie.

I rifled through the glove compartment until I found Nick's stash. He'd tucked it behind a Texaco road map. I rolled a modest joint—strictly for medicinal purposes—sparked it, and lay down in the back of the van. I closed my eyes and smoked, feeling the headache lighten and float away like a balloon. My ears were still ringing from the show, and the radio was barely a mumble in my head. After a while, I sunk into a hazy cloud of sleep.

Dewey woke me. "Shit, man. Are you trying to burn your ass up?"

He was holding the nub of the joint in his hand. He considered it with some reluctance, as though it were a dangerous item, before remembering what it was meant for and holding it to his lips.

I sat up and rubbed my eyes. "Fuck, I must have fallen asleep."

"It's all right," Dewey said. "You're entitled. Court dates do the same thing to me. It's a lot of stress."

"It's been a long fucking day," I told him. "I don't think I've ever been this tired in my life."

Dewey was looking fairly beleaguered himself. I think the Jack-and-Cokes had finally caught up to him. At the very least, they were nipping at his ass.

Dewey laid his head back against the side of the van. "Don't worry, things are gonna get better. You're gonna like living with us."

I asked him what had happened to the rest of the band.

"They oughta be here soon," he said. "Nick was trying to get Bev to leave. But you know how she is when she's doing that cocaine. Just yap, yap, yap, like a little Chihuahua."

There were footsteps on the pavement, clomping toward the van in a hurried manner.

"That sounds like Liberace," Dewey said. "He don't even have rhythm when he walks."

I raised my head and looked out the windshield. Carlton and his red shirt were headed our way. "Yeah, it's him," I said.

"He's always fucking me up onstage," Dewey said. "I've been telling Nick he's not working out, but he won't listen to me. I may be the heartbeat of the band, but I'm still low rung on the totem pole."

Carlton opened the driver's side door and stuck his head inside. He had this silly grin plastered to his face, and he was panting and trying to catch his breath. "Guess who's across the street?" he asked.

Dewey was playing possum, pretending to be passed out. So I went ahead and asked Carlton who he'd seen.

"It's Jack motherfucking Nicklaus, man. That's who."

"Bullshit."

"No, it's really him. I swear."

"Where?"

"Right across the street, at the Waffle House."

"Are you high? What the hell would Jack Nicklaus be doing at a Waffle House?"

"Hell, I don't know. Eating pecan waffles or some shit. Come on, I'm gonna get some autographs."

Carlton sounded so sure of his discovery that I crawled to the back of the van and looked out the window. The only car in the Waffle House lot was a blue Park Avenue. Two guys were walking away from it, and one of them was plump and blond, with big forearms sticking out of his baby blue knit shirt. He looked enough like Nicklaus to get my attention, but I still had serious doubts.

Carlton slammed the door and took off running across the four-lane avenue in front of the hotel, dodging the sparse late-night traffic and yelling at the top of his lungs, "Hey, Bear! How 'boutcha Golden Bear!"

"I think you're right," I told Dewey. "Some of that perm solution must have seeped into his brain."

But Dewey wasn't answering. By that time, he'd passed out for real. There was nothing left of the joint. His alligator clip smoldered between his fingers.

I heard more voices in the parking lot, so I crawled up front to take a look. Nick and Bev were walking out the hotel's side door. Bev was still wired up. She slung her backpack over her shoulder and took off walking really fast, as if she was mad about something. Nick, who appeared to be tore-up drunk, was weaving along the sidewalk, almost taking a header into the bushes on one occasion, struggling to keep pace with Bev. He was wearing his motorcycle jacket and a green sock hat.

The windows were down in the front of the van, so I could hear them arguing. Bev said something about "that fucking broadcasting school."

"Come on," Nick said, "you don't have to get all hostile about it."

She stopped and spun around to face him. "The hell I don't. You don't even tell me about it, like it's some big secret."

"I'm just thinking about it, is all. What's the big damn deal? It could be a good thing. I could get free concert tickets and shit."

"I don't give a fuck. It's still a job. What about all the stuff we do? Shit, do you think a job is gonna give you time to run off whenever you want?"

It was strange hearing a person try to talk someone out of pursuing an honest job. For some reason, I pictured Bev kicking Judge Knox's ass, just walking right into that woman's office and stacking some furniture. It gave me a thrill.

"You've got the perfect setup right now," Bev said. "You've got a job you don't even have to go to, and your parole officer's happy. The band kicks ass. Shit, this is the best we've ever had it."

He laid his hands on her shoulders, but she jerked away from him and started walking toward the van again. Nick stood by himself atop the damp pavement, looking whipped.

"Come on, Bev. I mean, goddamn."

About that time a pair of car doors thunked shut. The two brothers who'd bought the tickets stepped away from their Caddy and walked in Nick's direction. The one with socks was carrying a golf club.

Nick turned their way. He didn't appear to be all that concerned over their surprise appearance.

The sockless brother tossed the Masters tickets at Nick's feet. "Remember us, asshole?"

Nick gazed from one face to the other and held up his hands in a gesture of surrender. "Fellas, I'm in no condition to handle business right now. I'm only the slightest bit inebriated."

Bev had stopped in her tracks. She stood there watching while the club-wielding brother took a step toward Nick.

"Look," the guy said, "I'm pretty fond of my two-iron. So if you'll just give us our money back, we might be willing to let this shit slide."

Nick considered the club head. It glinted like a huge dental instrument in the hotel's floodlights.

"You know, the two-iron's a tough club to handle," Nick said. "I find that I'm always slicing the ball, so I usually pull out my three-wood and take a shorter . . ."

Just as Nick started into his shadow backswing, the guy swung the club and grazed the side of his head. Nick's cap went flying through the air. Nick staggered a little but didn't go down. He reached up and touched his scalp, then studied the tips of his fingers.

"Hey, man! What the fuck?"

"We want our goddamn money, you shit-ass sonuvabitch!" Mr. Socks whacked the pavement with the club head to emphasize the urgency of the matter. "I got a buddy who just bought tickets. He says there's no such thing as a green badge."

His brother stepped forward and grabbed Nick by the front of his shirt, but Nick shoved him away and popped him in the nose with the heel of his hand. The other brother took another swing with the two-iron, this time catching Nick in the back. Nick dropped to his knees.

"Goddammit," he said, "will you just give it a fucking rest with the Tommy Armours?"

I scrambled to the back of the van and tried to wake Dewey, but he was too far gone. "It's a four-four," he mumbled. "Try to keep up."

I looked out the back window to see if Carlton had finally realized that the guy in the Buick wasn't Nicklaus. But he was still standing in the Waffle House parking lot with the two men from the car. They were facing me now, and the blond one really did look like the Golden Bear. He was pressing a piece of paper against Carlton's back and signing it with a pen.

I needed a weapon. My first thought was a tire iron, but there was none to be found in the van. The best I could do was to snap one of the rabbit ears from the top of the Emerson. I pulled it out to its full length and swiped it through the air, Zorro style. It whistled like a fencing saber.

Bev reached the melee before me. She was screaming at the top of her lungs, "Stop it, you motherfuckers! You're killing him!" She waved the envelope over her head, apparently planning to return the brothers' money.

When Nick saw what she was attempting to do, he shook his head and tried to grab the envelope from her. "Bev, no. Just hold on a minute."

The guy with the club took the envelope from Bev, but Nick jumped up and grabbed him from behind. He took hold of the club shaft, too, and pulled it tight against the guy's windpipe.

I ran in soon after, drew back my antenna, and took a swipe at the sockless brother's ankle.

"Oww! Goddamn sonuvabitch! That fucking stings!"

He grabbed his ankle and started hopping around on one foot. I struck again while he was stunned, lining up his face and catching him across the cheek with the next shot. That one spun him and dropped him to his knees. He was holding his left eye, screaming that I'd blinded him.

"Oh, Jesus. I can't see. I can't fucking see."

Nick was still wrestling with the other brother, and Bev was chomping down on the guy's hand, trying to pry it away from the envelope. When Nick saw me standing at the edge of the fray, he told me to get the van.

"Hurry. Bring it over here."

I sprinted back to the vehicle and fired up the motor. Only after I'd dropped the transmission into drive did my heart fold itself up like a cold animal. I could hear Judge Knox's voice and see those steel gray doors in her eyes. *You better bring your damn toothbrush and a clean pair of underwear. Because your little fanny's going straight to the youth correctional institute.*

The tide had turned again, leaving Nick in desperate need of some backup. Both brothers were on top of him. The sockless one had seized the envelope. He reached out and shoved Bev to the ground. She hopped up, ran back to the van, and climbed in beside me.

"Well, what the fuck are you waiting for?" she said. "Run those motherfuckers over."

I gazed into her dilated pupils. "I can't. I don't have a license."

"No fucking shit, Sherlock." And then she laid her foot atop mine and stomped the accelerator to the floor.

Nick and the brothers scrambled to their feet and scattered like pigeons. The sockless brother ran right out of a shoe. The other one managed to scoop up the envelope but left his two-iron in my crosshairs. I clattered right over the top of it, then slammed on the brakes and cut the wheel to the left, trying to pull a bootlegger's turn. It was something Lyndell used to do when we were out driving in the night. I quickly learned that such maneuvers are best performed in Chevelles and not delivery vans, as we found ourselves traveling only on the two right-side tires. The van finally came back down on all four, but only after I'd broadsided a light pole. The collision sounded like a huge set of gears grinding together.

We sat there idling, with the two brothers crouched behind their Seville looking scared. Mr. No Socks still had his hand over his eye. He looked like he was taking an exam at the ophthalmologist's office.

I switched on my high beams and revved the motor in a menacing way, just to keep them guessing. Bev threw open the door, and Nick jumped in. He rolled over to the space between the seats. He was pissed at Bev.

"Goddammit," he said, "why did you give them the fucking money?"

"Because I was trying to save your ass," she said. "Those mother-fuckers were gonna kill you."

"Well, I had a plan," he said. "I had a fucking plan."

"Oh, yeah. Well, what was it?"

Nick threw his hands in the air. "Hell, I don't know. I was still working it out."

The brothers had worked up enough nerve to step out from behind their car. The one with socks eyed his mangled two-iron. He looked like he wanted to retrieve it. But I didn't give him a chance. I hit the gas again and took off for the road, nailing his club in the process. The brothers turned tail and jumped back behind their car.

I'd managed to put Judge Knox completely out of my head. I suppose Bev had beaten her ass down when she stomped the accelerator. I felt better than I'd felt all day. The smell of gasoline swelled the air as I careened around a row of parked motorcycles. *"Unwind and stomp that sonuvabitch."* I could hear the voice giving me instructions. I hopped the curb and intersected the quiet four lanes of asphalt, finally hitting the brakes and sliding to a stop in the Waffle House parking lot. Three men stood in the glare of the high beams, looking awfully frightened by what had just transpired in front of them.

Nick raised his head and gazed through the windshield. He narrowed his eyes and studied the vision before him.

"Holy fucking shit. Is that Jack Nicklaus?"

Nick, Bev, and I climbed out of the van. Somehow, Dewey had remained peacefully passed out through everything.

Carlton's mouth dropped open when he saw the dent and the

scratches running along the side of the van. "Oh, shit," he said. "My ass is grass."

He dropped the pieces of paper he'd been carrying. They were napkins from the Waffle House. They all had Nicklaus's signature on them. Carlton stepped over to the van and ran his fingers along the damage.

The man who I now understood to be Jack Nicklaus appeared shocked and frightened, almost unable to move. But then he surprised me and spoke. He looked right into my face like I was Ken Venturi or something.

"Are you okay, son?"

He sounded just like he did on TV, his voice as flat as a tee box. I lied in response.

"Yeah, I'm fine. The accelerator just stuck on me for a second."

I gazed over my shoulder to make sure the brothers hadn't followed us. They were nowhere in sight. I listened for sirens, too. Thankfully, the night remained silent.

By that time, Nick and Bev had walked around from the other side of the van. A gash had opened up on the side of Nick's head thanks to the now-deceased two-iron. Nick was pressing a bloody towel against the wound.

Nick's face was pale, his eyes bright and wild, hair swept all over the place. He offered his free hand to Nicklaus in a very gentlemanly way. "I'm a big fan, Mr. Nicklaus. A big fan."

Nicklaus eyed the towel. It looked like it had been soaked in a bucket of cherry Kool-Aid. The Golden Bear cringed and finally obliged Nick's handshake offer.

"That looks like a nasty cut." Nicklaus gestured toward the Waffle House. "Maybe you should let someone inside call an ambulance."

Nick was quick to put that club back in the bag, shaking his head and saying no.

"It's not a big deal," Nick said. "Actually, it's just a golf injury."

Nicklaus looked at his friend. His eyes were pleading with the guy. Unfortunately, the man in the blazer appeared even more frightened than Nicklaus.

Carlton got down on his hands and knees to gather up his autographs. Nicklaus's friend took the lapse in conversation as an opportunity to hustle the Bear out of harm's way. He placed his hand on Nicklaus's elbow and tugged him back toward the Buick. "Maybe we should go somewhere else," he said.

"There's a Huddle House up the street," I told them. "I saw it on the way into town."

We all stood there like a viewing gallery while the two men walked back to the Buick. Just as Nicklaus was ducking his head into the Park Avenue, Nick called out to him, "Hey, Jack. You don't know anybody who's looking to buy some Masters tickets, do you?"

Nicklaus shut the door without answering. His buddy hit the automatic locks and started the engine. Nick, Carlton, and I cracked up.

"I guess not," Nick said.

"Fuck him, anyway." Carlton had a sour look on his face.

"What are you talking about?" Nick said. "He was a true gentleman, considering the circumstances."

"Well, he wouldn't sign my autograph the way I wanted him to."

"What the hell did you want him to write?" I asked.

"To the guy with the biggest balls on the course . . ." Carlton said.

We started laughing again. Nick grabbed at his head and let out a groan. "Don't make me laugh, Carlton. My head's killing me."

We watched the taillights on the Buick shrink. Nick draped his arm around me and squeezed my shoulder.

"Look at that," he said. "One day with me, and you're already hobnobbing with legends."

"I think we scared the shit out of him."

"We may well have taken him right off his game."

I looked into Nick's glassy eyes. "You don't think we cost him the Masters, do you?"

Nick smiled and pulled me close with his free arm. "Thanks for coming to get me back there, bro. That was a rather impressive display of high-performance driving."

"Not impressive enough." I gazed at the damaged van. Carlton was running his fingers over the dent and the scratches. He looked like a faith healer, only without the faith.

Nick waved his hand through the air. "Don't worry about that shit, Carlton. I know somebody who can knock that out before the sun comes up."

Nick wobbled a little. His face was pale. I grabbed his shoulders and steadied him. "How's your head?"

He pulled the towel away from the wound. His hair was matted and sticky with blood. He studied the crimson towel for a moment, like it was an X-ray.

"It's nothing four stitches and some Percocet won't cure. I can tell you that right now."

6

Nicklaus missed a three-way play-off by one stroke, allowing some guy named Fuzzy to go on and win the Masters. Nick and I watched it all unfold at his and Dewey's place. Nick switched off the TV before they had even awarded that ugly green jacket.

"I think I've seen enough golf."

He sat down beside me on the sofa and lit a cigarette. It's fair to say a cloud of responsibility hung over the room.

"You don't think we—"

Nick swatted the air with his cigarette. "Don't even say it."

"But that was a makeable putt he missed on seventeen. Even Pat Summerall said it."

"Pat Summerall was a fucking football player. Hell, he doesn't know golf. Those greens down there are like fucking ice. Jack gave it a good ride, man. He's just getting older, is all."

We sat there for a moment in the silence.

"Well, at least I didn't run him over with the van."

Nick gave a sharp, affirmative nod. "There you go. That's looking at the bright side. You can't let one little scrape with the law make you think everything's your fault."

He stood up, walked back to the bedroom, and fetched his golf bag. He set it down on the living room floor and started rummaging through the zippered pockets, taking inventory of the company warehouse. Weed. Cash. Golf balls. Shoes. Costa Rican cigars in case of a hole in one. And a brand-new Daisy .22 air pistol to replace the old shooting wedge I'd stolen.

"You did what you had to do," Nick said. "Took those two assholes at the hotel out of play, got me and Bev out of a situation, and then swooped in to make sure Carlton was all right. If you ask me, it takes a real man to pull off that kind of shit."

I caught myself staring at the blank TV screen. I was wondering if watching a blank screen was worse than watching a test pattern. And then I had an actual thought.

"A real man eats pussy and drives a stick shift."

Nick burst out laughing. He was holding his head, groaning and laughing. "I know where you heard that one. I know exactly where you got that pearl. Lyndell Fulmer, the king of wisdom."

"Did he tell you the same thing?"

"No, but I used to hear him say it to his buddies down at the garage."

I settled back on the scratchy sofa and stretched out my legs. It had already become my favorite spot in the house, my private little cove— good sunlight from the window, perfect angle on the TV, telephone within reach, TV tray nearby for snacks and drinks. It was where I slept at night, too, always with the TV flickering, sometimes with Dewey sitting in the recliner, strumming his acoustic, or Nick and Bev going at it, one way or another, back in his bedroom. I'd drift off smelling the sweet aroma of beer and tobacco in the cushions.

Nick asked if Claudia had told me about Lyndell's unexpected rise to respectability.

"Yeah, she told me. I think it shook her up."

Nick was squatting on the floor, rolling up bags of pot and sliding them into a pocket of his golf bag. "What do you think?"

"No offense to Claudia, or anything, but I'm glad it all turned out okay for him. I just can't imagine Lyndell being sober and going to work every day."

Nick smiled. "It's a helluva thing to try to picture."

He zipped up the warehouse, and then he asked if Lyndell had ever told me any C.W. stories.

"Oh, yeah. I think I've heard them all."

Nick whistled. "He used to tell a story, that's for sure. If he talked for longer than thirty seconds, you knew it was bullshit."

He narrowed his eyes and looked to the front door as though some-one were standing there. "I bet that's probably the best thing about being a father, though. You don't have to be perfect, or even be around all that much, to make a big impression."

The afternoon light shone through the window, pale and tired. Its angle changed just a little, and I suddenly caught my reflection in the TV screen. I was merely an outline of a person.

"Are you and Bev ever gonna have kids?"

Nick laughed a little. "I doubt it. Hell, I think Bev doubles the dosage on her birth control pills just to be safe. She won't even talk about kids."

"Well, what about the radio thing? The Georgia School of Broadcasting?"

Nick looked away like I'd embarrassed him. "I don't know. Sometimes it seems like a good idea. Sometimes it seems stupid as hell."

"You should do it," I said. "Outside of Claudia, you know more about music than just about anybody."

"That's true," he said. "But I'd have to go to school for two years. And then, who knows what kind of job I'd get. Carlton says he could get me on at the Pond, but he'll have gotten his ass canned by then. Besides, it doesn't sound all that great. You know, they don't even let him choose his own songs, except once an hour. They got all the music programmed on these tapes. Everything comes in from this Florida company that owns the station: Whitlaw Broadcasting. Hell, Carlton's just a monkey in there pushing the buttons."

Poor Carlton. First, Dewey wanted to hire a monkey to play the bass, and now this.

"Why would you wanna go legit, anyway?" I asked. "It's like Bev said, you've got a pretty good setup right now."

Nick leaned his golf bag against the wall and stood up. He took a long drag off his cigarette, considering me all the while.

"Have you been selling?"

"Selling what?"

He made a face. "Don't fuck with me. You know what I'm talking about."

I shrugged. "A little."

"You've been stealing that shit from me." Nick pulled out his seven-iron and waggled it a little, staring down the shaft. "I thought you were just smoking with your friends. But you were going into business for yourself, weren't you?"

"Well, I smoked a good bit of it, if that makes you feel any better."

Nick leaned on his club like it was a walking cane. "Why the hell would you wanna go into business after all the shit you've seen me go through?"

"I don't know. I was just testing the job market. I wanted to see what it was like, maybe make a little money toward buying a car."

Nick shook his head. "And what'd you end up making?"

"About a hundred bucks. I smoked a little more than I meant to."

"Do you know what that hundred bucks could have cost you?"

"You don't have to start acting like a judge," I said. "I'm here, aren't I? I'm starting work at the Holiday Inn next week. I'm gonna be a good citizen of the world. And I'm sure as hell not gonna give Dot Knox an excuse to send my ass to Alto."

Nick frowned and slipped his seven-iron back in the bag.

"It's a goddamn impossible way of life," he said. "Bev talks it up, but there's a lot of stuff that she leaves out."

"That's what Dewey was saying. He was telling me about the cops, the competition, all that shit."

"It's more than that, even," Nick said. "It goes right on down to telling you who your friends are. They gotta be people in the business, or else your buyers. If I meet a girl out somewhere, say I'm at the grocery store or something—shit, I can't tell her what I do. I either have to lie or act all cagey about it. And that might be okay for a few days, maybe enough to get in her pants. But what if I fall in love? Shit, I'm screwed. The whole thing's a lie. If I tell her, it blows right up in my face."

"So where does Bev fit into all this grocery store talk?"

"Well, this is all speculation," he said. "I love Bev. I mean, she and I are looking at things long-term, but you never know when shit's gonna get thrown at you."

I was starting to feel like a real shit ass for stealing his pot and his BB pistol. I'd never considered Nick's life to be anything but great, at least when he wasn't in jail. And even then, it's not like he ever made prison sound terrible. All I ever heard him mention of it were the golf books he read in there and how he'd played all these famous courses in his head while he was doing his time.

"You're lucky ol' Sport Coat Charlie got you that job at the Holiday Inn," Nick said. "Times are fucking tough right now. We're in a god-damn recession. A lot of my customers are out of work, coming to me wanting to buy on credit or stealing shit so they can buy. Hell, that kind of behavior leads the cops right up to the door."

7

Nick set up shop in his usual stall at the far end of the range. He dropped his bag and started banging drives out at the two-hundred-yard flag. Needless to say, he didn't believe in working the irons first. "I can't reel in all my impulses," he said.

I'd been to the range a few times but hadn't exactly taken to the sport like a young Sam Snead. My biggest handicap, as I could see it, was being left-handed. That meant I couldn't use Nick's shiny Hogans. Instead, I'd adopted a rusty left-handed one-iron that we'd found sticking out of the range's trash can. It was like hitting with a shovel.

I bent over the red-striped sphere and prepared myself to take a swat at it, determined not to do all of that waggling shit like the pros on TV. I addressed the ball—"Hello, motherfucker"—and went right into my backswing, taking a big one, nearly wrapping the club all the way around me, not wanting to cheat myself in case I really got hold of one. Of course, I then proceeded to slice the shit out of the ball. It was a low, hard liner that skittered across the dirt and the browning clumps of crabgrass.

"That's a double, down the line," Nick said. "In the corner for extra bases."

He might have been laughing. But what came over me as I watched the ball mark its stray path was a sudden, and frightening, wave of fury, the kind that makes people pull guns at the dinner table and kill their relatives. Nothing outside of golf had ever had such an effect on me. I spiked my club into the faded patch of AstroTurf and glared at it.

Nick calmly reached into his golf bag, pulled out the shooting wedge, and offered it to me.

"You wanna finish it off?" he asked.

"You wanna eat me?" I replied.

I flipped him off, picked up my still half-filled bucket of balls, and set it down in his stall.

"That's it, I'm retiring," I announced. "This game is total fucking horseshit."

Nick just stood there laughing, leaning against his driver like he was Bob Hope. His hair was pulled straight back into a ponytail, and his left hand was sheathed in a black glove with a small golden bear stitched to the back of it. The glove matched his black golf shoes and black T-shirt. He was the only person I'd ever seen who could look cool while playing golf. He looked like a cross between a golfer and a hit man.

I sat down on the bench behind the stalls and took a swig from my can of Coke. I watched Nick hit for a while. The sun looked like a fiery Titleist teed up on the tree line at the far end of the range.

Pretty soon, a vehicle crunched the gravel in the parking lot behind us. Nick turned and raised his eyes in recognition. He smiled and waved in the direction of the engine's hum. It had the sturdy timbre of an American pickup truck. Music was trickling from the windows, the Stylistics singing "Betcha By Golly, Wow."

The truck was a white Ford, its driver a tall black man with a red-and-black Titleist bag slung over his shoulder. He was wearing a Philadelphia Phillies ball cap, jeans, and a white Izod.

"Cash Bishop," Nick said, "I got somebody I want you to meet."

Cash set his bag down in the stall beside Nick's, pulled out his pitching wedge, then walked over and shook hands with me. He smiled as if we were all preparing to play a round together.

"Cash, here, is a bail bondsman," Nick said. "He's a walking 'Get Out of Jail Free' card."

"Yeah, and your brother's my best customer," Cash said. "His next one's on the house."

Nick laughed. "He's full of shit. He only bailed me out once." He wagged a finger at Cash. "I have acted as a referral service, though."

Cash frowned. "Yeah, you sent me some fine customers. Most of them ran off in the middle of the night."

We were all standing there with our sticks in our hands. Cash was looking at my one-iron. "You play?"

"No. I just quit."

Cash sighed. "You don't have your brother's hook, do you? I keep telling him to open his hips a little, but he don't wanna listen. He thinks he's Lee Trevino playing that damn thing."

"I've got a slice," I told him.

Cash took my one-iron and held it up to the pale evening light. He looked at Nick and shook his head. "Damn, why don't you buy the man some decent sticks."

Nick grabbed the club and gave it back to me. "It's fine for him. He's just learning."

Cash smiled like he'd been let in on a secret. "Forget golf," he said. "I hear you're a pretty good wheel man."

"Well, I'm sort of between licenses at the moment."

"Cash owns a race car," Nick explained. "Runs it over at the mixing bowl on Saturday nights."

My ears perked up. "What kind of car?"

"I got a sixty-nine Cougar."

"Eliminator package?"

"Hell, no. I got the 428 Cobra Jet. Pure pussy."

"You need it with that thing. It's a heavy car."

"Damn right."

I asked Cash if he'd won any races.

He made a face and shook his head. "Not yet. I finished sixth in hobby stock last season. Too many motherfuckers in there don't know how to drive. I gotta give up spots to save my ride."

"Yeah, that's what Lyndell used to say. Of course, he'd take a tire iron to anybody who wrecked him."

"Cash's old man used to race out at the speedway, too," Nick said. "Back in the sixties, if you can believe that shit."

"In Green Lake?" I asked. From what I'd heard, the town had not exactly been a hotbed of civil liberties in those days.

"Oh, yeah," Cash said. "He knew most of the white boys from running whiskey with them. They didn't mind racing him—as long as he didn't beat them."

"So, did he ever win?"

Cash frowned. "You ever heard of Wendell Scott?"

I shook my head.

"Only black man to win a big-time Grand National race. That was back about the same time Pop used to run. When Wendell won his race, they disqualified him because they didn't want him kissing a white girl on the winner's stand. They finally got around to sending him a trophy in the mail, but it wasn't even the real one. It was about the size of a pissant, like a Little League trophy."

Cash was looking down the shaft of his wedge, waggling it a little.

"So, yeah, Pop won a feature race one night. It was small-time shit, but they still disqualified him, said he made an illegal pass."

Nick shook his head. "Auto racing is a hillbilly sport. You start combining all that inbreeding with exhaust fumes, and people just don't act right." He held up his driver and smiled. "Now golf, on the other hand, is a gentleman's game."

Cash just laughed. "Yeah, let's call some of those gents down in Augusta and see if they'll give us a nine-thirty tee time tomorrow morning."

Nick laid his hand on my shoulder and gestured toward Cash. "My bail-bonding friend here was telling me he needs some help at the track this season, and I told him you'd be the perfect guy."

I looked at Cash. "What kind of help?"

"Just shit work. Unloading the car off my hauler, loading it back up after the races. Checking stuff out beforehand. And I can't pay you nothing."

"I don't mind. As long as I get to see the races."

Nick was smiling. "Oh, you'll have plenty of time to watch the races. Cash never makes it out of the qualifying heats, anyway, so you'll be finished working pretty early."

Cash shook his head. "You just keep hooking that damn ball, Lee. And I'll keep taking all your fucking money."

About that time, another car pulled up, a white BMW.

"If you'll excuse me," Nick said, "I've got some business to do."

He walked over to his bag and started unzipping pockets, preparing to make a transaction. Cash and I stood there watching him.

Cash shook his head and whistled. "Damn, your brother sells some good weed."

Somehow Cash lured me back into the hitting stall. He claimed he could straighten out my slice, even though I was far past the point of caring.

I started off by whacking five bad ones. The slice on those shots was almost geometrically impossible.

Cash tapped my legs with his wedge, opening my stance a little. "All right," he said, "keep that elbow in and just relax. Slow everything down. Pretend that you're water and the moon is making you do all this shit. It's pulling you, and pushing you. You're not even yourself. You ain't got a mind, or nothing. You must become empty in order to gain totality."

I looked up from the ball. "What the fuck are you talking about?"

"I'm talking about simplifying."

"Simplifying. I can't even remember half of what you just said."

Cash shrugged. "Man, ain't you ever watched any Bruce Lee? Just pretend you're water and let that motherfucking club flow."

I gazed down at the ball again and thought of the lake. I could feel myself turning watery, could hear the murmurs of the deep in my ears. Time slowed to a trickle. And then . . .

THWACK.

The ball was shrinking, streaking off toward the two-hundred-yard flag, no more than ten feet off the ground. It was a helluva stroke. Even Nick and his customer turned to watch the ball fly.

"Jesus Christ," Nick said. "What the hell got into you?"

I hadn't even been aware of making contact. It felt like I'd awakened after the ball was in flight. I was already thinking of hitting another one. I lifted my scarred one-iron and lovingly wiped a smudge of dirt from its blade.

Cash was smiling, looking all wise. "Grasshopper," he said, "it is time for you to leave."

8

I picked up my first Holiday Inn paycheck near the end of April, feeling awfully proud of what I'd earned—a grand total of $80.57, after taxes. I ached when it came time to deposit the check in Mrs. Dee's Maverick repair fund. Even after Nick had kept his promise and reimbursed me for half the proceeds, I still had a hard time bringing myself to spend the money on anything. Nothing seemed worthy of my noble efforts.

Nick made me pose for a picture with the paycheck held up beside my face. Afterward, he took me out to dinner at the T-Bone King to celebrate my walk on the straight and narrow.

It felt different from any other time I'd followed a hostess to the table. Nick and I were laughing and joking with each other, not even worrying about being too loud. It felt like we had the right, like there was nothing wrong with us that other people might see.

Nick kept telling the waitress that I was picking up the tab. In the end, though, he laid down the cash. At the last second, I told him I'd cover the tip. I left a twenty, just like a high roller. The waitress hadn't been anything special. She'd even fucked up our order, bringing our steaks out medium well instead of medium rare. But I could see that she was having a tough night.

"Goddamn," Nick said. "You'd go broke fast at a titty bar."

I walked out of the restaurant feeling like that good citizen of the world. Then, about halfway across the parking lot, Nick and I noticed the cop car that was blocking Nick's Fury. A tall, uniformed figure stood there in the darkness, the sheriff of Green Lake County, Loyd Muskgrave.

I recognized Muskgrave from his photos in the *Green Lake Gazette*. He was embroiled in a scandal concerning the treatment of prisoners at the county jail. He'd been accused of pulling them off their normal work duties to perform personal chores for him. They had supposedly bush-hogged his pasture, repaved his driveway, painted his house, cleaned the swimming pool, and washed and waxed his Thunderbird for a guarantee of conjugal visits from prostitutes and access to booze and marijuana. Of course, Muskgrave denied all charges.

"Ah, shit," Nick muttered, as if Muskgrave's presence was only a minor nuisance. I wished I could have felt the same way, but my first instinct had been to turn and run like hell.

Muskgrave was lanky and young, with thick blond Robert Redford hair and the sort of blue eyes that people tend to recall fondly in the voting booth. He was leaning back against his Crown Vic. The scanner in his car was squawking away like a bird.

Nick took the initiative. "Hello, Loyd. What's up?"

The sheriff nodded. His eyes moved from Nick's face to my own.

"Lord help us," he said. "It looks like I'm seeing double."

Nick grinned. "What is it they say in that chewing gum ad? Double your pleasure, double your fun."

Muskgrave shook his head and sighed. "Double your trouble's more like it."

"Now that's not a very nice thing to say," Nick told him. "Young Luke here just collected his first paycheck from the Holiday Inn."

Muskgrave considered me. He was wearing this smirk on his face, like someone who knows that something bad is going to happen, only they don't plan on sharing the knowledge with you beforehand.

"So, I guess Dot Knox must have put the fear of God into you."

I couldn't help but answer that one. It wasn't like I'd exorcised all the smart-ass out of me.

"I ain't afraid of Knox and her flying monkeys."

It wasn't exactly top-drawer material, but the sheriff's badge had taken me off my game.

"Good for you." Muskgrave laughed. "That sort of attitude's gonna serve you well when you're under incarceration."

"I don't have to go to jail to wash cars for a living."

Now that one was top drawer, if not exactly judicious. Muskgrave narrowed his eyes and took a step toward me. Nick was staring at me, too, his mouth open as though he couldn't believe what I'd just said. Fortunately, he stepped between me and the sheriff.

"So, you want to talk, or what?" Nick asked.

Muskgrave and I were still eyeing each other over the top of Nick's shoulder.

Muskgrave pointed at me. "You had better watch your ass," he said.

Nick held up his hands and tried to calm Muskgrave down. "Listen, Loyd. Why don't you and I just sit in the cruiser and talk?"

Loyd finally turned his attention back to Nick. "No, I think it's best we talk right here, where both of you can get the message."

Nick looked back at me and frowned. "All right, then. What is it you want to talk about?"

"Business," he said. "Namely, yours."

"You mean landscaping?"

"Cut the shit, Nick. You know what I'm talking about."

Nick crossed his arms and sighed. He waited for Muskgrave to get to the point.

"I don't know if you even pay attention to this sort of thing," Muskgrave said, "but there was a report that came out a couple months back about the drug problem in this country. Morley Safer was talking about it on *60 Minutes* the other night."

"I must have been watching *Wild Kingdom,*" Nick said.

"Well, it's a serious problem. Usage is up seventy percent across the board, eighty-two percent among teenagers. Hell, there's even grade-school kids using."

He rattled off a bunch of statistics. It sounded like he was delivering a stump speech.

"It's a bad economy," Nick said. "People are always gonna look for a way to get through when times are tough."

Muskgrave snorted. "Well, I'm building my reelection platform on cleaning up this problem. We've let a lot of shit slide around here for too long."

Nick smiled. "Somebody must be planning to run against you this time."

The sheriff wasn't amused. "I'm not bullshitting you, Nick. You can play dumb if you want, act like you're just this little ol' pot dealer, Mr.

Nickel-and-Dime, or whatever. But I know what goes on around here. I know all about the cocaine that's been coming in lately."

Muskgrave fixed me with a stare, as though I might give something away. But this was the first I'd even heard of any cocaine trafficking.

"Cocaine's been coming through here for a long time," Nick said. "It ain't nothing new."

He shot me a glance, then set his sights back on Muskgrave. "Not that I've had anything to do with it."

Muskgrave chuckled. "Yeah, I know. You two have just been so busy earning those paychecks."

"Pretty much," Nick told him. "Between the landscaping business and my golf game, my days are pretty much booked solid."

Muskgrave sighed and shook his head. It was amazing how young he looked. Take away the sheriff suit, and he could have passed for one of Nick's friends.

"You know, I play some golf myself."

"No shit?" Nick smiled as though he was genuinely interested. "So, what's your handicap?"

"I got it down to a six last fall. Started off four years ago with a fourteen."

"Damn, you oughta quit law enforcement and get your tour card."

"Wouldn't that be a sweet life?" Muskgrave asked.

"You don't have to convince me," Nick said.

Muskgrave flashed a smug grin. "You ever played the Atlanta Athletic Club?"

He might as well have asked Nick if he'd ever humped the queen of England. The Atlanta Athletic Club was almost as exclusive. It had been Bobby Jones's home club when he was alive.

Nick acted as though the jab had missed its mark. "Can't say I have. I mostly stick to the public courses. I like a place where I can spit without getting fined."

Muskgrave smiled. "Well, I'm not a member or anything. I've just played there a couple of times as Senator McHugh's guest."

This caused Nick to smile. "I hear McHugh's retiring after his next term."

"That's right," Muskgrave said. "Sort of coincides with the end of my next term as sheriff."

"How convenient," Nick said. "Hey, maybe you could go down to Atlanta and work under the gold dome." They were both grinning now, clearly enjoying the give-and-take, each acting as though he held the upper hand. "Of course you have to get reelected sheriff first. Don't forget that."

"Don't you worry. I'm not taking anything for granted."

"I'm sure you won't," Nick said.

Muskgrave finally opened his car door. And then, before departing, he looked my way. He'd kept one last comment in the bag for my benefit.

"If I run into Dot Knox, I'll pass along your regards."

He chuckled a little, ducked inside the cruiser, and slammed the door, leaving us to ponder what had just transpired. I was left with one question for Nick.

"Are you really selling cocaine?"

Nick pretended he didn't hear me. He watched the sheriff's taillights as they headed down the street.

"Six handicap, my ass," he said. "I bet he cheats like a motherfucker."

9

The Holiday Inn's dishwasher was chugging away, keeping a rhythm that reminded me of Dewey when he was banging out "Heartbreaker" on his drum kit. The machine even sweated like Dewey when he played, the heat and the steam pulsing over me as I set a tub of dishes atop the drain board.

Stanley, the always-stoned room service waiter, stood there in the mist trying to eat a Reese's Peanut Butter Cup. The steam melted the chocolate all over his hands and his wrinkled white shirt. I pointed out the stain, not sure that he'd even notice without a heads-up.

"Jesus, Stan. It looks like somebody wiped their ass on your shirt."

Stan gazed downward, considering the situation with only the slightest concern. "It's cool. I'll just button my blazer."

He shook his hair out of his eyes, licked his fingers, and stared up at the ceiling in a thoughtful way. "I've been reworking the letter a little bit."

"How's that?" I asked.

"Well, what if the woman in the room were an amputee? Some people are into that shit."

Stan had been composing a letter to the Penthouse Forum ever since I'd started bussing tables at the hotel six weeks earlier. It involved the sexual escapades of a swollen-membered room service waiter and a busty hotel guest who looked like Cheryl Ladd.

"I think I'd lay off the amputee stuff," I told him. "Whenever I see those kinds of letters, I usually skip to something else."

Stan sighed. "Yeah, I wouldn't want to go over the top."

About that time, there was a commotion at the other end of the kitchen. Stan's eyes widened. "You might want to take cover," he said. "Fay's got a knife."

Before I could even turn around, I heard Fay's loud voice.

"Cough it up, you goddamn bitch!"

Fay was a tall blonde waitress who suffered from an affinity for blue eye shadow. She also had a temper, hence the butcher knife presently cocked behind her ear. She was blocking the double doors that led to the dining room, apparently ready to carve up a smaller, red-haired waitress named Eileen.

Eileen stood in front of Fay holding a tray with a couple of shrimp scampi dinners on top of it. She was overmatched but standing her ground like a left tackle.

"What the hell are you talking about?" Eileen asked.

"You know what I'm talking about, you ugly little slut. You lifted my tip off table twelve. I did everything but give that guy a hand job. He wouldn't stiff me like that."

Eileen let out a snort. "You're crazy," she said. "Look at your fucking eyes. You're so high, I bet you picked it up yourself and forgot about it."

Eileen took a step toward the door, but Fay blocked her path and gave her a shove to the chest. Eileen staggered backward. She grabbed the tray with both hands to keep the dishes from falling.

We had all stopped what we were doing to see if the tip dispute would result in bloodshed. Yuri, the executive chef, even turned his back on the grill to check things out. He gripped his spatula extra tight, as though he might whip some ass if need be, his ever-present Macanudo clenched in his teeth. Meanwhile, the burgers and steaks cooking behind him were slowly sizzling their way toward the grayer side of medium well.

Fay and Eileen sized each other up like a couple of heavyweight boxers. The shit hit the fan when Eileen threw the tray of scampi right at Fay's head. It sounded like a car wreck, all clanging metal and busting glass. Amid the clatter, Eileen let out a banshee wail and went in after the knife.

Stanley could barely contain himself. "Bitch fight," he said. "Hell, yeah."

We all looked to Yuri. He was a wide-bodied Russian with a full dark beard, and he lorded over the kitchen with the iron fist of a communist strongman. Fay had dubbed him "the Dictator," and the nickname had stuck to him like his shrunken chef smock.

However, Yuri didn't appear all that eager to wade into the scuffle. He began to scout the kitchen staff for help. His eyes quickly landed on me. He looked me up and down, then waved his hand in the direction of the melee.

"Come, beeg boy!"

Fay was straddling Eileen and still clutching the knife. Eileen had both hands wrapped around Fay's arm, trying to fend her off. Both women were grunting and straining, the muscles in their arms and legs flexed tight and shining from the garlic butter that coated the checkerboard floor. Fay's green polyester waitressing jumper had ridden up over her panties. They were the same light shade of blue as her eye makeup. The whole scene was like something out of a women's-prison movie.

I took up a position behind Yuri. Nick and I had been working out in the mornings, so it felt good to have Yuri pick me out as his henchman, even if he hadn't remembered my name.

"Stop this fucking madness!" Yuri screamed. "I will fire both your asses, tu twi!"

He reached in from behind and tried to grab the knife from Fay. But Fay struck like a coiled rattler, taking a backhanded swipe at Yuri. The shiny blade caught the meat of his spatula hand.

"Aaahh!" Yuri dropped to his knees and crawled over to the gas range. He cowered there, yelping like a hound. "Take the knife, beeg boy! Take the knife!"

The sight of blood gushing from Yuri's hand made us all go quiet. It looked like he'd stashed a bottle of Heinz up his sleeve. Even Fay paused for a second. She appeared surprised by what she'd done.

One thing the Augusta incident had taught me was that, in a dire situation, it's best to act first and think later. So, I jumped right in and tried to take the knife. My heart thumping like the dishwasher, John Bonham, and big Dewey all rolled into one, I grabbed hold of her wrist.

Fay grit her teeth and tried to jerk away. But then, she calmed down and hardly offered any resistance at all.

Once I had the knife under control, I tossed it onto the drainboard. Stan immediately picked it up. He studied the crimson stain on the blade and started grinning like he'd just hauled in a prize fish.

Another waitress handed Yuri a stack of white napkins. Yuri tried wrapping one of them around his hand, but the blood quickly seeped through. It was a serious bloodletting. The way Yuri was bleeding, someone might have thought that we'd gutted a deer in that kitchen.

Fay eventually climbed off Eileen. She stood up and pulled her dress back down over her panties. At first, she appeared to be embarrassed, but that feeling must have quickly passed.

"Well, what the fuck are all y'all staring at?"

She kicked at a couple of the shrimp lying on the floor. Then she put her fingers to her temples like she was fighting some kind of godawful headache.

"Jesus Christ," she said, "I need a fucking cigarette." And with that, she headed down the hallway to the employee dressing room.

"Don't come back to my fucking kitchen," Yuri shouted. "You are fired now."

"Fine," she said. "You can go to hell, you fat-ass."

Eileen was still lying amid the wreckage of shrimp and garlic butter. A sprig of parsley lay on her jumper like she was the nightly special, with prawns on the side. I asked her if she was all right. I was expecting a thank-you for taking the knife from Fay. Instead, she looked at me like I'd been the cause of all the trouble.

"What do you think, shit head?"

She held out her hand, and I helped her to her feet.

"That's it," she said. "I quit. This place is a fucking lunatic asylum."

She pulled her tip money out of her apron pocket and stuffed it into the top of her jumper, then she untied the apron and spiked it on the floor.

"You can't queet," Yuri said. "I am too shorthanded. Get your ass back to here, now."

He was half demanding and half begging, still down on his knees, looking like a casualty of war. But Eileen showed no mercy. She gave him the finger and kicked open the heavy back door. Before she walked out, she called down the hallway to Fay: "By the way, bitch. He only left you three dollars. Maybe you should've given him that hand job."

Yuri jumped up and intercepted Fay before she could head out the door and catch Eileen.

"No, no," he said. "Don't be rash. Maybe we can give you second chance. We can call this verbal warning. I cannot lose two waitress people."

Fay gave Yuri the once-over, clearly skeptical of his proposal. She gestured toward his hand, which was still wrapped in the bloody napkin. "So you're not gonna call the cops?"

Yuri sniffed at the air. He spun toward the grill and pointed to his spatula. "Beeg boy," he said, "flip the meat. I have to talk, now."

I went to work, even though the cause was a lost one. The burgers and steaks were past well done, working toward a nuclear singe. Another piece of flesh that I couldn't even begin to identify was smoking like an overturned tractor trailer at the back of the grill. I pried it loose from the scalding surface and flipped it to the less burnt side. I believe it may have been a chicken breast.

Yuri and Fay hashed things out, and then Fay stepped out back to smoke her cigarette. Yuri finally returned to the grill and reassumed control of his spatula and cigar. None of us had the gall to tell him he shouldn't have been handling food with that bloody napkin wrapped around his hand.

I gazed up at the big clock on the wall, surprised to see that it was already eight-thirty. Almost a half hour had passed since Fay drew back the blade. It hadn't even seemed like five minutes. I'd really come to enjoy working in the service industry.

Her name was Rachel Coyle, and she was a server, a position just above busboy since it actually required some flicker of brainpower to remember which meal belonged to which customer. That's not to say she was a model employee. I could tell by the slouchy way she walked back to the kitchen. Of course, I immediately took a liking to her.

Rachel walked in with a steak dinner and stopped to survey the aftermath of Fay's tizzy: the shrimp and the rice and especially Yuri's zigzagged trail of blood. She didn't bother to ask what had happened. She acted like she couldn't have cared less.

"The couple at table fourteen keeps asking about their scampis," she said. "The woman wants to know if we had to send out a boat."

"Ha. Ha," Yuri said. "People are so fucking clever."

Rachel tiptoed through the debris in her clunky black shoes. She carried the steak dinner over to Yuri. He considered it for a moment and grunted.

"What the fuck is this?"

Rachel shrugged. "That's your dinner special tonight. Remember those rib eyes that were about to go bad?"

"No," he said, clearly irritated. "I mean why are you bringing it back?"

"The woman at table nine says she ordered it medium well, and it's still rare. Her husband said he could see the marks where the jockey whipped it."

Yuri clenched his eyes shut. "I don't want to hear anymore what customers have to say."

He picked up the steak with his fingers. He held it to the light and studied the spot where the woman had cut into the flesh.

"It is fucking gray," he said. He slapped the steak back onto the plate, whipped his cigar out of his mouth, and tamped a coat of ashes onto the meat.

"There," he said. "Now tell her it is well done."

Rachel never batted an eye. She just stood there looking bored.

"What?" Yuri asked. "What is it? Tell me." He looked jumpy. It was obvious that Rachel had a way of unnerving him.

"You never gave me an answer about the shrimp scampi." Her voice was as flat as the spatula in Yuri's hand.

Stan and I were unloading the washer. I nudged his shoulder and pointed to the grill. "What do you think of her?"

Despite his penchant for pot and pornographic letters, Stan was no run-of-the-mill idiot. Apparently, he'd scored a 1,320 on his SATs after graduating from the Four Loaves Christian Academy. And yet he'd postponed college for Yuri's kitchen.

"There's something about her eyes," he said.

"Yeah, I know. They're kind of sexy in a weird way."

"No, that's not it," he said. "Something about her eyes reminds me of my older sister. The doctors told my parents she has a chemical imbalance."

"Is that a mental thing?"

"Yeah. She has to take medicine for it. Otherwise she goes out and wrecks cars and shit."

Yuri held up his bloody paw. "Can't you see I am wounded?" He sounded like he was pleading with Rachel. "I cannot make scampi now."

Rachel still refused to ask what had gone down in the kitchen. "Well, if it's that bad, you should go to the hospital. Either way, I'm not telling those people their scampis are on the floor."

She turned her back on Yuri and walked off to deliver the Macanudo-dusted steak. Along the way, she tramped through a pool of Yuri's blood. Before the kitchen doors swung shut, I could see that she'd left a trail of it on the dining room's gold carpet.

Yuri stood there looking butchered and beleaguered, like some kind of pro wrestling chef who'd come out on the wrong end of a Ginsu-knife cage match. He might have been six feet tall and two bills with change, but he'd proven no match for a couple of skinny women in aprons. He surveyed the shrimp that littered the floor, and then his blue eyes traveled to a stack of clean dishes that I'd just set beside the stove. He stroked his beard in a devilish way, as if he was considering the unthinkable.

Stan placed his hand on my shoulder and leaned in close to my ear. "I got five bucks that says he serves those shrimp."

All I could do was shake my head. "I sure hope this kind of stuff doesn't happen at the T-Bone King."

I found Yuri sitting at the bar after the dining room had closed. That's where he always doled out the checks to the kitchen staff. The bar was quiet and empty. Even the bartender had knocked off for the evening. Yuri had helped himself to a bottle of Courvoisier. He was nursing a snifter and watching *Cool Hand Luke* on the TV mounted above the bar. The wet, gnawed stump of a cigar lay smoldering in an ashtray.

"Sit," he commanded, waving his hand, which he'd finally gotten around to patching up with a roll of gauze. "This is good movie, yes?"

I gazed up at the screen. The card scene was on, the one where Newman bluffs his ass off with a worthless hand.

"Ha!" Yuri let out some strange hybrid of a laugh and a grunt. "I love that. He beats them with nothing. With pooey."

Yuri had a physical way of talking. Even when he was happy, you got the feeling he might just reach out and slap you shitless at any second. I nodded and smiled, trying to stay limber in case the need arose to bob and weave.

"Your name is Luke, yes?"

I was surprised. He really did know my name.

"Maybe we call you Cool Hand Luke," he said. "Cool Hand take knife from Fay."

"Yeah, I guess I did."

Yuri turned his attention back to the screen. The stack of checks was sitting between us. I could have thumbed through it and found mine, but I got the feeling he wasn't finished talking to me.

"Your parents like *Cool Hand Luke,* yes?"

"I don't really know. Why?"

"Why? Because they name you Luke."

I was worried I might have to explain that my name wasn't all that uncommon, and, anyway, Claudia had named me after the alter ego of Hank Williams: Luke the Drifter. I had a feeling Yuri didn't know who Hank was, and I wasn't in the mood for explanations.

Then Yuri started laughing. "Ha. Ha. Ha. I am kidding, beeg boy."

He poured a little more Courvoisier into his glass. Gazing into his bleary eyes, I could tell that he'd advanced past the stage of a light buzz and was working his way toward a full-fledged bender. Tomorrow was his day off.

"Paul Newman," he said, pointing at the screen. "I love that man."

"Yeah, he's cool," I said. "He races cars, you know."

"I know that. You think I am fucking idiot? Paul Newman stay in this hotel last year when he race at Lakeside Circuit."

Yuri pounded his fist on the bar to emphasize his point that it was *this* hotel and none other.

"No shit?"

"No shit. Yuri cook steak for Cool Hand Luke. I try to send him fifty eggs. Ha. Ha. Ha. But he like steak, medium rare. He even came back to kitchen, and we make salad dressing together."

"Make what?"

Yuri pronounced it as clearly and as slowly as he could. "Sal-eet dress-king. He makes his own. It is very good. I tell him he should start his own company."

There was a road course near Green Lake called Lakeside Circuit that hosted a big GT race every fall. I could see Newman showing up for it, as the race attracted all the top drivers. The story checked out until the salad dressing part.

"I met Jack Nicklaus once."

"Who?"

"Jack Nicklaus, the golfer."

Yuri waved his hand through the air. "I don't know golf. Paul Newman, though. I love that sonuvabitch."

I waited to see if he had anything else to say, but he kept his eyes on the screen. Finally, I decided to make a play for the checks. I eased my hand down the bar, toward the stack of paper.

"Let me tell you something, beeg boy."

I tried to jerk my arm back, but he clamped his bandaged hand over my wrist. He leaned over like he was going to tell me a secret.

"When I was small boy, they pack me and mother on railroad car."

"Who did?"

"Who? Who do you think? Joseph Stalin."

He jerked his head derisively. "Fucking cocksucker. Pooey. They take us from our village in Chechnya, and they burn it to ground. It was very cold, and mother, she die in cattle car. She die with her arms around me."

He wrapped his arms around himself and squeezed tight, like he was trying to dislodge a chicken bone from his windpipe.

"My father was killed in war, see. And then my mother, she was killed by Stalin. They throw her body to the snow. So I have nothing. I am eight years old, and I have nothing."

"Jesus, I'm sorry."

Yuri pointed to the TV screen. "That is okay, beeg boy. Don't feel sorry for Yuri. Sometimes nothing is a pretty cool hand."

He shoved the stack of checks in front of me. "What are you waiting for? Take it. Go buy Fay a drink. Tell her no hard feelings. Ha. Ha. Ha."

10

I stopped by the hotel gift shop on my way out. It was closed for the night, but the lock on the glass door was busted. I looked around to see if anybody was watching and then I let myself inside. I felt my way through the dark, past the peanut-shaped ashtrays and the little souvenir bales of cotton. I stopped at the magazine rack and waited for my eyes to adjust in the dim light. When I could read the covers, I picked up the latest *Road & Track* and stuffed it into my backpack. I considered lifting a Payday bar but resisted the temptation. I was still riding high on my wave of law-abiding citizenship, determined not to slip up. I even planned to sneak the magazine back into the gift shop when I came to work the next day.

I parked myself on the curb, right beneath the floodlights at the kitchen's back entrance. Nick and the band were playing a late set at Smokey the Bar, so I figured he'd be a while picking me up.

The night was still and warm, typical early May stuff, with a whiff of the swimming pool's chlorine hanging in the air. I pulled off the white oxford that I wore in the dining room and shook the hem of my T-shirt to stir some air around my body. I fired up a Winston that I'd lifted from Nick's soft pack and opened the magazine. I'd just started to read about the new Porsche Carrera when I heard Rachel's voice.

"Don't they cut off your fingers for stealing shit like that?"

She was standing over me, wearing her green waitress jumper and her bad girl leather jacket. She was slouching to one side to make up for the weight of the green backpack slung over her shoulder.

"Nobody except Fay," I told her.

"You're the one who took the knife from her, aren't you?"

"I didn't have much choice. Yuri told me to take it."

"The modest hero," she said. "How refreshing. Too bad you're a thief."

"What are you talking about?"

"The magazine," she said. "I was picking up my check in the bar. Anybody could have seen you stumbling around in the gift shop. If I were your guidance counselor, I wouldn't suggest a life of crime."

"Well, it's nothing you need to tell anybody. Besides, I'm gonna return it."

She let out a snort, as though she had no doubt whatsoever that I was full of shit. She hoisted her backpack a little higher and turned to walk away.

But then she stopped and looked back over her shoulder. "I knew a boy in Ohio who looked like you."

I figured this was a good thing.

"He was a fucking asshole," she said.

The statement just sat there, rotting like the shrimp in the Dumpster across the parking lot. She waited for a response, but I didn't know what to say. So, I decided to go with Nick's tactic. One morning when we were lifting weights on the front porch he told me that if I was ever with a girl and found myself at a loss for words, it was best to just keep quiet and look irritated. This was the same morning he'd told me to wash my Hanes pocket T's in hot water so they'd shrink up nice and tight. "Then you gotta stretch out the neck," he said. "Girls eat that shit with a spoon."

I tugged at the neck of my white Hanes, puffed the Winston, and tried to pull off a Clint-like squint. I looked at Rachel, and she looked at me. I was determined to wait her out.

"So is there anything to do around here?" she said finally.

I felt like I'd won a contest, only now I really did have to say something. I went back to the well again and asked myself, "What would Nick do?" The answer appeared like a burning shrub.

"You wanna smoke a joint?"

Rachel tilted her head and pushed her long spill of hair behind her ear. She appeared hopeful. "You got one?"

I was on empty at the moment, but I knew that Stan was equipped to handle all marijuana emergencies this side of a Rastafarian convention. "Stocking the pantry" is how he put it. I gazed out into the employee lot to make sure his van was still there.

"I can get one," I said.

"Where?"

I took one last drag off the Winston, then flicked it across the pavement. I stood up and turned to go back inside. "Wait here. I gotta call room service."

Rachel drove an old white Peugeot sedan with Illinois plates: *GS 8349—Land of Lincoln.* I remembered reading somewhere that Peugeots never wanted to start in cold weather, but I didn't see any need in telling her that. Besides, she went well with the car. It wasn't all that attractive at first glance, just a boxy European four-door. But it had its appeal if you kept looking, the slightest of curves around the trunk and the grill, small details that made it interesting, details you'd never see on a Ford or a Chevy. I suppose I would have been disappointed if she'd been driving an ordinary, dependable sort of car.

We were smoking in the Peugeot at the back of the employee lot. We had a real fog going in that thing. Rachel told me how she and her mother just moved to Green Lake a few months back. They were from Champaign, Illinois, though they'd lived somewhere in Ohio for a year before coming south. Rachel was seventeen, heading into her senior year of high school in the fall. Her mother was an English professor who'd just taken a job at Lakeside Community College.

"Why would your mother want to teach here?"

"Probably the only place that would have her. She's been at three schools in three years."

She handed me the joint and went to work on the radio dial. I took a quick hit and looked around the car. It was a mess, cassettes and paperbacks strewn all over the floorboard and the backseat. One of the books was called *The Tibetan Book of the Dead.* The car also had a distinct smell to it, like Juicy Fruit gum. It was strong, even amid the pot smoke.

"Does your mother have trouble holding jobs or something?"

Rachel paused amid the radio static. "Don't you think you're being kind of nosy?"

I held out the joint. "It's one of the lesser-known side effects."

It turned out Stan's pot wasn't half bad—certainly not in Nick's league, but passable. I felt loose, like a big Slinky snaking its way down a staircase. And I was craving a stick of Juicy Fruit all of the sudden.

Rachel took her turn with the joint and went back to the radio. She paused at "The Gambler." Kenny was singing about knowing when to hold 'em, and when to fold 'em. I was expecting her to say how much she hated that song.

"So where's your car?" she asked.

"I don't have a car."

"You mean Mr. *Road & Track* doesn't have a cool-as-shit Trans Am?"

"Only rednecks and Burt Reynolds drive Trans Ams."

"Sorry, I didn't realize you were a man of such discerning taste."

"That's okay," I told her. "I tend to enjoy the finer things. A good steak, maybe a plate of scampi."

"So, why don't you have a car?"

"I don't have a license."

She laughed. "What happened? Did you fail the driving test?"

"No. As a matter of fact, I fucking aced it. I got screwed on the parallel parking, because this dickhead patrolman was on some kind of fucking power trip."

Rachel looked confused. "So, you're saying they wouldn't give you a license because you can't parallel park?"

"No, they gave me a license. But then I had it suspended for six months. This juvenile judge cut it up right in front of me."

That little piece of information impressed her so much that she turned down the radio. "A judge?" she asked. "What did you do?"

I reached over and plucked the joint from her fingers. "Who's being nosy now?"

She gave me this beautiful sneer, just like the ones she'd given Yuri. I felt honored.

"Forget it," she said. "I didn't really want to know, anyway."

She turned up the radio again. Kenny was still singing. The Gambler was down to his last cigarette, just about to break even.

"God, I hate this song," she said.

She spun the dial, but the next station was playing the same thing. She let out a pained groan and turned down the volume.

"I went for a drive in my neighbor's car," I told her, "and I sort of neglected to notify the woman."

Rachel shut off the radio. "Jesus Christ," she said. "You mean you stole a fucking car?"

"No, I just had an errand to run. I was gonna take it back."

She started laughing again. "Yeah, right. Just like you're gonna take back that magazine."

I didn't see any point in trying to convince her that I really did plan to return the magazine, or the car. So, I just tried to look irritated again.

Rachel was excited now, more animated than I'd ever seen her in the restaurant. Her eyes were bigger, her mouth wider, stretched into a juicy smile. She took the joint out of my hands and sucked on it until it almost burned her lips, until there was almost nothing there, and the glowing ashes tumbled onto the front of her leather jacket. Then she grabbed my arm up under the shirtsleeve.

"Come on," she said, "I want to show you something."

I stood at the back of her car while she emptied her backpack into the trunk. The bag was crammed full of stuff: more books—*The Bell Jar* and *The Flowers of Evil*—a hairbrush, a pink cardigan with the price tag still attached, mascara, lip gloss, and about a dozen packs of Juicy Fruit. The yellow packs were raining down into the trunk.

She held up the pink garment and let it drop inside the empty spare-tire well. "That's my mother's," she explained.

I pointed to the gum supply. "Can I have a stick?"

She slammed the trunk and slung the empty backpack over her shoulder. "Follow me," she said. "I'll get you all the Juicy Fruit you want."

It didn't take me long to figure out where we were headed, or what we were going to do when we got there, but I followed her to the gift shop anyway. I followed her the way that some people talk about following that light when they're near death. I leapt right off my wave of good citizenship, sheriffs and judges be damned. The next thing I knew, I was crouched low inside the darkened gift shop.

"You gotta stay down," she whispered. "I mean, that was your first mistake. Really amateur. I could see your head bobbing around in here from the back of the bar. You looked like you were on a fucking pogo stick."

Rachel told me to wait by the door and tell her if I saw anybody coming. Then she unzipped her backpack and went to work.

She hit the newsstand first. She pulled down an armful of magazines and swept them right into the bag: *Cosmo, Rolling Stone, Vogue,* and *Glamour.* After that, she went for the gum rack and then the sunglasses. She grabbed a tacky white pair of cat's-eyes. She looked my way and modeled them for me, cocking her head to the side and shrugging her shoulder in a sexy way.

She was brash and fearless, like Cale Yarborough on a short track. Watching her in action gave me a boner right there in the gift shop. It beat the hell out of any letter Stan could have written to *Penthouse.*

The next thing I knew, she had slithered out of sight. She was behind the glass counter that housed the cash register. I could see her arm reaching up and pulling stuff off the medication rack. That's when I noticed Yuri. He was walking slowly, practically teetering in his Courvoisier fog, gradually making his way out of the bar. He appeared to be up to something, looking over his shoulder and then peeping around the corner to check out the action at the front desk. Satisfied with his surveillance, he turned and headed toward us.

I crawled across the floor and ducked behind the counter with Rachel. She was still wearing the sunglasses.

"What the fuck are you doing?" she said. "I told you to stay up front."

"It's Yuri," I said. "He's coming."

"Here?"

"Yes, here."

About that time, the bells on the door jingled. We dropped fast, like there'd been gunfire. We lay there on our sides, facing each other.

Yuri bumped into something almost as soon as he walked through the doorway. We heard glass banging together and then Yuri mutter, "Fucking ashtrays." The wind chimes were the next indication of his location. He must have walked right through them. As prowlers went, he had the finesse of a blind mule.

His destination was the glass counter. He jiggled the sliding door in front until it finally opened. Then he reached inside and went for the cigar box. We could see his bandaged hand above us groping around in the darkened case. He scooped up a couple of face turds and slammed the case shut. It made a loud noise. Yuri whispered, "Shhh, little box."

Rachel and I were trying not to laugh. She clamped both hands over her mouth, and I buried my face in the front of her leather jacket. I breathed in the smoke and the cowhide, and, for a second, it smelled like Lyndell's Chevelle. Maybe that car wasn't the only fun place to be late at night.

I lifted my head when Yuri had gone, and we both let ourselves laugh. The gum in Rachel's mouth fell on the floor, but I could still smell it on her breath. Juicy Fruit, like she'd promised.

"If I'm an amateur, then what's Yuri?"

"Oh, he needs a remedial course," she said. "That's way beyond my tutoring skills."

I started to feel bad about making fun of Yuri. I pictured that open-sided railroad car and Yuri rattling through the cold of Russia with his mother's stiff arms around him, not knowing where the hell he was headed.

"What's the matter?" Rachel asked.

I shook my head. "Nothing."

"What? Did you forget to return something you borrowed?"

I didn't even bother to look irritated. I pushed her cheap, almost stolen sunglasses up on her head and looked down into those dark eyes. I leaned in to her mouth. I did it quickly, silently, like a burglar stealing his way across a darkened room.

11

Dewey had just finished playing his song for me and Nick. He was sitting in the recliner, cradling his Western Auto guitar, staring down at the floor and the lyrics scrawled in his red spiral notebook.

"Fuck," I said. "That's good. That's really good."

Dewey had strummed the chords to the melody, laying it out there like a pretty tiled roof above his singing. It was his voice that carried the song. While his pipes might have been a little rough around the edges, they were also sturdy and elegant in the way of an idling '63 Corvette. Which is to say that he could make the hair stand up on your arms.

Nick had been working with Dewey, helping him learn to write music. This had been Dewey's first shot at a song, so he was eager to earn a good word from his mentor.

Nick hopped off the bar chair, scratched at his chin, and sighed, extending Dewey's misery a few seconds longer.

"I don't know, Dewey. It's kind of predictable."

"Well, what's the matter with it?" Dewey set his guitar down beside the recliner. He looked awfully glum.

"It's just kind of simple," Nick said. "I like to be challenged, you know. I like some wild-ass chord progressions, some adventure in the melody."

I felt like Nick's criticism was a little harsh. After all, it wasn't like he ever played any of his own songs for us. He was real private about his blues compositions, always grumbling about how something sucked, or needed more work.

Nick sat back down on the bar chair and grabbed the *Green Lake Gazette* that he'd been reading. He tried to go back to the Sports page, but Dewey wouldn't quit staring at him. He finally got the message and set the paper down in his lap. He gazed from me to Dewey, and then back again.

"Oh, all right," he confessed. "It's good. There, are you satisfied? You write one damn song your whole life, you asshole, and it beats the shit out of anything I ever wrote. I hate your guts, you big tub of shit."

Dewey was beaming. He grabbed his PBR can off the floor and took a long, satisfied swig.

"So who was the song about?" I asked.

"Well," Dewey said, "it's actually about two different girls. But I combined them. It's what they call a composite."

Nick peered over the top of his newspaper and rolled his eyes. "Now he's gonna fucking talk shop."

I asked Dewey the girls' names.

"Pearl Nicklaus and Cheri Lovely."

Nick dropped the paper and started laughing. "Those are strippers at the Booby Trap."

"So what?" Dewey said. "There's no law against writing songs about strippers. They've got sad stories to tell."

Nick shook his head. "As much money as you spend at that place, they oughta be listening to your sad stories, not the other way around."

Dewey's regular forays to the Booby Trap were no secret. Nick joked that Dewey kept the Shoreline Cab Company in business with his titty-bar excursions to Atlanta.

"Pearl was telling me about this boyfriend of hers," Dewey said. "She told me how he got her drunk on her birthday and gave her some blotter paper with Tweety Bird on it, because he knew how much she liked Tweety. Anyway, it was some bad shit. She was down on the floor tripping, and he was hauling all her stuff out to his truck. TV. Stereo. Her grandmother's wedding ring. She's lying there seeing these fucking elephants on the ceiling, scared out of her damn mind, and he's stepping over her, stealing everything she owns. Even took the damn mattress. Headed down to Slidell, Louisiana. Never even called to see if she was okay. And it just got me started to thinking, you know, that what he did was the opposite of love, that if you loved somebody, wouldn't you be willing to give them everything you had? I mean, that's the real shit, when you'd give your life, or go to jail, for somebody."

Nick lit a Winston and exhaled wearily. "Dewey, this is why you need to get out and meet a real woman, instead of somebody who dances on a table for a living. I mean, these girls, they know what a guy wants to hear. They know who wants to be told they're hot shit and who wants to hear a sad story. Whatever it takes to keep those greenbacks coming in, they're gonna say it."

The phone rang, long and loud, the way it used to when a phone call really meant something. It startled us right out of our conversation. Nick picked up the receiver, since he was the most likely candidate to receive a call. He stretched the cord back to the bedroom, talking in a hushed tone. I assumed it was a business matter.

Dewey stood up and groaned. He was rubbing at his belly and making a sour face.

"Damn," he said, "I had me a sackful of Krystals at lunch, and they've just about torn my guts out."

"Well, you don't have to announce it," I told him. "This ain't a Pepto commercial."

"Why don't you go ahead and lay out the buffet?" Dewey said. "I'm gonna go back here and try to grunt."

It was almost four o'clock, time for the ever important two-hour stretch on channel 17. That meant *Andy Griffith, Leave It to Beaver, The Beverly Hillbillies,* and *The Munsters,* as fine a foursome as you could pull down with a $4.99 UHF antenna.

Dewey and I were quite familiar with these shows. By our calculations, we'd seen each episode an average of seventeen times, and we were not ashamed to admit it. We had even turned our expertise into a daily contest called Name the Plot. The loser coughed up a dollar every time he was beaten to the punch. I'd been on a roll the past week, lightening the load in Dewey's wallet to the tune of fourteen dollars. He'd been itching for payback.

I laid the snacks on a tray and set the tray down on the middle cushion of the sofa. It was the usual spread: pretzels, barbecue potato chips, and peanut M&M's. I grabbed a Coke for myself and another Pabst for Dewey.

Dewey walked out of the bathroom, grabbed a handful of chips, and proceeded to plop his ass down at the other end of the sofa.

"Everything come out all right?" I asked.

"Yep, just fine."

Andy's whistled theme song had barely ended when Dewey started snapping his fingers and batting his eyes as though his memory was taking a severe jarring. The man had never owned a poker face.

"I know this one already," he said. "This is where Uncle Joe from *Petticoat Junction* guest-stars. Only he ain't playing Uncle Joe. He's Mr. Wheeler, this flimflam fellow, and Aunt Bee gets the hots for him."

The facts were pouring out of him like a trumped-up confession, and I wasn't buying it. He was already rubbing his fingers together, gloating over the dollar bill he was expecting me to hand over.

"You sorry sack of shit," I said. "You looked at the *TV Guide*."

Dewey snorted and tried to act offended. "The hell, I did."

"Yeah, right. Like there's any fucking way you could have already figured that out. All they show is a pickup truck, and you got it nailed. That's bullshit."

"Bullshit, my ass. I recognize the truck. I've got a photographic memory."

"Yeah, from the fucking *TV Guide*."

"Oh, so you're gonna turn it around now. Make me the bad guy."

"If you're cheating, I am. We agreed not to look at the *TV Guide*."

"Well, I didn't cheat. What are you gonna do anyway? Call the NCAA? Have 'em put me on probation?"

"I can handle my own damn investigation."

"You got no proof."

"Oh, yeah? Then what were you doing in the bathroom just now?"

"I told you already. I had to lay some pipe. Drop the kids off at the pool. Shit, shat, shut. Do I need to make it any clearer?"

"That's bullshit," I said. "You're like clockwork, every morning at seven-thirty, as soon as you come out of the bedroom and set your eyes on the Sports page. It's like God's own laxative."

"Well, a man can shit more than once a day. That don't mean he's a criminal."

"I bet if I went in that bathroom, I'd find the *TV Guide*. Where'd you hide it, anyway? Under the sink?"

Dewey didn't have anything to say about this. He pulled his Marlboros out of his shirt pocket and shook one from the box. He always smoked when he was nervous. I could see him eyeing me as he snapped his thumb down the back side of his Bic lighter.

"Look at yourself. You're sweating like a cheap refrigerator."

"I ain't done shit," he said. He wiped at his brow, took a drag off his cigarette, and pointed at the TV. "Let's just watch the show, all right? This is a good one."

I pulled a dollar bill out of my pocket, wadded it into a ball, and tossed it in his lap. He couldn't even look me in the eye when he stuck the dollar in his shirt pocket. But I gave him the skunk eye for a good long while, just to let him know that I'd be watching him from now on.

"Don't get too attached," I said. "Ol' George is coming back to my side of the sofa once *Beaver* starts."

Nick walked out of the bedroom wearing his leather jacket and carrying his motorcycle saddlebags. "What the hell's going on out here? Sounds like a fucking cockfight."

"Your brother's a sore loser," Dewey said.

"Yeah, most people are pretty damn sore after they get screwed," I said.

Nick raised his hands in a plea for calm. "Look, I gotta go to work. Y'all try to play nice while I'm gone."

Dewey looked up at Nick and frowned. "You mean you're not gonna watch Andy with us?"

Nick shook his head. "You know how much I hate that show."

"I don't see how you can hate Andy," Dewey said. "Hell, I'd move to Mayberry if I could."

"It's a little too white bread for my taste," Nick said. "If I had to live somewhere like that, I'd probably blow my damn brains out."

I asked Nick if he'd be home in time to drive me to work.

"I gotta be out late tonight. I'll call Bev and tell her to pick you up."

"What about band practice?" Dewey asked. "I thought we were gonna jam tonight."

Nick made a face and looked down at the floor. "You better call up Carlton and tell him we're off for tonight. And while we're on the subject, I might be sidelined for Friday night, too."

"But that's our fucking gig at Whatchamacallit's," Dewey said. "Hell, we can't cancel on them. That's a good venue for us."

Nick offered up an apologetic shrug. He was already backing

himself through the doorway. "I'm sorry, Dewey. It's out of my hands."

We finally went back to watching *Andy*. Mr. Wheeler, the flimflam artist, was pumping something out of a can onto Aunt Bee's roses. "My goodness," Aunt Bee said, "you've got a spray for every bush."

Dewey nudged me with his elbow. "Wonder what kind of spray he's got for Aunt Bee's fur bush."

"Man, that's sick," I told him. "She could be your grandmother."

We kept the jokes coming until Andy had to run Wheeler out of town. That's when Aunt Bee gave her sad speech about pitying the poor soul of the drifter, pitying the fact that he misses out on so much in life: family and friends and home-cooked meals. Dewey and I got real quiet then, like we were in church or something.

"You know, I really could live there," Dewey said. "I don't care what Nick says."

I told him I could see Nick's point. Thirty minutes a day was probably enough of Mayberry. "It'd get old in a hurry. You'd probably be better off living in Mount Pilot."

"Nah, that's the concrete jungle," he said. "I'd get me a little house out in the woods near the Darlings, so I could jam with them. Then I'd find a good creek where I could grow me some pot. Hell, me and Barney could get lit together."

I tried to picture him and Barney sitting at the counter of the Bluebird, scarfing down pie after they'd gotten stoned, but it was hard to imagine Dewey in black-and-white.

"What about you?" Dewey asked. "You still wanna buy you a trailer and move to the ocean like Rockford?"

"I don't know about that anymore. I've been thinking maybe it's not too bad right here." I leaned over and sniffed the sour arm of the sofa. "This sofa needs some fucking Lysol, but otherwise . . ."

Dewey grinned. He had these big pearly white teeth, like something out of a toothpaste commercial.

"Oh, hell," he said. "You've got a girl, don't you?"

"What makes you think that?"

"Well, I didn't read it in the *TV Guide*. I can assure you of that."

"I guess that's why you're wrong this time."

Dewey let out a deep sigh. "If you don't want to admit you've got a girl, I mean if she's ugly or something, and you're ashamed of her, I understand. But when you're ready to talk, I'll be here. Ol' Dewey will always be here, a sounding board, a shoulder to cry on, whatever you might need. I mean, I'm sure there'll probably come a time when you could use some advice, and old Dew——"

"All right," I said. "Just shut the fuck up."

Dewey piped down and waited, his face full of anticipation.

"I met this girl at the Holiday Inn. We work in the kitchen together."

It felt good to get it out, like speaking of Rachel had actually made her real.

"What does she look like?" Dewey asked. "No, wait. Let me guess. Tall blonde with nice, full tits. Kind of a Susan Anton type."

"She's got dark hair, actually."

"Well, that's okay. Jaclyn Smith's got dark hair, and there ain't no flies on her."

"She doesn't look like Jaclyn Smith, either."

"Kate Jackson?"

"Nope."

"Well, what famous celebrity would you say that she looks like?"

"I don't know. She doesn't remind me of anybody. That's why I like her."

"Well, is she good-looking?"

"Of course, she's good-looking. At least in my opinion, she is."

Dewey lit another cigarette. "So, you snaked her yet?"

"Jesus, Dewey. I don't think that's any of your damn business."

Dewey slid the cigarette out of his mouth and drew his head back to get a better look at me. Something about the pose reminded me of Barney Fife.

"You're already in love with this girl, aren't you?"

"What the hell are you talking about?"

"You sound like you got it bad," he said.

"Man, that's crazy talk."

"Then why did you say it was none of my business?"

"Hell, because it's not. You don't see me asking who you're snaking, do you?"

He shook his head and grabbed a handful of chips. But then he tossed them back in the bowl like he'd decided he didn't like barbecue potato chips anymore. Instead, he took a long drag off his cigarette.

"You need to go listen to that song," he said.

"Which one?"

"'Love Hurts.' That's which song. That just about sums it up."

"Listen, I didn't ask for any advice."

We watched the opening to *Beaver,* saw June handing everybody their lunches as they headed out the front door. It made me hungry for a ham and cheese sandwich, only I didn't want to go fix one for myself.

I cracked the episode after a couple of minutes. I told Dewey it was the one where Beaver spills paint on Wally's suit jacket and then Eddie Haskell helps cover for the Beav, proving that he's not such a motherfucker after all. It wasn't one of my favorites. Eddie was more entertaining when he acted like a jackass.

Dewey pulled the dollar out of his pocket, straightened it, folded it, and passed it down in a gentlemanly fashion.

"Nick's right," he said.

"About what?"

"I gotta find a woman. I'm starting to sound like a bitter asshole. A bitter, just-before-turning-thirty asshole."

"Well, what about Pearl? Why don't you ask her out? Strippers have to date somebody, you know. And it sounds like this last guy was nobody's bargain."

His face shone with a little hope. The sun had changed directions in the window. It was hitting the back of Dewey's neck, shooting across the room and clipping off the bottom corner of the TV screen.

"I really like Pearl," he said. "She even told me her real name."

He turned his head and considered me. "I mean, Pearl Nicklaus is just a stage name."

"Yeah, I kind of had that feeling."

"She told me she didn't want to use that fake name when she was talking to me. She said it felt different with me, that I wasn't like the other customers."

"So, what's her name?"

He smiled. "Melissa. Just like that Allman Brothers song. It was playing on the jukebox one night, and I started singing it to her. When I was done, she leaned into my ear and told me that was her real name."

"That's a good song," I said.

Dewey nodded in agreement.

"But I liked your song, too," I said.

He gave me a long disbelieving look. "You're not shitting me, are you?"

"Swear to God," I said. "It made my nipples hard."

We'd forgotten all about Wally and the Beav.

"Melissa's got this blonde hair," Dewey said. "It's real long, and she uses this shampoo that smells like bananas. Damn, I love that smell."

"Yeah, this girl at the Holiday Inn smells like Juicy Fruit. She stole ten packs of it for me."

Dewey squinted and cocked his head like a lap dog pondering a treat. "Juicy Fruit?"

"Yeah. I used to be more of a Dentyne man, but I've switched over to the Juicy Fruit camp."

The phone rang before we realized how stupid we sounded. Dewey settled back into the sofa cushions.

"That's probably for Nick," I said.

Dewey looked at his watch. "*The Hillbillies* are starting in five minutes."

The phone was sitting atop the TV tray at my end of the sofa, still ringing away.

"Damn," Dewey said. "They're persistent, aren't they?"

"I guess I better take it off the hook," I told him. "We won't get any peace unless I do."

I lifted the receiver and set it down on top of an old *Creem* magazine. Angus Young was on the cover, one leg kicked up, arm high in the air, ready to strike a power chord. He was the only guy I'd ever seen who could look cool in a pair of shorts.

I settled back into my hollow of the sofa, figuring whoever was calling would eventually hang up. But something wasn't right.

"I think you might want to take that call," Dewey said.

I looked over at the receiver. "Shit."

* * *

"That is so rude," Claudia said. "I can't believe you'd leave somebody hanging on the line just so you could watch a TV show."

"Well, I thought it might be somebody else. We get a lot of people calling this time of day, trying to sell us stuff."

"How much TV are you watching, anyway? I thought you agreed to cut back."

"Oh, I've cut way back. Me and Dewey were just getting ready to watch one of those *National Geographic* specials."

"On what?"

I looked to Dewey for help. "What's this one about, anyway?"

"Elly May fucks Mr. Drysdale," he said.

I clamped my hand over the mouthpiece and gave him the finger.

"You're running that thing twenty-four hours a day, aren't you?" Claudia asked.

She had me dead to rights. Hell, I even slept with the TV on. She let out a sigh, but I knew that she wasn't really mad. "As long as you're going to work and staying out of trouble, I guess it's all right."

"I'm holding up those bargains. I might even add some hours to my work shift when school gets out for the summer."

"Are you keeping up with your schoolwork?"

"Nick makes me show him my homework every night."

Technically, that was true. Of course, I'd been showing Nick the same set of geometry problems for the past month. He hadn't caught on. As for grades, I'd become the master of the C-minus.

"So, you actually enjoy bussing tables?"

"Yeah, I enjoy seeing how a hotel operates. It's a fascinating industry."

Truth be told, I enjoyed talking to Rachel, and getting stoned with Rachel, and robbing the gift shop with Rachel, and lying on my back while Rachel squirted Coke out of the bar fountain into my mouth.

"Well, don't work too hard," Claudia said. "I might have to disown you."

"You've got nothing to worry about. Too much Fulmer blood in me."

There was a pause. I could picture her cradling the receiver on her shoulder, firing up a Virginia Slim. I stood up and carried the phone back to Nick's bedroom so that Dewey could watch the *Hillbillies* in peace.

"So everything's going okay?" she asked.

I tossed some dirty clothes onto the floor and sat down on the foot of the bed. "Yeah, everything's great. I think this was a good idea for all of us."

"What about Nick? What's he doing?"

"He's not home right now."

"He hasn't been leaving you there by yourself all the time, has he?"

"Nah, he's here a lot," I lied. "He's keeping pretty regular hours these days."

"I just want him to be careful," she said. "Wade Briggs told me that Sheriff Muskgrave is on some sort of drug crusade right now. There's an election year coming up, you know."

My arms went numb when she mentioned Muskgrave. I wasn't sure what to say, so I tried to steer us elsewhere.

"Yeah, I know. Nick said that Jimmy Carter might be out on his ass if he doesn't get the economy back up."

"You better hope he doesn't get voted out of office," she said. "He's a fine man. All people care about these days is filling their cars up with cheap gasoline. They don't even bother to see all the good that he does."

I knew that Jimmy Carter would distract her. It seemed that everyone had some strong feelings about our homegrown president. I was pretty neutral, though. His didn't appear to be an easy job. I couldn't even imagine where you would have gone to smoke a joint in the White House.

I tried to change the subject again. "So, when did you talk to Wade Briggs?"

"We talk from time to time," she said. "I asked him to keep an eye on you guys for me."

"So he's moonlighting as a private eye now?"

"He's doing it as a friend," she said.

I heard a noise in the background, like a power drill. "What's that?"

"Oh, Charlie's got the blender out. If it's five o'clock, you can bet he's making frozen margaritas."

"So, how's life with Mr. Forty-eight Long?"

"Well, we drink a lot." She laughed. "Charlie fixed us up a batch of banana daiquiris this afternoon. It's a new mix his stores are carrying. It was actually pretty good. I poured them into these big Solo Cups, and we took a walk on the beach until Charlie got a stitch in his side."

"Well, what else are you doing?"

"Actually, I've been thinking about going to school. I'd like to be a voice coach, or maybe teach music somehow. Charlie said he'd pay for it."

"That sounds like a good idea."

"Doesn't it, though?"

I thought she might tell me more, like where she was planning to go to school, or when she was getting started, but she didn't. She blew a mouthful of cigarette smoke away from the receiver. It sounded like a sigh.

"Charlie's new stores are doing great," she said. "He's even got a drive-through place down here. Can you believe that? I told him he needed to start making home deliveries next. Just place an ad in the paper: IF YOU HAVE A DRINKING PROBLEM, CALL THIS NUMBER."

12

Once summer kicked into gear, I began to spend as much time with Cash as I did with Nick. We worked on the Cougar in his garage every Saturday afternoon, getting the suspension and the throttle just right. Cash knew his shit where cars were concerned. That Cougar was always tuned to perfection, the body all shined up and dent free. It looked like it belonged in a museum instead of on a dirt track.

Cash was a top-shelf driver, too, probably the smoothest in the hobby stock class. The only thing that kept him from winning races was his tendency to shrink away from contact. He was racing to survive instead of to win, just like Lyndell in the old days.

I invited Rachel to the races one night. I wasn't sure she would take me up on the offer. The Green Lake Speedway didn't seem like her kind of scene.

But she showed up right at nine o'clock. She came walking out of the dust after the first qualifying heat, wearing a black T-shirt, hiking boots, and Levi's, toting her backpack and looking totally out of place among all the other girls in their fake French jeans and spaghetti-strap tops.

She crossed the track with that walk of hers and started scanning the pit. The pit was the beehive between races, cars parked nose to bumper, tires and tools strewn like a tornado had just blown through. The place smelled downright flammable, with a cloud of gas fumes hanging overhead. Not that it ever stopped anybody from smoking. Almost every man there had a cigarette snagged in his teeth. The whole crowd was smoking and clanging wrenches and revving motors and pouring gasoline.

I was down on my knees checking Cash's tire pressure since his qualifying heat was next. I called out Rachel's name, and she jerked her head in my direction and walked over to the Cougar. She was smiling, her lips shiny from the raspberry lip gloss she'd stolen out of the gift shop.

"I think I know some of these people," she said.

"From where?" I asked.

She smiled. "The bulletin board at the post office."

"Most of these fellows are law-abiding citizens," I told her.

She raised her eyebrows. "So, I guess those are fake prison tattoos?"

I showed her around Cash's Cougar, let her look inside and under the hood. She indulged my enthusiasm, even tried to appear mildly interested, though I was extra careful not to overdo things. I just couldn't help being excited, what with her standing there and the car gleaming under the track lights, scarlet red with a white roof and white circles on the doors sporting black number twelves. Since Cash was his own sponsor, *Cash Bail Bonds* had been scripted across the rear quarter panels in black paint. The only other artistic touch was a small yin-yang symbol on the driver's side door. Rachel noticed that right away.

"Is your driver Buddhist?" She sounded hopeful.

"In a way," I said.

She appeared skeptical. "What does 'in a way' mean?"

"It means he really likes kung fu movies. He's a big Bruce Lee fan."

She rolled her eyes. "So, where is he? Praying in the temple?"

I told her that Cash was, in fact, underneath the stands at that very moment doing his "pre-race meditation." What I didn't tell her was that the meditation entailed the consumption of half a joint and a bag of Doritos.

Rachel stepped away from the car and did a slow three-sixty, taking in the whole scene, the oxblood track and the packed bleachers along the straightaways, the plywood press box with the checkered-flag paint motif and the light poles rising out of its roof like a huge set of claws.

"So, this is why you never work on Saturday nights?"

"Yeah, this is why."

I told her that my father used to race. "He brought me with him a few times when I was a kid. I just liked it, that's all."

She narrowed her gaze like she was trying to see inside me. "That's all?"

"Well, he sort of taught me how to drive, too. He used to let me drive his Chevelle on some of the streets around here."

"How old were you?"

"About ten, I guess."

"Jesus!" She looked away and laughed. "How did you reach the pedals?"

"I just scooted up to the edge of the seat. It wasn't that hard."

"Did you drive fast?"

"Not really. I mean, I'd get it up to about ninety or ninety-five on a couple of the quarter-mile stretches, but that's about it."

"At ten years old?" Rachel asked. "You could have gotten killed."

I couldn't really argue with her there.

"So where is your father, anyway?" she asked.

The question caught me by surprise. "Don't you think you're being kind of nosy?"

"I thought you said it was one of the side effects of smoking pot."

"It is, but I think you become immune after a while."

"Maybe I have a strong resistance," she said.

I decided to lay it all out on the table for her. I trusted her not to say anything stupid.

"Lyndell's got a new family up in Bristol, Tennessee. He builds engines for a racing team."

"What about your mother?"

"She's living with her boyfriend down in Jacksonville right now."

Rachel had just slid a fresh stick of gum into her mouth. She paused in midchew and studied my face. I supposed she was trying to think of what to say, so I decided to save her the trouble and change the subject. I eased up beside her and made a sweeping gesture with my arm, as if the track were a green orchard, or some other lush landscape, that I wanted her to appreciate.

"If there's one key to having fun at the track, it's taking the time to learn a little something about the drivers. Once you get to know them as human beings, you start to feel like you have something invested in the outcome of the race."

She let out a sharp little bark of a laugh. "Oh, really?"

She sounded skeptical, but she was smiling, too. She was willing to play along.

"Take Carl Bettis over there, for example." I pointed Carl out to her. He was a heavyset guy, sporting wall-to-wall tattoos and a grungy green-and-red Mountain Dew baseball cap. Carl had a crowbar in his hands, and he was cussing and trying to pry a dent out of his collapsed front fender.

"So tell me something about Carl," Rachel said. "I mean, outside of the obvious fact that he's got superb taste in headwear."

"Well," I said, "it might interest you to know that he is currently drunk off his ass."

She put her hand over her mouth in fake horror. "Oh, his poor mama." She incorporated a lame Southern accent into her exclamation. She thought it was pretty funny, but I kept quiet. I didn't want to encourage her to do it again.

She went back to her regular voice. "Will they let him drive like that?"

"Oh, yeah. He's been driving on the sauce for years. Used to do it back when my father ran here. He even tried to hook up a beer tank in his car one time. Mounted a wiper fluid case to the floorboard and ran this long tube up to his mouth so he could drink while he was racing."

"Did it work?"

"No, not really. All the vibration made the beer too foamy."

Rachel pointed to a slight, glassy-eyed fellow who was sitting atop a stack of tires, chewing gum and steadily rocking back and forth.

"What about him?" she asked. "What's his story?"

"Oh, that's Ebo Mitchell."

"Is he drunk, too?"

"No, he rocks like that all the time. Even when he's driving. Keep an eye on him during the race. You can see him rocking through the window."

"He looks kind of sad," she said. "Like a little stray puppy. Maybe I'll pull for Ebo. I mean, if your guy doesn't win."

"Well, Ebo doesn't usually do that well. You might want to pick somebody else."

"But you said to pick somebody that I might like as a human being."

"I know I did. But you picked Ebo because he reminds you of a stray dog."

"So?" she asked. "What's the matter, you don't like strays?"

"I don't have anything against strays. I'd just rather have a grey-hound if I was in a race."

"Well, strays have more common sense," she said. "Good breeding is highly overrated."

"Suit yourself," I told her. "You just better hope Ebo doesn't start chasing his tail."

Seeing how she was such an expert on dogs, I asked if she had a canine of her own.

She shook her head. "Not anymore. My mom doesn't like animals. She claims she's allergic, but she's really just a hypochondriac."

"What about your father? Where's he?"

She looked away again, scanning the crowd in the pits. I think she was looking for someone else to poke fun at. Finally, she gave up. She turned and offered me that blank stare of hers.

"He had leukemia," she said. "It was two years ago."

She said it like it had been an event, something that happened all in one day, like Pearl Harbor or the moon landing or Evel Knievel jump-ing the Snake River Canyon. I didn't know what to say next. Our con-versation had slammed into a wall.

It was closing in on race time, and still no Cash. I began to worry. And then, finally, I caught sight of him and Nick. They were making their way through the crowd, grinning and smoking cigarettes. Cash was wearing his white coveralls and black suede Converse.

I wasn't expecting Nick, not with his busy schedule. He threw his hand up in the air and gave me a goofy wave. Then he draped his arm around Cash's neck.

"You need to keep a closer watch on your driver," he said. "I just found him under the stands experimenting with mind-altering substances."

Both of them were giggling, severely red-eyed and stoned. Cash had clearly exceeded his prerace half-joint limit. He shoved Nick away, stumbling over his own feet in the process.

"Your brother's a bad influence," he said. "Somebody oughta lock his ass up."

"They've tried," Nick said. "But there's always some asshole bail bondsman willing to spring me."

They were practically doubled over laughing. Neither of them had noticed Rachel standing there beside me.

"Listen," Cash said, "me and Nick already got the postrace meal planned. We're gonna hit the Varsity. Chili dogs, onion rings, fried peach pies, PC, Frosted Orange, milk shakes, glorified steaks, pimento cheeseburgers . . ."

Cash closed his eyes and swayed his head as he recited the menu. He looked like a preacher who was feeling the power of God move through him.

In closing, he made this proclamation: "We're gonna eat the whole motherfucking menu."

Nick moaned like a porn actor in the throes of carnal pleasure. "I don't think I can wait two more hours, Cash. Why don't you go ahead and wreck your car in this first race and get it over with. Hell, you're not gonna win tonight anyway."

"Man, shut the fuck up," Cash said. "That shit affects my chi."

"Horseshit," Nick said. "Your chi just got affected by some bad-ass weed."

Cash snorted. "Considering the source, I probably got some paraquat poisoning. My goddamn kidneys are probably shutting down as we speak."

Nick frowned. "That's not funny," he said. "You know I sell the best shit around."

They started laughing all over again. They didn't even hear the loudspeaker crackle. The announcer tapped the mike and spoke up in his high, inflamed-sinus voice that always reminded me of Mr. Haney from *Green Acres.*

"Heat Two drivers, report to your cars."

Tools rained down on the infield dirt. Everyone started to get their shit together. Everyone, that is, except for Cash.

Rachel was wearing that beautiful smirk of hers. "I thought you said he was meditating."

"He was. They smoke pot in the Shaolin temple, you know. It calms the nerves before they whip somebody's ass."

I decided I'd better try to do something, so I started yelling at Cash and Nick.

"Quit dickin' around. The race is gonna start in five minutes."

I picked up Cash's helmet and the bandanna that he wore underneath it. I set them on top of the car, and then I pointed an accusing finger at Nick.

"I'm holding you responsible if he comes in last. This is all your fault."

Nick was selling a ferocious sens hybrid that summer. Rachel and I had actually smoked a little of it secondhand—by way of Stan—and it had knocked us on our asses. We'd ended up stripping down to our underwear and taking a 2 A.M. dip in the Holiday Inn swimming pool. Lyndell would have been proud.

Nick held up his hands in a plea for leniency. "Guilty as charged," he said. *"Nolo fuckin' contendere."*

The two of them finally made the connection between Rachel and me. It had only taken about five minutes of seeing us standing right beside each other.

"Did we pick up another crew member?" Cash asked.

I proceeded with the introductions, explaining that Rachel and I worked together at the Holiday Inn. It looked as though things might settle down. And then, just as Cash was swinging his leg through the car window, we heard an engine snarling on the backstretch. Everybody on the pit road craned their necks to see who was causing the racket. A black El Camino. The car was just sitting there, quivering, nose stuck low to the dirt, poised like a mountain cat ready to pounce. The big V-8 would bust out with a roar and then settle down into a *pop-pop-pop* growl. Very predatory.

The people in the stands ate it up. They stood and cheered and started to chant something that I couldn't make out right away.

And then the loudspeaker crackled again.

"Ladies and gentlemen—we have a late entry. In the black El Camino at the back of the field. Number eighty-eight in the program and number one in your hearts . . ."

This is where the announcer paused for effect, letting all that yelling and clapping percolate like a big pot of Maxwell House.

"Yes, he's back from a short stay at a county facility. You've voted him the most popular driver in the hobby stock class four years running. You know him, you love him, and you had better get the heck out of his way. It's Leee-roy 'Speedy' Brown!"

The crowd just went ahead and let themselves go ape shit, chanting, "Spee-dee! Spee-dee! Spee-dee!" They were jumping up and down and waving their arms and stomping the metal bleachers on the backstretch. All that clanging metal sounded like a freight train blowing through.

As if that wasn't enough, the PA guy started cranking "Bad, Bad Leroy Brown" over the speakers. Before long, everybody stopped chanting and started singing along, adding special emphasis to the word *Bad!*

While the crowd celebrated, a cloud of dismay settled over the pits. The drivers were shaking their heads and looking as solemn as if they'd just learned that OPEC had embargoed every damn barrel of oil in the Middle East. Ebo was chewing and rocking a lot faster than before, and Carl Bettis kicked at the dirt and looked skyward in a helpless way.

"Well, just fuck me where I stand," he said.

Although most of the drivers appeared unnerved by Speedy's presence, Cash was flat-out agitated. He'd already taken off his helmet and unzipped his coveralls. He was all puffed up like a bullfrog, looking like he was getting ready to kick somebody's ass.

"What the hell are you doing?" I yelled.

Cash pointed at Speedy's car. "I'm fixing to grab that motherfucker's ass and put him in my trunk."

I asked why he felt persuaded to do this.

"Because I posted a five-thousand-dollar bond on his skinny little ass last month. And then he up and beat feet the day before his court date."

Nick scratched at his chin like he was thinking over a problem in a crossword. "What's his name again?"

"Leroy Brown," Cash said. "But everybody calls him Speedy. Dirtiest motherfucking driver on the track."

Nick snapped his fingers. "Oh, yeah. I was in the can with his brother, Walt. He got busted for cooking crank in his attic. From what I heard, Speedy used to snort that shit like it was going out of style."

Cash just nodded. "That's Speedy, all right. Broke into a Scientific Atlanta truck and got off with about a hundred cable TV boxes. Can you believe that shit? Out here in the boonies, half the damn county ain't even wired yet, and he's going around thinking he's gonna sell illegal hookups. Wade Briggs hauled his ass in."

Cash picked up his helmet, all the while keeping his eyes on Speedy's El Camino. Speedy was in the midst of a slow, celebratory lap. It was the first time I'd ever seen one taken before a race rather than after. He had his arm stuck out the window, waving to the crowd.

As Speedy came up the front stretch, I got my first look at him. He was no Burt Reynolds, that's for sure. Just a skinny guy with tattooed arms and barely a suggestion of a chin. His helmet had been spray-painted black, and a scraggly mop of brown hair poured out from the back of it.

Cash leapt onto the hood of his Cougar and pointed at Speedy. "Hey, Speedy!" he screamed. "Remember me?!"

Speedy turned his head. When he got a load of Cash standing there, his eyes lit up like a pair of high beams. He made a futile attempt to shield the side of his face with his hand, as though Cash might not notice it was him.

Cash may have had a legal right to be pissed, but Speedy had numbers on his side. He might as well have been Richard Petty, the way all of those people were cheering him. Once this fact had dawned on him, he lowered his hand, narrowed his eyes into a diabolical squint, and stuck his arm back out the window. But instead of waving to the crowd, he looked Cash square in the eye, smiled at him, and gave his crooked middle finger a little bit of the up-and-down. The gesture almost appeared courtly.

Cash fired his helmet at Speedy's car. It ricocheted off the Amoco advertisement on the driver's side door. Speedy ducked down and hit the gas, kicking up a rooster tail in the dirt. That's when the crowd's cheers turned to boos. They aimed their wrath squarely at Cash. I even saw a few drink cups fly onto the track in our general direction.

Nick started laughing. "Don't worry," he said. "They're not booing. They're yelling, 'Caaash! Caaash!'"

Cash jumped off the top of his car. He wasn't smiling anymore. He was severely pissed. "Fuck them," he said. "Redneck motherfuckers."

He stalked the length of the car a couple times, like a restless dog on a short leash. Rachel moved in behind me. She was standing real close, with a concerned look on her face.

"Do they ever have riots at these things?"

"Not that I've ever seen," I told her. "Of course, anything's possible."

Carl Bettis had fetched Cash's helmet. He handed it back to him with a look of resignation. "He's gonna wreck us all now."

Bettis turned to go back to his own car, stumbling a little as he changed directions. Rachel and I grabbed his shoulders and steadied him.

"Are you okay to drive?" I asked.

He laid his hand on his belly and fixed me with a sad and practiced gaze. "Oh, yeah. I'll be fine. I've just had me a touch of that stomach bug that's been going around."

The drivers eventually set their apprehensions aside. They climbed into their sleds and fired up their big blocks, ready to go racing. It sounded like a pit of giant wasps had been stirred up. Even Rachel clamped her hands over her ears.

I leaned inside the Cougar to give Cash a last-minute pep talk.

"Try to move up front in a hurry," I said. "Maybe Speedy'll get hung up in traffic."

Cash grunted, rolled his neck around a couple of times, and romped on the pedal in an angry sort of way. That 428 Cobra Jet let out a nasty roar of its own. It was a reassuring sound, filling the car with the sharp smell of gasoline.

"Tell Nick to watch the gate," Cash said. "And you get the truck ready to go. I don't want Speedy slipping out of here when this race is over."

"I'll unhook the hauler and start the truck," I told him. "Don't worry about any of that stuff. You just be aggressive out there. Kick some ass."

Cash slid his goggles down over his eyes. "It's time to break out some Iron Monkey kung fu driving."

"Does that mean you're gonna bang the shit out of some people?"

"You're goddamn right it does."

The drivers circled the track, their cars packed together as they waited for the green flag to be waved. Even with the engines cooking at a simmer, the ground quaked from all of the horsepower.

Nick took his spot behind the gate in turn four, and I unhooked the hauler from Cash's white pickup. I reached inside the window and slid the key into the ignition.

"What are you guys planning to do?" Rachel asked.

"I don't think we have a plan, exactly. But it looks like Speedy might be a flight risk. We just wanna make sure we keep him boxed in."

We sat on the roof of Cash's truck to watch the race. Cash started near the back, on the eighth row, but moved up steadily, overtaking two cars on the first lap and one each on the next three. He was catching most people on the backstretch, driving high and then diving down into turn three, where he'd go into a smooth, controlled slide. By the twelfth lap, he was sitting fifth. He laid off Carl Bettis's bumper while Carl tried to ram his way through the car in front of him. Finally, Cash went high again and cut in front of Carl as he was coming out of turn three.

"We've got a mover," the announcer said. "Cash Bishop, sliding into fourth place ahead of Carl Bettis."

The crowd had not forgotten Cash's dispute with their golden boy. They poured another wave of boos on him when he passed Carl.

Speedy, who had started last, was also making hay, bumping and banging his way to the front of the pack. Any time I'd hear the clang of sheet metal against sheet metal, I'd look back to see Speedy laying his El Camino into the hip of a cowering Chevelle or Matador. He moved into sixth place on the fifteenth lap and bore down on poor old Ebo. Ebo was eyeing his mirror and rocking to no end inside his white Caprice. You'd have thought a shark was chasing him. After living through two laps of sheer terror, Ebo just flat-out surrendered, pulling down onto the track apron and letting Speedy go by. Devastated by fear, Ebo laid his head on the steering wheel. He was dead still.

Cash worked his way into the lead with five laps remaining, giving the first-place driver a little fake-high, drop-low move coming out of the second turn. Rachel grabbed hold of my arm with both her hands. She actually had an excited look on her face.

"Is Cash going to win the race?" she asked.

The only response I could muster was to cast a wary finger in the direction of Speedy's El Camino. He was sitting third. Shortly thereafter, he applied a savage blow to the second-place driver's rear axle. The car shot down the track and slammed nose-first into the infield retaining wall.

"Damn!" I said. "That's a Goody's headache."

It wasn't long before Speedy had Cash lined up in his crosshairs.

"Cash is gonna have to play dirty to win it," I told Rachel. "He's gonna have to put Speedy into the wall. Either that or Speedy's gonna put him into it."

"How do you know?"

"I just do," I told her. "Closest my father ever came to winning a race was this one time when he was leading with five to go. Some guy who drove like Speedy waited until the last lap and then pushed him right up into the fence."

Speedy caught up to Cash with two to go. He gave Cash a little love tap to let him know he was there. But Cash refused to drift high. He held his position like he was willing to fight for it. Speedy bumped him again coming out of turn four. This time Cash fishtailed a little, and Speedy rushed underneath, into the sliver of daylight that had opened up. Cash straightened the Cougar and went right back at Speedy, bashing into his rear bumper on the front stretch. The crowd was loving it, I was loving it, and the dust was swirling around like God himself had gotten all stirred up over the race.

Cash stuck to Speedy's bumper and gave him another shove going into the last lap. Speedy slid high and Cash ducked back into first.

They were hurtling down the backstretch with Speedy on Cash's bumper. Rachel was holding my arm, and I was holding her arm, and the bleachers were throbbing.

Cash left Speedy a little bit of room going into turn three. It wasn't enough for Speedy to move completely underneath Cash, but it was plenty for him to slide up under there and give Cash a firm shot to the rear axle. And that was pretty much all she wrote. Cash spun sideways, and Speedy darted under him. The back side of Cash's Cougar slammed into the wall right as Speedy took the checkered flag.

Rachel and I sagged against each other.

"What a fucking dick," she said. "He did that on purpose."

She looked like she wanted to fight Speedy, herself. I just shook my head.

"I told you it was coming."

Cash climbed out of his car, and Speedy proceeded to cut his victory lap short. He steered the El Camino toward the back gate.

Rachel and I jumped off the truck in a hurry. I climbed inside and started the engine. Rachel rushed to the window. She had a concerned look on her face.

"Wait. What about your license?"

I dropped the truck down into drive. "Don't worry. I'm just going over to pick up Cash. I'll call you tomorrow."

At least that was my plan. But when I got out to the track, Cash dove in on the passenger side and told me to floor it.

"Hurry the fuck up," he said. "We're never gonna catch him."

"I can't. I don't have a license. Remember?"

"The fuck you can't." And to illustrate his point, he reached over with his own foot and stomped the accelerator, à la Bev.

We headed off down the backstretch. It was even more fun than I'd imagined as a kid, the way the lights played off the red dirt, the little bump-bump-bump feeling of the ruts on the track, and the way the banked turn seemed to pull me around it with no effort at all. I even did a nice little slide for Rachel, who was still standing in the pits looking bewildered. I tapped the brakes right before the last light pole on the backstretch and then eased back on the throttle, spraying up a wave of dirt. At the last possible instant, I hit the brakes again and whipped the steering wheel back to the right, launching us through the gate and into the parking lot.

"There he goes," Cash shouted. "Look! Nick's got his skinny little ass."

That might have been overstating things just a bit. What Nick had was an armful of Speedy's hood. He'd jumped onto it as Speedy was driving through the parking lot. Now Speedy was jerking the El Camino back and forth, trying to pry Nick loose. Nick was flopping around like a fish in a frying pan.

Speedy finally threw him, though the effort had given us enough time to close the gap. Nick picked himself up off the gravel and ran over to the truck. He dove into the back and screamed for me to go.

The roads around the track were crooked, country two-lanes, rutted and void of any illumination except the occasional bare lightbulb shining from a front porch. Naturally, Speedy shut down his headlights in an attempt to shed us. It was like trying to tail a shadow. But I managed to keep him in sight. I was pushing Cash's truck right to the edge of collapse. The motor was screaming for mercy.

"You think maybe I oughta pull over and let you drive?" I shouted to Cash.

"Man, we can't pull over now," Cash said. "We'll never find him."

"But I've only got three months left until I get my license back. If I get caught doing this, they'll send my ass to Alto."

"Don't worry about that shit," Cash said. "These are extenuating circumstances. You're in pursuit of a fugitive from the law. Man, they oughta give you a goddamn medal."

I wasn't convinced by Cash's logic, but I kept on following Speedy. Putting his ass behind bars did seem like a worthy goal at the moment. Unfortunately, he made a right turn and a quick left and then seemed to disappear into thin air.

Cash waved his hand so I'd let off the gas. "Easy," he said. "I think he pulled into one of these houses."

We cruised past the houses on the street. They were ramshackle affairs, about the same size as Nick's place, but not nearly so cheerful. They possessed the frail posture of long-lost relatives who'd been scarred by disappointment and cheap liquor.

"Whoa," Cash said. "See that?"

He pointed to a house with an Alabama Crimson Tide flag hanging in the front window. A light shone behind it, and a dog was barking inside. It sounded like a rabid dog.

An old green and white Chevy truck sat in front of the house, but that wasn't what caught Cash's eye. There was a trail of dust running the length of the dirt driveway, all the way around to the back side of the house. Obviously, a car had just pulled in.

"Cut the lights," Cash said, "and pull over."

The three of us devised a plan. Nick would take the back door, Cash the front, and I'd guard Speedy's truck.

Nick gazed down at Cash's empty hands. "So, where's your Magnum?"

"Man, I don't take it to the track with me."

"Okay, then let's get a tire iron and a couple of wrenches out of the truck."

"I don't need that shit," Cash said.

"Well, what the hell are you gonna do if he comes out armed?"

Cash didn't say a word. Instead, he crouched into a kung fu stance: one foot up in the air, hands poised in front of his face like he was holding a camera.

Nick tried not to laugh.

"What's so goddamn funny?" Cash said.

"I can't help it," Nick told him. "You look like Elvis doing all that kung fu shit in a jumpsuit. What are you gonna do, throw him a scarf?"

I asked Cash how long he had actually been studying kung fu. He informed me that he had recently earned a gold belt, which sounded pretty good to me.

"In case you're wondering," Nick said, "gold's the one they give you after your white belt. That means you're certified to break paper plates."

Cash dropped the kung fu stance. He was scowling at both of us. "Just give me a goddamn tire iron and shut the fuck up."

Nick happily doled out the hardware. He tossed me a cold and heavy monkey wrench, and then we all took our spots. I crouched in front of Speedy's truck while Cash walked up the steps and rapped on the door with the tire iron. The dog started up with his barking again, even louder and more vicious than before. It was a deep, hoarse bark, unmistakably the sound of a very large and ill-tempered creature. Cash instinctively backed up a couple of steps.

"Speedy!" he yelled. "Get your ass out here. You know what I'm here for."

Speedy didn't answer. There was nothing to be heard from the inside except barking.

Cash pounded on the door again. He even gave it a kung fu kick with his foot. He let out a loud "Waaaahhh!"

The door buckled a little but refused to give way. This really made the dog crazy. It sounded possessed, like it was barking in the tongues of satanic mongrels.

"Goddammit, Speedy, I'm not messing with you. Do you hear? If I have to come in there, I'm gonna take it outta your ass."

About that time, the door opened a sliver. All I could see was the dog's head. It looked to be the size of a football. I suppose it was God-given instinct that caused me to scout the yard for a tree to climb.

The dog was snarling and stripping his teeth and trying to get at Cash. Cash backed up even farther, until he was standing at the edge of the porch steps.

"Speedy," he said, "don't you be pulling any shit. Now you better keep that fucking dog inside the house."

Speedy still didn't answer, though he was obviously standing on the other side of the door, holding the dog by its collar. The dog was thrashing his head from side to side, trying to break the door with his skull.

Finally, Speedy flung the door wide open. There was a blast of light from inside the house, and then the dog burst right out. He was airborne before he even took a step, like Bruce Lee with four legs.

The dog appeared to be part chow, part rottweiler, and mangy as hell. He latched on to the crotch of Cash's jumpsuit in a very purposeful manner.

Speedy shot through the doorway in the dog's wake. He looked like a tailback scampering behind his lead blocker. He leapt over the porch railing, shouting instructions to the dog as he made his escape.

"Get him, Brute! Chew his goddamn nuts off!"

Cash lay flat on his back. He was holding Brute's big head in his hands, trying to keep the dog from latching on to anything more valu-able than the inseam of his Dickies, screaming Nick's name as loud as he could.

Nick raced around from the back of the house. The first thing he saw was Speedy scrambling toward me and the truck. Then he caught a glimpse of Cash wrestling with the dog. Nick almost jumped out of his shoes.

"Holy fucking shit. That's a goddamn wolf."

He took off running for Cash, yelling all the while for me to put the skids on Speedy's getaway.

I stood up and blocked the driver's side door. I drew the wrench back behind my ear, ready to impart some pain. This caused Speedy to stop in his tracks. He squinted at me like I was some kind of apparition.

"Who in the hell are you?" he asked. "I don't owe you any god-damn money. Now get the hell out of my way. I got places to go, if you don't mind."

He took a step toward the car, and I drew the wrench back even far-ther. He was a short guy, five-six at most. I could have easily smacked him right on top of the head.

"Call off the dog," I yelled. "Call him off, or I'm gonna split you wide open."

Speedy raised his hands in a gesture of surrender. "Whoa," he said. "Easy there, fella. I'll do whatever you want, okay? There's no need to get all shitty ditty about it."

He turned and looked back at Brute like he was going to be agree-able and call him off. He even put his fingers up to his mouth to whis-tle. But instead of whistling, he bolted for the road, churning his arms like a marching-band leader. I froze for a second, not quite believing what I was seeing, and then I took off after him.

Speedy and I ran right down the middle of the two-lane road. Lucky for me, his short legs weren't fit for this type of racing. Three of his strides matched one of mine. I caught up to him after about fifty yards. I could have jumped him and knocked him down right then and there, but instead, I eased into step behind him. I stalked him for a good thirty yards, just letting him wonder what was coming. Finally, I gave him a sharp whack between the shoulder blades with the wrench.

"Oww! What was that for?"

"That's for Ebo," I said. "And this one . . ."

I cracked him across the lower back.

". . . is for Cash."

He let out a chuff of air and stumbled, veering toward the shoulder of the road. He had one hand on his back, the other out in front, preparing for touchdown with the grass. But I wouldn't let him fall. I ran up beside him, grabbed the neck of his shirt, and straightened him. Then I shoved him back toward the middle of the road. He went down on the yellow stripe.

"What the hell is your problem?" he asked. "I ain't got no gripe with you. That's just racing, what I did out there. It don't mean nothing. It don't mean you can't be civil to one another."

"Cash had your ass beat, fair and square," I said.

Speedy snorted. "He didn't have jack fucking shit. He should've wrecked me when he had the chance."

Nick and Cash came running up the road. The crotch of Cash's coveralls was missing, but his red Jockeys were still intact. Nick looked like he'd been through the wringer as well. One of his shirtsleeves was ripped and flapping in the breeze. By the time he and Cash reached us, they were both out of breath. Nick had to bend over and rest his hands on his knees.

We all stood there looking down at Speedy like he was a deer that we'd run over and didn't know what to do with. Nick eventually straightened himself. He slapped me on the shoulder and smiled.

"Congratulations, bro. You just bagged your first bounty."

"Damn right," Cash said. "Maybe we oughta mount his ass over your TV."

I couldn't help but smile. This felt better than taking the knife from Fay. I might have even stumbled onto a career, a legitimate line of work. Luke Fulmer: Bounty Hunter. It sounded like a TV show.

Speedy looked up with a pained expression on his face. "Where's Brute?" he asked. "What'd you do with my little puppy dog?"

"We threw his ass in the house," Cash said. "And that dog better have had his damn shots, because he broke the skin on my hand."

Speedy appeared bewildered. "What shots?"

Nick and Cash groaned. Speedy finally pushed himself up to a sitting position. He reached around and grabbed at his back.

"Any of y'all got a cigarette?"

"Fuck you," Cash said. "Telling that dog to rip my goddamn nuts off, and then you think I'm gonna give you a smoke."

I guess Nick found it hard to refuse a man who was about to be incarcerated. He reached into his pocket and pulled out his Winstons. He tossed one to Speedy, along with a book of Waffle House matches.

Speedy blazed up, took a long drag, and let the smoke drift out amid a deep sigh. "Are y'all gonna take me in right now?" he asked. "I sure could use a little something to eat."

Cash laughed like that was the funniest thing he'd heard in a long time. "So what are you saying? You want me to buy you a steak dinner? Maybe I oughta massage your feet, too."

Speedy shrugged. "I'd settle for a hamburger."

"Get your ass up out of the road," Cash said. "I'll buy you a fucking hamburger. But that's it. After that, your ass is going back to the county. And you better not start any more shit. I've had it. I've had a bad fucking night on account of you. I go to the track to relax. And then you come out there driving all crazy and wrecking people, with an outstanding warrant on your ass, no less. You've given me a big damn headache so you better just shut the fuck up from here on out."

Cash carried on like that all the way back to the truck. He wasn't going to let Speedy get that hamburger without a good ass-chewing. Speedy took it as best he could. He walked along behind Cash, staring at his shoes and frowning like a scolded child.

14

The chili dogs and hamburgers were forty minutes out of our way, in downtown Atlanta, but Cash didn't mind the detour. When it came to tracking fine eats, he had the nose and tenacity of a good bird dog. He'd follow a scent to the end of the earth if there was some chance of finding decent onion rings or a superior chopped pork platter. Best of all, he always saw to it that we put on the feed bag in a very serious way after the races, no matter what the results might have been. One night we'd driven all the way to Macon—and that was ninety miles one way—just for barbecue. Not that it wasn't worth it. Best sauce I ever put in my mouth: kind of lemony, but sweet, too, a nice balance of tang and smoothness.

The Varsity was this sprawling, neon-trimmed grease emporium perched at the edge of the interstate. The big sign out front laid claim to the "world's largest drive-in restaurant," but you could also eat inside. The best part about going inside was the TV rooms. There were five of them, each the size of a classroom, filled with school desks and lorded over by nineteen-inch mounted Zeniths. Each room monitored a different station, so that you'd have your pick of the channel 2 room, channel 5 room, channel 11 room, and so on.

Claudia took me to the Varsity once, when I was little, and our food turned cold while I walked around trying to decide which room to sit in.

"For Christ sake," she said, "can it be that hard to decide?"

It was, I told her. And that's why we ended up eating our chili dogs in the channel 17 room, thereby catching the last ten minutes of *Mr. Ed* before moving over to the channel 2 room to eat our fried pies and watch *Match Game P.M.* with Gene Rayburn and his telescoping microphone.

The Braves. were playing a late game in L.A., so me, Nick, Cash, and Speedy took our plastic trays with their piles of chili dogs, onion rings, and fried pies and settled into the WTBS room. We found a big round table that we could all sit around. It was nestled up against the wall, a good ten feet from the TV. We plopped ourselves down in the plastic chairs and started to dig in.

"They'll have to get more TVs in here before long," Speedy said. "Cable is the wave of the future."

He sounded like he'd memorized the last part from a brochure. We all laughed at him. He lowered his hamburger from his mouth and looked at us like we were a bunch of idiots.

"I'm not shittin' y'all. You can pick up fifty channels with one of those boxes." He leaned forward, as if to approach us in confidence. "You can even watch titty movies," he whispered.

"We know all about cable," Cash said. "We also know they've gotta run the coaxial in from the street before those boxes work."

Speedy bristled. "Hell, I know that. But they was supposed to have half of Green Lake wired by last spring. Damn cable company don't know their ass from a hole in the ground. Left me holding all those boxes."

"Yeah, those boxes you stole from them," Cash said.

I asked Nick if we were ever going to get wired for cable.

"I already called the cable company," he said. "They told me the house was set too far off the street. They're going after the subdivisions first. Those and the apartment complexes. That's where they'll make money fast."

Speedy pointed up at the TV. Bob Horner was settling into the batter's box, adjusting his batting helmet, the one with the small letter *a* on the front. He had the beginnings of a beer gut and golden curls that made him look like a little boy dressed in baseball pajamas. But, Jesus, he could knock the shit out of a ball. He cut loose with that short swing of his and sent one out to the palm trees behind the left field fence, causing that junk-balling Don Sutton to step off the mound and shake his head.

"Ted Turner's done made a load off the cable," Speedy said, "broadcasting his ball games and all those old TV shows. Hell, I was just trying to get in on a little of it."

"This ain't the racetrack," Cash said. "You can't go running Ted Turner into no wall."

Cash was talking through a mouthful of chili dog. He and I were really going to town, shoveling those dogs into our mouths. I could feel the grease welling up on my chin after each bite.

For all his talk of being hungry, Speedy was only halfheartedly nibbling at his burger. And Nick hadn't even touched his food yet. He fired up a cigarette and sat there looking at the ball game in a distracted sort of way, checking his watch every now and then.

"Do we need to get you somewhere?" Cash asked.

Nick shook his head. "In a little while," he said. "But take your time. I don't have to meet these people until one." He dipped a french fry into Cash's pool of ketchup and slid it into his mouth.

"Damn," Cash said. "You've been keeping some fucked-up hours lately."

"Yeah, it's not like it used to be." Nick appeared wistful, like there had actually been a string of good old days in the dealing business.

Cash's eyes widened into a look of recognition. He pointed at me, then reached into his back pocket. He produced a fifty-dollar bill and slid it across the table. "Speaking of work, that's for the assist. Take your little lady out dancing."

I thanked him, though I tried not to appear too happy, seeing how Speedy was sitting right beside me.

Nick smiled and nudged Cash with his elbow.

"Look at our boy," he said. "He's in love, ain't he?"

Cash nodded like that was old news. "Oh, yeah. I saw him walking around that track with a hard-on. He's gonna have to strap that thing to his leg or something."

I flung an onion ring at Nick. "Come on, we've just been hanging out together, that's all."

Cash took a gulp of his chocolate shake and swiped at his mouth with a little paper napkin. "So, here we sit," he said, motioning with his hand to let me know he meant himself and Nick. "A panel of experts on the ladies, at your disposal. Now's the time to ask questions. The secrets of the universe shall be revealed."

They both crossed their arms and sat there expectantly, like a couple of elders. But I couldn't think of a thing to ask.

"All right," Cash said, "I'll start off. When you're kissing a girl, you always gotta play with her hair. You start off twirling the ends, that and those little baby hairs down there on her neck. And then, when things start to get hot, when Teddy Pendergrass starts singing *'close the door, let me give you what you've been waiting for,'* you move your hand in deeper, grab a fistful of hair and give it a little tug. Not too hard, just enough to pull her head back so you can get down on her neck. Women love that shit. And don't forget the Teddy Pendergrass, either. That motherfucker is cooler than this milk shake."

Cash swirled his cup and took another drink. Then he gestured toward Nick, turning the floor over to his fellow expert.

Nick tamped his cigarette into the ashtray. He did it slowly, like each little jab might actually have been revealing secrets of the universe. Finally, he offered a sly grin.

"You remember that thing Lyndell used to talk about?"

I knew exactly which thing. "What about it?"

"Well, he was right. It's something you gotta know how to do the right way. It's a natural part of a man and woman's relationship."

Cash appeared confused, so Nick leaned over and whispered in his ear. Cash's eyes widened and a smile spread across his face. He nodded his head with conviction.

"Oh, yeah," he said. "You gotta go downtown. That's your key to the city, right there. Because listen, she's gonna be telling all her little buddies about what you do. And when they hear that, man, they're gonna be jealous. You're gonna be getting all you want. You're gonna be having to take vitamins and shit."

"What are y'all talking about?" Speedy asked.

Cash leaned over and whispered to Speedy. Speedy jerked away like Cash had stuck his tongue in his ear. "Ah, hell," he said. "That's disgusting. You wouldn't catch me doing that."

"See right there?" Cash pointed at Speedy. "It's already whittling down your competition."

I slid my tray aside. I set my arms on the table and leaned forward to hear Nick's instructions.

"It's all a matter of tempo," Nick said. "Like music. You know how some songs start out slow? You got the acoustic guitar going for a while and then the bass comes in a little bit, then the drummer. You got these layers coming in one at a time, applying more force, and then the tempo starts to pick up, and it builds and builds until the power chords just start raining down."

"You mean like 'Stairway to Heaven'?"

Nick grinned. "Exactly."

He grabbed his uneaten chili dog and held it up as a visual aid. The tube steak was tucked into its bun, caked with a pasty coat of chili. A thin stripe of mustard ran right down the middle of the creation.

"Imagine yourself trying to lick that mustard off without disturbing the chili. It's a very delicate affair."

"And that's the acoustic part?" I asked.

He pointed at me and winked. "You got it. Now what comes after that is all instinct. You gotta look at her as your drummer. She's gonna be the one giving you the cue. She's gonna let you know what kind of tempo to keep. And if you follow her along and don't try to rush things, you're gonna be bashing out some hellacious power chords before that song ends. You're gonna be bending notes, hammering, getting major feedback. The whole nine yards. But you gotta listen to your drummer."

I could picture Rachel sitting behind a drum kit. I was thinking she could probably bash the shit out of those skins. All of the sudden, I felt something like a wave of electricity run through me. In my head, I heard the opening chords of "Back in Black." My appetite came back in a big way, and I unwrapped my peach pie and took a bite.

"You know you could always give her a puppy," Speedy said. "That's what I usually do."

Nick and Cash started laughing. Speedy cut his eyes in their direction, looking like he regretted having said anything.

I wiped a glob of pie filling off my chin. "That's not a bad idea."

Speedy's face brightened. "You know, I need somebody to keep Brute for me. I mean if Cash is really gonna turn me in and all."

Cash's mouth dropped open. He looked like he couldn't believe what he was hearing. "Man, what do you mean, *if*? There ain't no *if* about it. If hell froze over right now, I'd put chains on my tires and drive your ass back to the courthouse."

I pointed out to Speedy that Brute wasn't exactly a puppy.

"He's only a year and a half," he said. "That's just a baby. And he's pretty easy to take care of, too."

Speedy gave me the rundown on Brute's upkeep, the kind of food he ate, the times that he liked to go outside to use the bathroom. It turned out his favorite snack was Krystal cheeseburgers. Speedy would put one end of a burger in his own mouth and let Brute take the other end and eat away until he was licking Speedy's face.

"Giving me some sugar," Speedy said with a smile.

Cash and Nick looked like they might puke.

"What you gotta do, though," Speedy said, "is get yourself a thick strand of rope and double-knot it from a tree limb so it hangs to about five feet off the ground. Then take Brute out there and let him jump up and latch on to it with his mouth. Man, he loves that. He'll hang there for an hour, just jerking his head all around and swinging his body. It'll take some of the piss out of him, too, so he don't bite too many people."

Nick had a frightened look on his face. "You're not bringing that mongrel into my house," he said.

"I wouldn't give it to a girl, either," Cash said. "Shit, she might lose a hand or something. You don't wanna be dating no one-handed girl."

"I think it'd be all right," I told them. "In fact, I think Rachel might like Brute. She told me, for a fact, that she likes strays."

"God himself would put that dog to sleep," Nick said. He grabbed the flap of fabric that Brute had torn loose from his shirtsleeve and held it out as material evidence.

"Yeah," Cash said. "Trust me. Once she sees this dog, she'll be sending your ass out to buy one of those poodles."

"Or a goldfish," Nick said.

I didn't trust their opinions on every matter of the heart. I knew Rachel well enough, and that's why I struck a deal with Speedy. I agreed to take Brute off his hands, but only if it was permanent. He couldn't come back for him once he'd gotten out of jail.

"It's probably for the best," Speedy said. "I don't hardly have time to look after him, no ways. That's why he's so wild."

I asked Speedy if Brute had really been a stray.

"He sure was. Somebody tossed him out of the car right in front of my house. Poor little thing. I cleaned him up and fed him, then I tied a bow around his neck and gave him to this woman I was seeing. She told me she was gonna name him after me. That's how he got the name

Brute. She used to call me her little brute, on account of the way I race and all."

Cash was polishing off the last of his rings. "She should have named him Asshole."

Nick asked Speedy what had happened with him and the girl. He sounded genuinely interested, for some reason.

"Ahh, she left." Speedy swatted at the air with an open hand. "She said if I could channel some of my tenacity on the track into other stuff, I might really make something of myself."

"So why didn't you?" Nick asked.

Speedy shrugged. "Hell, I don't know. I guess I care more about racing than I do about anything else."

Nick leaned back and drummed his fingers on the table. "My girl doesn't even want me to get a real job. She gets mad at me when I start talking about going legit. Ain't that a kick in the ass?"

"It's blind luck," Cash said, "who you bump into when your dick gets hard."

"That's why there's so many sad songs," I said. "Claudia told me ninety percent of the people aren't with the person they really want to be with."

"More like ninety-nine percent," Cash said.

Nick studied my face for a moment. "You just be careful," he said. "Sometimes you get hooked up with somebody, not really meaning anything to come of it. And then, the next thing you know, ten years have gone by and you're stuck with one another."

"Sounds like you're speaking from experience," Cash said.

Nick got this embarrassed look on his face, like he'd just dropped a bag of pot on the floor in plain view of everyone.

"I didn't mean it like that," he said. "Me and Bev aren't the Cleavers, but we're good for each other."

He took a sip of his Coke and made a grab for his cigarettes. I understood this to mean that he'd said all he was going to say on the matter of himself and Bev.

It was hard for me to understand their relationship. They'd fight and drive each other crazy most of the time, but then Nick would go out of his way to act like they were some kind of old married couple. He'd call Bev "dear" in between their scraps and carry that Nikon camera along when we'd all go out fishing or on a picnic or to a Braves game. He'd ask other people to take our picture. Bev and I hated it, but he loved to save photos. He had shoe boxes under his bed filled with photos, going all the way back to when he was a little baby and Claudia looked about twelve years old.

Cash scratched at his neck and chuckled. "So, y'all wanna hear my sad story?"

"Go on," Nick said. "Break our hearts."

Cash wadded up his napkin, dropped it inside the empty onion ring box and shoved his tray off to the side.

"Well, I used to go out with this girl back when I worked at the chicken farm," he said. "First girl I ever loved. Her name was Cassandra. And man, let me tell you, I had it bad. She was all pretty and quiet, and her father was a Baptist preacher. Made me want to be a good man, have babies and all that other shit. But after I came in to work late one too many days and got my ass fired, she told me she didn't want to see me anymore, said she didn't see me going nowhere, that all my friends were thieves and card sharks and I was headed down the same path. It shook me up, too. Man, I wanted to go out and knock off a liquor store and get my ass caught just to make her feel bad."

"Trust me," Nick said, "you would have ended up feeling a lot worse about it than her. Right after the cops shot your ass."

"Well, it never came to that," Cash said. "I was in this bar drinking, when I started talking to this guy. I was telling him what Cassandra had said to me. So he tells me he's a bail agent, and if I got connections like that, if I know all these criminals, then maybe I should go into the bonding business myself. I set down my beer, and I thought: Shit, I'll go legit. That would piss her off. So I went to work for that guy. I stayed two years, took a class and got my own license."

He looked down at the hole in his coveralls and laughed in a sad and quiet sort of way. "I built my whole life out of spite for a girl. That's the only reason I'm not in jail."

The three of them stared off into space with these gloomy expressions on their faces. They made me think of those three figures: see no evil, hear no evil, and speak no evil. But with different warnings, of course. I guess they all should have been sitting around that table with their hands over their hearts. Either that, or their dicks.

Speedy was the one who broke the silence. He slid his chair back from the table and stood up. "That hit the spot," he told Cash. "I appreciate it, but I'm ready now. We can get going, if you want."

Cash looked like he'd been shaken from a deep sleep. "Yeah, okay," he said. "Listen, Speedy. I'll tell you what, man. I'll drive you to the county lockup, but you can go up the steps and turn yourself in. All right?"

Speedy just stood there holding his tray. He didn't say a word. I suppose he thought that Cash might be playing a trick on him.

"It always looks better that way," Cash said. "It might save you a couple of months on the tail end."

Speedy nodded in a slow, appreciative way. He walked over and dumped his and Cash's wrappers into the trash can. Up on the TV, the Braves were headed into the ninth, trailing by a pair of runs. Ernie Johnson uttered his almost nightly refrain: "Time to go get 'em, Braves."

Nick draped his arm around my shoulder as we walked out into the lights on North Avenue. He was smiling and looking content.

"What a fucking night," he said. "Man, I wish I'd had my camera with me."

15

It's amazing how lawful you can feel driving on a suspended license. There I was out on the streets under a bright Sunday afternoon sky, steering toward Rachel's apartment in Nick's old Plymouth Fury. Nick had given me the okay, impressed by the skills that I'd exhibited during our high-velocity pursuit of Speedy. He'd tossed me the keys that morning right before he left town with one of his customers, a fellow who drove a white BMW. Nick had his Hogans and his suitcase propped up by the front door. He told me he was headed down to Pensacola for a couple days to do a little business and rattle some jars. My driving liberties extended only as far as the Holiday Inn and Rachel's apartment.

The Fury smelled like grilled onions from the sackful of Krystals sitting at my feet. I'd bought an even dozen to keep Brute in line. I picked him up from Speedy's disaster of a house, where I also adopted a cable box and about six feet of coaxial that was lying on the bedroom floor. I didn't think that Speedy would be needing that stuff for a while.

Brute was riding shotgun and smacking on a burger while I made my way back across town. The big fella needed a trip to the vet in a bad way. His ears smelled like sour milk, and his black and brown coat had been hacked up by the mange. It looked like somebody with the DTs had come after him with an electric razor.

I was doing everything by the book, watching the speed limit, staying off the busy roads, keeping the radio volume low even though the Pond was in the midst of a Van Halen rock block. I was incognito as well, my disguise a pair of drugstore aviators and a Braves cap pulled low on my forehead. I could have been headed somewhere to relieve Danno on a stakeout.

The chances of encountering Wade Briggs at a three-way stop must have been pretty damn slim. But it happened. I was sitting there waiting to make a right onto Green Lake Road when his truck crossed my path. He was off duty, driving his black Ford F-150 with his crippled teenage son sitting beside him in the cab.

I tried to pull a Speedy, sliding down in the seat, shielding the side of my face with my hand. It was no use. Wade recognized the car right away. And once his eyes latched on to me, it was like he couldn't stop looking. You'd have thought he'd seen a long-dead relative sitting behind the wheel. He almost hit the stop sign at the other side of the intersection.

I groaned, punched the steering wheel, and said, "Fuck me," about a half dozen times. That was right before I remembered the joint in my shirt pocket, the one that I'd intended to share with Rachel. I fished it out and dropped it inside the Krystal sack for safekeeping. Then I tossed my cap and sunglasses onto the dashboard.

Naturally, Wade made a U turn. He followed me down the road, blinking his lights so I couldn't even pretend to ignore him. I went ahead and pulled over into the weeds by the side of the road.

The steep embankment led down to a dirty cove of the lake. When I got out of the car, I could smell the water, the steamy fishy stench of summer. Out in the distance, the wide blue carpet was dotted with sails and the slim silhouettes of speedboats, most piloted by Atlantans who came out for the weekend, hauling their beer coolers and turning the volume way too high for "Margaritaville."

Wade climbed out of the truck, leaving Danny inside. Danny was the product of Wade's troubled first marriage. He looked like Wade, even had a junior set of bags under his eyes, though he'd dyed his hair blond and had grown it down his back. He was wearing a *Dark Side of the Moon* T-shirt over his bony shoulders and smoking a cigarette, and he looked pissed off about something. I figured he had a right to be, considering how he'd been wrecked by muscular dystrophy.

I leaned against the Fury's trunk and tried to act like everything was normal.

"Hey, Wade. How's it going."

"It's going okay, Luke. Not too bad."

Wade was wearing jeans and a Western shirt with snaps on it. His hair was slicked back like he'd just taken a shower.

"Would you believe I'm on a rescue mission?"

Wade couldn't help but smile a little. It made me feel better, like seeing me had brightened an otherwise gloomy afternoon.

"Probably not," he said, "but go ahead and convince me."

"It's a stray dog." I pointed at the rear windshield. "I found him a new family, and I'm on my way to deliver him."

Wade tilted his head and gazed through the window. Brute's head was bobbing, and his tongue was hanging out of his mouth. It looked like a huge piece of bacon.

"Good God." Wade's eyes widened. "That looks like Speedy Brown's dog."

"That's impressive," I told him. "You must know all the outlaws' dogs."

"I just remember thinking I'd never seen a case of the mange that bad before."

I glanced in at Brute again. "Yeah, I know. He's gotta see the vet about that."

Wade straightened himself and considered me with some measure of bewilderment. "So, what the hell are you doing with Speedy's dog?"

"Well, he sort of needed a new home, seeing how Speedy turned himself in last night. So, I volunteered to locate a proper and responsible caretaker."

Wade stepped up to the driver's side window and bent low to take another look. As soon as Brute caught a glimpse of Wade, he made a lunge for him. Wade gasped and jumped back a couple of steps.

"Jesus, he's quick."

After Brute had finished bashing his head into the window, he shook himself all over and stared down at the Krystal bag. His nose started twitching, and he proceeded to stick his snout in there with all those hamburgers and the joint I'd hidden. I tried to get him away by banging my fist against the window, but he didn't pay me any attention.

"I hope you know that he's been hauled in a couple of times, himself," Wade said. "He pulled a woman off the back of a motorcycle out in front of Speedy's house. Thirty-seven stitches in the upper thigh. Somebody called Animal Control, and it took five of them to get him in the truck. He almost chewed off a man's testicles."

"Yeah, he's got this thing for the balls. But he's not a bad dog. Once you throw him a couple of Krystals, he's pretty loyal."

Wade turned and looked up at the treetops across the road. The cicadas were up there, throbbing in time with the heat.

"I don't even wanna know how you ended up with Speedy's dog," Wade said. "Just tell me why you're driving. Why couldn't Nick drive?"

"Well, he sort of had to go out of town for a couple of days."

Wade turned from the trees and looked right at me. He had his hands on his hips. "So, where are you staying?"

"Nick's house. Dewey's there."

"Well, did Nick tell you where he was going?"

"Yeah, he told me."

"Mind if I ask where?"

"It depends. Is this a police question, or a friendly question?"

A speedboat streaked by near the cove, hauling a water-skier behind it. The boat's wake caused the water to slosh against the shore below us.

"You know, I told Claudia I'd keep an eye on you two. Not to throw you in jail, but just to look after your best interests."

"Yeah, she told me."

He gazed down the embankment and watched the waves lapping against the muddy banks. Pretty soon, his face turned serious again.

"I understand you had a conversation with Loyd Muskgrave not too long ago."

The comment caught me by surprise. But then I figured there were probably few secrets in the Green Lake Police Department.

"Yeah, Sheriff Loco seems to have this idea that me and Nick are the cocaine kings of Green Lake. You know, I'd appreciate it if you could help straighten him out on that. All it'd really take is pulling his head out of his ass."

Wade smiled. "I don't have a whole lot of access to the sheriff these days. Ever since the whole jail scandal broke, he only talks to about three people. He's not the most trusting sort."

"He's not the most likeable sort, either. I don't know how you can stand to work for an asshole like him."

"I don't elect the sheriff," Wade said. "The voters do that."

"Well, I hope they vote his ass out of office next year."

"It's a possibility. That's why you and Nick need to be about as cool as possible for the time being."

I held up my hand so he could save his breath. "Muskgrave already read us the riot act."

Wade frowned. Then he looked down at the dirt and nudged a beer bottle over into the weeds with the toe of his cowboy boot.

"Muskgrave's got your picture on a bulletin board in his office."

I felt a tick of concern inside my chest. "For what? Because I mouthed off to him at the T-Bone King?"

Wade shook his head. "He's got a bunch of pictures up there. Nick's, too. Muskgrave's looking to do something big."

"But I'm clean. And so is Nick, at least as far as this cocaine thing goes."

"I know you're not involved," he said. "But I'm pretty sure Nick is."

My chest tightened even more. It felt like somebody was holding me against a wall.

"Are you sure?"

Wade looked me right in the eye. He didn't appear to be happy about passing along the news.

It made perfect sense, though. The crazy hours and the business trip to Florida. Most of all, the way that he changed the subject when I brought it up. He'd never been cagey like that about his pot business.

The only question was why he'd want to take such a risk. It's not like he was living any better.

"So, is Muskgrave gonna haul him in?"

Wade let out a sigh. "He'd like to. But I don't think he can. I mean not just yet, anyway. Muskgrave can hardly run any sort of investigation when he's spending all his time defending himself. But he wants to do something big before next year's election. He's already looking down the road to eighty-four. He wants that state senate seat that McHugh is vacating. He's bending McHugh's ear. He wants the senator to get the GBI and the FBI involved. Muskgrave says he's gonna trace it all the way back to the source."

"The source?"

"Yeah, he keeps saying he wants to nip it in the bud. He's got this notion in his head that Morley Safer's gonna come out and interview him for *60 Minutes* if he does."

We stood there under the sun, Wade staring at the ground and me picturing the possible outcomes to all of this. It was hard to imagine a good one.

"You know, he was talking about going into the radio business," I said.

Wade looked up as though I'd awakened him. "Who? Nick?"

I shrugged. The radio thing didn't seem very likely right then.

"I'd do anything I could to help Nick," Wade said. "I've tried calling him, but he always puts me off, says he's gotta go somewhere or that somebody's waiting for him. It's just hard for people to change when they've been doing things a certain way for so long. That's the hardest thing about this job: taking people back in. Every time you carry them back to jail, you can see they've had a little bit more of the life sucked out of them."

"I believe they call it recidivism," I said.

Wade stared at me for a long time, leaving me to feel a little uneasy. I wondered if he was thinking about running me in, or maybe telling Knox about my little excursion.

But I had it all wrong.

"Outside of the Muskgrave thing, I've been hearing good stuff about you," he said. "I hear you've been working and sending money to Mrs. Dees. That's good. Real good."

What he said felt like a compliment, so strong a compliment that I had a hard time looking him in the eye.

"I guess I never said thank you for what you did. You know, getting rid of the—"

Wade held up his hand before I could let the words out into the air.

"Anybody can change," he said. "I mean, look at me. Nobody's born to be a drunk. Or a drug dealer, for that matter. God gives us choices. Not all the ones we want, but plenty enough."

He was looking at Danny while he said the last part. He waved at his son to let him know he'd be just another minute, then he stuck out his big hand for me to shake. I gave it a firm squeeze.

"Get the dog taken care of," he said, "then go on home."

I told him I would, and then I watched him walk back to the truck. Inside, Danny slowly raised the cigarette to the general vicinity of his mouth, then leaned over to take a puff. It was painful watching him move.

Wade opened the door to the truck and looked back one last time. "Tell Claudia hello for me."

I waved again before I remembered the joint inside the Krystal bag. I stood there by the trunk and waited for Wade to pull away. As soon as he'd driven out of sight, I bolted for the car to see if there was anything left to salvage.

16

Rachel and her mother lived in the Lake Breezes apartment complex out near the community college. They rented a two-bedroom on the second floor of building 2112—easy to remember, thanks to Dewey's obsession with the so-dubbed Rush album. It was smaller than Nick's house, but without the cracks in the ceiling. It also had a tiny balcony that overlooked a murky run-off pond. Rachel said the pond looked like a good place to dump a body.

I took her hand and led her down to the parking lot. She was barefoot, wearing cutoff army fatigues and a tattered gray T-shirt. Her nipples looked like the tips of balloons pressing against the fabric. I got a thrill watching the flex of her leg as she padded down the stairs, the faint outline of a muscle at the back of her leg. Her body looked perfect to me, though I sometimes wondered if she could stand to add a few pounds, just for the sake of good health. She hardly ever ate, and when she did, it was usually gum or M&M's. She was like a hummingbird, always craving sugar. She also took a lot of Dexatrim. She called it her "go fast."

"How did you get here?" she asked. "Are you fucking driving again?"

"I've got special permission from the police. One day only."

I led her over to the Fury and pointed inside. She had to cup her hands against the side window because of the glare. Naturally, Brute had a go at her, barking like an idiot and crashing into the glass. Rachel leapt backward, screamed and hid behind me. She had her hands on my shoulders, using me as a shield between herself and Brute.

"Does he bite?" she asked.

"A little."

"What do you mean, a little?"

"Well, he's pretty even-tempered if you've got Krystal hamburgers. I brought a sackful with me, but he already ate them."

Rachel peeked over my shoulder. Brute was eyeing us, tongue wagging in a cute sort of way. He actually looked like he was trying to put forth his best self.

"My God," she said, "he looks like he's got the fucking mange."

"He's a stray. I thought you might like him, since Ebo's not currently up for adoption."

"You mean you got him for me?"

I looked back over my shoulder. "He's for you, if you want him."

She made a little sound in the back of her throat—sort of like a gasp—and then stepped out from behind me. She slid her hands into her back pockets and looked from me to Brute and then back again.

"His name's Brute," I told her.

Her dark eyes widened and flashed with a tenderness I'd never seen in them before. It was quite a sight, like watching murky water turn perfectly clear. It made me feel like Moses. I had this feeling that something had changed forever, in a good way. It was hard to believe I owed it all to Speedy.

"My mother's going to shit," she said. "And besides, you can't have any pets here that weigh over eighteen pounds."

"You want me to take him back?"

She shook her head in an urgent way. "No. Let's just get him upstairs." She looked all around to see if anyone was watching. "We'll figure something out."

Rachel's mother was at the community college, so I led Brute through the small living room on his chain leash. The place was a mess. It looked like they'd just moved in two days ago, rather than three months ago. Cardboard boxes were scattered all around, still packed and marked with labels. And there were no pictures on the walls, just plastered holes from the previous tenants' stuff. The only two items that didn't appear ready for a middle-of-the-night getaway were the sofa and the TV. The Zenith lacked a cable box, but I noticed a coaxial outlet on the wall. It provided the room with an instant dose of charm.

After we'd gotten Brute settled into Rachel's bedroom, I told her all about the shit that had gone down with Speedy.

"I can't believe you hit somebody with a fucking wrench." She fell back on her bed, laughing. "You guys are like the Three fucking Stooges or something."

She was lying on top of a tan comforter, and I was sitting on the floor with Brute. He'd already plopped himself down on the splotchy gray carpet. His eyelids were at half-mast, well on their way to sleepy town. I couldn't help wondering if the joint that he'd eaten had made him drowsy.

Rachel sat up again. "So Cash paid you fifty dollars for catching the guy?"

"Yeah. He even said he was gonna call me the next time he had to bring somebody in."

"You mean you're thinking about this as a career?"

"Absolutely," I said. "Bounty hunting is a legal profession, you know. Plus, you get to work for yourself. That's the best career to have, according to Cash. You don't have to answer to anybody. Plus, crime is recession-proof."

She studied my face for a moment and started laughing. I asked her what the hell was so funny.

"You," she said. "Already worrying about your career. Most guys could give a shit about that stuff."

"Well, they probably haven't met the juvenile magistrate who took my driver's license. She told me if I ever came back in her office, I'd better bring my toothbrush and clean underwear. That's enough to get you thinking about a career."

"Well, don't be insulted," she said. "It's sort of cool that you think about that kind of stuff. Even if you do want to hit people in the head for a living."

Brute was asleep, snoring quietly but in a hoarse tone, like an old man who'd smoked Pall Malls his whole life. Rachel slid off the bed, got down on her knees, and stroked one of the bald spots on his head.

"Poor little guy," she said. "He needs to go to the vet."

Her room was tiny, but with a more permanent feel to it than the living room. It smelled good, too, like the fat vanilla candle burning atop her dresser. She had a New York Dolls poster hanging over her bed and a David Bowie poster stuck to the back of her door. There was also a bookcase sitting against the wall beside her bed. It was crammed with paperbacks, and it harbored a cheap stereo system on the middle shelf.

Everything in the room fit together, except for the clutter of papers tacked to the back wall. There must have been twenty of them, each displaying a charcoal sketch of a frog. They were gawky little creatures with gangly legs and crosses on their backs. They'd been drawn on notebook paper and tacked up with pins.

"What kind of frogs are those?" I pointed to the drawings.

She glanced over her shoulder, still stroking Brute.

"Spring peepers," she said. "But I didn't draw them. My father did."

"Did he draw them for you?"

She crawled over to the bookcase and crouched there, playing with the buttons on the stereo. "Yeah. I used to go frog hunting with him every spring."

"You mean like frog giggin'?"

She laughed. "No, Jethro. Not frog giggin'. We caught them with our hands. We'd creep around the edge of a pond right after dark. That's when they come out to breed."

She studied the drawings for a moment, then turned her attention back to the stereo. "The loudest males are the ones that have the easiest time getting laid 'cause they let out this god-awful squeal. Anyway, Dad had these helmets with lights on them, and we'd just follow the noise. He collected the frogs for his work. He was a herpetologist."

I was struck with the vision of Jim Fowler wrestling an anaconda on *Wild Kingdom*.

"So he studied reptiles?"

Rachel nodded. She had the stereo going now, whipping the tuner around the dial, stations coming in and out so fast it sounded like some strange new instrument.

"And your mother's an English professor?" I asked.

"When she can get out of bed," Rachel said.

I scanned the bookcase. The only name I recognized was Anne Frank. Based on the titles, though, I concluded that Rachel was very interested in death.

"So I guess you're pretty smart?" I asked.

She gave me the sneer.

"I didn't mean it as an insult. I mean, look at all these fucking books."

She considered her collection as though she were looking for one to pull down and offer to me. I would have read it if she had.

"I read what I want to read," she said, "not what some dumb-shit teacher tells me to read. You think I actually wasted my time on *Moby-Dick*? Fuck, no. I hated that fucking book. Like the whale represents life, or something. Yeah, right. I refused to read it. I got an F because of it."

She smiled at the memory of this. "That really pissed off my mother."

She finally stopped the dial on WPND. It was the clearest station she'd come across. Neil Young was singing "Southern Man" while Rachel pulled a stack of record albums out from the bookcase.

"I bet you I can guess what song they'll play next," I told her.

She was thumbing through the albums. "Oh, yeah? Which one?"

"'Sweet Home Alabama.'"

I told her the whole story, how Skynyrd had recorded the song to tell Neil Young that not everybody in the South was as backward-thinking as George Wallace. I also told her how the late Ronnie Van Zant and Neil Young had become friends after all was said and done. At least that's how Nick told the story. Personally, I'd always been partial to Neil Young and was never much of a Skynyrd fan. It was a preference that would have gotten my ass kicked by a number of people.

Rachel didn't appear to be all that impressed with the history lesson. "Yeah, like Neil Young's gonna be listening to this crappy station, anyway."

She slipped an album out of its sleeve. She was smiling. "You're gonna like this," she said.

"Who is it?"

She clutched the record against her chest. "Just wait. You'll find out."

Neil faded out, and the opening notes of "Sweet Home" started thumping. Just as Ronnie grunted, "Turn it up," Rachel pressed phono and laid the needle on the vinyl. It crackled a little as she slid the volume lever up to eight.

"You need to turn this up, too," she said.

There wasn't any kind of intro, or even somebody saying, "One, two, three." The music just started, like some kind of assault. It had this way-too-fast 4/4 beat, like a mad dash to the bathroom. At first, I thought that she'd played the record at 45 by mistake. But then this guy started singing, telling a girl good-bye, he was glad to see her go. And even though he was keeping up with the tempo, he sounded like he'd swallowed a handful of painkillers.

The song was even shorter than Dewey's, maybe two minutes, tops. When it was over, Rachel turned down the volume a little and gave me an expectant look.

"So, what do you think?"

"Are they on crank or something?"

"Seriously," she said. "What do you think?"

"Seriously, I think that might have been the stupidest song I've ever heard."

"Yeah, I know," she said. "They suck, but in a good way."

She finally told me it was the Ramones. I'd seen their picture in one of Nick's *Rolling Stone* magazines but had never heard their music. All I knew was that they didn't sound like anything I'd ever heard before. And like that car of Rachel's, their music just seemed to go with her.

"Don't worry," she said. "It'll grow on you."

I nodded. If she liked it, then I was willing to give it a chance.

"My brother has a band," I told her.

"Really? What kind of stuff do they play?"

"Nothing like this."

She stretched out her legs and crossed her feet at the ankles. "So what's the deal with your brother, anyway?"

"What do you mean?"

"Come on." She smiled like we were in on some sort of conspiracy together. "Don't act stupid. You know what I mean. What does he do?"

"For a paycheck?"

"Yeah, for a paycheck."

"He's an English professor," I said.

"Seriously, what does he do?"

I thought about those photos again, mine and Nick's tacked up on the bulletin board in Muskgrave's office. I could see Muskgrave sitting there, staring up at them, pondering his options. It felt like he was in the room with us, like he and his deputies had bugged the place or something.

"He's in the landscaping business," I told her. "Commercial stuff. You know, like golf courses and office parks."

Joey Ramone was touting the benefits of shock treatment. Rachel smiled and shook her head. "You are such a fucking liar," she said.

She reached onto the bed and unzipped her backpack. She slipped her hand inside and fished out a pack of Juicy Fruit. I could smell it before I saw it. Since I'd met her, Juicy Fruit did something to me. It had this mysterious power, like radio waves loaded with pheromones, or whatever it was that Marlin Perkins talked about antelope being attracted to just before they rutted.

I couldn't help looking at the frog drawings again. There must have been fifteen of them tacked up there. Their eyes were huge. It felt like they were staring me down. I found myself wanting to ask more questions about her father, about their trips to the pond. But I knew that she wouldn't really want to talk about those things.

Rachel slid closer to me and Brute. She snapped her finger, as if to break me from a trance. When I looked down, she was petting Brute and chewing a stick of gum.

"What's the matter?" she asked. "Do those pictures make you wanna go frog giggin'?"

"No, I was just thinking it seems kind of cruel to snatch up those frogs when they were about to screw for the first time."

She was sitting cross-legged, facing me and Brute. She laughed and threw a wadded gum wrapper at me. I bobbed my head, and the little ball of foil whizzed past my ear.

The Ramones were already into another song. Rachel was right. I didn't know why, exactly, but I was already starting to like those guys.

"You must have liked giggin', yourself," I said, "to save all of these pictures."

She smiled. "I bet I know what kind of peeper you'd be."

"What kind is that?"

"A quiet one," she said. "Quiet and brave. A real Southern gentleman of a frog."

I felt some of the air seeping out of my tires. "I thought you said the loud ones had the easiest time getting laid."

"Yeah, but the quiet ones never got caught."

I took my hand off the bald spot on Brute's head and reached for Rachel's hair. I twirled the fine, curly strands right behind her ear, and she shuddered a little.

"I start off quiet, but I get louder as I go along."

We kissed. The inside of her cheek tasted like Juicy Fruit. It was like she manufactured the stuff in there. I felt myself come to life immediately, the blood rushing to all the right places.

"What are you talking about?" she asked.

I told her to lie back. When she did, I lifted her T-shirt a little and kissed her belly and then her hips just above the top of her shorts. Her skin smelled like bread, warm and moist and sweet. I worked on the button and the zipper of her shorts while I kissed all around down there.

"It's sort of like 'Stairway to Heaven,'" I said. "You know how it starts slow and quiet and then gets louder and faster."

"I hate that fucking song," she said.

"Well, what about Teddy Pendergrass?"

"Who?"

"Just relax," I said. "It'll grow on you."

I slid her shorts and her panties below her knees and over her feet. She never resisted. She pointed her toes like a diver to make the job easier.

The Ramones hadn't slowed down a lick. It was hard to think about doing anything acoustic with those guys going at it full throttle. And I had a feeling there weren't any slow songs on the album.

Rachel grabbed the neck of my T-shirt to pull me back up to eye level. But I stopped halfway. I kissed her hips again, and then I slowly worked my way down to her music room. It was damp, and it smelled like ivy after a rain shower. Lyndell and Nick had been right. It felt like a perfectly natural place to be.

Rachel giggled a little. "What are you doing?"

I stopped and looked up at her. "The acoustic part. Why? Do you want me to stop?"

She shook her head. She had this curious expression on her face, a little reluctant but a little impatient as well. Her cheeks were flushed, her lips full. She reached down with her hand and pulled my face against her.

"That's okay. You don't have to stop, if you don't want."

There was no use fighting it. I gave in to the music on the turntable. I listened to my drummer, to the hell-bent tempo. Rachel was playing right in time. *Hanging out on a night like this/I'm gonna give her a great big kiss.*

17

SHWOOOK! Nick smacked the range ball with his driver. We both stood there watching the grungy, dinked-up sphere shrink in the pale sky.

"Get legs!"

Nick grunted and performed a pelvic thrust, like a stripper.

"Now fade, goddammit! Fade!"

The ball picked up a nice little tail as it eclipsed the two-hundred-yard marker and zeroed in on its target like a heat-seeking stone.

CLANK.

The guy collecting balls atop the Massey Ferguson flinched a little as the ball ricocheted off the chicken-wire enclosure that protected him. He shook his head as though he'd just heard the same joke for the thousandth time.

Nick grinned and pumped his fist into the air. He couldn't have been any happier if he'd dropped in a sixty-footer at Pebble Beach. "Did you see that? That was head high. Not a bit of fucking hook to it."

"Right between the eyes." I laughed.

"Now that's what they need in golf," Nick said. "Moving targets."

"Yeah, and a shot clock. Give the players some fast carts and twenty seconds to get to their balls. Cut out all of that wagglin' shit."

"Fuckin' A," Nick said.

I was parked on the bench behind Nick's stall, sipping a Coke and listening to the Braves–Phillies game on Nick's transistor radio. I'd returned my one-iron to the trash bin earlier in the summer, right after I'd sworn off the royal and ancient game for good. Not even Cash's Iron Tiger brand of golf had been enough to win me over.

It wasn't long before Chuck Sosebee pulled up in his white BMW.

He was one of Nick's regular customers, as well as his traveling companion on the recent trip to Pensacola. Chuck flew the commuter birds for Delta Airlines and also owned a Piper Cub. That's how he and Nick had gotten down to Pensacola.

Chuck walked over to where I was sitting, still wearing part of his Delta pilot's uniform: the black pants and the white shirt with the gold wings over the heart. I'd met him twice before, though only briefly on each occasion, so I didn't know all that much about him, except that he was married and had a young daughter. I wasn't too sure of his age, though he appeared to be at least a few years older than Nick. He owned a shaggy blond head of hair that looked like it belonged on the PGA tour.

"So, how've you been hitting 'em?" Chuck grinned and stood over me with his hands on his hips. A sweat bead trickled down the side of his face.

"I'm not."

"What do you mean, you're not?"

"I mean, I quit—retired—hung up the spikes—*vaya con Dios,* my one-iron."

I hoped a string of simple explanations might help to satisfy his curiosity, though I doubted it would be that easy to get rid of him. During our other encounters, he'd tried to engage me in some sort of half-assed conversation before taking up his true business with Nick. I could never tell if he was trying to convince me, or himself, that he was an interesting guy.

"Don't tell me we lost you to tennis," he said. "That's what all the kids are into these days. They want to be like that crybaby, Jimmy Connors."

"I'm not playing tennis, either."

"Man, that guy Connors is a jerk. You know, I had him on one of my flights." Chuck shook his head sadly. "What an asshole."

I gave him a Rachel stare, blank and disinterested. I knew that he was full of shit. Nick had already told me that Chuck only flew between Greenville and Mobile. And the last I'd heard, neither of those metropolises were hosting a big-time tennis tournament.

Nick rescued me. He walked over, driver in hand, and draped his arm around Chuck's shoulder. I went back to listening to the baseball game. Phil Niekro had his knuckler dancing, and the Braves were up 2–1 heading into the ninth. Ernie Johnson was making his plea: "Time to hold 'em, Braves."

Chuck turned his attention to Nick. "So," he said, "you got those golf shoes for me?"

I looked at Nick and rolled my eyes. That was another thing about Chuck that got on my nerves: the way he talked in code around me, as though I weren't aware of Nick's pot business.

Nick flashed me a grin. He scratched his head and tried to appear confused. "Well, I don't remember you saying anything about golf shoes, Chuck. But I do have that Moroccan yum-yum you were asking about."

Chuck tried to shush Nick. He gazed back in my direction, obviously hoping that I hadn't caught the drift of things.

But I'd already placed my thumb to my lips, miming a long toke on a hash pipe. Chuck just stared at the tops of his wingtips and frowned.

With Nick hustling around like a blue-ass fly, and me bussing tables and spending as many hours as I could with Rachel, he and I hadn't exactly spent a lot of time together. That's why he'd asked me to come to the range with him. He'd said that we should have us a visit for old times' sake. It sounded good to me. I didn't expect that there'd be any more to it.

Nick finished off his bucket after Chuck had left. When he was done, he slipped his hand into a pocket of his golf bag and pulled out a can of Budweiser. He popped the top, clattered across the cement walkway in his spikes, and sat down beside me on the bench.

"I lost my tempo, all of the sudden. It just up and left me." He swiped an Atlanta Athletic Club towel across his face.

"Listen to your drummer," I told him.

He considered what I'd said and broke into an approving smile. "Oh, yeah. How'd that go, anyway?"

"It went fine." I didn't want to sound too cocky. But then I couldn't help myself. "Let's just say we've added that one to the set list."

Nick jerked the Budweiser can away from his mouth. He had his lips puckered, trying not to spew the mouthful of beer onto the sidewalk. After he'd finally managed to swallow the brew, he allowed himself to laugh.

"That's the Fulmer touch," he said.

"Well, I followed your directions. But she didn't linger on the acoustic part for very long."

Nick raised his eyebrows. "Oh, really?"

"Yeah, she's definitely more of an up-tempo kind of girl. She likes the Ramones."

"It's all rock and roll," Nick said.

We sat there staring out at the broad spread of ground, trampled and brown and dotted with golf balls. The sun was pale as a stone, perched high in the ashy blue sky. On the radio, the Braves were making a pitching change, bringing in the sidewinder, Gene Garber, to finish up for Knucksie.

I asked Nick if he and Chuck were planning any more trips to Florida. I'd heard Chuck mention something about Pensacola during their conversation.

Nick clucked his tongue. "Yep. Next weekend, in fact. So, I guess you'll have driving privileges again."

"What are y'all doing down there, anyway? What's the business part of the trip?" I took a casual swig of my Coke so as not to appear like I was grilling him.

Nick didn't answer right away. He took out a Winston and lit it.

"Chuck knows a guy down there who's in the entertainment business. He promotes concerts, wrestling events, stuff like that. Even owns a couple of radio stations."

He grinned and raised an eyebrow when he said the part about the radio stations.

"Well, why the hell does Chuck need extra work? Doesn't he make enough flying for Delta?"

"He should," Nick said. "Of course he's got that BMW, the airplane, a wife, a kid, plus several expensive habits on the side. That guy could teach a college course on liquidation."

"So what, exactly, are y'all doing for this guy in Pensacola?"

"Just legwork right now. I'm trying to show the man I've got some ambition."

Naturally, I had a strong suspicion the legwork involved the movement and/or sale of cocaine. I'd walked into Nick's bedroom right after he'd returned from the first trip, just as he was slipping several stacks of hundred-dollar bills out of his golf bag. They were crisp, clean bills, not the kind you earn making nickel-and-dime pot sales.

"I saw all of that money, you know."

Nick didn't even flinch. I suppose he'd trained himself to take an accusation the way a wrestler takes a chair to the back of the head.

"Listen," he said, "I've got a good reason for not telling you everything. You're just gonna have to trust me, okay?"

He waited for a reassuring gesture, but I wasn't offering.

"I saw Wade Briggs a couple of weeks ago. He was asking about you. He mentioned the cocaine, just like Muskgrave."

Nick's expression remained calm, but his Adam's apple took a slow dip.

"When was this?"

"The night after we bagged Speedy. I didn't tell him anything, but he said that Muskgrave had our pictures stuck to his bulletin board."

Nick's eyes widened. "For what?"

"What do you mean, for what? You heard him that night as plain as me. He thinks we're the fucking Dalton boys or something, running cocaine into Green Lake County."

Nick took a drag off the cigarette, held it in front of his face, then flicked it out over the range stall. It carried a good ten yards, even faded a little. There were some balls scattered in the grass that hadn't traveled that far.

"I haven't even heard from Muskgrave lately, not since that night you smarted off to him."

"Well, you will," I told him. "If you're doing what he says, you'll be hearing from him. Wade said he's trying to get the GBI and the FBI involved in a little crusade."

Nick gave me this long, disbelieving look. I expected him to say something, or to ask me something, but he just kept quiet.

We listened to the final out of the ball game. Geno got Larry Bowa swinging. Pretty soon, Ernie was interviewing Phil Niekro, awarding him a pair of Coosa slacks as player of the game.

Nick pointed to the radio. "So what's Knucksie's record now?"

"That makes him ten and eleven."

Nick shook his head. "That poor, pitiful bastard. He'll probably win twenty and lose twenty, the way the Braves are playing."

"That's better than not winning twenty at all."

"Yeah, but who wants to finish at the bottom of the heap every damn year?"

Nick lit another cigarette and sat there with his elbows on his knees, gazing out at the range. There were only a few golfers hitting, all of them parked at the other end of the stalls. One guy kept pounding drive after drive out past the two-hundred-yard marker. He was like a fucking machine.

"I've been wanting to talk to you," Nick said. "In fact, it's sort of the reason I asked you to come out here with me."

"So, what is it?"

He sat up straight and sighed. "It's about this Florida business."

I couldn't help myself. "Are you guys running cocaine, or what?"

Nick smiled and held up his hand. "Ease up, there, Barnaby Jones. That's not the kind of business I meant. What I wanted to tell you is that I've been talking to this entertainment big shot down in Florida—Whitlaw's his name—about working at one of his radio stations. We've got this deal where he pays me off for the other work I'm doing by making me program manager of a station. It'll be sort of a promotion."

"So, what's the other work?"

Nick laid his head back and sighed in an irritated sort of way. "You don't need to know about that part."

"Why not? You tell me everything."

"I know I do. But not this. What you don't know won't get you thrown in jail."

"If Muskgrave nabs your ass, it's gonna be lights out. You've got two priors, don't forget that."

"It's all right," Nick said. "What I'm doing right now is only a short-term thing. It's an *A* to *B* proposition, with *B* being a management position."

I finally realized that no amount of cross-examination was going to uncover the truth. I knew what he was doing, and he knew that I knew. Now I understood. It all went back to the music and going legit.

I decided to get off his case. I owed him that much for letting me come live with him and for setting me up with Cash and for so many other good things that had come about in the last few months.

"So what kind of station is it?"

Nick's face brightened. "It's Top Forty right now, just a bunch of disco and shitty stuff. But I'm gonna change all of that. My format's gonna be blues based. All kinds. Delta. Memphis. West Coast. People are gonna get an education in the blues. Plus I wanna have live music, people coming into the station at night to play. We'll get some of the old blues guys and unknown bands. And I'd also like to give guitar lessons on the air. I think that'd be pretty cool."

He took a quick puff on his cigarette. "And you know how they make radio stations have one hour of public service programming each week? Well, I'm gonna use mine to lobby for the legalization of marijuana. We'll have round table discussions, with doctors and scientists talking about the medicinal benefits and how cannabis is less harmful than alcohol."

He shrugged. "At least, that's what I'd like to do. I just don't know how the FCC would react to it."

The station sounded cool. I would have given it a button on my car radio, if I'd had one.

"So, where's the station?"

Nick smiled. "Shreveport, Loo-zee-ana."

I wasn't sure if he was being serious. I'd never considered Nick living anywhere other than his house or the big house.

"Why the hell would you want to move to Shreveport? Doesn't this guy own a station around here?"

Nick laughed. "Hell, I wanna go somewhere different. I'm tired of the same old routine. Same scenery. Same people. Same old shit. Besides, Shreveport's an up-and-comer. They've got horse racing down there. Riverboats. Golf courses."

"Are you tired of me staying with you?"

"Hell, no," Nick said. "I didn't mean it like that. It's hard to explain. Maybe it's because I'm older. People my age have these midlife crises, you know."

"But you're only twenty-six."

"Well, better to get it out of the way," he said. "I just wanted to let you know what I was planning, so that when the time comes, and things fall into place, you won't be surprised."

Naturally, I started to wonder where I'd land if all of this came about. I was in no hurry to move out of Nick's house. Things had been going far too well since I'd gotten there. I didn't want to mess with the recipe.

"When are you moving?"

"Pretty soon. There's no real timetable, but me and Chuck are planning to take on a little more responsibility."

He shot me a concerned look. "Are you all right?"

I was staring out over the range, already feeling as though I'd lost something.

"Yeah, sure. I mean, I'm happy for you. Shit, this is what you wanted. You'll be in the music business."

Nick grinned. "Fuckin' A."

I really was happy for him. It seemed the both of us now had operational plans for becoming good citizens. But my enthusiasm belied a number of concerns, and at least one question.

"What about Bev? Is she going with you?"

Nick sighed. He made a visor out of his hands and considered an airliner flying high above the range.

"I'm gonna be straight with you," he said. "Things haven't been all that good between me and Bev, not for a long time. I mean, I've tried to act like they were, tried to act like we were a normal couple. I guess, in some way—at least, since you moved in—I thought I was doing it for you. I wanted you to see that not every man-woman deal has to fall apart."

He brought his hand down from his eyes. He was still squinting, though. "Of course, I may have just been trying to prove it to myself."

"What happened with you two?"

Nick polished off the rest of his beer and fixed the trash can with a weary gaze. "Only thing we have in common anymore is getting high. And I'm pretty tired of that, too. I mean, it's never a relaxing thing with her. It always has to be an ordeal of some sort."

He crinkled the can and arced it into the middle of the trash can. He swiped his hands against each other and drew back his elbows, resting them atop the bench.

"Back in high school, when I first moved out of Claudia's house, I used to sleep in Bev's parents' garage. I was supposed to move in with some guys, but they got evicted from their house, so Bev started sneaking me in after her parents went to bed. She'd bring me blankets and cherry Pop-Tarts and then we'd lay there together with just a scratchy blanket between us and the concrete floor. We'd do our thing, you know, right there beside her daddy's Bonneville, and then we'd share those Pop-Tarts and talk about what we were gonna do when we got older."

"What was that?" I asked.

Nick smiled. "Oh, you know. The usual stuff. Babies and houses and cars and jobs. The funny thing is that it was mostly me doing the talking. I wanted those things more than her. Hell, she was just happy to be dating a dealer, a guy who played in a band. She thought that was pretty cool."

He laughed and shifted in his seat like he was embarrassed. Then he got this dark, reflective look on his face. "You know, she did get pregnant once."

"Bev did?"

He nodded.

"Right before I went to jail the first time. She found out during the trial. She didn't tell me, though. Said she didn't want to worry me. She went out and got an abortion and told me about it later, while I was serving my sentence. I don't guess there was really anything else she could have done."

I agreed with him, but then I told him I was sorry it had happened like that.

"That's okay. I don't think I would have made a very good father back then."

"Well, what about now?"

Nick took a draw on his cigarette and blew a puff of smoke into the air, as if that were a reply in itself. "I wouldn't mind stocking the pond with a couple of Fulmers."

"I'm guessing Bev's still against that idea."

"You guessed right. And I can't wait forever, you know. I can't wait forever to start a life."

I found myself wondering what Rachel might look like pregnant. What I saw was her with this basketball-shaped belly, crawling around the gift shop floor, clutching a stolen box of Pampers. I could see myself keeping a lookout, doing my part.

"I'd like to meet me a girl who's smart," Nick said, "and athletic, too. I figure if our kids get my music genes and athletic skills, then combine that stuff with her brains and even more athletic skills, they'd be okay. We could have us some little doctors and musicians, and they could get golfing scholarships to college."

"That sounds like the fucking *Stepford Wives.*"

"Well, I wouldn't want her to be perfect," Nick said. "I think a few flaws are kind of sexy." And then he laughed. "Of course, women must think the same thing. I mean, look at Lyndell. He's never lacked for pussy."

Nick stared at me a while longer. "You know, I ran into Lyndell a while back."

Now, there was some news I hadn't been expecting. "When was this?"

He let out a deep breath, like he'd dived under water to retrieve the information. "It was about a year ago, I guess."

"Where?"

"Me and a buddy were up in Virginia fencing some Alpine car radios we'd come across. Just getting out of state, you know. A day trip, in and out. So we stopped at this T-Bone King on our way home to get a bite of supper, and there was Lyndell sitting over in the corner with his new woman and their kid. He had the little girl up in the high chair feeding her baked potato, making car noises and waving the spoon all over the place, getting her to laugh. He finally saw me. Man, you should have seen his face. It just sort of melted, you know, the smile and everything. That baby was still banging on the high chair, laughing and wanting her potatoes, but Lyndell was looking at me. Finally, his woman turned around to see what the hell he was looking at. She asked him something, and he just looked down at the table. He didn't say anything to her. It was weird seeing him, you know. Kind of like running into a ghost."

That's how I felt hearing the story, like somebody was blowing a warm breath on the back of my neck. This was the only firsthand account of Lyndell that I'd heard since he left Green Lake. Claudia's information had been so vague as to make it almost impossible to imagine.

"Did you say anything to him?"

"Nah, I didn't see how that'd help anybody. You know, they'd looked pretty happy when I came in, like a regular family and all. I just didn't feel I had a right to ruin their meal. I mean, after all, it had been a long time. So I told my buddy, 'Let's go somewhere else,' and we got up and left. I thought that was it,' too. But then we were heading back out to the van, and I heard somebody clomping through the parking lot behind me. Sure enough, it was Lyndell."

"Well, what'd he look like? Did he look older?"

Nick cocked his head, trying to get a better angle on his memory. "A little bit. I think he might have been dyeing his hair, though. It looked a little darker. Of course, he was still slicking it up nice and high."

"What about the burns?"

Nick smiled. "Oh, yeah. He still had the chops. Little shorter, maybe. But he still had them. I'd say he was still spending a good half hour on the 'do."

I could almost smell the hair wax, along with the Old Spice and the Kools and the gasoline.

"Well, did he say anything?"

"That's the thing," Nick said. "He opened his mouth like he was going to, but then he couldn't seem to get the words to come out. I don't think he really knew what he'd come out there to tell me. So I just told him what a cute kid he had. He told me the kid's name—I think it was Mary Beth—and he told me about his woman and their house and how they lived near the speedway there in Bristol. He even had a shop out back for working on his cars."

"What else did he talk about?"

"That was pretty much it."

"You mean he didn't ask about Claudia?"

Nick shook his head and looked at the ground. He waited for the next question, but I felt certain that I already knew the answer to that one as well.

"It was an awkward situation," Nick said. "I could tell he wanted to ask how we were all getting along. He just couldn't get it out. So, right before I got in the van, I told him Claudia was doing fine. And then I lied and told him you were a good kid and never got into any trouble."

Nick smiled. "I don't know if he bought that one or not. Though he did ask if you had your driver's license yet. He asked if you still talked about racing."

"What'd you tell him?"

"I told him you still had some time to go. Hell, you didn't even have a learner's license then. But you know how he is. He's always had a little trouble keeping track of time."

We both nodded our heads. It felt like Lyndell was there with us, nodding along.

"It was sad, though," Nick said. "Man, he looked pitiful out in that parking lot, like he wanted to come with me. I think he would have, too, if I'd asked him. Last thing he said to me was, 'Nick, I'm too god-damn old to be raising a baby.'"

"Well, was he drunk?"

Nick shook his head. "That's the thing. He was stone-cold sober. It was quite a state to see him in, too, almost like he was wearing somebody else's eyes. It was kind of pathetic, really. Hell, I wanted to buy him a beer."

Lyndell's new life had sounded pretty good to hear Claudia tell it. But now that I could draw the picture in my head, I wasn't so sure.

"Do you think he's still sober?"

"If I was a betting man . . ." Nick said, but then he never finished the thought.

I knew what he meant, and the truth of it jarred me a little. After all, I'd pocketed Lyndell's success story as if it were an inheritance of sorts, or at least a promissory note for tags and title. And now it all appeared to be as flimsy as any piece of paper you could have written it down on.

Nick finally grunted, setting us back into motion. "Fuck, we better get going."

He jumped up and started packing his golf bag in haste. "I was supposed to pick up Bev fifteen minutes ago. Man, she's gonna be pissed."

18

As it turned out, Yuri had not been shitting me. Paul Newman really did stop in for dinner one night. It was early August, and Newman had come into town to test a GT car at the Lakeside Circuit. I suppose he had to eat somewhere.

The restaurant was crowded and buzzing with conversation. I was clearing dishes near the bar when I heard Fay talking to someone at the table beside me. She was speaking in an overly pleasant tone of voice, an immediate tip-off that something wasn't right.

"Welcome back, Mr. Newman. It is so nice to see you again." She flashed the Hollywood legend a phony beauty-pageant smile.

Newman gazed over the top of his menu and smiled like he actually remembered her from his previous visit.

"Oh, hello."

It might have been a bullshit gesture, but he managed to pull it off with grace. Unfortunately, it only served to encourage Fay. She licked her shiny red lips and drew in a breath to accentuate her bustline, eyeing Newman all the while with this wolfish gaze. I wouldn't have been surprised if she had just gone ahead, dropped to her knees and tried to give the guy head.

I'd almost finished sweeping the dishes into my tub, but I slowed the excavation project and readjusted my angle so I'd have a better look at Paul Newman and Fay. Newman was sitting with another guy at a small table by the back window. His companion looked like a driver, too, mustached and wearing a silver jacket with a Datsun racing patch on the sleeve. Newman himself didn't favor other GT drivers

I had seen. He didn't have the shaggy hair or the vacant, self-satisfied expression. He was wearing regular pants and a pale blue sweater, nothing fancy or movie star about them, though he did have this cool Rolex strapped to his wrist. It had a black face with white chronos for racing purposes. It was not the sort of watch he would have wanted to leave unattended in my presence.

Fay lingered at the table a lot longer than usual, going over the specials and telling Newman her favorite items on the menu. "I'd stay away from the seafood. We get it in on Tuesdays, so it's close to going bad about now. But the rack of lamb is yummy. That's always my favorite. That and the onion soup with the cheese on top. I could get you that and a nice green salad with creamy Italian. That's what I'd recommend if you were asking."

Newman, of course, had not asked her a damn thing. Fay simply could not shut her mouth. She was like one of those talking Barbie dolls, but with a hundred yards of string running out from between her shoulder blades.

Newman managed to speed up the process by smiling again. That sonuvabitch could have disarmed a bomb by smiling. Fay immediately shut her mouth.

"I tell you what, dear." Newman stroked the sides of his movie star chin and batted those blue eyes that kept his pockets full. "I think I'll have a Budweiser while I'm trying to decide."

Fay just stood there nodding her head. She looked like a trained seal awaiting a signal from her trainer. She didn't even ask the other guy if he wanted a drink. The poor bastard had to grab her by the arm as she was walking away.

I swept the rest of the plates into my tub and headed back to the kitchen. I tried not to gawk at Newman as I walked past him. I tried to be respectful. I told myself that he was just a guy, like myself, and not a very big one at that. I could have whipped his ass if he'd gotten out of line. I could have pulled a George Kennedy on him.

Of course, I also couldn't help imagining the two of us striking up a conversation at some point in the evening, maybe when I came back later to clear his dishes, him leaning back in his chair, giving me that smile and saying, "You look like a driver." I'd shrug modestly, right before he offered me a race car and a sponsorship. I allowed myself to take that dream out for a spin. I didn't see any harm to it. God only knows what Fay was imagining.

I could hardly push open the kitchen doors because of the crowd standing on the other side, peering through the porthole windows. Stan was there with three of the waitresses. A desk clerk had even fled her post to get in on the action. Fay strolled in behind me wearing that grin of hers. When she saw the other waitresses, she grit her little corn teeth and scowled at them.

"If any of you cunts go near that table, I'll fucking cut your hearts out."

A wave of black smoke drifted over from the grill, which for some reason had been left unattended. A strip steak flamed up in the back corner, while a chicken breast did a slow burn near the front. I nudged Stan and asked if he'd seen Yuri.

Stan tugged at the lapels of his hospitality-green blazer. "He's in the back, changing. He wanted to break out the fine threads for Cool Hand Luke."

About that time, Yuri marched around the corner looking way too sharp and professional. He was wearing blousy houndstooth pants, a blindingly white chef smock, with his name stitched to the breast, and a toque that must have been two feet tall. He looked like an artist's rendition of a chef, like something on a pizza box or a can of ravioli. I'd never seen him so dapper. He usually worked hatless, in a pair of Dickies dungarees and a shrunken smock with yellow sweat stains under the arms.

Stan and I gave Yuri a polite round of applause, just like we were at the opera or something. Yuri got this badass look on his face, squatted like he was going to take a dump on the floor, and then rotated his hips back and forth while he pointed his finger way out in front of his face. It took me a moment to realize he was doing the Travolta thing from *Saturday Night Fever.*

"It's the gallopin' fucking gourmet!" Stan announced.

"Graham Kerr," I added, "but with bigger balls."

Yuri hated Graham Kerr. He was always talking about how he could have done a better cooking show when he was drunk. At the mention of Kerr, Yuri stopped dancing and stood up straight. He wagged his finger in my face.

"And don't you forget that, beeg boy." Then he smiled and slapped my back so hard it hurt.

Yuri crouched a little and peered through the door's porthole. He stared for a long time, like he was lining up a putt. He finally straightened himself, tugged at the hem of his shirt, and burst through the doors with the confidence of an island dictator.

"Paul Newman, my friend! Ha! Ha! Ha!" He stretched his arms out wide, ready to give Cool Hand Luke a bear hug.

Newman flinched as though someone had just lobbed a grenade into the room. But then his eyes lit up in recognition. He grinned, pushed his chair away from the table, and stood up with his own arms outstretched. Stan and I stared at each other in disbelief.

"Well, fuck me up the ass with a pineapple," Stan said. "He really does know him."

I shook my head in bewilderment. "Either that, or Newman's a better actor than I give him credit for."

Rachel walked over with a tray full of garden salads, destined for the dining room. Naturally, she acted like she could have cared less about the acting and racing legend currently in our midst.

"Could I get by, please?" Her voice had an edge of irritation.

Stan and I parted to give her an open lane, but Stan appeared confused by her lack of interest in our famous guest.

"Do you know who the fuck is out there?" he asked.

Rachel looked at him like he was an idiot. "Yeah, he walked right by me when he came in. I mean, big fucking deal."

"He walked right by you?" Stan touched her shoulder, genuinely impressed. "So, what did you think?"

Rachel shrugged. "He's short."

Stan smiled as if that explained something. "All actors are short," he said. "That's what drives them. They've got a Neapolitan complex."

Rachel snorted in a scornful way. "It's Napoléon, you retard. A Napoleonic complex. Neapolitan is a fucking ice cream."

"She's right," I told him. "It's that ice cream with the stripes in it."

Stan, the former SAT wizard, squinted as though he were trying to think his way through a complex word problem, one of those involving trains leaving stations *A, B,* and *C.* He finally shook his head, dismissing us both. "No, I think Napoléon had a different complex."

Rachel let out a hopeless groan. "You really need to lay off the weed for a while." Then she backed her way through the door, and disappeared into the dining room.

Rachel and I took our usual nine o'clock break. Stan called out to us as we were walking to Rachel's car to get stoned. He was standing at the kitchen's back door.

"Hey, man! Hold up a second!"

We waited for him in the middle of the parking lot, beneath a buzzing light pole and the fat moon. Stan looked like a TV detective jogging across the asphalt in his blazer. I half expected to see a piece strapped to his side.

"So, what's up?" I asked him.

He was winded, his face flushed in the warm night air.

"I was gonna check out Paul Newman's car," he said. "Tammy at the front desk saw him pull in. She said he's driving this cool-as-shit 280-Z. You guys wanna go?"

I looked at Rachel. "That's a cool ride," I assured her.

She just rolled her eyes. "Why not?" she said. "Let's go see the car that Paul Newman drove to the Holiday Inn. I'm sure it'll end up in the fucking Smithsonian someday."

Stan led us across the lot to the other side of the hotel. The car was parked near the swimming pool. Newman had tucked the white Z between a black Caddy and a green LeSabre.

"Well, there it is," Stan said triumphantly. He extended his arm like he was Monty Hall showing off a grand prize on *Let's Make a Deal.*

Now that we were there, we didn't really know what to do. Stan and I stood at the rear bumper of the car considering the vehicle as though it might come to life and give us profound instructions. Rachel stood behind us with her arms crossed, looking bored.

The car was a '78 model, smaller than the new ones and cooler, in my opinion, more of a real sports car, a two-seater with none of those stupid jump seats in the back.

"How much would one of these things set you back?" Stan asked.

"About twelve grand," I told him. "Thirteen if you did some after-market stuff and jacked up the horsepower." I ran my finger along the sharp edge of the hatchback lid.

"It's a cool car," Stan said, "but you'd think he'd have something tougher than this. You know, like a Ferrari or a Lamborghini."

"He races Datsuns," I said. I remembered this fact from having read about Newman winning the Le Mans twenty-four-hour race. "They probably just gave him this to drive while he's in town. Look, it's even got Georgia plates."

"So, basically," Rachel said, "you've gone out of your way to look at Paul Newman's loaner car."

"It's not your ordinary loaner," Stan said. "I mean, it's like the man has driven it, you know. It's been fucking what do you call it? Validated?"

Rachel wasn't offering any help, not after the Neapolitan episode.

"It's like it's got a fucking stamp of approval," Stan said.

He fixed Rachel with a satisfied gaze. But then it seemed to dawn on him that the experience wasn't going to get any deeper than this.

"I guess I better get back inside," he said. "Gotta go serve some Yuri grub."

After Stan had tramped off, I stood there a while longer.

"Let's go," Rachel said. "I feel like a total fucking loser out here."

But I stepped up to the driver's side door and peered inside. I couldn't help myself. I always liked to peek into nice cars. It didn't matter who owned them.

"Whoa," I said, "look at this."

Rachel sighed impatiently. "Let me guess. It's Paul Newman's fingerprint, and it's got the face of Jesus on it."

"No, it's not that. It's this."

I clutched the door handle, gave it a squeeze, and felt the latch pop open—*kachink*. I looked at Rachel and held up my hands in an innocent way, as if the door had opened itself.

"Well, what do you know," I said. "It's unlocked."

Rachel's body jerked as though someone had startled her from behind. She glanced over her shoulder and all around the lot. Once she realized the coast was clear, she smiled.

I waved her over, and she rushed to where I was standing. She had a gangly way of running. It made me think of those lanky creatures on

Wild Kingdom that were always hightailing it away from the lions. Me and Dewey always pulled for those guys.

Rachel grabbed my shoulder and jabbed a finger into the small of my back. "All right," she said. "Up against the car. I'm making a citizen's arrest."

I pried her hand away from my shoulder. "Take it easy, Deputy Fife. It's not a crime if the doors are unlocked."

She snorted. "Yeah, like I'm going to trust you."

I looked around again to make sure no one was coming, then I slid right inside. The back of my poly work pants squeaked against the black leather when I wiggled myself down into the seat. The hide had a familiar smell to it, like a late-night drive on an empty road. I felt twitchy all of the sudden, my reflexes tuned up. I wanted to share that feeling with Rachel.

"Go around and get in," I told her.

She was crouched below the roof of the Buick parked beside us, trying to stay out of sight. She was still smiling, but also picking at one of her fingernails in a nervous way.

"This is so fucking stupid," she said. "But in a good way."

Once she was inside, we shut the doors. We sat quietly in the dark for a moment. I had one hand on the wheel, the other on the stick shift—no way Newman would have driven an automatic—poised like we were set to do some traveling.

"So, where are we going?" she asked.

"It's your call," I told her. "I haven't thought about it."

She stared out the windshield for a moment, over the long scoop-nosed hood of the car, out at the bushes and trees planted around the swimming pool. Shadows from the lighted pool rippled across the milky paint job.

"What about Champaign?" she said.

"What the hell's in Champaign?"

She thought it over. "Not much, really. It's kind of flat and dull."

"We've got that here," I said. "Plus a big lake."

She agreed. "I guess I'm open to suggestions."

"What about California?"

She shook her head. "It seems kind of unoriginal, don't you think? Everybody goes to California."

I checked the radio dial to see which station Newman had been listening to. It would have been cool to tell Carlton that Newman had been cranking WPND, listening to one of his Pink Floyd supersets. But the radio was set at 89 on the FM side. I thought that might have been the public radio station. I slid the dial over to WPND's 102 spot just for the hell of it.

"I used to wanna live in California," I said.

Rachel had already opened the glove compartment. She was rummaging through it. "Oh, yeah?"

"Yeah, I wanted to live in a trailer like Rockford. You know, right on the beach. Do some surf-casting, keep my pistol in a cookie jar."

I flashed her my Fulmer smile—which would not have been able to disarm a bomb—just to let her know the trailer thing was old news and I realized it had been a stupid idea.

She shut the glove box, turned, and studied my face. She was smiling like I'd just said something sweet and endearing. "That doesn't sound so bad."

"Are you serious?"

"Of course I'm serious. I like your ideas. They're original."

"But that's not an original idea. I stole it from a TV show."

Rachel shrugged. "Hey, the best I could come up with was Champaign. I mean who the fuck would steal a car and go to Champaign?"

She stared at me like she was really expecting me to answer, like maybe she was hoping I'd say it wasn't such an unusual choice.

"So do you really know how to hot-wire a car?" she asked.

"Nah, I'm pretty useless unless somebody leaves the keys inside."

"Well, I guess that limits our options." She sat there looking out the windshield, and then she grinned in a sly way. "Though I guess we could always stay here and get stoned."

I noticed a pair of sunglasses lying on the corner of the dashboard, Ray-Ban aviators. They were the real deal, not the drugstore kind like I wore. I slid Paul Newman's sunglasses onto my face and looked at Rachel. I could barely see her in the darkness. She was like a shadow.

"That seems kind of inevitable, doesn't it?"

She smiled. "Sad, but true."

She fished our pot pipe out of her leather jacket, and we packed it and sparked it right there in Paul Newman's loaner. Soon, the smell of rope blanketed the grease stench that had soaked into our clothes and hair. We just sat there smoking, passing the pipe between us. Whenever our eyes met, we'd burst out laughing.

"This is even better than knocking off the gift shop," Rachel said. "It's got its own kind of righteousness, you know. I mean, everybody's in there kissing this guy's ass, and here we are."

She reached over and slid the glasses off my face. She put them on and leaned in to kiss me. "Are you my car thief?" she teased. "My grand theft auto darlin'?"

She was doing the Southern accent thing again. But that wasn't the reason I pulled away from her.

"What's the matter?" she whispered.

"That's not why you hang out with me, is it? Because you think I'm a criminal?"

She pulled back a little to get a better focus on me. The glasses swallowed her small, heart-shaped face. They made her look like a little girl.

"What's the matter with you?" she asked. "Is Stanley's skunk weed making you paranoid?"

My thoughts sloshed around in my head like water. It sometimes happened that way when we were smoking. I wasn't exactly sure of what I was going to say until half of it was already out of my mouth.

"My brother told me he might leave his girlfriend," I said. "He told me he was gonna move to Shreveport, Louisiana."

She pulled back even farther now. She settled into her seat and leaned back against the door.

"Are you going with him?" She narrowed her eyes, appearing concerned.

I shook my head. "Probably not. I don't really know what I'll do."

"You like living with him, don't you?"

"Well, yeah. I mean, I know it's only been a few months, but it seems like I've been with him forever."

She gazed down at the floorboard, twirling the glasses around by an arm. "It works that way, you know."

"What way?"

"Well," she said, "any time you have people living under the same roof, there's bound to be a disaster. It doesn't matter how well things are going, they'll eventually get fucked up. In fact, if things are going well, that's when you should start getting really worried."

"You think so?"

"Oh, fuck, I know so."

Rachel handed me the pipe. I raised it to my mouth but stopped at the last second.

"You know what Nick told me?"

"What?"

"He told me that he used to talk to his girlfriend about having kids, about having a house, a regular job, all of that stuff."

"He doesn't seem like the type," she said.

"Yeah, I know. But he even wants to join a golf club. That's the whole nine yards right there. He says he's gonna manage a radio station. That's gonna be his line of work."

My hand was resting against my thigh, clutching the smoldering pipe. I took a halfhearted toke and passed it over to Rachel.

"I don't ever want to have kids," she said. "No fucking way."

That didn't surprise me. She said this sort of thing from time to time. But I knew that it wasn't entirely true. It was a different story when we had sex, the way that she liked to play Russian roulette. No pill, no rubber. She was like a fucking Rolex, she said. She marked her calendar with green, yellow, and red dots, and she told me we'd work around the colors. Just like a traffic light. But there was this one time that she'd wanted to run the red light. She was different that night, more urgent in the way that she moved her body beneath mine, her legs pressing against my hips as though she didn't want me to pull away, her face almost crimson, her eyes locked onto mine. "Stay inside. I don't want you to pull out." We were on the floor in her bedroom, and she was clutching my shoulders, digging her tiny fingers into my skin. I told her it wasn't a good time to be talking crazy, and what if I belted one past the third baseman? Then what? But she told me she didn't give a fuck. "I don't care what happens" is what she said. Hearing those words, I was sold. I was ready to enlist, to keep the Fulmer banner flying. It wasn't two seconds later I was about to explode. She must have seen it in my eyes, like cherries on the face of a slot machine. And I guess the reality of everything kind of smacked her upside the head. The next thing I knew, she was pushing me away, acting real urgent. "No! Pull out! We can't. I'll get pregnant." I barely made it in time, spilling myself right there on her pale tummy. Neither of us said anything. I just stayed there on my elbows and knees, panting and staring down at the sad puddle of Fulmer spunk on her belly. All of my boys stranded out there in the desert with no ride home.

The smoke inside the car had gotten thick. I cracked the window to stir a breeze. "You mind if I ask a nosy question?"

Rachel grinned and rolled her eyes. "Okay, that's it. No more pot for you."

"No, I'm serious. I just don't want to piss you off or anything."

"Okay," she said. "You can ask. But I'm not promising an answer."

"It's about those frog pictures," I said.

Rachel laughed. "Jesus Christ," she said. "You're fucking obsessed with those frogs. What is it? Do you want me to take you frog giggin' next spring?"

"No, it's not that. It's just that I thought it was kind of strange how you have all of those drawings up but then you don't have any pictures around of your father. Not in the whole place."

She turned to the side window and stared into her own faint reflection.

"We don't have photographs of anybody," she said. "I mean, what's the big deal? We're just not camera people."

"Nick takes a lot of pictures," I said.

"Your brother's pretty old-fashioned, isn't he?"

"In a way, I guess. He's got tons of photos, though, like ten shoe boxes worth under his bed. Old stuff, too, like black-and-whites. He gets them out all the time. What's funny is how he'll lay them out in order on top of the bed. You know, what do they call that order that goes in time?"

"Chronological order," Rachel said.

"Yeah, that's it. Only he won't talk about the pictures themselves. He'll start talking about what happened between the pictures. You know, like, 'This was the year I sold my first bag of pot,' or 'Two weeks after this picture, I got laid for the first time.' Shit like that. It's fun because you can see the difference, you know. Like how he's smiling a lot bigger in the pictures after he got laid."

"So what does this have to do with the frogs?" She sounded confused.

"I'm not sure," I confessed. "I guess it just feels like something's missing. You know, after those frog pictures."

She gazed down into the pipe. What with us doing so much talking, it had almost burned itself out. There was barely a glow inside the bowl.

"I was thinking about telling you," she said.

"Telling me what?"

"What you just asked," she said.

"You mean my question made sense?"

"Yeah, it made perfect sense."

"So, tell me," I said.

It took her a moment. I could sense that she was fumbling through her brain for the right words.

"So," she said, "what do you think happens when two fucked-up people have a kid?"

"Are you talking about us?"

She shook her head. "The thing is, my parents were college professors. They wouldn't have gotten together otherwise."

"Why is that?"

"Well, my mother used to say that the thing that attracted her to my father was his intelligence. Isn't that fucking ridiculous?"

"Well, you're smart, too," I said. "There's nothing wrong with that."

"Yeah, but come on. There's gotta be limits. I mean, that's always been the most important thing to her. It's so cold, you know. Like when I wanted a dog, my mother had to do all this homework first and find out which was the smartest breed. She didn't want a stupid dog. So we drove out to this breeder and bought a sheltie. Well, you know what? The dog was fucking retarded."

"Seriously?"

"Yeah, seriously. He used to bark all night, couldn't be house-trained, used to run into the sliding glass doors whenever he saw a squirrel outside. So she gave him away."

"Now I know why you like strays."

"Bingo," she said. "And it was the same thing with my father. She used to say that she loved his brilliance and his intensity. It never occurred to her that he was crazy as a fucking bedbug."

"What do you mean, 'crazy'?"

"How about two suicide attempts in the same week? Does that sound crazy to you?"

"Fuck. I guess that qualifies."

She opened the glove box again and took one last look through it, then slammed it shut.

"So, did he jump off a bridge or something?"

Rachel laughed. "No, he wasn't that dramatic about it. Bottle of aspirin the first time, sleeping pills the next. He went to a hospital for a while after all of that."

"Well, what was he like? Was he mean?"

"Oh, fuck no," she said. "He'd have these great flashes, you know, like when we used to hunt the frogs. He could act all goofy and make me laugh. It was like when you're driving along and you pick up a song you really like on the radio, but the station keeps going in and out. That was him. It gets to your favorite part, and then *buzzzzzz*." She swiped her hand through the air. "Nothing but static."

She reached out and touched her thumb to the fogged-up windshield. It seemed to amuse her, how the print of it slowly vanished.

"My mother was such a fuck, though. She never tried to help him, not after she realized he was defective. It was just me and him at the end. She'd taken a semester's leave in Oregon. She was fucking some anthropology professor out there. So Dad and I stayed behind in Champaign."

I still hadn't met Rachel's mother, but the picture that she painted of the woman grew less flattering all the time. She was always saying that her mother needed to boost the dosage on her mood stabilizers.

"So your mother was screwing around while he had leukemia?"

Rachel looked at me with those dark pools of hers. "He didn't have leukemia," she said. "I lied about that. I don't know why, so don't bother asking."

"Then what happened to him?"

"Well, he was doing okay while my mother was gone. I mean, all things considered, he was doing okay. But like I said, you never knew when he was going to come and go. So there was this one night around Christmas when he decides we needed to go driving around looking at

the Christmas lights. He liked doing that kind of stuff. You know, traditional stuff, kind of like your brother. Problem was, he'd been mixing Borden's egg nog with Captain Morgan's. Plus he and my mother
had gotten into this fight on the phone. Of course, I was proud of him
about that part. He'd really stood up to her that night. He said, 'Goddammit, Maggie, I'm tired of your fucking shit.'"

She smiled proudly, as though she were telling me about some
important science prize her father had won.

"Anyway, we're driving around these neighborhoods looking at the
lights, when this dog runs out in front of the car. This little beagle. So
my father, he's looking off at some plastic Santa on a rooftop or something, and doesn't even see the dog. And *splat*."

She slapped her hands together.

"Jesus," I said, "do you have any happy dog stories?"

She laughed. "Brute's still alive. That's a happy one."

"So what about the beagle?" I asked. "Did it kill him?"

"It was a she," Rachel said. "And we killed her good. Jesus, that was
the last thing my father needed. He could take something like that and
really run with it, you know. He was cussing and kicking dents in the
side of the car. And then he started crying. Kneeling in the middle of
the street, crying."

"Over the dog?"

"Absolutely. He kept thinking we could save it. He thought it
belonged to some little girl, that it was like a Christmas present or
something, and he'd ruined this little girl's Christmas. He wanted to
take the beagle to a real hospital to see like a fucking internist or something. But I knew that dog had pranced across her last green lawn. I
mean, she was on the express elevator to doggie heaven."

"So what happened?"

"I had to get him in the car and drive him home," she said.

"How old were you?"

"Thirteen."

"You mean you were driving at thirteen, and you gave me shit about
driving when I was ten?"

She smiled. "Ha. Turns out you were right. It really is important to
learn young."

"So, did your father get over the dog thing?"

She was holding the sunglasses, tilting them in different directions, studying the reflections from the hotel's floodlights.

"He was better, you know. For about a few months, I guess. He took his medication and stayed busy doing stuff. That was always a good sign, though a lot of times it meant that he'd charge up the credit cards really high. But he seemed more balanced this time. He bought new tires and brake pads for the car, got a new toaster for the kitchen. Then he went out and bought us all of this ski stuff. I'd been asking him to take me snow skiing, so he got me the bibs and the jacket and gloves. He said we were driving up to Michigan for the weekend. I was so fucking happy, I didn't even care that the ski suit he'd bought me was this awful green color. Plus I was fat back then, so I looked like this big fucking avocado."

"Come on," I said. "You weren't fat."

"You wanna bet?" She stuck out her hand. "I was like a butter butt. Oh, and I had braces, too. I was ugly."

"So this was before the Juicy Fruit diet?"

"Bingo," she said. "Juicy Fruit and Dexatrim. They changed my fucking life."

"All right, so get back to your father. What happened?"

"Well, he was seeing somebody, too. I forgot to mention that. But at least he wasn't an asshole about it, not like my mother. He didn't moon around the house and act like he hated everybody. She was this woman off campus, a waitress from a bar that he went to. So he told me he was going to her house for a while. Remember, now, this is the same day he bought all of the ski stuff, the brake pads and everything. And what he did is he went over there and they polished off some coke that they'd bought together, and then they fucked, I guess. And after that, he went to the drawer in her kitchen where she kept her cocaine and this forty-four pistol. And he took the pistol and left without telling her good-bye. And then he got in the car with those new tires and brake pads, and he drove way outside of town, and he parked the car there and walked out into the woods and stuck the forty-four in his mouth and killed himself."

After she'd finished the story, she pulled a stick of Juicy Fruit from her pocket and slid it into her mouth. Nice and calm, like the story had been mostly about her father buying the new brake pads. She turned to me and held out the pack of gum. She pushed her hair off her face and gave me a smile.

For a time, I couldn't even speak. It felt like someone had kicked me in the chest.

"Are you okay?" she asked.

"Why didn't you tell me all of this before?"

She pocketed the gum and threw her wrapper onto Newman's floorboard. "I don't guess I had a reason to tell you before now."

"So what's your reason?"

She slipped her hands into her jacket pockets. "Maybe it's because I had this idea. I was thinking, you know, that if your brother moves to Shreveport, you could come live with us. I just thought that maybe I should tell you all of this first."

She was being careful not to look at me. It made me wonder if she was worried I might say no.

"But what about that stuff you said? You know, about things going bad when you get people under the same roof?"

She locked her eyes onto mine again. She flattened the gum against the inside of her front teeth and popped it.

"Maybe it's not always like that," she said. "I could be full of shit, you know."

I ran my finger along the steering wheel. All of the car's gauges were resting on zero, but we might as well have been moving. After what Rachel had just said, it felt like we were headed somewhere. I couldn't help but punch the accelerator just a little.

"You know, Nick believes in this evolution kind of thing," I told her, "like that his kids will have all of the stuff that he's missing. He thinks that if he marries the right woman, they'll be like doctors and pro golfers and shit."

"So what are you saying?"

"Well, I don't know if I buy into any of that. But I was thinking, you know, that me and you could have some pretty smart little convicts."

Rachel didn't say anything. A breeze drifted in through the side window, warm and reassuring. It made what we were doing seem of less consequence, at least for a moment.

Finally, I couldn't help but look over my shoulder. "Come on," I said. "We better get back inside."

Just as I reached for the door handle, Rachel laid her hand on my arm. "Here," she said, "you forgot something."

She was smiling, holding Paul Newman's sunglasses. I slipped them over my eyes and flashed her the Fulmer grin.

"You're probably right," she said. "Our kids would be running the prison library."

19

I could feel the stretch run approaching. It was mid-August, six weeks and counting until my return engagement with Dot Knox. Rachel drove me home from work one night in her Peugeot. The air was warm and heavy, like a hand pushing against my chest. We were parked in Nick's driveway, talking some more about how I was going to move in with her and her mother. I was ready to make the jump. It felt like the right thing to do, never mind that Nick was planning to leave town and Claudia appeared to be entrenched with Charlie and his Hamilton Beach blender.

Heat lightning flickered in the distance. The occasional raindrop plinked against the windshield. Rachel had the windows cracked and a Damned cassette playing in the dash. She was talking over the music, telling me she had an even better idea, something to top the simple notion of our living with her mother. She was just about to reveal the details, when Bev started up with her screaming from inside the house. She was in full throat, and not even the mighty drumming of Rat Scabies could drown out her wrath.

"I wanna know who you're fucking, goddammit!"

There was a noise like breaking glass, and then the front door flew open and Bev ran down the steps. Rachel forgot all about her bright idea. She turned off the radio and pointed, her mouth open in total surprise.

"Who is that?" she asked.

"Oh, that's just Nick's girlfriend."

"Is she the one he's going to break up with?"

"Actually, he did break up with her. About ten days ago. She just hasn't taken it very well."

"No shit."

Bev was running around holding Nick's car keys over her head. Nick walked out the door barefoot in his jeans and T-shirt. He had his palms pressed together, pleading with Bev.

"Come on, Bev. Get hold of yourself and quit acting crazy. You're not a teenager anymore."

Bev stood on the opposite side of her Matador, taunting Nick by jiggling the keys over the roof of the car.

"Let's see what you do without these," she said. "Let's see you make your little cocaine run with your rich friend, Chuckie."

She started waving her arms like a cheerleader. "Chuck—Chuck—bo buck—banana fanna—fo fuck. Chuck, Chuck is a fuck, a big fat, rich, ugly, airplane-flying fuck."

Nick rubbed his temples and let out a sigh. "Look, Bev. I don't know what else you want me to do. I've been honest with you. I told you how I feel."

"Did you think it was gonna be that easy?" she screamed. "After ten fucking years?"

Nick shrugged. "I don't know. I mean, yeah. Maybe."

"Then you must be fucking high," she said, "if you think you're gonna throw me away like some piece of dog shit on the bottom of your shoe."

Nick appeared completely exasperated. "I'm not throwing you away. I'm just saying it's time we looked at some alternatives."

"I wanna know who you're fucking!" she screamed. She started pounding the top of the car with her fists. "You owe me that much, you motherfucker!"

Rachel watched the episode with a fair amount of disbelief. "Jesus," she said, "this is brutal."

"High school sweethearts," I declared. "This could be us in a few years."

Rachel shook her head at the sorry sight in front of us. "No way. We've gotta fucking call it quits before it ever gets that ugly."

"Of course, we might be different," I said.

"Trust me," she said, "everybody thinks they're different."

"You've got a point there."

Bev's tantrum soon turned to flat-out grief. She was bawling and screaming but still pounding the roof of the car. Nick stood on the other side, trying to reason with her. I don't think he wanted to get too close.

"I'm not fucking anybody," he pleaded. "I wouldn't do that to you. It's just not working anymore. We don't want the same things."

"Since when?"

"I don't know. I mean, hell, probably since we first met. You just wouldn't ever listen to me."

"Okay, goddammit. Quit blaming me for everything. You make it sound like I'm some kind of selfish bitch."

"I never said that."

"Well, you didn't have to."

She looked like she might try to get hold of herself. She stopped her blubbering and drew up the muscles in her face until she appeared halfway composed.

"So when are you leaving for Shreveport?"

"Probably after Labor Day," Nick said. "I still have a couple more jobs to do with Chuck."

Bev snuffled and wiped at her nose. "Well, can I come?" she asked.

Nick looked away from her. His gaze landed on Rachel's car. He squinted to see who was inside. Our eyes met, and he shook his head in a hopeless way. He turned back to face his troubles. "No, Bev. You can't come."

She stood there, staring at him in disbelief. Her lower lip started to quiver, and then she began to whimper.

"My God," she said, "you really aren't fucking anybody else, are you?"

Nick stared at the ground.

"That's even worse," she said. "That means you don't love me at all. You'd rather be alone."

Nick started to walk toward her. "Bev, you know I love you."

"Stop it!" she screamed. "I've heard enough out of you!"

She tightened her face up even more, until it was full of spite, just like when she sang "Hair of the Dog."

"I hate you!" she hollered. "I wish you were dead right now, and I mean that. I mean it more than anything I've ever meant in my life. If you were to die right now, I'd laugh at your fucking funeral. Hell, I'd get drunk and throw a goddamn party. Then, I'd fuck every man in the house. Twice!"

Bev climbed inside the Matador.

"You've still got my damn keys," Nick yelled.

But she didn't pay him any attention. She fired up the motor and backed up to turn around. Nick moved to the front of the car. He stood there while she slid the shifter into drive. He planted his hands on the hood like he was going to hold her back.

Rachel grabbed my arm. "She wouldn't run him over, would she?"

"Oh, yeah. I think she would. She asked me to run over a couple of guys in Augusta, once."

They stared each other down, Nick lit up by the high beams and Bev clinching the wheel, gazing out at him with an incendiary mix of love and hate. Hate eventually got the upper hand. She stomped the gas, and the Matador kicked up a shower of gravel and lurched forward. Nick jumped and landed facedown on the hood. His and Bev's eyes couldn't have been more than a foot apart, separated only by the thick pane of glass, before he rolled over and fell onto the ground.

"Bev, honey. Wait a minute. Don't do this. I need my fucking keys."

Bev barely missed Rachel's car as she headed out to the street. Nick sprinted back to the porch and hopped on his Triumph. He kick-started the engine and took off after her in the moonless night: no shoes, no helmet, and not a whole lot of sense behind his actions. Of course, he smiled and waved at me and Rachel as he passed the car, acting as though this sort of thing was not out of the ordinary.

Dewey stood waiting for us on the porch, a can of PBR in his hand. He wore the expression of a doctor who had just emerged from an operating room with tragic news.

"Well," he said, "there goes the fucking band."

He shook his head sadly before turning to Rachel and making a game attempt at smiling.

"I'm Dewey," he said, extending his free hand.

Rachel introduced herself. And then, true to his nature, Dewey said something completely inappropriate.

"I sure hope you're not a crazy bitch like Bev."

Rachel came inside to watch some TV. She'd been curious about our digs for a while. Dewey took the recliner, and I settled into my driver's seat on the left-hand side of the sofa. Rachel examined the dirty couch. She sat down slowly, as though the upholstery might scald her.

It was just past midnight, so I switched over to Johnny Carson on channel 2. Buddy Hackett was riding the guest chair, giving Johnny grief about all of his marriages.

After a while, the phone rang. I leaned over the edge of the sofa and grabbed the receiver. I was surprised to hear Nick's voice. He sounded like he was out of breath.

"I'm in jail," he said.

"Oh, fuck." I sat up straight and scooted down to the end of the sofa. "What happened?"

Dewey and Rachel cut their eyes my way, appearing concerned. I motioned for Dewey to turn down the volume on the TV.

"I got stopped for speeding on my bike," Nick said. "Plus I had some pot in one of my saddlebags. I'd forgotten all about it."

"How much did you have?"

"Enough to cause me some problems. Let's just put it that way."

"Does Muskgrave know about this?"

"Not yet, but I'm sure they'll call him in. He beats off to this kind of shit."

"Well, what do you want me to do? Should I call Cash?"

Nick started whispering, his voice so low I could barely hear him. "Yeah, call Cash," he said. "But that's not all. I've got another problem that's gonna be worse than this one if it's not taken care of. I'm supposed to pick up some stuff that Chuck's dropping off in a little while. That's why I needed my fucking car keys."

"What kind of stuff? Cocaine?"

Nick shushed me. "You don't need to know. But I need you and Dewey to go pick it up for me. Do you think you could borrow your girlfriend's car?"

"Yeah, she's still here."

"All right. Now listen close and write this down, because I can't repeat myself. God knows who might be listening."

I grabbed the *TV Guide* and a pen from the floor and looked for a place to write. Thankfully, Bea Arthur was on the cover in a white gown.

"Do you know where Grimes Road is?"

"Yeah, me and Lyndell used to go driving around there. It sort of runs parallel to Green Lake Road."

"Good," Nick said. "That's good. Well, there's an old horse farm out there, it used to be called Grimes Stables. It sits way off the road, and it's pretty much abandoned now. They've got three big pastures in back."

"I know where you're talking about."

"Okay, then. That's where you need to go. Chuck's supposed to be there around two o'clock. It's the back pasture. Just grab the duffel bag and bring it back to the house. Put it in the attic."

I told him that sounded fine. And then something dawned on me. "Wait a minute. This doesn't make any sense."

"Why not?"

"Well, if Chuck's got something for you, why can't he just bring it by the house?"

"Oh, yeah," Nick said, "I almost forgot. Chuck's gonna be dropping the bag from his Piper."

He said it like it was the most natural thing in the world to be doing.

"You mean from the sky?"

"Yeah. But don't worry. He's pretty accurate. You just have to take my flashlight and wave it around when he flies over."

I was having a difficult time picturing all of this in my head.

"Are you still there?" Nick asked.

"Yeah, I'm still here."

"Listen," he said, "I wouldn't put you on the spot like this if it wasn't extremely fucking dire. You know that, don't you?"

"Yeah, I know."

"And you know how I didn't want you getting caught up in any kind of crap like this."

"It's okay," I said. "Don't sweat it. I've got things covered."

I heard him exhale, and I figured they must have been letting him smoke a cigarette.

"So you're leaving for Shreveport after Labor Day?" I asked.

"Hopefully," he said. "But it was looking a lot better about an hour ago."

"Well, don't worry about this end of it. Me and Dewey will take care of it."

"Okay, bro. And, hey. Listen."

"What is it?"

"I'm sorry you had to see that stuff with me and Bev."

"That's all right. I guess you did what you had to do."

There was a long pause. He blew out some more smoke. "Yeah, I sure hope so."

20

My plan was to drop Rachel off at her apartment. That way, if Dewey and I stumbled onto any trouble, we could always say that we had stolen Rachel's car, shielding her from any heat.

But she insisted on going with us. "You're not taking my car without taking me," she said.

She agreed that I should drive. She also let Dewey ride shotgun, accepting his lame-ass explanation about getting carsick when he rode in back. I knew that what really made Dewey sick was not being able to exert absolute control over the radio. He couldn't ride in a car unless he was constantly fiddling with the knobs.

The rain had picked up. Heavy drops thunked against the windshield as we made our way outside of town. Rachel's wipers were a beat slow and her headlights a little off kilter, kind of like her eyes, one aimed straight ahead, the other off into the mysterious woods beside the road.

I flipped on the defroster, and my face caught a blast of musty air. Dewey was playing with the radio, and Rachel was leaning up into the space between the front seats, her face lit by the pale glow of the dashlights.

"Should I even ask what we're going to pick up?"

Dewey scratched at his chin like a sleuth. "Cracker barrel logic tells me it's a white, powdery substance."

In the rearview mirror, I could see Rachel cutting her eyes my way. "Cocaine?" she asked.

I waved my thumb in Dewey's direction. "I think Barnaby's right."

Someone had planted a For Sale sign at the edge of the road in place of the Grimes Stables sign. I slowed up, checking the rearview mirror to make sure that nobody else was around before turning onto the gravel road that led to the stables and back pasture where Chuck was supposed to make the drop. The road was narrow and rutted and overhung by tree branches and bushes. Between the leaves swirling through the air and the rain peppering the windshield, it made for a spooky scene.

"I could be home watching *Don Kirshner* right now," Dewey said. "Thin Lizzy was gonna be on tonight."

"Well, nobody made you come."

"I know. I was just saying."

The trees finally broke and the gravel road took its route to the edge of a wide, flat pasture. I followed the fence line to the back of the property. I stopped the car at the edge of the woods, turned off the headlights, and pulled up the emergency brake.

Dewey sat in the car with the radio playing. Rachel and I waited outside, leaning back against the warm hood of the Peugeot. I'd brought along Nick's motorcycle jacket for myself, and she had her own leather jacket zipped up to her neck. We both ducked our heads against the rain.

"So, I don't guess your brother's really in the landscaping business."

"I had to lie when you asked me. It was nothing personal."

"It's okay," she said. "You're loyal. Most people would have spilled their guts."

"I just thought that I should keep quiet. The sheriff has been leaning pretty hard on Nick lately. He even thinks that I've got something to do with it."

"Well, you do. I mean, now, at least."

"Thanks for reminding me."

She looked at me. Her cheeks had turned scarlet in the rain. It looked like she'd stolen blush from the drugstore and dabbed it on herself as a joke.

"So, what would happen if you got caught?"

Normally, I wouldn't have wanted to discuss those possibilities. But now that I'd started telling things to Rachel, I didn't want to stop. It almost felt like I was protecting myself from the very things that could get me.

"For starters, I'd spend a couple of years at the youth correctional institute. After that, they'd probably transfer me to a real prison. Maybe Reidsville, or somewhere like that."

Rachel was quiet for a moment. I got the feeling she was trying to imagine what I'd look like in prison garb.

"So," she said, "why are you taking this kind of chance?"

"I could ask you the same thing."

"That's easy. I don't trust you with my car. Your checkered past speaks for itself."

"Trust me, that Peugeot is not worth going to jail for."

She shrugged.

"Nick's not a career criminal, you know. He's planning to go legit. I'd just like to see him get what he wants."

"You mean the house and the family and the radio job?"

"Yeah, and some respect. I think he wants that as much as anything. Just to have people respect him for what he does."

"You think that if he goes legit and gets all those things, then you'll be able to do the same."

"I never said I wanted to spin records."

"Okay, then. Bail bondsman. Bounty hunter. Maybe you'll have a garage full of cars and a house with cable TV in every room."

"The bathroom, too?"

"If that's your dream . . ."

She was making some sense.

"You think you might like to live in that house with me?" I glanced at her from the corner of my eyes.

"Not if it was tacky," she said. "I mean, if you went all Elvis on me, with the jungle shit, I'd have to say no fucking way."

"So," I said, "what kind of house would you like?"

"Nothing ridiculous," she said.

"What do you consider to be not ridiculous then?"

She was chewing on her bottom lip, smiling faintly. "We lived in this little Cape Cod the last few years that my father was alive. It was just a rental, you know. Pretty rough around the edges. But it was cool. My father had all these birdhouses and feeders that he hung in the backyard. He had birds flying in from all over the place. They'd all stop in to fill up. It was like a fucking Waffle House for birds. My father had these bird books that he kept on the kitchen table so we could figure out what was what. We'd get up in the morning and sit there checking them all out. Goldfinches and hummingbirds and little sparrows. He'd have a class to teach, and I'd have school, but sometimes, he wouldn't even notice. Or at least he'd pretend not to notice. And of course, I didn't remind him. So we'd end up bailing. Both of us, we'd just take the whole fucking day off."

The corners of her mouth quivered a little, as though she was trying to hold back an even bigger smile.

"So, we'll have birdhouses," I said. "Birdhouses and cable TV."

"And we can let our little convicts skip school," she said.

"I didn't think you wanted any little convicts."

"I said I didn't want any kids. You know, like regular kids."

"Well, fuck, yeah," I said. "They can skip all the time, if they want. They can just take the GED when they get older."

She smothered a laugh with her hands. "I can't believe you just said that. I've been thinking about taking the GED. That's what I wanted to tell you about back at your brother's house."

"Are you serious?"

She grinned and looked down in a bashful sort of way, like it was some kind of big news, an acceptance to Harvard or something.

"My mother's talking about moving again," she said. "Like sometime after the fall semester. And I'm just sick of it, you know, following her around while she tries to get her shit together. All she does now is go to these AA meetings. She's addicted to them."

I felt a nudge of recognition. "Where does she go to the meetings?"

"At the Baptist church in Green Lake."

"Hey, I know the guy who leads those meetings. Wade Briggs. He's the cop who arrested me when I took the car."

"Is he a tall guy, with dark circles under his eyes?"

"Yeah, do you know him?"

She told me her mother had dragged her to a meeting one night. "That was enough for me. All those people sitting around, patting each other on the back for being such fuckups. They started talking about how they'd been to hell and back. Ha! What a laugh. They don't know what hell is. Hell is having to live with people like that."

The wind picked up again, howling through the trees, beating the grass flat and blowing the rain against our faces. We ducked our heads to our chests and waited for it to let up.

"So, you're really gonna take the GED?" I asked.

She smiled, her face becoming animated again. "Yeah, and I was thinking about moving back to Champaign, maybe getting a job and renting a room. And I just thought that since your brother was planning to leave and all, and since I'd already asked you to move in with me anyway, that you might want to come, too. You could drop out of school now that you're sixteen. You can just take the GED when you turn eighteen."

Her idea shot right through Nick's jacket. It caused my heart to bounce against my rib cage like a speed bag. I liked the thought of us being together. Birdhouses and TV sets and all of that. Champaign probably wouldn't have been my first choice. It sounded kind of land-locked. But Rachel would make up for the lack of water.

"So when are you thinking of leaving?" I asked.

"I don't know. Maybe in the fall."

"I get my license back October first."

"Are you serious about this?"

"Fuck, yeah," I told her. "Let's do it."

I reached over and shook some of the water from her hair, and then I draped my arm around her shoulder. When we finally heard the faint buzz of Chuck's Piper, we snapped our heads back as though a fire-works display might break out. Alas, all we got were three tiny red lights bobbing above the tree line.

21

Dewey climbed out of the car. "That's gotta be him. Nobody else would be flying around in this shit."

I pulled the flashlight out of Nick's jacket, turned it on, and waved it in the direction of the plane. As if on cue, the Piper's wings tilted back and forth. It headed for the road, made a lazy banked turn, and flew back in our direction again. At this point I stepped away from the car and started to move the flashlight around in a circular motion.

Dewey stepped up beside me. We stood there as the plane circled a few more times, descending lower with each pass. The closer the Piper came to the treetops, the more it fluttered against the wind. The wings tilted wildly, and the tail swung from side to side.

Rachel had a concerned look on her face. "Jesus, he looks like he's going to crash."

"It's this fucking wind," I told her.

Dewey flinched as the plane dropped straight down and then bounced back up like it was tied to the end of a rubber band.

"Are you sure this guy's really an airline pilot?" he asked.

"Yeah, I've seen him in his Delta uniform."

"Well, he's making a damn good case for Greyhound."

Finally, the Piper dipped low enough for us to read the tail letters: N634CS. It was flying just above tree level. That's when something came tumbling out the door.

"Ta-daa," Dewey sang. "There's your money shot."

The bag dropped straight down into the middle of the pasture, like a turd from a giant pigeon. The plane's motors sputtered a couple times and then picked up a louder, throatier hum before the nose lifted and the lights slowly shrunk in the distance.

Rachel opened the Peugeot's trunk while Dewey and I tromped across the soggy grass to retrieve the bag. It was a huge blue duffel, about four feet long. We stood over it for a long time, both of us reluctant to move forward with the operation.

"You still got that flashlight?" Dewey asked.

I held up the light and jiggled it for him.

"Well, I think we should look inside," he said. "I think we should know what we're getting ourselves into before we go any farther."

"Yeah, you're probably right."

I held the beam on the bag while Dewey ripped open the zipper. As soon as we saw what was inside, we both stepped back as though it might jump out and bite us. We'd gotten what we expected, which was cocaine, but a lot more of it than we could have ever imagined. White bricks were packed together like the foundation of a sand castle. There must have been twenty of them.

"Oh, Wilbur," Dewey moaned. "That's a lot of fucking cocaine."

The only answer I could muster was a slow nod. All of the sudden, my wet clothes made me shiver. My knees turned watery, and my pulse started to thrum behind my ears.

Dewey pointed a shaky finger at the bag as it lay there glistening in the rain.

"How much do you think that is?"

He appeared frightened by the answer that I might give. He was looking all around, like somebody might throw a net over us at any second.

"I'd say that's enough to get us a matching set of leg irons."

"Why don't we just leave it?" he asked. "Let's just get the hell out of here."

"We can't leave it. Let's just finish what Nick told us to do. Do you know how much this shit is probably worth? If Nick were to lose this stuff, somebody would probably kill him."

I was waiting for Dewey's response, but he'd stopped paying attention. He was looking over my shoulder, up into the black sky.

"Luke?" he murmured. His voice was high and unsteady.

"Yeah?"

"Did Nick say anything about a helicopter?"

Before I could even ask what he was talking about, I heard the *thump-thump-thump* in the distance. When I turned around, I could see the spotlight shining down. It was way out beyond the road, but headed in our direction.

I think our first inclination might have been to leap into each other's arms. But that quickly passed, and we set about the task of getting ourselves—and the bag—the hell out of there. The duffel must have weighed a hundred pounds, but we hardly felt it. We each threw a strap over our shoulders and headed back to the car. We ran like sturdy beasts, like a couple of those rhinos that we always watched on *Wild Kingdom.* By the time we tossed the bag between the barbed wire strands of the fence, the helicopter was hanging over the middle of the pasture, shining its light down on the drop zone. I told Rachel to crank the car while Dewey and I dumped the bag into the trunk.

I left the headlights off and turned around on the gravel road. I floored the little Peugeot and prayed to the Italian god of automobiles to please be kind and channel a little bit of Ferrari blood into that sled. The chopper's beam was still dancing around in the field, searching for the bag of cocaine.

Dewey sat dead still beside me, his hands in his lap, staring straight out into the darkness. He appeared to be bracing himself for a sudden and terrible fate. Considering the situation, it was not very reassuring to see a 240-pound man in such a state.

I checked the rearview mirror for Rachel. She was sunk low in the corner of the backseat, clenching the sides of Dewey's seat with both hands. Her eyes were following the spotlight as it danced behind the car.

"Who is that?" she asked.

"It's gotta be the cops," I said. "Maybe GBI, or FBI. It's somebody with badges. I know that much."

"Well, what are you going to do?"

"I'm gonna get us the hell out of here."

I cut the wheel at the top of the gravel drive and slid onto the asphalt of Grimes Road. Without the headlights I could barely see beyond the hood of the car. But that was enough.

"Trust me," I told them, "I could drive this road with my eyes closed."

Without hesitation, Dewey reached for his lap belt. Rachel didn't waste much time groping around for her own. But, thanks to Lyndell, I really did know the road well enough to drive it with my eyes closed. It was all about feel and recognition, knowing the bumps, curves, and dips. It really wasn't all that different from Nick shutting his eyes when he played slide guitar. I'd probably covered a mile, when Rachel's voice rose from the backseat.

"I think they're gone. I don't even see the light anymore."

Dewey turned around and blew out a big breath. "She's right," he said. "I don't see 'em."

"That doesn't mean they don't have any cruisers out here," I told them. "I'm gonna switch over to another road, just to be safe."

I flipped on the cockeyed headlights, slowed to the speed limit, and cut over to Green Lake Road. It seemed an unlikely route for the county police to take if they'd been headed out to the stables.

"The cops know something," Dewey said. "They're gonna get that pilot. I guarantee you."

"Somebody tipped them off," I said. "That's for sure. We're just lucky they were a couple of minutes late."

Rachel leaned up again. "Maybe we shouldn't take the bag back to the house. What if they're waiting there?"

"But what the hell are we gonna do with it?" Dewey asked.

He and I were staring at each other, trying to figure that one out, when Rachel screamed.

"Oh, shit! Look out!"

A set of high beams was barreling toward us, way over on our side of the road. Dewey grabbed the dash, and Rachel wrapped her arms around the back of Dewey's seat, and I did the only thing I could do to avoid a head-on collision. The wheels clunked over the shoulder and the trees came into view. The trunks and limbs looked like bars on a cage. There were too many of them to count, too many even to consider the possibility of avoiding contact. I stomped the brake pedal, clenched my eyes shut, and waited for a blow to the head.

22

"Ho-lee shit! Are y'all all right in there?"

The guy was banging on the side window, looking in at me. Dewey, Rachel, and I were checking ourselves out to make sure that none of our bones was sticking through the skin.

Rachel stared at my head, cringing. When I reached up, I found a lump the size of a Titleist on my left temple. It throbbed like somebody was taking whacks at it with a sand wedge.

I asked Dewey and Rachel if they were okay.

"Forget us," Dewey said. "What about the car? Is it driveable?"

The Peugeot had been smashed up pretty good, the hood buckled and steaming against the trunk of an oak. One headlight was out, the other shone toward the dark water's edge.

"I don't think so."

The man knocked on the window again. "Hey! Is everybody okay in there?" He had a really loud voice, like an auctioneer.

"Who is that fucking idiot?" Rachel asked.

"Probably the asshole who ran us off the road," Dewey said.

I held up my hand to signal that all was well, hoping the guy would pipe down. He finally stepped back and gave me a chance to climb out. I had to kick the door in order to open it.

As soon as I stepped onto the wet turf, the man rushed toward me. "God almighty, damn. I am so sorry." He laid his hands on my shoulders and whistled at the size of the knot. "Goddamn, looks like you got tagged pretty good."

The guy appeared to be in his fifties, tall and broad across the chest, with a thick neck and a hypertensive flush. He had a big head, too. It was crowned with a salt-and-pepper flattop.

I assured him that I was all right, that we were all just fine.

"Thank God for that," he said. "These roads are fucking treacherous."

He was obviously half in the bag, his breath practically flammable and his clothes (Bermuda shorts, boat shoes, and a tank top) best suited for a two-day bender.

"I must have hit an oil patch back there," he said. "Pushed me right over to your side of the road. That was a hell of a piece of driving you did to miss me."

He draped his arm around my shoulder and led me toward the road. From the looks of it, we'd slid a good thirty feet down the embankment before we hit the tree. Rachel and Dewey climbed out of the car and tramped up the hill behind us.

"Listen," the man said. "I'm gonna be honest with you about something. I've had me a little bit to drink tonight. I'm not drunk, but I'd just as soon not get the police involved in this. You know how they can be."

Dewey grunted. "Oh, yeah. I know how they can be."

It was right about then I gazed over the man's shoulder and caught my first glimpse of his car sitting by the side of the road. There was no ignoring it, not even in a time of crisis. It was a 1968 GT 390 Shelby Mustang, the same kind of car Steve McQueen drove in *Bullitt*. It was sitting there with the engine idling and the headlights glowing, sparkling under a blanket of rain.

"Holy shit," I said, "is that victory green?"

The man jerked his head in a surprised way. His face beamed. He reached out and gave my shoulder a squeeze like I was his son or something.

"That's pretty damn good," he said. "You know your cars."

He led me toward the Shelby. For the first time, I noticed that he walked with a limp. He winced and jerked with every step like somebody was jabbing a pair of scissors into his hip.

"I bought that thing brand-new back when I was offensive line coach for the Rams."

It all came together then: the big jaw, the limp, the thing about being a coach, and then, finally, the specialty plates on the back of the car: TBREX. We'd been run into the trees by none other than Lance Hillin, the T-Bone King himself: former All-American lineman for the University of Georgia and pioneer of the mega-all-you-can-eat food bar.

Hillin patted his pants pockets as though to make sure they were still full of money. "Listen, I think I can work this out. I got a friend who runs a garage. He takes care of my cars for me. So how about I get him out here first thing in the morning to haul your car in and fix it? All charges covered by me, of course. I can give y'all a ride back up to the house, and you can borrow one of my cars until the other one's fixed."

He turned and winked at me. "I ain't loaning you the Shelby, though. So don't ask."

"I think we could live with that," I told him. "But we've got some valuables in the trunk. We can't just leave them out here like this."

"What kind of valuables?" Hillin asked.

Naturally, he would have to be the curious sort.

"It's birdhouses," I replied, surprising myself with how easily the cover-up slid out.

Hillin cocked his head in a puzzled way. "Birdhouses?"

"Yeah. Rachel, over there, makes them. Her family's been doing it for generations. They're sort of famous for their birdhouses."

"Well, I'll be goddamned," Hillin said. "Maybe I'll buy a couple from you. I wouldn't mind having some of those bat houses. I hear they run off the fucking mosquitoes in the summertime."

He turned and slid the key into the trunk of the Shelby. When I looked back up, Dewey was shaking his head and Rachel was applauding in a silent and sarcastic way.

Hillin's house sat way off the road on a big lot that fronted the lake. It was one of those rustic log cabin designs, but with four bedrooms, a Jacuzzi, central air, and a big satellite TV dish out front. Hillin had built a huge fucking garage beside the house.

"That's the showroom," he said as we climbed out of the Shelby.

And he wasn't lying. He pulled up one of the garage doors and hit the light switch. Soon, we were standing amid an automotive paradise. There must have been fifteen classic cars in there, lined up side by side, poised to rush through the doors and wreak havoc on the streets: a '69 Corvette with side vents, a Plymouth 'cuda, a Buick Wildcat, a pair of Porsche-outfitted VW Beetles, a GTO, an Olds 442, a Jaguar XKE. Hillin even owned a '66 Chevelle Super Sport—white with blue stripes—just like Lyndell's. That one gave me a jolt.

Hillin limped over to a metal cabinet and rummaged through a drawer full of keys, finally fishing out a particular set. "I was thinking y'all could take my fishing vehicle, if you want. I've got insurance and everything on it. So you don't have to worry about that."

When he walked back over to me, I was staring into the Chevelle.

"You've got good taste," he said.

I backed away from the car. "Yeah, it's a favorite of mine."

"I didn't catch your name," Hillin said.

"I'm Luke. Luke Fulmer. And that's Dewey and Rachel."

He gave them a friendly nod, then led us all the way down to the end of the garage. There, parked last in line, sat a long, mud-splattered Buick hearse. It was black, of course, and it appeared ready for a trip to the graveyard, except for the numerous fishing decals plastered all over the vehicle. There were largemouths in midleap on the side windows, bream, crappie, and catfish, too. The rear gate of the hearse was wall-to-wall bumper stickers. *I'd Rather Be Fishing. Fishing Is My Religion. Let Me Tell You About My Grandfish.* Hillin had also jacked up the rear end and slapped on a set of fat truck tires. The specialty plates read: GONFSHN.

Needless to say, I was underwhelmed by our new set of wheels. It was not the most understated way to haul around a large quantity of contraband. But considering the circumstances, I knew better than to complain.

Hillin handed the keys to Rachel. "You can take this for now. I should know something tomorrow about the Peugeot."

Rachel returned Hillin's jovial gaze with a sour expression. I thanked him profusely before she could object, and then I asked the King if he went out driving in his cars every night.

Hillin smiled as if we were kindred spirits. "I try to get out a couple nights a week," he said. "It keeps the engines clean. More than that, it keeps my head clean."

He finally bid us a farewell, heading back to the cabin to fix himself a beverage. Thankfully, he'd forgotten all about the birdhouses.

I gazed down the row of vehicles, savoring all the fine automobiles that we wouldn't be driving, and then Dewey and I opened the trunk of the Shelby and lugged the bag of cocaine over to the hearse. Rachel held the rear gate open for us.

"I'm not driving this thing," she said. "There is no fucking way."

I told her to calm down. "It could be a lot worse," I said.

Dewey and I were about to toss the bag into the back of the hearse, when I noticed all of the fishing gear inside: rods and reels and tackle boxes and Styrofoam ice chests. There must have been a dozen Budweiser cans scattered around as well. I told Dewey to drop the bag.

"Let me clear a spot first."

I stuck my head inside the vehicle and was promptly assaulted by the most heinous odor I'd ever come across. The culprit was a Styrofoam bucket. Inside lay the spoiled fruits of an angler's labors: four dead bream of a less-than-recent vintage. By the looks of things, Hillin had probably caught the fish a few months back. Removing them from the hearse must have slipped his mind.

We finally loaded the bag into the back of the hearse. Then we lowered the windows and jacked up the AC, trying to clear the air a little. As I pulled out of the garage, I felt something roll from under the seat and bump against my heel. It was a half-drained bottle of Jim Beam. Hot on its heels was a bottle of Listerine and a Popeil Pocket Fisherman.

Rachel was sitting between me and Dewey. She gazed down at the floorboard. "I'm guessing those are the basic tools of survival around this place."

Dewey leaned over and took a gander. "One of 'em sure as hell is."

Before he could even ask, I'd already reached down and snagged the bottle of Beam. I took a long drink and then another before passing it along. Afterward, I sat there with the engine idling, considering the glow coming from the windows of Hillin's cabin.

"So what do you think of his place?" I asked Rachel.

"Log cabins aren't supposed to be that big," she said. "I mean, that's like a fucking log mansion. It's all out of proportion. Just look at it."

I sat there a while longer, thinking of houses and birdhouses and the like. Rachel finally nudged me.

"We better go," she said.

23

There were no cops at Nick's house, only Cash and Nick. They were in the bedroom, emptying money out of Nick's golf bag. They spun around like a pair of gunslingers when we walked through the door.

Nick let out a big sigh. "Jesus Christ. Thank God you made it."

Dewey frowned. "Well, if you didn't think we were up to it, why'd you ask us to go?"

Nick shook his head. "I thought you were up to it. I just didn't expect Chuck to get his ass pinched by the cops."

Needless to say, I wasn't surprised. "Yeah, a chopper showed up about two minutes behind Chuck. We knew something was up."

Cash grunted. "How the fuck did y'all get out of there?"

"No headlights," I said. "We flew under the radar."

Cash pointed to the knot on my head. "I say you didn't fly low enough."

"Well, they found Chuck," Nick said. "The dispatcher at the police station was saying they'd forced a plane to land at the Green Lake Airport. You should have heard all the chatter on that shortwave. They were calling in the GBI, the FBI, the ATF, everybody but fucking McCloud and the Texas Rangers."

I asked about Muskgrave.

"He was on his way in. Cash posted my bond, and we got the hell out of there before he showed up."

"So they don't know that you and Chuck are working together?" I asked.

Nick tossed his golf bag onto the floor. He reached under the bed and pulled out his suitcase. "Fuck, no. I was in jail when they grabbed Chuck."

He started pulling clothes out of his closet. "But if Chuck runs his mouth, it's gonna be bad news for everybody."

"But we picked up the bag," Rachel said. "What can they do if there's no evidence?"

Nick topped off his suitcase with jeans and T-shirts. He tossed his shooting wedge on top and zipped up the bag. Then he sat down on the edge of the bed and fired up a Winston.

"Chuck had a planeful of those duffels," he said. "He was supposed to make four drops tonight. I'm just one person in all of this. He probably still had a couple in there when they forced him down."

Cash stood beside the bed trying, ever so subtly, to count the wad of bills that Nick had just given him for posting his bail.

Nick looked up at him. "It's all there, asshole."

Cash looked away like he was embarrassed. He rolled up the money real fast and stuffed it into his jeans. Then he looked at his watch. "You better hit the road," he told Nick.

Nick sighed, took one last drag off his cigarette, and dropped it on top of an old Sports page that was lying at his feet. He crushed the Winston under his boot, stood up, and grabbed his golf bag and black Samsonite.

"Are you jumping bail?" I asked him.

"I might have to," he said. "It's just a possession charge. I can take care of that later, if need be. But if Chuck starts naming names, I damn sure can't be around."

We headed outside. Of course, the first thing Cash and Nick wanted to know was where the hell we had gotten the hearse.

"You mean you didn't work out a deal for free steaks?" Cash asked. "How the fuck could you not get some free steaks out of this?"

Dewey and I looked at each other and frowned. We'd been under such a heavy burden that the possibilities of free beef had never even dawned on us.

We transferred the duffel to Nick's car while Cash hot-wired the ignition. It only took a couple of minutes to get everything into place: the cocaine in the trunk and the motor humming. The rain had stopped, and the night had turned cool and damp. I took off Nick's jacket and handed it to him. He tossed it into the car and pulled me aside to talk. Everyone else headed back inside the house.

"This isn't exactly what I had in mind for us parting ways," he said. "I wasn't thinking it would be this sudden."

"It's okay," I told him. "It makes sense for you to get out of here."

"So, are you set?" he asked. "I mean, can you stay with your girlfriend?"

"We're working on some plans," I said. "She's thinking about moving to Illinois. I'm going with her if she does."

Nick pulled a wad of cash from his jeans, unhooked the rubber band that was wrapped around it, and peeled off ten Jacksons.

"Take this," he said. "And before you go anywhere, be sure to pay off that old woman for the car you wrecked."

I took the money and stuffed it deep inside my jeans pocket. "Thanks."

"Now if the cops link me to this," he said, "then Muskgrave's probably gonna haul your ass in and ask you a bunch of questions. He'll make threats and shit, but don't say a word. Just play dumb. Believe me, there's nothing they can do to you. I've got all the evidence with me, and Chuck didn't know a thing about you being there to pick up the stuff. You're in the clear, so just cover your ass."

Nick leaned back against the trunk of the Plymouth and sighed.

"What's the matter?" I asked.

"I was just thinking how one of us has gotta call Claudia. We can't just hightail it out of town without letting her know."

I knew what he was getting at. I told him it was no problem. But I wasn't exactly looking forward to it. I thought to myself that I had better call early in the morning, before Claudia and Charlie had a chance to get the blender running.

"Just don't go into too much detail," Nick said. "Not that Wade Briggs won't fill her in once he gets wind of it."

"So where are you going, anyway?" I asked.

Nick fished a Winston and a pack of matches from his shirt pocket, turned his back to the wind, and lit up.

"I guess I'll head down to Pensacola and take that bag to the people it belongs to. I can't do anything else with it now. Not with all the shit going down around here."

"Does this hurt your chances with the radio station?"

"Who knows?" he said. "I'm just one guy who was supposed to make a pickup. I pulled that off, thanks to you. So that should count for something. Of course, if Chuck starts giving out names, a lot of people, including myself, are gonna be fucked."

He stepped away from the car and stuck out his hand. When I shook it, I noticed him shivering a little. His T-shirt was soaked, same as mine.

"I don't guess I thanked you for everything," I said. "You know, the room and board, the golf lessons, getting me hooked up with Cash."

Nick grinned. "That's what we like to do at the Nick Fulmer Boys Ranch."

He took a long drag off the fresh cigarette, then flipped it out into the soppy grass. "Let's not make this a farewell," he said. "Maybe everything will smooth out after a while, and I can give you a call from Shreveport. You and the girl can come down and visit. I'll let you spin some wax for me at the station."

"Can I play anything I want?"

He smiled. "Yeah. Within reason."

24

Chuck made the local paper two days later. The *Green Lake Gazette* devoted the entire front page to the bust, knocking Muskgrave's county jail scandal over to page three. The headline announced: PILOT NABBED IN DRUG BUST—30 KILOS OF COKE SEIZED. There was a photo of Chuck's Piper beneath the huge type, along with Chuck's mug shot. He was wearing a yellow V-neck sweater with a Masters logo on it. His hair was messed up, and his eyes were bulging with fear. He looked like he'd been dragged behind a golf cart for a couple hundred yards.

I carried the paper along when I drove down to the airport in Atlanta to pick up Claudia. She'd booked a morning flight from Jacksonville as soon as I'd called to tell her about Nick's sudden departure. I hadn't gone into any of the details with her. I'd merely said that there'd been a "scrape with the law."

I found a stretch of curb space in front of the terminal and slipped Hillin's hearse right into it. There couldn't have been more than an inch to spare on either bumper. It was a major-league parallel parking job.

Needless to say, the sight of the hearse gave Claudia pause as she walked out into the sunshine carrying her suitcase and holding her straw cowboy hat down against the breeze. I couldn't read her eyes because of the big sunglasses she was wearing. But her jaw sure dropped. She mouthed the words "Oh, my Lord."

I pulled my Braves cap down over the knot I'd acquired courtesy of the T-Bone King, and then I hopped out and swung open the rear gate.

"Come on," I told her. "Most people don't get to ride in one of these until they're a lot older."

She finally walked over and handed me the suitcase. She was reading all of the bumper stickers and shaking her head.

"Where in the hell did you get this thing? It looks like something Herman Munster would drive."

"It's a long story," I told her.

"It's not stolen, is it?"

"No, it's a loaner."

"Are you sure?"

"Yeah, I'm positive. Do you think I'd steal something that's this easy to spot?"

I shut the gate, and we stood there for a moment, enjoying the sight of each other. She looked pretty much the same, only skinnier and awfully pale for someone who'd spent so much time in Florida.

"So, is this the first time you've driven since I left?" she asked.

"Second, actually."

I knew better than to try and sell her on a 100 percent good behavior record.

She frowned and shook her head. "I knew something would go wrong. I knew it from the start."

I told her to look at the bright side. "We made it a whole four months. A bookie would have probably set the over-and-under at about two."

I'd already dialed in her favorite country station. Willie was singing when we got into the car. He was saying how he'd trade all his tomorrows for just one yesterday.

Claudia's nose started twitching as soon as she sat down. She made a face and reached for the door handle as if she might flee. "My God, what's that smell?"

I yanked the strawberry air freshener off the rearview mirror, reached over to her side of the car, and waved it around in circles.

"It's dead fish," I told her. "I think somebody left a bucket in here about five years ago."

She rolled down the window and fanned the air with her hat. Then she waved off the strawberry. "Go on with that thing. It smells like a whorehouse."

I cranked the hearse and jacked up the AC fan. Then, I slid Paul Newman's sunglasses over my eyes.

"Maybe it'll smell better in here if I light a cigarette," she said.

I dropped open the ashtray and pushed in the cigarette lighter while she fished around in her bag for the Virginia Slims. I couldn't help but notice the stash of airline liquor bottles inside her purse. There were a couple of Jack D's, a Smirnoff, a Bacardi, and some Dry Sack sherry.

"What the hell did you do, hijack the drink cart?"

She ignored the inquiry. A couple of tugs on the cigarette seemed to acclimate her to the death stench. Finally, she pulled one leg up under the other and let out a relaxed sigh. Her cowboy boot creaked against the leather seat.

I gassed the hearse and merged into the morning traffic on I-75. A truckful of construction workers pulled alongside me and started laughing and pointing at the car. I flipped them off, as I had most everyone who'd seen fit to comment on my unfortunate automotive situation.

"So what's this about Nick and cocaine?" Claudia asked.

"I never said anything about cocaine."

"I know you didn't."

I glanced at her. "You must've called Wade."

"Actually," she said, "he called me."

I reached up under the seat and pulled out the newspaper.

"It's all there," I told her. "But Nick's not mentioned. As long as this guy keeps his mouth shut, Nick should be in the clear."

She laid her cigarette in the ashtray and unfolded the paper. She swallowed hard at the sight of the headlines.

"Do you know this guy?" She pointed at Chuck's picture.

"Yeah, I've met him a few times at the driving range. He's a Delta pilot."

"Great," she said. "That's who I flew home."

She studied Chuck's mug shot as though it might reveal something about him.

"He looks like he'd start singing for a ham sandwich," she said.

"Yeah," I agreed. "We're kind of worried about that."

She read the article, folded the paper, and reached for her cigarette. "Wade thinks they'll offer this guy some sort of deal. Maybe tell him he's looking at twenty years versus eighteen months, depending on how helpful he is."

She opened her purse and pulled out the Smirnoff. "Do you mind?"

she asked. "I don't usually drink this early, but I've had a splitting headache."

I started to tell her it was fine with me, but she'd already whipped off the cap and turned up the bottle. She looked like a scientist drinking from a test tube.

Once she'd drained the vodka, she screwed the lid back on the bottle and dropped it inside her purse, as natural as applying lipstick.

"You're not involved in all of this, are you?"

"Are you crazy? I don't want to go to Alto."

She stared at me for a moment, trying to get a read on my expression. I supposed that Wade had probably spoken up in my defense, telling her that I'd been a good citizen.

"So where's Nick hiding?" she asked.

"He didn't say exactly."

Technically, that wasn't a lie. It's not like Nick had provided a specific address in Pensacola.

"That's okay," she said, "just promise you'll tell me if things get bad. Will you do that?"

Claudia didn't wait for an answer. She turned up the radio and hummed along quietly to Willie. Once she'd slipped off her sunglasses, I noticed how her green eyes had retreated into their sockets a little. I saw some wrinkles at their corners, too. For the first time ever, I would have said that she almost looked her age.

After the song ended, I asked about Charlie. "Why didn't he come home with you?"

She ground out her cigarette. "He offered," she said. "But I don't think he really felt up to it. So I told him to stay."

"What's the matter with him?"

"He's having some problems with his liver," she said. "His gallbladder, too."

I thought she was finished. I was just about to ask what kind of problems, but then she remembered a few other things.

"His prostate's not so hot, either," she said. "And after he climbs the steps, his heart sounds like Buddy Rich."

"Good Lord," I said. "Is he seeing a doctor?"

"He's got a chiropractor."

"For his heart?"

"Well, no. That's for his neck. He backed into a light pole leaving one of his stores."

We rounded the bend on I-75 and wheeled past Atlanta-Fulton County Stadium, where the Braves played, and lost, most of their games. The stadium looked like a big blue doughnut sitting there beside the highway.

Claudia took another drag off her Slim. "It's a little strange being with an older man," she said. "Their bodies are different, you know?"

"I'm not sure I want you to go any farther with that," I told her. "At least not before lunch."

"They've got different smells, too," she said.

"Jesus Christ, Claudia. I'm gonna have to pull over and throw up."

She laughed. "I'm sorry. I shouldn't complain. Charlie's about as generous as they come."

The traffic stayed thick until we had moved well north of the city, out past spaghetti junction, where the perimeter freeway linked up with the interstate highway. Closing in on Green Lake, the highway became quiet, lined with pastures and Ted Turner's billboards. The Holiday Inn sign streaked by off Claudia's side of the car. *Come Meet Our People Pleasin' Staff,* it boasted.

"What's happening with your music?" I asked. "Are you still thinking about going to school and getting a teaching degree?"

She made a face like she wished I hadn't reminded her. "Not yet. Charlie says he's ready when I am. He'll write the checks."

"So what's holding you up?"

"I don't know. It's just a big commitment."

"Come on," I said, "you already know all there is to know. The school stuff would just be a formality."

"I don't mean like that," she said. "I mean it's a big commitment to our relationship. Sweet as Charlie is, I'm not sure I want to be that indebted to him."

I could smell a breakup coming. The only question was, who did she have pegged for a replacement? Claudia always had somebody in her sights.

"Besides, I'm looking forward to getting back to the fish camp," she said. "Me and Wade are gonna do some new songs."

And there, potentially, was my answer.

"Wade's married," I told her.

She looked at me coolly. "Wade's my friend. And that's how it's going to stay."

Maybe she was right. If anyone could say no to Claudia Fulmer, it was Wade "Been to Hell and Back" Briggs. I'd heard somewhere that he'd gone five hundred–plus days without missing an AA meeting. That was some serious fucking willpower.

Claudia took a drag off her cigarette, held the smoke, and eyed me suspiciously. "So tell me about this girl you've supposedly moved in with."

"How'd you know about that?"

"Dewey told me."

"Dewey? When the hell did you call Dewey?"

"I didn't. He called me. Last night."

"For what?"

"I don't know. I think he was drunk." She lowered the window and flicked her cigarette into the wind. "He's lonely, too. I mean, with Nick leaving town and you moving out, it's hard. Plus, he's real upset about the band breaking up. That was the biggest thing in his life. I don't think he had anybody else to call."

I veered onto the exit ramp, stopped at the light, and hung a left onto Green Lake Road. The lake was shining like a big mirror. Claudia watched quietly as we drove alongside it. She watched the wind move the branches on the trees, and then she checked out all the sights in town: the Big Star, the Krystal, the T-Bone King.

"So I don't guess you're gonna stay at the house," she said.

I shrugged in an apologetic way.

She waved me off like the question had been a joke in the first place. "That's all right. I'm happy for you. It sounds like you went out and got yourself a life while I was gone."

"What about your life with Charlie? Is it good?"

Her lips parted as though she meant to speak, but the words never came out.

"This girl you're living with," she said finally. "I don't mean to pry, but I hope she's not a lunatic, like Bev."

I shook my head. "She does get kind of crazy with her mother, though."

"In what way?"

"Just yelling at the woman about stuff, giving her a hard time about nothing in particular."

I'd finally met the infamous Margaret Coyle a day earlier, when I moved my stuff over from Nick's place. I'd been expecting some sort of crazy-eyed devil woman. But she hadn't been that way at all. She might have had this shroud of melancholy about her, but she appeared to be quite sane. She'd even welcomed me into the apartment, set up the sofa for me, and brought in a big bag of Chinese food for dinner. The only blight on the evening had been Rachel yelling at her mother and then refusing to eat because the woman had forgotten to order kung pao shrimp.

"I can't pretend to understand mothers and daughters," Claudia said. "But I had some problems with my mother's cousin."

I turned onto our street. The big pie-plate sun beamed right through the windshield at us. Claudia grabbed her shades off the dash and slid them over her eyes. "I used to go round and round with that woman."

"You mean, like fistfighting?"

"A few times," she said. "But mostly lots of screaming."

"Why didn't you get along with her?"

Claudia sighed. "For starters, she hated me because I looked like my mother. And then I hated her because she wasn't my mother."

She turned her head and frowned. "That was right before I met Lyndell."

Our conversation was interrupted by the sight of Mrs. Dees. She stood at her mailbox, mouth agape, as we rolled past. We smiled and waved sunnily from the hearse, but she just stood there, frozen in her tracks, not quite believing what she was seeing.

"I hope you've been sending her that money," Claudia said.

"I have. In fact, I've got some with me right now. I'm gonna drop it off before I leave."

"That's good," she said. "I'm glad you're holding up your end of the deal."

Rolling up to our house at a funeral-procession pace, we were both struck silent by the condition of the place. Amazingly, it appeared that someone was still living there, most likely a family who took much better care of the place than we ever had. This was all Charlie's doing, Claudia told me. He'd paid a landscaping crew to come in and cut the grass and plant some pansies. By the looks of things, he'd also sent over a painter to slap a fresh coat of white paint on the house. We sat there for a while before we even had the nerve to climb out and take her bag inside. I think both of us half expected someone to storm out the front door and run us off the premises.

25

I headed over to Lance Hillin's log mansion to get an update on the Peugeot. I'd been putting it off for a couple of days, wondering if Hillin would even remember me. Considering just how piss-drunk he'd been on the night he wrecked us, I worried he might even accuse me of stealing the hearse.

But that wasn't the case at all. He waved me out onto his boat dock, just like Bob Barker on *The Price Is Right*.

"Lucas J. Filmore!" he shouted. "Come on down!"

It was one thing to butcher a person's name, but, for the life of me, I couldn't figure out how he'd managed to grant me a heretofore nonexistent middle initial. Not that I was complaining. At least he wasn't threatening to call the cops.

I tramped down the fescue-blanketed hill behind the house and walked right out onto the dock. It was the size of a ballroom dance floor, plywood floating atop aluminum pontoons. Hillin stood at the door to the boathouse, fiddling with a ring of keys.

"You wanna take a boat ride?"

He was wearing baggy shorts, flip-flops, and a pink golf shirt, and he didn't even bother turning around to greet me. In the daylight, I could see that his body was a mess. His fingers and toes were gnarled and doglegged, and both knees bore the jagged marks of surgical knives. One kneecap was set off to the side and the other might have been missing altogether.

He kept on plugging keys into and out of the big padlock that swung from the metal door, growing more agitated each time a key wouldn't fit. "Goddamn these sons of bitches," he growled.

I stood behind him with my hands stuffed into my jeans pockets, taking in the desolate spread of water. It wasn't exactly a stellar day for boating, the afternoon thunderclouds gathering above our heads, ready to raise some hell. The lake reflected the sky's gray pall, its surface dull like a tarnished coat of primer.

"Actually, I just wanted to check in with you about the car situation. Have you heard anything on the Peugeot?"

The padlock clicked. Hillin turned and smiled like he'd just cracked a safe. He peeled off the bifocals perched at the edge of his nose and looked me up and down as though I had overdressed for the occasion.

"Well, we can talk about that shit in the boat, can't we?"

The clouds spit a few raindrops on us, but Hillin didn't even seem to notice. He slapped me on the shoulder and marched right into the boathouse without waiting for an answer. There wasn't much left for me to do but follow him.

I untied his twin-outboard nineteen-foot Kona so we could back out of the boathouse. I hadn't even taken a seat when he slapped the throttle with the heel of his hand and sent us charging out into open water. The bow shot up into the air and pitched me backward. I made a grab for the back of Hillin's captain's chair but missed and thumped the floor of the boat with the back of my head. The pain felt like an explosion. That was two good head shots I'd now taken courtesy of Hillin.

"You better grab a fucking seat," Hillin yelled, as though I'd brought the tumble upon myself.

I waited until the boat had leveled off and then climbed into the passenger seat, directly across from Hillin. We skimmed across the flooded valley, heading straight out to the dam. A jag of lightning stabbed at the north end of the lake while the ashen clouds peppered our faces and arms with raindrops.

"So how's that knot on your head?" Hillin shouted so I could hear him above the screaming Evinrudes.

"It's not too bad. Looks a lot worse than it feels." I lifted my cap to give him a better view. Hillin puckered his lips and shook his head like I'd given him a case of the willies.

"I had one like that a long time ago, back when I played for the Packers."

I expected a football story.

"I ran into a goddamn telephone pole," he said. "We'd just lost to the Lions, and I was piss-drunk, driving this brand-new Cadillac DeVille. I hadn't played worth a shit, and my hip and my knee were bothering me. Plus, me and my second wife were having some problems back then. Anyway, I hit some water. Hydroplaned, you know."

I was beginning to wonder how many cars he'd wrecked in his day, how many phantom oil slicks and ice patches he'd actually come across. I couldn't help worrying that he might have had a few boating mishaps under his belt as well. One thing was certain: he believed in making eye contact with his passenger while he drove.

"I talked to my mechanic," Hillin said. "Besides all the body damage, your girl's car has got a busted radiator. He said it's hard getting parts for that thing. Could take a month. So you can just go ahead and keep the hearse until it's ready."

The big dam loomed off to the right. It hulked over the water like a broad set of granite shoulders, Hillin's maybe, or those of a pro wrestler. The shoreline was bordered by tall stands of pine trees. The only evidence of the houses tucked back into woods were the boat docks scattered along the water's edge.

"Just as long as it's ready by October first," I said.

"What's so special about October one?" he asked.

I'd forgotten he was a curious sort. I told him that Rachel and I were planning on moving that day. He smiled like he was pleased, his flattop fanning back and forth in the wind like rows of wheat stalks.

"Where you moving to?"

"Champaign, Illinois."

"Champaign," he repeated in a singsong way. "Sounds like a shot-and-a-beer kind of town."

He pulled back on the throttle, slowing the boat with a jerk. The wake disappeared, and we sat there bobbing like a cork in the middle of the lake. I thought he was going to turn around and head back to the dock. It felt like the sensible thing to do. Thunder rumbled all around us, and the rain was pelting the lake like buckshot.

But Hillin had no intentions of turning back. It was like the man had no sense of weather. He reached up under his seat and pulled out a pint of Maker's Mark.

"So, what are you gonna do in Champaign? Build birdhouses?"

"No, I'm probably gonna work at a restaurant, at least until I can find me a job working for a bail bondsman."

"Why do you want to do that?"

"I wanna go to school and get my license eventually—open up a bonding and bounty-hunting outfit."

Hillin pulled the bottle away from his mouth. "No shit?"

I assured him it wasn't. I even told him about Speedy and the car chase. Hillin was rapt, sitting there with that big jaw of his dropped open like a cash register drawer.

"I tell you something," he said. "If I was fifteen years younger and had any knees left, I'd go in on it with you. To hell with the restaurant business. I'd just pack up and do something crazy."

He sat there staring at me, smiling like I was someone to be admired, like I was the one with the big ideas. It made no sense whatsoever. For all I knew, I might be incarcerated by nightfall.

"I don't think you'd be making the same kind of scratch," I said.

Hillin snorted. "Let me tell you a little secret." He leaned forward as though he was about to share something in confidence. "The thing is, I didn't know what the hell I was doing when I started off in the restaurant business. In fact, I was trying to go broke."

"Why the hell would you want to do that?"

Hillin threw his hands in the air. "Hell, I don't know. My first wife used to say that I was self-destructive, but I never cared much for her from the start. Anyway, I got into the restaurant business because somebody told me it was the best way to lose your ass. I opened me a steak house with a big ol' bar where I could drink every day. Put everything I liked on the menu. All you could fucking eat. I thought, Shit, I'll just go there every day and enjoy it until I'm broke. And you know what happened?"

"Forty locations," I said. "Six states." I remembered the info from the back of the menu.

Hillin sat there shaking his head, wearing this bewildered look, as if he couldn't understand how his life had gone so right. "I've always been lucky. Got the big bones for football, you know. Had a heart murmur that kept me out of World War Two. My big brother, Buck, now he was something. He had talent and brains. Smart, good-looking, and a hell of an athlete. Hit .560 his senior year in high school, had Yankee scouts coming to the house. Hell, he could have played center field for those fuckers. They'd of moved that gimpy-assed DiMaggio to right field."

He was on a roll now, and I didn't know how to shut him up. The rain was slanted, the boat swaying. I couldn't even see the shore. It was getting close to five o'clock, punch-in time at the Holiday Inn. The last thing I needed in my current predicament was to lose that job. Rachel and I had planned to squirrel away as much money as possible before our October getaway.

Hillin went on about Buck for a long time, about big hits he'd gotten and pretty girls he'd dated. The stories eventually turned as dark as the sky. Hillin's old man used to beat on the King, and Buck would often intervene. Apparently, the father respected Buck more than he respected himself. And then Buck was sent to Fort Benning to become a paratrooper, to train to be dropped over the fields of Normandy. But "some stupid bastard" crashed the plane he was in before he ever got a chance to go overseas and become a war hero.

"So don't tell me I ain't lucky," Hillin said.

He let out a chuff of air, like he'd just finished running a sprint. I took the opportunity to steer our conversation toward land.

"I need to get back, if you don't mind. I have to be at work by five."

Hillin didn't say anything for a moment. He just sat there, staring at the floor of the boat. Finally, he looked up at me.

"Champaign, huh?"

I nodded.

"Champaign fucking Illinois."

I shrugged, not exactly certain where he was going with the conversation.

"I don't suppose you could stand to earn a little extra money before you go."

Even in the downpour, those words got my attention. "What have you got in mind?"

Hillin smiled, then gazed skyward as if he'd just taken notice of the weather. "Let's talk about it back at the dock," he said. "Looks like it's fixing to get ugly out here."

26

The first sign of trouble was the patrol car that followed me and Rachel home from the Holiday Inn one night. Rachel was driving the hearse, and I was riding shotgun and keeping an eye on the action in the rearview mirror. I caught a glimpse of the cop's head while we were sitting at a traffic light near the bank. It was someone I didn't recognize, probably sent out at Muskgrave's behest. He followed us all the way to the entrance of the apartment complex, where he pulled off to the side of the road and sat as if he was going to stay for a while.

Rachel parked the car, slid the keys out of the ignition, and grabbed my arm. "What the fuck was that all about?"

"I don't know, but he sure as hell didn't mind us knowing he was there."

"No shit. It's like having the KGB follow you around."

I told her not to worry about it. "Muskgrave's probably just trying to scare me. He hasn't got jack shit to haul me in on. If he did, I'd be sitting in a cell right now. You can be sure of that."

"You mean you're not worried?"

"Hell yeah, I'm worried. I'm not stupid. I just need to play it safe for now. No slipups. Don't give Muskgrave a reason to grab me."

She sat there staring out the windshield at the sad brick face of the apartment building.

"I don't think you should drive anymore. At least not until you get your license back."

"I agree. But I can't quit running errands for Hillin. We need the money."

Hillin's offer to earn a little cash had quickly turned into a minor windfall. What he'd needed was a "Sonny, or Red," as he put it, referring to Elvis's famed gophers. He even gave me a pager, which had seemed a little formal at the time, although in the two weeks since we'd set up the arrangement, he'd called me at least once a day to go to the liquor store, grocery store, and/or pharmacy to pick up his pain medication, whiskey, and favorite dessert, which was Breyer's mint-chip ice cream. It was shit work, but Hillin paid for everything with hundred-dollar bills. And he always told me to keep the change. Thus far, I'd managed to net just over two hundred dollars in gratuities. Fay would have shot someone and dumped his body in a ditch for those kinds of tips.

"I'll just have to be really careful," I told Rachel.

"That's not exactly reassuring," she said. "Your definition of the word *careful* is not in any way similar to what's in Webster's dictionary."

What I wanted to explain to her was how I felt safer behind the wheel of a car than anywhere else. It didn't matter if I was driving on a suspended license, or if someone was looking to put me under the jailhouse. A car was just about the only place where you could take absolute control of your circumstances. Of course, I realized this was no time for such an explanation. All I needed to do was ease her mind a little.

"I'll take it easy," I told her. "Seriously, I will."

We finally got out of the hearse and made our way up the steps to her mother's apartment. I was already starting to feel comfortable there, if not quite rooted. The sofa wasn't as long, or as comfortable, as Nick's, but it smelled a lot better and offered a clear view of the illegal cable hookup that I'd acquired courtesy of Speedy.

Rachel and I spent a lot of time on that sofa, Brute curled up at our feet. We'd stay up late after we got home from work, watching movies on HBO. *Jeremiah Johnson* and *Midnight Express* were in heavy rotation that month. We must have watched them both a half a dozen times.

Sometimes, Rachel would fall asleep as we lay there together. I wouldn't move, even if I was uncomfortable, because I didn't want to wake her and have her go and get in her own bed. I'd reach for the pale blue afghan and pull it around her shoulders. And then I'd lie there and watch her instead of the TV. I liked the way she slept with her lips parted, as though she were about to tell me something.

We made the most out of Fridays. I'd ignore the fire marshal's edict and crank up the hibachi out on the apartment balcony, grilling us a couple of strip steaks that I'd slipped out of Yuri's freezer. Rachel would take care of the Ore-Ida fries, and we'd chow down in front of the TV, using a couple of unopened moving boxes as trays. We'd watch the *Rockford* and *Dallas* reruns (I'd missed a lot of those when our TV was stolen), stepping onto the balcony during the commercial breaks to get stoned. If I was really lit, I might even do my J.R. impression for Rachel, seeing how she liked it so much.

" 'Sue Ellen, you are a drunk and an unfit mother.' "

"Now do the other one," she'd say. She was an easy audience when she got high.

" 'Cliff Barnes, you and that drunk daddy of yours better not mess with ol' J.R. You're outta your league, boy.' "

We'd stand there smoking and laughing and fine-tuning our moving plans while the moths gathered around the floodlights. It just felt like the place to be.

I'd always grab a steak for Rachel's mother, too. She didn't come home until eleven, after she'd finished teaching her summer-school class and going to her AA meeting. I'd soak the strip in some Worcestershire and soy sauce, à la Yuri, and throw it on the grill for her after she came in.

As far as I could tell, Mrs. Coyle didn't have a problem with me, or Brute, staying in the apartment. I suppose it helped that I tried to pull my weight, that I tended to Brute's needs, and went to the grocery store and brought home those steaks. On the other hand, she might have been frightened of what Rachel would do if she tossed my ass onto the street.

Rachel could be a real shit to her mother. In fact, I'd come to learn that she was the main instigator of tension between herself and Mrs. Coyle. But it wasn't like she fought the woman every second of the day. She'd let her guard down at times, and I'd see a side of her that I didn't even know existed. It might sound strange, but the more Rachel confused me, the more I liked her.

It was still difficult, at times, to imagine any of our plans coming to light: like living in Champaign, or visiting Nick after he was settled in Shreveport. And not all of my doubts were seeded by the shadows of patrol cars. Once, in the late afternoon, I came in from working in

Cash's garage to find Rachel and her mother together on the sofa. A record played on the stereo, Chet Baker blowing softly, and darkly, into his trumpet. Rachel lay with her head in her mother's lap, while Mrs. Coyle stared sadly at the blank walls, absentmindedly stroking her daughter's hair. The record sleeve was on the floor beside an opened moving box. It was one of the boxes that had been sitting, still taped together, in the living room for months.

They hadn't noticed me when I walked in, the music concealing the sound of my borrowed key in the door. I stood in the tiny foyer, behind the sofa, watching, not understanding. Mrs. Coyle had dark hair, like Rachel, but sad, murky green eyes. Her hands shook a little as she worked on Rachel's hair. Rachel lay still, running her own fingers along the hem of her mother's skirt. The sight caused my heart to sway a little. And then our secret plans began to ache inside me. For the first time, I didn't feel as if I belonged there. I finally backed out the door and left them alone. I went for a drive along the lake in Lance Hillin's hearse, and I didn't feel that I was in control of a single thing.

27

The local prosecutor placed a gag order on everyone involved in the Chuck Sosebee case, including Muskgrave, making it difficult to gather much of anything from the daily articles in the *Gazette*. Some days I'd try to forget the whole mess, at least for a little while. My success was limited. I'd pick up the Atlanta paper, where Green Lake was largely ignored, but the news there was even worse. A fourteen-year-old boy had been missing for a week, his bike found on a deserted road. The last anybody had seen of him, he was heading out to run an errand for his mother.

I tossed the front page aside. Cash offered the Sports section, but I waved him off.

"I don't even want to see it, not unless the Braves pulled off a trade for J. R. Richard."

Cash glanced at the headlines, then set the section back in his lap. "Keep on dreaming," he said.

We were sitting on the bow deck of the *Cash Register*, the rechristened houseboat that Cash had just acquired from one of his clients, a guy who'd been sent up the river due to a penchant for check forgery. His final payment to Cash had been the boat's title, which, to everyone's surprise, had turned out to be an authentic document. Cash held this notion that he'd eventually spruce up the vessel and live there like some sort of TV character, partying with all of his friends. I could relate, even though that tub was not, in any way, fit for habitation. It would have taken God, Noah, and a whole set of Time-Life repair books to bring that thing up to par.

There truly was no end to the boat's deficiencies. Its cabin was infested with mice, the deck slick with fetid bilge water, the hull decrepit, the paint peeling, and the twenty-horsepower Evinrude flat-out dead in the water. It also gave off an odor reminiscent of the hotel Dumpster during Yuri's Seafood Extravaganza.

I pushed myself up from the lawn chair and walked over to the railing, gazing across the line of boats docked in the marina. Labor Day had just passed, and most of the vessels were battened down for the season. They creaked and clanged against the sway of the water.

"What would you do first?" Cash asked.

I understood he was talking about the houseboat, so I turned and tried to evaluate the entire spectacle. Cash was sitting in the lawn chair while his future home slowly took on water.

"I'd probably buy some insurance and sink the damn thing."

Cash made a face. "I fucked up, didn't I?"

"Welcome to the team."

I leaned back against the railing, though not before I'd tested its sturdiness. "To hell with this boat," I said. "Are you ever gonna race again?"

Cash shrugged. He'd been dodging the question for a couple of weeks, ever since we'd gotten his Cougar back into fighting shape. His duel with Speedy had done some serious damage—to the tune of $600—and he wasn't eager to jump back into the fray.

"That's not exactly an answer."

"All right, then. Here's your answer: I don't know."

"What's not to know? You own a race car, you've got a damn good pit man, and you're probably the best fucking driver in hobby stock. You could be out there winning trophies if you weren't afraid of getting a scratch on your car."

Cash looked up from the newspaper. "Why are you trying to start this shit with me?"

"I just want to know if you're ever going back to the track. I wouldn't mind winning a race before I leave town."

Cash smiled. "So how's Little Miss Tempo doing, anyway?"

"She's fine."

"Where is it y'all are running off to again? Chicago?"

I reminded Cash that it was Champaign and not Chicago. His response was a grunt and a shake of the head.

"It's cold as shit up there," he said. "Wouldn't be my first choice."

"So where would you suggest we go?"

He tapped his chest, acknowledging the Philadelphia 76ers T-shirt he was wearing. It was the exact response that I'd expected.

"Yeah, like it's fucking sunny and warm up there," I said.

"At least they've got good teams."

Cash's affinity for the City of Brotherly Love was a fairly recent phenomenon and could be traced to the previous spring, when he drove to Philly in pursuit of a bail jumper. When he finally located his man, the guy was scalping Sixers tickets outside the Spectrum. Cash was a big Dr. J fan, and it was a play-off game against George Gervin and the Spurs, so Cash obliged himself to a couple of ducats, even taking his bounty along so he could keep an eye on him. The guy still snuck away at halftime, while Cash was at the souvenir stand loading up on T-shirts and hats. But the lost business didn't seem to bother Cash. The experience had somehow transformed him into a Philadelphian. He started talking about moving up there and joining forces with a bondsman he'd met. He wore his Sixers stuff all the time and even pulled for the Phillies when they played the Braves. That shit got annoying. But I understood where he was coming from. Like Nick had said: Who wants to finish in last place every year?

"You think you'll ever move up there?"

"Couple years, maybe," Cash said.

"Why a couple years?"

"Man, I've got responsibilities," he said. "Hell, I own a boat."

I seriously doubted that Cash was going anywhere. For starters, he wasn't one to take those kinds of chances. And unlike myself and Nick, he actually had a few good reasons to stay in Green Lake: his business, for one, plus a couple of women I'd seen him with, and, yes, even the boat. His wasn't a first-place life, but it wasn't the cellar either. He'd always have his Philly teams to make up the difference.

Dewey finally showed up. He hadn't seen the boat yet. He hollered out to Cash while he was still halfway down the dock.

"Arrr, matey! Let the pillaging begin."

Cash just shook his head. "What the fuck is he talking about?"

The plank groaned when Dewey crossed it. I went to shake his hand, but he gave me a hug instead. It was the first that we'd seen of each other since I'd moved out. We'd purposely maintained a communication blackout after the cocaine incident.

I probably should have said hello, or congratulated him on getting his driver's license back. But instead, I asked if anybody had followed him from Nick's house.

"Why?" he asked. "Has Muskgrave been tailing you?"

"Not him, but some of his Oompahs."

Dewey sighed. "They came in and tore up the house a couple days after Nick left, but I haven't seen any action lately."

I wished the same could have been said for Rachel's apartment, but that cruiser was parked out front almost every time I needed to go somewhere. Muskgrave had to be aware of my driving habits. One of his numb nuts had even tailed me to Hillin's house a couple of times. But he'd passed on the chance to haul me in. My guess was that Muskgrave wanted to see if I might lead him to something more valuable than my own sorry ass.

Dewey asked how I'd gotten to the marina without a Crown Vic escort.

"I walked through the woods in back of Rachel's apartment. Cash picked me up at the 7-Eleven."

"Just like some TV bullshit," Cash said. "I felt like I had Wo Fats riding around with me."

Dewey lit a cigarette and tossed the match into the slimy water on the boat deck. I was more than a little worried the sludge might be flammable.

"So, still no word from Nick?" Dewey asked.

I told him I hadn't heard anything. "But that's not a bad sign. Nick said he was gonna lay low for a while. He said he'd be back in touch when he got to Shreveport."

"What about Claudia? How's she getting along?"

"I'd say fair, at best. She's still in town. I don't think she's in any hurry to get back to Charlie."

"She still talking to Wade Briggs?" Dewey asked.

"Yeah, they talk on the phone every day. According to Wade, Chuck's father went out and hired a good lawyer. So, Chuck's not talking, at least not yet. He's trying to make a deal first."

Dewey blew out a mouthful of smoke. "I don't have a good feeling about any of this. I think that motherfucker's gonna hang Nick out to dry."

Cash agreed. "They'll use this guy Sosebee if they can. He ain't no big deal to them. They're hunting for the big boys."

"Well, what about us?" Dewey asked. "You think there's any way they can tie us in?"

"Compared to Nick, you two are sitting pretty," Cash said.

We finally dropped the subject. It was hard to consider it all for more than a few minutes at a time. My thoughts always returned to Dot Knox and how I'd felt that she had gotten me all wrong. I couldn't say that about myself anymore. Even if I slipped the noose on all of this, I still had its shit all over my shoes.

Cash treated Dewey to the grand tour. When he asked for Dewey's opinion of the boat, Dewey made no attempt to sugarcoat the reality of the situation.

"Somebody fed you a shit sandwich, my friend."

Cash frowned. "And held the goddamn mayonnaise."

The sad captain walked over to his mop and started slopping the bilge water. Dewey and I retired to the rear deck before he could put us to work. We watched for a moment as a Chris-Craft worked its way out to the NO WAKE pylon, its wooden hull shining in the sun.

"I hear you've been doing some work for T-Bone Rex." Dewey patted his belly. "Is he paying you by the pound, or what?"

I told him I wouldn't exactly call it work. "All I do is make pickups for him."

Dewey narrowed his gaze. "What kind of pickups?"

"Mostly liquor and pain pills, but some crazy shit, too. Banana cream pies, rat traps, ammunition. He paged me the other night because he wanted the *Street & Smith's* college football preview. Hell, it was almost midnight. I had to drive to Atlanta to find a place that was still open."

"I wouldn't put up with that shit," Dewey said, "not unless I was getting paid some big bucks."

"Well, he's an all-pro tipper," I said. "There's no doubt about that."

"What kind of cash are we talking?"

"I got fifty bucks on a case of Michelob last week."

Dewey whistled. "Damn."

"Tell me about it. I can't decide if he's the most generous person I've ever met, or the craziest."

"Well, maybe you should fix him up with Claudia. It'd be kind of nice to have a filthy-rich stepdad."

"I don't think so. Money or not, you could only take this guy in small doses. Besides, I think Claudia's got a crush on Wade Briggs. The only thing she's done since she got home is drink Smirnoff and wait for Saturday night to roll around. That's when she goes over to the fish camp to get her weekly dose of the singing deputy."

"Sounds like a vicious circus," Dewey said.

"I think you mean a circle."

"Whatever," he said, "it's vicious."

And the circus wasn't pulling up stakes anytime soon. Claudia had been ignoring Charlie's pleas to come back to Jacksonville. She even lied and told him the house was infested with termites. When Charlie sent over an exterminator to take a look, she told Charlie that I'd gotten into more trouble with the police and needed her help.

I had to take offense at that one.

"Well, it's believable." She smiled in a sly way. "And Charlie didn't bat an eye. He even offered to send me some extra money in case you needed a lawyer."

"You didn't take it, did you?"

"Well, of course I did." She laughed.

I'd stopped by the house after a Hillin run (Percocet, nail clippers, and peanut M&M's), and now she and I sat at the kitchen table trying to be civil to each other. It was not a problem that we'd ever encountered in the past.

"I can't believe you're talking shit about me."

"Relax," she said, "it's just Charlie."

She was sipping Smirnoff and Tropicana from a coffee mug, as if the vessel might convince someone that a screwdriver was the sort of thing you should be drinking at eleven o'clock in the morning. The radio in the window was playing "Good Hearted Woman."

"Are you going through the change?" I asked.

The question caught her in midsip. She snorted and set the mug down hard on the table. "What's that suppose to mean?"

"It's just something I saw in one of Rachel's *Cosmo* magazines. Menopause."

She waved her hand through the air and laughed.

"Well, this article said it could cause some emotional—"

"Luke, this is not a subject I'm going to discuss with my sixteen-year-old son. Now if you want to know my opinion, I think that maybe you should stick to looking at the busty women on the cover and not worry about the articles."

She had a point. One minute I'd been gazing at Adrienne Barbeau's rack, the next I was reading about hot flashes. It wasn't right.

"Either way," I told her, "you oughta think about cutting down on the screwdrivers a little. Charlie's turned you into a booze hound."

She was standing up now, checking her reflection in the oven window. She was already dressed in her singing clothes, the jeans and the Western shirt, even though the fish camp didn't open for another six hours.

She turned around slowly and fixed me with a somewhat sober gaze. "I know what you're saying. And believe me, I appreciate the concern."

"I'm not trying to be an asshole," I told her. "You just don't seem yourself lately."

She tried to smile in a reassuring way. "It's hard to explain. So much has happened since last spring, I've just kind of let it all get away from me. I think maybe it happens to everybody at some point or another. I don't see how it couldn't, anyway."

"Is it because I got in trouble?"

"No, of course not. It's not that at all. And I don't want you thinking that, either. You're nobody's burden. Do you understand?"

I didn't know what to say, so I just nodded.

"Besides," she said, "this right here is the first time anybody's ever acted concerned about me. Even since I was a little kid. So, how could I be mad at you?"

"I was just saying you might want to ease up on the Smirnoff a little."

"I'll be okay," she said.

She finally turned the tables and asked me about school. It was a question I'd been expecting. I decided to lay it out for her in the simplest and most direct way.

"I quit."

Her shoulders sagged like another burden had just fallen upon them.

"Oh, Luke." She said it like she felt sorry for me.

"It's all right," I told her. "I'm planning to get my GED eventually."

She left her cup on the counter and sat back down at the table. She seemed puzzled by something, but then she smiled.

"I never liked it either," she said. "And Nick was the same way, always cutting classes and getting caught. I don't think anybody in our family is cut out for a routine like that."

We sat there for the longest time without even saying a word. Even when the phone started ringing—and we both knew it was probably Wade—we still sat there a few seconds longer. I suppose she was thinking the same thing as me: Just what the hell was a Fulmer cut out for?

28

The Peugeot came back better than before, but our escape plan was in jeopardy. The longer the whole Sosebee affair dragged on, the less confident I felt that I'd ever see Champaign.

I began to have trouble sleeping, and even when I made it to dreamland, the cops would burst into Rachel's apartment and roust me from the sofa, Muskgrave leading the charge.

"We know you've got the cocaine, Fulmer. Now where is it?"

I'd try to protest, but I couldn't even speak. My tongue, arms, and legs were pure liquid. And then one of Muskgrave's guys would unscrew the back of the TV, releasing an avalanche of cocaine bricks. The same story when they opened the closet doors, the kitchen cabinets, and the refrigerator door. Muskgrave would flash his Pepsodent smile, and then Dot Knox would walk into the living room with those big scissors of hers. That's when I'd realize I wasn't wearing any pants. I couldn't run or scream or do anything.

Most nights, I'd check the window every hour or so, just to see if there was a cruiser out in the lot. Some nights, it was there. Some, it wasn't. There was no pattern, no rhyme or reason. It was hard to figure what Muskgrave was thinking, or more important, what he did or did not know.

Hillin paged me one evening, in need of hemorrhoid cream and Raisin Bran. It was around midnight, and the coast was clear, so I hopped in the hearse and started the motor. He'd allowed me to keep the death wagon even after Rachel's Peugeot had been fixed, just so I'd have a vehicle to make his pickups.

When I stepped inside the log mansion, Hillin was perched in his

La-Z-Boy, reading the Sports page. As always, the Panasonic TV was blaring. Wayne Newton was singing a Barry Manilow song on the *Tonight Show.*

I set Hillin's stuff beside his chair. He noticed and started to fish through his pocket for some cash. "Did they have the Prep H?"

"Yep, the tube says it's good for burning and itching."

"To hell with the burning," Hillin said. "It's the goddamn itching that's driving me crazy."

He spotted me a crumpled fifty, then raised the Sports page and went back to reading about his beloved Georgia Bulldogs. I headed for the door, but then Hillin started bitching about the Dawgs' 0-and-2 start on the gridiron season.

"Goddamn that Dooley," he said. "All he wants to do is run, run, run. He ain't ever gonna win a national championship playing that kind of ball."

I already had the doorknob in my hand. But Hillin was gazing over his shoulder at me, waiting to hear my opinion on the crucial matter. I searched for a reply that might hasten my exit.

"Maybe he just needs a really good tailback."

Hillin snorted and waved me away like I was a fool. "Good luck finding one who's *that* fucking good."

The police car was sitting in front of the apartments when I got back. Something about its presence unnerved me even more than usual that night. I lay on Rachel's sofa and tried to watch a table tennis match on some new all-sports station. But the quiet started to agitate me, so I switched off the TV and tiptoed back to Rachel's room. I stood there in the dark for a long time, just watching her breathe. I couldn't help remembering what she'd told me, how when things are going so well, you have to be on guard for the worst.

I took Brute out for his predawn dump. The cruiser was gone by that time, so I eased my nerves with a joint as we walked through the apartment complex, watching the smoke coil in the cool morning air.

After Brute finished his business, I padded down to the 7-Eleven to buy a box of Krispy Kremes. It had become a Saturday-morning ritual for me and Rachel's mom. We were always up before Rachel, so Mrs. Coyle would make the coffee, and then we'd sit at the little table off the kitchen, eating doughnuts, drinking beans, and reading the newspaper.

"Look at this," Mrs. Coyle said. She was sitting there in a baggy Illinois sweatshirt, eyeing the front page of the *Green Lake Gazette* with weary amusement.

I glanced up from the Sports section. "What is it?"

"It's the lead story." She sipped her coffee and set the mug back down on the table. "They misspell the word *trafficking* twice, and in two different ways."

"You mean, like drug trafficking?" I craned my neck to get a peek at the article. Sure enough, Chuck was back on the front page. The headline read: DOPE PILOT GRANTED BAIL—TRIAL PUSHED BACK.

The doughnut that I'd just eaten ceased its downward journey and lay heavy against my windpipe. Chuck had struck a deal.

"Are you okay?" Rachel's mother looked over the top of the paper.

I tried to swerve my thoughts back between the lines of our budding conversation. "Yeah, I was just thinking that kind of stuff must drive you crazy, seeing how you're an English professor."

"No, I just thought it was funny."

Her gaze remained fixed on me. I couldn't help wondering if she held me in the same bemused light as a misspelled word. We both sat there staring at each other until it seemed inevitable that one of us would speak.

"I know about your and Rachel's plan," she said.

She didn't sound mad or anything, just matter-of-fact about the whole affair. I didn't see any reason to play dumb, so I nodded. I felt I owed her that much.

"She's done this before, you know."

"Done what?" I asked.

"Made plans to run away," she said. "With a boy."

The doughnut tightened its grip on my windpipe. "When?"

"About a year and a half ago," she said, "right after we moved to Ohio."

She folded the paper and laid it on the table between us. Chuck stared up at me, appearing as stunned as I felt. I could imagine how fast his heart must have been pounding when that mug shot was snapped.

"There was this boy," she said. "His name was Ward. Rachel met him at the university."

"You mean he was a college student?"

"No, he and Rachel were taking advanced placement classes together."

"Is this about Rachel being smarter than me?" I asked.

She smiled and stared down at the mahogany tabletop. She traced one of the knots in the wood with the tip of her finger.

"Trust me," she said. "You're a lot smarter than Ward."

"So what happened?" I asked. "What kind of plans did they have?"

She bit her lip and looked back up at me. "They took Ward's car and drove to Champaign. Rachel was planning to get a job, and Ward was going to start a band. He already had the name picked out and everything: Ass Disaster, or something like that."

"Ass Disaster?"

I had to admit, it was a pretty good band name.

"But then Rachel turned up pregnant," Mrs. Coyle said. "So Ward disappeared. He was so scared he drove all the way to North Dakota. I was the one who went down to Champaign and picked up Rachel. I took her in for the abortion and looked after her."

My head crackled and buzzed as if I'd just run into another tree. I had no idea what to say or do.

"You have to understand," Mrs. Coyle went on, "that Pete's death was hard on me, too."

"So his name was Pete?" I realized that I'd never heard either of them speak the man's name.

Mrs. Coyle nodded, then she gave me this look that begged for reassurance. "I hope you understand."

"Understand what?"

"Understand that I don't want to lose her."

The doughnut had finally begun to sink. My hopes were racing along ahead of it, clearing a path. "So, I guess you're expecting me to talk her out of it."

She opened her mouth to speak, then stopped to reconsider the words.

"I can't stop her," she said. "Not after I ran off and left her and Pete at the worst possible time."

I lifted the Sports page and gazed dumbly at it for a few seconds, finally dropping it on top of Chuck's photo. I trumped him with a picture of a high school place kicker. The kid was booting one through the uprights from forty yards out. The caption read: LIGHTS OUT FOR GREEN LAKE.

"Maybe you and Rachel need to talk about this stuff," I said. "I mean, instead of me and you."

Mrs. Coyle shook her head. "This man who runs the AA meetings I attend, he was talking about how hard it is to win back a person's trust. It takes a long time, years maybe, especially when you've disappointed someone again and again."

Wade Briggs. I could see him sitting beside Danny in the truck, trying to start a conversation with his angry, crippled son. It must have felt like playing Ping-Pong with a person who keeps catching the balls and slipping them into his pocket.

"I've only had six months," Mrs. Coyle said. "I haven't even begun to make up for things. But now I've got a job offer at Vanderbilt. It's more money, we could rent a house. I just need more time, because she's all I have. I can't lose her."

My head went back to buzzing again. It felt like birds were pecking at my skull. I had no idea what I was going to do about any of this. All I knew was that I had to get out of that apartment. It felt as small as it was, all of the sudden. I needed to take a drive.

I stood up and looked back across the table at Mrs. Coyle. I opened my mouth, but nothing would come out. It was like I'd forgotten how to speak, forgotten how to spell my own name.

29

I wasn't really expecting the siren and the blue lights, but I suppose my heart lacked the motivation to jump up and down about much of anything after my little talk with Rachel's mother. And so I pulled over into the weeds and waited for the routine to begin. Thirty minutes later, I was sitting in Muskgrave's office.

"Well, well. If it ain't Mario Andretti, himself."

Muskgrave burst into the room, carrying a cup of coffee and acting all sunny, like a man who didn't have a care in the world. It was quite a contrast to his red-assed mood back in the spring, and I can't say that I didn't envy him for it.

He parked himself behind his desk, right across from where I was sitting. His deputy had gone to the trouble of cuffing my hands in front of me.

Muskgrave leaned forward and gazed into my lap. He was grinning like a jackass, his blond hair blown back from his face, feathered and firmed with hair spray.

"Kind of hard to drive a car that way, ain't it?"

I flipped him off, ever so casually. He sat back and chuckled, as though we'd just shared a joke.

"Ah, I'm just kidding with you," he said. "Here, let me take those off."

He walked over from behind the desk and proceeded to unlock the cuffs. I'd already had plenty of time to look around the office, to view the infamous bulletin board that hung on the wall behind his desk. There must have been thirty photos tacked to the corkboard, mostly mug shots. Nick and I were situated about halfway down, near the middle of things. I was still wearing my long hair in the picture.

The rest of the office was pretty much what I would have expected. The requisite photos of the wife and kids atop the desk, a big American flag in the corner, and a bevy of framed awards and citations. There was also a wall devoted to photos of Muskgrave coupled with more successful people: folks like Senator McHugh, Vince Dooley, Jimmy Carter, and Anita Bryant.

"So, I hear you're working for the T-Bone King." Muskgrave tossed the handcuff keys onto his desk and settled back into his big leather chair.

I didn't see any need to confirm the obvious. So I just sat there.

Muskgrave shrugged. "What? Are you taking the Fifth or something?"

"I'm not saying anything until you tell me why I got hauled in here."

Muskgrave scratched his chin in a gesture of deep thought. "Hmm. Let's see, now. If my memory serves me correctly, Judge Knox and her flying monkeys suspended your driver's license for six months."

I could never understand why people only seemed to remember your worst lines.

"You know damn well I've been driving on a suspended license. Hell, your boys have been following me around for three weeks. I don't think that's got anything to do with this."

Muskgrave gave me this disappointed look, like I'd gone and spoiled all the fun. Then he reached into a cardboard box sitting atop his desk and pulled out a nearly empty bag of pot. I recognized it as my own stash.

"Is that enough reason to haul you in?" he asked.

"There's barely enough there to roll a joint."

Muskgrave reached into the box again and produced a wad of cash and my pager. He lifted his brow as if he'd just produced a royal flush. "This right here," he said, "is a recipe for possession with intent to distribute."

He sat there expectantly, with a grin plastered to his face, all of the evidence piled in front of him. But I still didn't say a word. Even in the face of all this, I couldn't help thinking about Rachel and her mother, lying together on the sofa that day, listening to Pete Coyle's records.

Finally, Muskgrave's smile melted away. He actually fixed me with a concerned expression.

"What's the matter with you, anyway? I don't recall you being the gloomy type."

"It's nothing you'd want to know about, seeing how it doesn't have any bearing on your reelection."

Muskgrave reached back and closed the office door. He sighed, leaned forward, and set his arms on top of the desk. When he started talking, it was in a quiet voice.

"I've got a proposal I'd like to float."

I didn't offer up any sort of reaction. I just sat there and waited for him to lay it all out. Needless to say, my expectations were pretty low.

"Listen," he said, "I take a lot of shit from people about not being a real cop, about being a politician. They just think I'm some pretty boy who wants to go to the state capitol. But let me tell you something, I paid my fucking dues. I was a police officer for seven years before I ran for sheriff. I did a lot of investigating in that time. I honed my skills."

"So what are you getting at?"

"What I'm getting at is this: I'm pretty sure that I know what happened that night when we brought in the pilot. I know what happened to one of those bags of cocaine."

My heart suddenly caught its second wind. It jumped right up and started flapping away inside me.

"I don't know what the hell you're talking about."

"Bullshit, you don't. We had helicopters up there. They saw Mr. Sosebee circling over the Grimes horse farm. The GBI boys said he dropped something out of the plane. But when they got there, it was gone."

Muskgrave leaned back and fixed me with a hard stare. "Now I had been thinking all along that Nick was probably involved in bringing this stuff into the county. Naturally, he would have been the one out there to pick it up. But to my surprise, I found out that he'd been sitting right here in the station during all the excitement."

Here, Muskgrave leaned forward again. The slightest of smiles formed at the corners of his mouth. "Now, Nick made one phone call while he was here. And come to find out that phone call was to you. Of course, you didn't come to bail him out. No, sir. You sent that bondsman over here to take care of things. Which leads me to believe that you were the one who covered Nick's ass on the pickup."

He was full of himself, that's for sure, just sitting there smiling away. He might as well have been posing for another picture with Anita Bryant.

I didn't want to give anything away with my reaction, so I tried to imagine Nick's poker face, how he could smoke a cigarette and appear totally at ease even in the face of serious criminal allegations.

"So, prove it," I told him.

I fed Muskgrave a smile of my own. It caused him to blink hard.

"I can't," he said. "In fact, it looks like I'm pretty much shit out of luck. I mean, if Sosebee didn't know that you were making the pickup, and if you got rid of the goods, there's not much I can do about it, really."

"Then why the hell have I been sitting here for the last thirty minutes?"

"That's a good question," he said. "And here's the answer. First off, I can still send your ass away for what's lying here on my desk, not to mention your little driving habit. And number two, your big brother's going away for a while no matter what. He already missed his arraignment on the possession charge. And when Sosebee starts crowing, Nick's gonna have even bigger problems."

"Then I guess it looks like you got what you wanted: the Fulmers in leg irons."

Muskgrave let his shoulders sag. "Contrary to what you might believe, I'm not an asshole. And here's where it all comes back around to us helping each other out. Now the way I see it, Nick's going to jail, no matter what. There's not much I can do about that, even if I wanted to. But you, I can help. We can forget all about what happened today. I might even be willing to have a word with Judge Knox, maybe get your license reinstated a couple weeks early and have this stuff wiped off your permanent record."

"And what's the favor?"

He paused and stared at the wall, appearing to reflect on his many awards. "I want you to tell me where Nick is hiding."

"You're fucking crazy," I told him. "I'm not gonna be a snitch. Especially against my own brother."

Muskgrave sighed. "I understand how you must feel. But you need to take some time and think through all of this in a rational way."

"There's nothing rational about it," I told him. "If you're so sure that Nick's going to jail, then why do you need my help?"

"Because," he said, "I wanna break this thing open before the Feds do it."

And then it dawned on me. "Has this got anything to do with Morley Safer and *60 Minutes*?"

"How'd you know about that?"

"Maybe I've done some investigating, myself. Speaking of which, aren't you the one who begged the FBI to get involved in the first place?"

"That was a mistake," he said. "Sons of bitches froze me out. I did all the shit work in the beginning, and then they come in here with their little candy-ass windbreakers and reap the fucking rewards."

"So, why Nick?" I asked. "Why do you think he's some sort of key to whipping the Feds' ass?"

"Because he's the only one smart enough to be working with the top people. I've talked to this guy Sosebee, and he's a fucking dumb-ass. Certified, grade-A. I don't even know how he got a pilot's license. I sure as hell wouldn't fly with him."

I had to admit that Muskgrave's investigative skills were impressive. Of course, his understanding of me lagged far behind.

"I'm not gonna be a snitch," I told him. "I wouldn't even do it if he wasn't my brother."

He nodded as if he understood. But then he clucked his tongue and smiled in a satisfied way.

"So, tell me about your girlfriend, Miss Rachel Coyle."

I couldn't see where he was headed with all of this. "What are you, the fucking school counselor all of the sudden?"

Muskgrave chuckled a little. Then he opened the desk drawer, pulled out a file, and opened it up. "I can see what y'all have in common," he said.

"What's that?"

"Well, she's got a rap sheet almost as long as yours."

I sat up straight. This had been a day of far too many revelations on the Rachel front.

"What the hell did she do?"

Muskgrave slipped a pair of reading glasses onto his nose. "Well, it's all from out of state," he said. "Illinois and Ohio, mainly. Mostly shoplifting stuff. She must have some sticky little fingers. Let's see, here. She took some record albums, makeup, earrings, a hair dryer. Oh, yeah. And here's my favorite. A Girl Scout uniform from Sears."

He closed the file and laughed. By that time I'd abandoned any attempt to appear unfazed by the day's proceedings.

"Oh, and you might want to take a look at these," he said.

He slid a stack of black-and-white photos across the desk. They documented a recent weed purchase that Rachel and I had made from Stan in the back of the Holiday Inn parking lot. I gazed up at the bulletin board, scouting the field for Stan. Sure enough, I'd overlooked him the first time around. He was stuck way down in the lower left-hand corner, a bit player until now.

Muskgrave brought my attention back around to the matter at hand. "Seeing how she's still on probation with the juvie courts in Illinois and Ohio, I think that a prosecutor might try to tie her in with you on this trafficking thing."

I felt a little wobbly, my head buzzing again.

"I'd say that you have some things to think about," Muskgrave said. "It's a lot to consider, so I'm gonna give you a week to get your head around it. And just in case you're thinking of running off somewhere, don't forget that I've got friends with windbreakers."

He pushed himself out of his chair and walked to the door, stopping to consider me one last time. "I'm here if you want to talk about things. My door's always open."

30

"Little faster," I told Rachel. "Step, slide."

Somehow, I'd coaxed her onto the floor for a two-step lesson. We'd come to the fish camp for the Saturday-night dancing, the special occasion being Claudia's forty-third birthday. The Green Lake Gang was playing "Why Don't You Love Me?" on the stage above us, Wade singing Hank's goofy lyrics as the herd shuffled in circles down front.

"Slow down, I'm gonna fall."

Rachel's voice had an edge of panic and irritation to it. She was having some trouble, stumbling backward every few steps. It didn't help that she was wearing those clunky black shoes of hers, or that I was gaining a fair amount of pleasure watching her troubles. I'd never seen her so vulnerable. She kept gazing over her shoulder at all the other couples around us, most of whom were gray-haired and decked out in Western wear.

"Slow down," she said again. "We're gonna bump into one of these geezers and break their hip."

"No, we're not. Besides, we gotta keep up with the beat."

"Well, why can't I go forward for a while?"

"Because it's not allowed," I lied. "They'd ask us to leave. Besides, you wouldn't know what to do."

She gave me a dirty look. "What's the matter with you, anyway?"

"Nothing's the matter," I told her. "I'm happy as hell. I'm getting on the good foot."

I still hadn't said anything to Rachel about all the stuff I'd learned that morning. I'd run through my mind the different ways that I might approach her, but nothing seemed appropriate. Mostly, I couldn't decide if I was mad, or sad, or if any of it even mattered at all.

I swerved around the octogenarian gent who'd plucked Claudia off her chair. The guy was sporting a denim suit with pearl snaps. Claudia glided along the sawdust floor with the old-timer, smiling her new, drunken smile and making eye contact with Wade as he stood beneath his gray hat, strumming his Gibson.

Dewey had tagged along, just to get out of the house for a while. Even though he'd reclaimed his driver's license, he seemed to be falling evermore into a funk without Nick or the band around. Dewey had lured Wade Briggs's wife, Cassie, onto the floor. Cassie was a public defender who'd handled a number of Dewey's drunk driving cases. He swore that she owned the best legal mind in Green Lake.

I didn't know if Cassie was aware of her husband's friendship with Claudia, if she knew about the phone calls or Claudia's particular affection for the singing deputy. She was an attractive woman, blue-eyed and tall, with a good figure for her blue business suit. She could have been in that perfume commercial where the woman sang about bringing home the bacon, frying it up in a pan, and never, never letting you forget you're a man. Maybe she'd even married beneath herself.

Claudia patted Methuselah's shoulder midsong and excused herself. She fetched her purse from the table and headed for the bathroom, weaving just a little, no doubt longing to take a pull from whatever bottle she had tucked inside her bag. Wade eyed her sadly as she disappeared, still singing about how he'd had no hugging, or kissing, or squeezing in a long, long while.

Rachel and I stepped outside to get some air. The breeze felt good after floating among the stew of warm bodies on the dance floor. We tramped across the gravel parking lot and settled in at a picnic table beside the runoff pond. This was what passed for the fish camp's lake. The real lake was two miles away.

Rachel took a seat beside me. Pretty soon, she was talking plans again.

"I called a friend of mine in Champaign, and she was telling me a room in her group house is opening up in two weeks. That's perfect timing for us."

I just stared at her. I didn't have the heart to say anything, or to even play along anymore.

Rachel had a puzzled look on her face. "So, what do you think?"

I shrugged and looked away, staring off at the fish camp. It was little more than a long shed, really, with cinder-block walls and a tin roof. The building practically hummed a 2/4 beat, the twang of the steel guitar slipping through the windows.

"You've been like this all fucking day," Rachel said. "Did you get your period or something?"

I ignored the remark. "What is it with you and Champaign, anyway?" I asked. "What's so fucking special about that place?"

She eyed me with a fair amount of suspicion. "I thought we already talked about this. There's nothing special about it. I just have contacts there. I can find us a place to live, jobs, shit like that."

"Well, how do you know it hasn't changed? I mean, when was the last time you were even there?"

She just sat there staring at me, batting her eyes nervously.

"What is your fucking problem?" she asked. "You have got the shittiest attitude right now."

"I don't have a fucking problem. In fact, I was just thinking how I'd heard this band the other day that I thought you might like."

"Who?"

I fixed her with a hard stare. "I think they call themselves Ass Disaster."

She was dead still for a moment, stunned. Finally, she clenched her jaw and nodded as if she was starting to figure some things out.

"That fucking bitch," she said. "What did she tell you?"

"The whole thing," I said. "She told me the whole thing. The pregnancy, the abortion, everything."

"I'll fucking kill her." Rachel clenched her fists. "I swear to God, I'll fucking stick a knife in her heart. Goddamn her." She pounded her fists on the table.

"You can't kill her," I said. "They'll send you to the juvenile prison up in Alto. And, believe me, that'd make Champaign look like Paris fuckin' France. Besides which, there's nothing wrong with your mother. You make her out to be some kind of monster or something. And it's not true. She's no more fucked up than anybody else."

"How the hell do you know?"

"Because I've talked to her."

Rachel snorted. "You can't believe anything she says."

"Look who's talking. You've got more secrets than a twelve-dollar motel room."

"So, name some."

"How about all your shoplifting arrests? Turns out you're not the master thief you made yourself out to be."

"Motherfucker! Did she tell you about that, too?"

"Believe it or not, I got that information elsewhere."

I turned my back to her and straddled the picnic table's bench, gazing out at the cluttered parking lot. The rows of headlights stared back at me like sad pairs of eyes.

"It's not gonna be the same if you go back to Champaign," I said. "It's only gonna feel worse."

I waited for the smart-ass remark, but it never came. For some reason, she was willing to listen to what I had to say.

"I've seen it enough, the way it happens when people have to go from a place. Like when Lyndell left our house. It never was the same. Nick's house, too. I don't even like going there since he left, and poor Dewey, he's miserable. It'll be the same one day with that apartment you and your mother live in. I'll probably go out of my way to avoid driving by there."

"What are you talking about?" she asked.

"What I'm saying is that it doesn't matter if all you have are good memories of a place, or a person. Once it's over, it's over. And that's the worst memory of all, the day something ends. And believe me, that's the one that's gonna slap you into next week when you get back to Champaign."

We sat there without saying anything for a while. The ash-colored moonlight spilled mournfully across the tin roof of the building. When I finally turned back around, I could see that she'd been crying. She'd wiped the tears on the sleeves of her leather jacket.

She studied my face, her cheeks flushed and her eyes still watery. "They say your last thought before you die affects what happens to you in your next life."

"What's that got to do with Champaign?"

"The thing is," she said, "I've tried to imagine what my father must have been thinking when he died. And I just can't, you know. I mean, he was so unhappy that whatever it was, whatever he was thinking, it couldn't have led to anything good. And now he's got this new life somewhere, and it's bad, too. And he's in the same pain, and he'll end up like that again and again, with no way to stop it."

I had no business answering that question. Hell, I didn't know what Pete Coyle had been thinking. I didn't even know how Pete Coyle had died. I didn't know which of Rachel's stories was true, if any of them.

She had this desperate look on her face, like she was staring across the table at a doctor, hoping for a good prognosis, maybe a fifty-fifty shot. I wanted to deliver. I wanted to say the right thing.

"Maybe he's just dead," I told her. "Maybe that's all there is to it. And now he's not suffering anymore."

I felt like banging my head on the table. After the words had left my mouth, I realized they hadn't sounded hopeful at all.

But Rachel thought differently. "It would probably be better like that," she said. "For him, at least. Not for everybody, but maybe for him."

The breeze picked up and beat back her curtain of hair. It thrilled me to see her face. It was like a veil being lifted from a beautiful paint-ing. And I knew that I would have done anything to keep her from see-ing any more trouble or pain.

She ducked her head and wiped her arm across her eyes.

"I know that you don't hate your mother," I said. "I saw you one day with her, on the sofa. You were lying across her lap."

She stared off at the ground, embarrassed.

"I used to worry that something would happen to her," she said. "Back when she was drinking and staying in bed all the time. I worried that I'd come home from school and find her dead."

"She needs you," I said. "She's trying to change."

Rachel shook her head as though she couldn't begin to figure me out.

"Why are you doing this?" she asked. "Why do you care so much about my mother and I getting along?"

"I just don't want you to end up like Claudia. I think she may have run off with Lyndell just to spite her mother's cousin. Now, look at her. She's a mess. I mean, this is the shit you get yourself into with these kinds of decisions. You end up twenty years down the road, asking, 'What the hell have I done?' You end up miserable and sad, and then you have to hurt a lot of people to make it any better."

She narrowed her eyes, confused. "What does that have to do with us?"

I leaned forward and laid my hands on top of hers. "The thing is, I don't want to be the man who fucks up your life. I don't want to ever see you with a bottle of vodka in your purse, or your hands shaking."

She sat there with the moon's net draped over her, waiting for me to say more.

31

The next couple of days proved as awkward as our turn on the dance floor. It became apparent to the both of us that we'd lost our rhythm— in conversation, at work, in bed. Even the silence was grating. It was all pauses and squeaks, like fingers sliding up and down guitar strings but never stopping to play any music.

I still had a little time left before Muskgrave came calling again for his favor, a few more sleepless nights, lying there while the TV flickered, wondering what the hell I should do. I wasn't convinced that Musk-grave could pin anything on Rachel with those photos. Then again, I could never be certain. And if it came down to making a choice, I knew that I would spare her at Nick's expense. It was awful to consider. I kept hoping things wouldn't go that far, but I couldn't see any way out.

Regardless, it seemed to me that packing up and moving out was probably the best thing that I could do for Rachel and her mother. At least it would give them a chance to make things right between them-selves. With me out of the picture, Rachel didn't have anyone except her mother. And so I slipped my stuff out of their apartment in the middle of the night, while Rachel and Mrs. Coyle were still asleep and while the parking lot was free of police vehicles. I told Brute good-bye, and then I tossed my bag into the back of the hearse and drove over to the Cove Road Marina. I spent the rest of the night aboard the *Cash Register,* rumpled and damp and longing for the smell of Juicy Fruit.

I can't say that I ever had this concrete idea about calling Lyndell. But somewhere in the night, while the lake ticked against the side of the boat—over and over again with those same lake noises—I began to ponder his dusty image: the sideburns and the crooked smile, a steering wheel in his hands and cigarette smoke streaming from his lips. It was the day that he'd planned to leave for Bristol, and he'd come by the school and checked me out early to say good-bye. We cruised over to the Krystal, took the drive-through and sat in the car, working on a sackful of cheeseburgers while a Charlie Rich tune trickled out of the dashboard.

"Well, there he is." Lyndell pointed at the radio dial. "Claudia's favorite."

He grinned and took a drink from his Miller High Life. The can was wrapped in a brown paper bag.

"So, anything good happen at school?"

I swallowed the burger that I'd stuffed into my mouth. "Marty Atkins had a bottle of MD 20/20 in his locker. He said he stole it from his old man."

Lyndell was about to take another sip of beer. He reconsidered, lowering the can to his lap as if I might not notice. "That's what winos drink."

"Marty says his old man calls it Mad Dog. He told me his mother poured out a bottle one time, and his father got so mad he threw all her clothes out in the yard and ran over them with his lawn mower."

I could tell that Lyndell was none too impressed by Marty's father. Nevertheless, he smiled as if the lawn mower stunt had been a clever one.

"Listen," he said, "I want to tell you something."

He reached over and switched off the radio. I'd only seen him do that once before.

"Is this about C.W.?"

Lyndell shook his head. "No, I already told you all there is to know about that sonuvabitch. This is more important."

"Is it about Claudia?"

He scratched at his head. "Yeah, it's about her. But it's also about Nick. I just want you to know that if either of them ever gets into any sort of mess, I want you to call me. Okay?"

"Well, where would I call you?"

He made a face like he hadn't considered that part of the instructions. "Well, I suppose you could ask somebody from the track. I'll probably be keeping in touch with that gang. One of those fellows will know how to get me."

I told him I'd call, but I didn't really think much of his offer at the time. All I knew was that I'd miss riding in that Chevelle.

"Of course, I don't expect any problems from you," he said. "Just as long as you don't start drinking that Mad Dog."

He smiled and switched on the radio, jumping in with Charlie Rich, singing about the most beautiful girl in the world, asking someone to relay a message, to "tell her I love her."

And then he seemed to remember something important. He turned down the radio again.

"Drinking MD 20/20," he said, "is one step removed from drinking Aqua Velva. You remember that, okay?"

I drove to the Amoco the following morning to speak with Carl Bettis. I expected he would know the name of the racing team that Lyndell worked for and how I might get in touch with him.

"Well, look here," Carl said. "Where you been hiding, boy?"

I shrugged. "Oh, here and there."

He was sitting by the front door of the service station, atop a cannibalized backseat, working on a ham biscuit and a Miller High Life. As always, he was wearing his Mountain Dew baseball cap, just like Darrell Waltrip.

"I haven't seen you around the track since that night you and Cash took off after Speedy."

"Well, Speedy did some damage to Cash's car, if you'll recall. He's been out of commission for a while."

Carl shook his head at the craziness of it all. "I'm glad they locked that little peckerhead up. He put me on the sidelines for a month. Hell, I was seeing double after he ran me into that wall."

It was a warm morning, the sun low, a gash of jaundiced light cutting through the skinny pines. Most times, I would have welcomed the track talk. But not right now. Muskgrave's clock was ticking.

"I was wondering if you could help me out, Carl."

He wadded the empty biscuit wrapper and gazed up at me, his face knotted and flushed with an alcoholic burn.

"Well, sure. But I hope it's not for that thing." He pointed at the hearse and smiled. "I don't work on those. I figure I'll be riding in one soon enough."

"No, that's not it. What I was hoping is that you could maybe help me get in touch with Lyndell. Claudia had told me that you two talked every now and then. She said you knew who he worked for up in Bristol."

Carl appeared startled by the question, his eyes suddenly clear and sober. He tilted his head to get a better look at me but didn't say anything. And then he removed his cap and scratched at his head in a dodgy sort of way—a classic Lyndell gesture.

"Goddamn," he murmured. "Well, shit."

He was looking past me, out toward the road. It was like he'd suddenly remembered a head-on collision that had taken place out there.

My heart jumped out of its hole and gave my rib cage a nudge. "What's the matter, Carl?"

He pushed himself off his perch and started shaking his head. "This ain't none of my business," he said. "I think you better talk to Claudia."

I grabbed him by the shoulder before he could walk away from me. "About what? What the hell are you talking about?"

"I can't believe she didn't say anything about it."

"About what?"

He tried to steel himself, fighting his natural tendency to shake. He swallowed hard. "Lyndell's dead, Luke. He died last winter."

He closed his eyes, flinching as though I might hit him. Of course, I never would have done such a thing. I actually let go of his shirt and straightened the wrinkles. Only after I'd taken care of that piece of business did I realize my own hands had begun to shake. It might have been from lack of sleep, lack of food, lack of options. All I know is that the air felt as heavy as it had all summer, a front of gray clouds already moving toward the lake. They were always there, just like the water lapping at the shore, always the same thing and for no good reason.

Carl brought me a bottle of Coke. I was sitting on the old car seat, the sun beating against my face. He settled in beside me. Out of habit, I'd taken the left-hand side, the driver's side.

Carl sighed. "I told Claudia about it not long after he'd died. I fig-ured she'd want to know."

I took a sip of Coke. The liquid scorched my gut when it hit bot-tom. "All she ever told me is that he was living up in Bristol. She said he was working for a race team and had a wife and a kid. She even told me he'd quit drinking."

"Well, that's true," Carl said. "He did all those things."

"So, what happened? How'd he die?"

He scratched at his head again and looked out toward the road. I could tell by his body language that it was not a pleasant story.

"Old habits die hard," he said.

"Listen, Carl, you can tell me what happened. It's okay."

He took a deep breath. "Well, the thing is, he'd started drinking again. I hear it was nothing terrible, nothing to make him lose his job or anything. But, you know, he liked to go out and have a pop after work. Anyway, he was at this bar one night drinking with a buddy of his. Both of them were about three sheets to the wind, full of shooters and Bud-weiser, but Lyndell figured this other fellow was in the better shape to drive them home. He was being responsible, you know, trying not to get a DUI. But this other fellow fell asleep and drove head-on into a culvert."

"So, that's how . . ."

Carl nodded. "It killed the both of them. From what I hear, it was quick."

I could see Lyndell fiddling with the radio, maybe hammering out a little Chet Atkins on the dashboard. I wondered if he'd even had time to make a grab for the steering wheel. Probably not. He would have saved their asses if that had been the case.

"I wonder why she didn't tell me? All this time, I'd been thinking he was . . ."

Actually, I wasn't sure what I'd been thinking.

"Well, try not to be mad at her," Carl said. "She was pretty broken up about it."

"Don't worry, I'm not mad. This explains a whole lot."

Carl leaned forward and spat on the asphalt. Somehow, it appeared to be a thoughtful gesture.

"It's hard to figure," he said. "I just can't see Lyndell dying in a car wreck."

"Me either."

"Now, I could see a jealous husband shooting his ass, but other-wise . . ."

We both got a laugh out of that one.

"I tell you something," he said. "After I got the news, I must have thought of a hundred funny things that Lyndell had said or done. I got a lot of good stories to tell on account of him. And every one of them is the truth."

God knows, I had my own stories, but there was at least one more I would have liked to add to the list. As I walked back to the hearse, I found myself wondering what Lyndell might have been thinking just before his head hit that windshield. My hope was that he never saw it coming. Maybe he just had his eyes closed, singing along with the radio.

32

I suppose anyone else might have driven over to Claudia's place and asked what the hell she'd been thinking. But I didn't have the heart for that. And besides, she didn't deserve any more grief. Love had already been mean enough to her.

I ended up sparking a joint and taking a drive beside the lake. I tried, for at least a moment or two, to steer my thoughts away from Claudia and Lyndell. I still lacked a plan for dealing with Muskgrave, for saving Nick's ass and keeping Rachel out of trouble. And now I knew for sure—it had all fallen on my shoulders.

I stamped out the fresh joint and flicked it into the wind, hoping the gesture alone might produce an idea or two. The options before me were sparse and none too appealing. I thought of going on the lam. Despite Muskgrave's warning, I felt that I could probably outsmart the FBI for a little while. And with my ass out of Dodge, Muskgrave probably wouldn't bother to hassle Rachel. His only benefit would have been spite, and whatever other flaws he might have possessed, I didn't really see him as a vengeful person.

I'd just begun to consider a life on the run when the siren started to wail behind me. My already beleaguered spirits fell right through the floorboard. I drove along for a while, steadily, slowly, watching the rearview and hoping the Crown Vic might pass me and head off to a real emergency. But it never happened. And seeing how I was driving the hearse, fleeing was out of the question. So I pulled over to the side of the road and, once again, awaited the inevitable.

I was surprised to see Wade Briggs step out of the car. We met at our usual talking spot, between the two vehicles. Wade was smiling, and I took this to be a good sign.

"Muskgrave didn't send you, did he?"

Wade shook his head. "No, but I heard about him hauling you in a few days ago."

I leaned back against the hearse and rubbed my hands up and down my face.

"What's he got on you, anyway?" Wade asked.

I laid it all out on the table for him, everything that had gone down, even how I'd gotten mixed up in the cocaine delivery. And then I told him about the choice that Muskgrave had given me.

"If I don't lead him to Nick, he's gonna charge me and Rachel with distribution."

Wade frowned and stared out at the quiet lake. "Jesus Christ," he mumbled.

"I'm thinking about taking off, maybe heading out of state somewhere. If I'm gone, then maybe Muskgrave won't bother with Rachel. He wouldn't have anything to gain by it."

Wade turned. "Well, what about Claudia?"

"What about her?" I asked. "She's not one of the people who might go to jail if I stick around."

"I know that. But she's gonna be real upset if you disappear, especially when Muskgrave takes out a warrant on you."

"Trust me, she's got worse things to be upset about."

Wade fixed me with a concerned gaze. "What do you mean?"

"Has she ever mentioned the name Lyndell?"

"Once or twice," he said. "It sounds like she and him had a real complicated relationship."

"I suppose that's one way of looking at it." Of course, it went beyond complicated. They were each the center pole in the other's circus tent.

"So, what about him?" Wade asked. "Is he back in town?"

"He's dead. He was killed in a car wreck."

Wade peeled off his sunglasses and swallowed hard. "That's awful. Does she know yet?"

"Yeah, she's known about it for months. The thing is, she hasn't told anybody, not even me."

"So, how did you find out?"

"Carl Bettis, over at the Amoco."

"I'm really sorry, Luke. That's just terrible."

Wade stared out at the lake for a long time. I suppose he was trying to decide if he should run me in or not. No offense to Lyndell, but I was hoping the sad story might convince him to let me go.

When he turned back around, he appeared resolute about something. He pulled his sunglasses out of his shirt pocket and slid them over his eyes. Then, he turned and started walking back to the Crown Vic.

"Get in the cruiser," he told me.

I couldn't believe it. "Ah, come on, Wade. Don't run me in. That's not gonna help anybody out."

Wade never even looked back. "I'm not taking you in. I wanna show you something."

"Show me what?"

"Just trust me," he said. "You won't be disappointed."

We grabbed some coffee at the Waffle House, swung by Wade's place to pick up his truck, and then headed over to the Holiday Inn. Wade parked behind a trash Dumpster like we were on some sort of stakeout, never even offering a clue as to why we were there. We sat in the truck, drinking coffee and listening to the radio. George Jones was singing "Your Heart Turned Left."

Wade kept staring up at the balcony on the back side of the hotel.

"I hope this is important," I told him. "You know, I could already be in Tennessee by now."

He touched a finger to his lips and shushed me. Then he pointed across the lot to another truck, a silver Dodge W200. I immediately recognized it to be the off-duty ride of Loyd Muskgrave.

I slid low in the seat, mostly out of instinct. "What the fuck is he doing here?"

Wade took a sip of his coffee. "Just wait. You'll see."

Muskgrave stopped the truck, and a girl climbed out of the passenger door and scampered up the steps to one of the hotel rooms. I say girl because she looked to be about sixteen years old. She had curly brown hair and skinny hips. She was wearing tight jeans and a red gingham shirt.

I pushed myself back up in the seat. "Who's that?"

"Her name's Molly Tillman," Wade said. "She's a junior. I'm surprised you don't know her."

"I haven't been to school in a while."

"Anyhow, she's in charge of SOBA."

"What the hell is that?"

"It's Students Outraged by Alcohol. Muskgrave just started it this year. It's his antidrug, antialcohol program for the school system."

"I've never heard of it."

Wade shrugged. "Loyd thinks these sorts of things are gonna be big one day."

Muskgrave circled the hotel in his truck, allowing Miss Tillman time to open up the hotel room and slip inside. Finally, the sheriff parked the Dodge and stepped out into the sunshine. He was dressed in his golf-course attire, minus the spikes. His polo shirt was baby blue, same as his eyes.

"Isn't he afraid of getting caught?"

"That's just Loyd," Wade said. "The boy likes taking chances. I don't think he'd even know what to do if he didn't have some sort of mess to get himself out of."

Muskgrave bounded up the stairs. The girl must have left the chain lock wedged into the door so that he could let himself inside.

Wade filled me in on the particulars, how Muskgrave had a deal with one of the Holiday Inn's desk clerks, a woman whose husband had a towing contract with the county. She reserved a room for Muskgrave every Monday, Wednesday, and Friday, the days that Molly Tillman had early work release from the high school. They always met during Muskgrave's lunch hour, when he was supposedly at the driving range working on his six handicap.

I asked Wade how long he'd known about all of this.

"Couple of months. I got called over here because some money was missing from a room. Anyway, I saw Loyd and Molly leaving in his truck."

"Did he see you?"

"Oh, yeah. I wouldn't have thought much of it, but then he

DRIVE LIKE HELL **265**

reached over and pushed the girl's head down like he was trying to hide her."

"So, I'm guessing he brought you into his office for a little powwow."

"Yeah, we talked about it. He apologized, got all teary, said he'd been going through some pretty bad stuff with his wife. He said he was in counseling with a minister, and he just didn't want to let one weak moment ruin everything he'd worked for."

"And you believed him?"

"Hell, no. That's why I started staking the place out, checking to see if he was still seeing this girl."

"So, why haven't you turned his ass in?"

Wade let out a deep sigh, then reached over and turned off the radio.

"Selfishness, mostly. I mean, whatever flaws he might have, Loyd is a talented guy. He's a smart cop and a damn good politician. I just felt pretty certain that he'd be moving on after his next term. Going to the state capital. And I suppose I thought that if he owed me something like this, then maybe he'd throw his support behind me if I decided to run for sheriff. I guess I sort of rationalized it by thinking that I'd do a better job than him once I got into office. You know, clean things up, get rid of the scandals."

He looked away from me, plucked his sunglasses off the dash and put them on. I could tell that he felt some measure of shame, though I couldn't understand why, seeing how his goal all along had been to make things better in the end.

"So why did you bring me over here?" I asked.

"Because it's time," he said. "Enough's enough. And I don't want to see you have to go running off. You don't deserve that. Claudia doesn't deserve it, either."

We sat there a while longer, staring up at those long, neat rows of doors, numbered and painted a dark blue. It was a fairly quiet morning. A dog barked in the distance. Birds squeaked in the bushes beside the swimming pool.

My stomach ached in a hollow sort of way. I felt empty and light-headed, but it was not an unpleasant feeling. The lack of food and sleep only added to the dreaminess of what was happening. After all of the bad news, I finally saw a way out. I could feel myself nearing the surface of something.

"I'm guessing you'll be able to handle things," Wade said.

"What makes you think that?"

Wade smiled a little. "Well, you have been known to bust into hotel rooms unannounced."

Neither of us had to say another word. Wade started the truck and dropped it into gear. Just as we had taken our place among the other motorists, the people out running errands and taking their lunch breaks, I remembered something that I'd meant to tell him.

"He wasn't driving, you know."

Wade glanced in my direction. "Who wasn't driving?"

"Lyndell. He wasn't driving the car."

33

I headed out that night to pick up the two items that I would need come Wednesday morning. One of them was Nick's camera. I grabbed the Nikon out of his closet and then swung by the Holiday Inn to talk to Stan.

"So, you're saying the sheriff has got my picture on the wall of his office?"

Stan was sitting in the front of the hearse with me, working on a Pabst Blue Ribbon and looking scared.

"Not just yours," I told him. "Muskgrave's got a lot of pictures on his wall. He's gonna haul in a bunch of people if somebody doesn't stop him."

Stan rolled down his window and sucked in some of the fresh air. It was past midnight, and the hotel's parking lot was almost empty.

"So what are you planning to do?" he asked.

"I can't tell you."

Stan blinked and swallowed hard. "Oh, shit. You're not gonna kill him, are you?"

"Of course I'm not gonna kill him. Do you think I'm an idiot? Let's just say that he's doing something he shouldn't be doing. And if I can dig up some hard evidence, so to speak, then we all might be in the clear."

Stan considered me for a moment. Despite the beer and the weed that we'd just polished off, he looked as sober as an astronaut.

"So what do you say?" I asked. "Will you loan it to me?"

He finally reached into his blazer pocket and pulled out the key ring. "This is the master," he said as he slid one of the little gray pass-ports off its hitching post. "You can get into any room with it."

He dropped the key into my palm, and I wrapped it up with my hand. I squeezed it tight for a few seconds, a gesture meant to assure him that I'd guard it accordingly.

My final act of preparation was to sabotage that goddamn hearse. I performed the act just down the street from Hillin's place, puncturing the radiator hose with an ice pick. This allowed me to cruise up to his garage with steam pouring out from under the hood. Seeing how Wednesday was stocking-up-on-liquor day, he was more than obliged to toss me the keys to his Chevelle.

"Keep it under eighty," he said. "Fucking thing gets squirrelly in the curves if you're not careful."

"Don't worry, I used to drive one just like it."

The Chevelle was fast and loud, just like Lyndell's. It was also blessedly stealthy, at least when compared with the hearse. I parked behind the Holiday Inn Dumpster and waited. Muskgrave and Molly Tillman showed up just past noon. They went through the same routine as before, with Muskgrave circling the hotel before parking and heading up to the room.

I waited a few minutes, then started the Chevelle and pulled around to the side staircase. I parked at the curb and left the keys in the ignition. Then I popped off the camera's lens cap and headed upstairs.

Standing in front of Muskgrave's room, I could hear Donna Summer making out with a wah-wah guitar. I could also hear Molly Tillman giggling. Assuming the show was in full swing, I carefully slid Stan's key into the lock, turned, and pushed.

The music on the clock radio was so loud they didn't notice me standing there. Molly Tillman lay atop the sheets, naked and with her eyes closed. Muskgrave was situated somewhat lower, his head between the girl's thighs, following her musical lead. From the looks of things, she enjoyed a steady disco beat.

Despite the dire circumstances that had brought me into that room, I can't say that I didn't suffer a fair amount of shame over what I was doing. In fact, I felt like a pervert. And so I tried to get things over with as soon as possible, raising the camera and calling out to my subject in the hearty voice of a school photographer.

"All right, Sheriff! Say, 'Pussy!'"

It's hard to imagine Muskgrave having not suffered some degree of whiplash. That's how fast his head popped up from the sheets. He turned and looked right into the camera, mouth agape and eyes wide open.

I fired off four shots, catching him and the girl in each frame. She was screaming and trying to cover herself with a pillow.

Muskgrave tumbled onto the floor, cussing me the whole time.

"Goddamn you, Fulmer. Give me that fucking camera."

"I'm sorry, Sheriff, but I can't do it. I already promised the negatives to Morley Safer."

I was backpedaling, Muskgrave stumbling toward me, trying to get into his pants. He finally gave up on clothing himself, chasing me out onto the balcony in nothing but his bare ass. A family who was packing their car noticed the commotion and stared up at us. When Muskgrave saw them, he dashed back into the room, allowing me plenty of time for a getaway.

I let Muskgrave sweat for a couple of days before stopping by the Justice and Administration Building to have a talk with him. He couldn't have been more accommodating, tossing a prosecutor out of his office just so he could visit with me. I settled back into the chair that I'd occupied a few weeks earlier, feeling much more at ease and in control of things.

Muskgrave shut the door and offered a weary gaze. He looked like one of those dumb-ass hunters who get lost in the woods for a few days and have to be rescued: scared, exhausted, dark circles under his eyes.

"You look like shit," I told him.

He flipped me off, but only halfheartedly. Then he sighed, walked behind the desk, and flopped back into his chair.

"What the the fuck do you want, Fulmer? Just go ahead and spill it. Get your fucking paybacks."

I found myself smiling. "Come on, Loyd. You know I'm not gonna rub your face in it." I sat back and touched my hand to my mouth. "I'm sorry, that was a poor choice of words."

Muskgrave smirked. "That's very funny, Fulmer. You oughta take that shit on the fucking *Gong Show.*"

He pulled a bottle of Tylenol from his desk drawer and downed a couple of pills with a Tab. "So, where are the pictures?"

"You mean the originals, or the copies? Because I went ahead and got two sets. It's pretty easy these days. Did you know they're developing film at Eckerd's?"

I was lying out of my ass. Not about Eckerd's but about there being originals and duplicates. Somehow, I'd managed to load the film the wrong way. The entire roll had been ruined.

Muskgrave rubbed his temples. "Just get to the fucking point."

I leaned forward and set my hands on his desk. "I'm not gonna blackmail you. All I want is for you to back off Nick and Rachel. And me, too, while you're at it."

"Fine, it's done. But let me tell you this. I've got nothing to do with how this shit goes down for Nick. That's in the hands of the Feds."

"What are they gonna do?"

Muskgrave turned his head and stared out the window. "Hell, I don't know. They don't tell me anything."

"Bullshit. Now tell me what's going down, or I'll send those fucking pictures to the *Gazette.*"

He gave me a long, pained look. This was about as pleasant as having a pole shoved up his ass. He checked the door, then leaned forward.

"Sosebee's been talking to the Feds, giving up names left and right. That's why he's out on bail right now. He told them about a guy in Florida, a concert and wrestling promoter who owns some radio stations. His name's Whitlaw, and they say he's shipping in all this coke from Central America and parceling it out to four states. He's been laundering the money through his other businesses. From what I hear, they're gonna move on this guy in the next few days."

"You mean a bust?"

"I mean a megabust. So if Nick's down in Florida, then he better get the hell out."

That pretty much cemented my next move. I was done with Muskgrave, so I stood up and headed for the door. Before I could reach the hallway, he called out to me.

"It was Briggs, wasn't it?"

I stopped and looked back. I told him I didn't know what he was talking about.

Muskgrave's face had gone slack with resignation. "Don't worry,

I'm not gonna hold it against him. Any other asshole would have black-mailed me from the get-go."

"Like I said, I don't know what you're talking about. But now that you mention Wade, maybe you oughta consider backing him for sheriff when you leave office. I mean, that's just my opinion."

Muskgrave swallowed hard. "Maybe I'll do that."

I reached for the doorknob, but he called out one last time.

"Say, Fulmer. You didn't really take that film to Eckerd's, did you?"

34

Cash, Dewey, and I knew exactly where to locate Chuck Sosebee on a sunny Friday afternoon. We piled into the Chevelle and took a ride over to the Green Lake Municipal Golf Course. Cash had bailed their starter out of jail once on a public urination charge, so the tall guy in the Crimson Tide cap was more than happy to loan us a cart and inform us that Chuck had, in fact, teed off about an hour earlier.

"Is he on the loose for something?" the starter asked.

Cash smiled. "Not for long, he ain't."

"Well, just try to stay off my new greens," he said. "I got some Bermuda number-six out there I'm trying to nurse along."

Cash gave the man our assurances, which weren't exactly worth a handful of wooden tees, and then we headed off to find Chuck.

I drove the cart, Cash rode shotgun, and Dewey stood on the back like a fireman. The two of them kept an eye out for Chuck while I negotiated the cart path.

The course was practically empty, despite the nice weather. We were on the third hole before we even came across a group of players. It was a foursome, all of them scattered along the edges of the fairway. They were older men, dressed in bright sweaters and sun visors, taking turns flailing away at their Titleists, spraying the air with faded, brittle blades of grass.

Dewey finally spotted Chuck on the seventh fairway. It was a par-four with a slight dogleg to the right. From the looks of things, Chuck had sliced his tee shot into the rough. He was sitting about 180 from the pin, and he was playing all alone.

"Rat, ho!" Dewey hollered.

I veered off the cart path and onto the bumpy fairway.

"Look at that asshole," I said. "Strutting around out here like he's Tom fuckin' Weiskopf."

Cash grunted. "Somebody oughta put a five-iron up his ass."

Chuck was standing in front of his cart, three-iron in hand, eyeing the green as though he had a shot at it. He was wearing his red V-neck with the sleeves pushed up to his elbows. The sweater made for an awfully inviting target.

Chuck had just begun his backswing when he noticed us bearing down on him. He jerked his head around like a startled deer, freezing for a second before making a dash for his own buggy. He dropped his iron on the turf and laid the pedal to the floor.

We raced him up the seventh fairway, across the green and back onto the path at the eighth tee box. He had us by about two cart lengths at the start, but I closed it to nothing with some nifty driving around the hairpin at the tee box. I gave his rear bumper a love tap coming out of the turn, but I couldn't keep the pace when the cart path straightened.

Cash jerked his thumb back over his shoulder. "We've got too damn much weight on the back. Dewey's slowing us down."

"So, tell him to hop off. We'll come back for him."

Cash leaned out the side of the cart. "Jump the hell off," he hollered. "We'll come back and get you."

"Hell, no," Dewey said. "I ain't gonna break my fucking leg."

Cash leaned out farther and tried to push Dewey off the back. Failing at this, he ducked back inside. "Motherfucker's got a kung fu grip on the back of this thing."

"Well, I can't stop and let him off. Hell, we'll never catch him as it is."

Chuck had opened up a comfortable lead. He was nearing the eighth green and another hairpin around the ninth box.

"Fuck this," I said. "Y'all better hold on."

I swerved across the tee box. The foursome on deck, all of them white-haired gents in double-knits and wool sweaters, scampered for cover like a pack of arthritic dogs. The move also got rid of Dewey. When I glanced back, he was rolling across the turf like Mannix.

We T-boned Chuck as he was coming out of the turn. He never even saw us coming. I nailed him on the driver's side of the cart. Chuck let out a gasp and fell sideways across the seat. His cart veered off the path and pitched over onto its side. If it had been gas-powered, it probably would have burst into flames.

The foursome at the tee started hollering like they'd just witnessed a train wreck. I even heard one of them cussing me. "That goddamn, cowboyin' sonuvabitch!"

I clamped down the emergency brake, then Cash and I hopped out to have our talk with Chuck. His cart lay in the grass with a new set of MacGregor wing-backs scattered around the perimeter. The clubs looked like a spilled box of matchsticks. Cash grabbed a seven-iron and waggled it in front of him.

"Sweet, sweet balance," he said. "I gotta get me some of these motherfuckers."

Chuck's head popped out of the wreckage. He looked like a jack-in-the-box who'd just suffered an ass beating. There was a cut over his right eye and blood trickling down the side of his face. When he saw me step toward him he raised a white FootJoy over his head like it was a mace.

"Drop the shoe, Chuck. We just wanna have a little talk."

Of course he flung the shoe at me as soon as I'd gotten the words out of my mouth. The spikes hit me in the forearm just as I raised it to guard my face.

"Oww! Goddammit, Chuck! Those things are sharp. Now cut it out."

I reached out to help pull him from the wreckage. But when I got close enough, he whacked me across the back of the hand with the other shoe.

I grabbed my hand. "Fuck! What is your problem, dickhead?"

Before I could even ask for it, Cash handed me the seven-iron. It really was a nice club, chamois grip and everything. Cash was holding the sand wedge. We drew back our sticks to let Chuck know that we hadn't come to fuck around.

Chuck studied us for a moment. Finally, realizing he was outgunned, he pitched the shoe onto the path and held his hands up in the air.

"Go ahead and kill me," he said. "I deserve it. I just can't live like this anymore. It's too much. I can't sleep. I can't eat. I can't even get a hard-on anymore."

Cash laughed. "From the looks of that lie you were playing back there, you still can't hit your driver worth a damn, either."

Chuck buried his face in his hands and started sobbing.

"Is he fucking crying?" Cash asked. He stepped back as though someone were puking in the vicinity of his Converse Pros.

"We don't want to kill you," I told Chuck. "We just want to talk. Now quit crying. People are starting to stare."

In fact, the four guys we'd almost bumper-stunned were standing around us like a viewing gallery. One of the geezers was even threatening to find the course marshal and call an ambulance for Dewey and Chuck.

About that time, Dewey hobbled up to the wreckage. He assured the foursome that he was all right. "We're with the Green Lake Police investigative unit," he explained. "Undercover division."

The group appeared skeptical until Cash whipped out a phony badge and explained that we really were there on police business and that Chuck was a mentally disturbed fugitive. Seeing how he was crying and throwing shoes all over the place, it was a pretty easy sell.

"You gentlemen just go on back to your golf," Cash said. "Save your energy for the back nine. You're gonna need it on that par-five seventeen."

The old guys got a chuckle out of that. A couple of them pondered Chuck one last time, and then headed back to the tee box. The straggler of the bunch, a bandy-legged fellow with wisps of white hair sticking out the sides of his baseball cap, went so far as to give me the thumbs-up.

"Helluva crash," he said. "Looked like a Joey Chitwood move."

We helped Chuck out of the cart and set him in the grass beside the cart path. He was gashed up pretty bad, his elbows bleeding and his khaki pants ripped at the knees. Cash gave him a handkerchief for the cut on his forehead.

"I didn't want to do it," he said. "I'm not a snitch. But I've got a family to look after. I've got a wife and a little girl. I already put them through too much shit: the cocaine and the screwing around and all the money I pissed away. I didn't want my little Helena growing up and seeing her pop-pop in jail."

"Well, did you ever think that maybe Nick might wanna have kids someday?" I was standing over him with the seven-iron still very firmly in hand.

"Yeah, that's a bullshit excuse," Dewey said. "You got sloppy and got your ass caught, and now everybody else is gonna pay for it."

"Oh, God. I'm so sorry." Chuck buried his face in the handkerchief. He'd worked himself into a full-fledged sob.

"Where's Nick?" Cash asked. He was obviously growing impatient with the bawling.

Chuck blew his nose. "I honestly don't know. I haven't heard from him since those GBI goons hauled me in."

Cash took a short backswing and whacked Chuck across the ankle. Chuck yelped and fell over onto his side. "I deserved that," he sobbed. "I deserve it all, everything I've got coming to me. Just hit me again. Go ahead and put me out of my misery. Do the world a favor."

Cash dropped the club and threw his hands in the air. "That motherfucker's crazy. It ain't gonna do any good to beat on him."

Dewey frowned. "The guilt's eating him up. He knows he's done wrong."

I squatted beside Chuck. By the look in his eyes, he was somewhere else, somewhere sad and dark. He was holding his hands up against his chest, wringing them to no end.

"Listen," I told him, "you could go a long way toward making things right by telling us how to find Nick. Wouldn't that make you feel better?"

I wasn't sure he'd even heard me. But then he started mumbling. "I wish I could feel better. Oh, God, I wish I could feel better."

"You just fucked up," I said. "And nobody's gonna blame you for trying to stay out of jail for your kid's sake. But you can still help Nick. They're getting ready to move on this ring. Now, all I need to know is where I can find Nick in Pensacola. We need to get him out of there."

I helped Chuck sit up again. He sniffed and wiped at his nose, trying his best to get himself under control.

"The Sandbar Deluxe," he said. "That's where we always stay down there. It's a motel across from the beach. If Nick's in town, you'll find him there."

Cash had already whipped out his pen. He was writing the name of the motel on the back of a scorecard.

"But listen," Chuck said. "This guy Whitlaw is nobody you wanna fuck with. He's a bad dude."

Cash chuckled. "Well, I guess he won't be too happy when he hears you've been running your mouth to the Feds."

Chuck swallowed hard then pulled out his wallet and showed us a photo of his six-year-old daughter. It was a school shot of her, dark pigtails and a gap-toothed smile, dressed in a little plaid jumper from the Four Loaves Christian Academy.

"She never asked to be a part of this," Chuck said. "She's just a little girl. She's the only innocent one involved in all of this. That's why I had to do it. For her."

Cash laughed. "She'll find out soon enough. She'll find out what kind of man you are. Kids always do. And you know why?"

We all waited for him to answer his own question.

"Because you ain't ever gonna change, that's why."

Chuck shook his head. "That's not true. If this hasn't changed me, nothing ever will. I want to be a good father and a good husband. I realized that's all that matters. It's the only thing that matters in this whole world. When I was sitting in that cell, all I wanted was to hold my little girl. All the other shit, the cars and planes and drugs, that didn't mean a thing."

Cash smirked. "People like you always say that shit when they got their ass in a sling. But you just wait until things get better. You'll start getting that itch again. You'll start wondering, Who the fuck is Chuck Sosebee? And pretty soon you'll be putting that shit up your nose again, partying around, spending money you ain't got. Man, I hear this shit every time I bail somebody's ass out of jail. And it's a tired motherfucking song and dance. If you really want to do your little girl a favor, you oughta leave right now. Leave fucking town and give her mama a chance to find a decent man."

Chuck cut his eyes my way. I think he was hoping that I'd shoot down everything Cash had just told him. But it all rang too true.

"She's a cute kid," Dewey said. "You oughta be ashamed of yourself."

I stood up. I wasn't really in the mood to help Chuck to his feet. That's not to say the sight of him didn't make me sad. I hoped his daughter never had to see her father in such a sorry state.

We climbed back in the cart to leave. As I pulled away, Chuck called out to us. I tapped the brakes and waited to hear what he had to say.

"If you guys find Nick, will you tell him I'm sorry?"

I couldn't bring myself to say anything. Finally, Cash stepped on my foot, clamping the accelerator to the floor and vaulting us back across the empty tee box.

"Man, let's just get the fuck out of here," he said.

35

We decided to wait until morning to get a start on Florida. I hated wasting any more time than was necessary, but Cash had a bond hearing, Dewey a court-mandated defensive-driving class, and Hillin had been paging me all afternoon.

After making a drugstore run for T-Bone Rex, I asked if I could keep the Chevelle for a brief excursion. I lied and told him I'd been planning a beach getaway with a girl I'd met. I knew that he'd never stand in the way of a man's opportunity to get laid. "Screwing," he once said, "is about as sacred an act as God ever contemplated." This was during the same conversation in which I'd asked him to recount the number-one highlight of his football career. His response, after careful deliberation: "Fucking half the Sigma Nu sorority in 1945."

"Don't buy any cheap rubbers," he warned as I turned around in the driveway, ready to leave him there with his Percocet and mangled knees. I could still see him in the rearview mirror, watching me crunch my way down the long gravel driveway, unsmiling, his reflection so small, just like the TV characters who would keep him company after I disappeared.

I spent another night on Cash's boat, lying beneath the chalky moon, my thoughts jumping around with every slap of water against the dock, from Lyndell to Claudia to Nick to Rachel. At some point, I let them all go. And then I was dreaming, treading water, bodies floating all around me, facedown. I'd turn them over, looking for someone I knew, someone I could drag to shore, but their faces were all the same, with the same long hair and stupid sneer and stupid eyes. It's not like I didn't recognize the mug. God knows, it had stared back at me plenty of times: from Muskgrave's bulletin board and, for the briefest amount of time, from the front of my driver's license. The thing was, it just didn't seem to be worth saving.

I drove to Claudia's house early the next morning. Even as I turned down her street, I told myself that I wasn't going to stop, wasn't going to ask about Lyndell.

Needless to say, I was surprised to find Wade's truck parked in front of her house at 7 A.M. I went ahead and let myself in, stopping my forward progress almost as soon as I'd walked through the carport door. The kitchen was still dark, the house quiet except for the hum of the air-conditioning. The evidence lay there in abundance: an empty bottle of Smirnoff standing atop the counter, a dead carton of Tropicana lying beside it. Cigarettes littered the kitchen table ashtray. Only half of them wore lipstick rings.

I reached back for the doorknob, as much to steady myself as to make an escape. I could feel my heart swelling up, beginning to pound a little faster. And then I heard a stirring in the den, Claudia stumbling through, on her way to cook the Maxwell House. She started as a shadow, a shadow in a bathrobe, her hair mussed and her makeup dulled.

When she saw me, she gasped. She stepped back and laid her hand to her chest. Her mouth dropped open to form a perfect little O.

"I didn't hear you come in."

"Oh, Lord," I said. "Tell me you didn't."

She cast her gaze to the floor, walked over to the counter, and pulled the coffee can down from the cabinet.

"It's true," she said. "I got him drunk. He came over yesterday and tried to get me to go to AA with him, but I got him drunk instead. He stayed the night."

"You mean to sleep it off, or to sleep with you?"

She switched on the coffeepot, turned back around, and faced me. She was frowning.

"Oh, shit." I let go of the doorknob and took a seat at the kitchen table. Claudia sat down across from me. She fired up a Slim and tossed the pack onto the table.

"How did you do it?" I asked. "I mean, he came over here with good intentions."

She paused, blew out a cloud of smoke. "I guess we were both tired of the bullshit. I don't know, I guess it was inevitable."

"But how the hell did you talk him into drinking? The man hasn't taken a drink in two years. He's like the Lou Gehrig of AA meetings."

"Believe me, it didn't take a lot of encouraging. And it wasn't pretty either. You see a lot of truth in a person when they're drinking, a lot of stuff they try to hide otherwise. I guess that was one of the good things about Lyndell. He wasn't hiding a thing."

And there it was. She'd mentioned his name before I'd even found a way to come around to it.

"He was drunk the day I met him." She shook her head at the memory. "Straight-up noon on a Tuesday."

It would have been easy to force her hand, but I couldn't do it. Instead, I asked about the first time she and Lyndell met. I realized that I'd never heard that story.

"I went to the garage with my cousin to pick up her car," Claudia said, "and he was out front working on this old pickup. He didn't see me standing there by the Coke machine, so he reached back in his pocket and pulled out a little whiskey bottle. Just as he was wiping his mouth, I stepped out of the shade."

"What did he say?"

"He didn't say anything. He just grinned and pressed his finger to his lips, like it was our secret. I'd never had a secret with a man before, so I thought it was about the most exciting thing that had ever happened."

Claudia went to the counter and poured her coffee. After she'd sat down again, she stared at me for a long time. It made me wonder if she understood that I already knew about Lyndell.

"He wanted all the right things," she said. "He just wanted to trade in the girl every couple of years."

"What about you?" I asked. "What did you want?"

"I wouldn't have wanted him to change," she said. "Because then he wouldn't have been Lyndell. And you wouldn't have been who you are. And Nick . . . Well, maybe I wish he could have stayed out of trouble. But that's all I'd change, really, that and I wish I could have met somebody decent after Lyndell."

I heard Wade's singing voice working its way through the house. It was a whole lot cheerier than usual. "You get a line, and I'll get a pole, and we'll go fuckin' at the crawdad hole."

Claudia laid her hand to her forehead. "Good Lord, I think he's still drunk."

Wade stepped into the kitchen doorway, buck naked, clutching a bottle of Kahlúa that Dewey had given to Claudia for her birthday. I'd never seen such a wide grin on the man's face, like he'd been possessed by the spirit of a dead rodeo clown.

When he saw me, his shit-eating grin went south. In fact, he dropped the Kahlúa bottle and screamed like he'd seen a ghost. He didn't waste any time turning tail and retreating into the den.

Claudia called out to him, her voice calm and flat, "Wade, get on some shorts and come back in here. Luke already knows."

It took him a minute. When he returned, trudging slowly, he had the bedsheet wrapped around his shoulders. From the look of things, that sheet must have felt like a hundred pounds of lead.

Claudia nudged a chair out from the table with her bare foot, and Wade took a seat between us. He sat there hunched over the coffee she'd poured him, looking timid. I was embarrassed for him. Every time our eyes met, we'd both look away.

Claudia looked as sober as I'd seen her in some time. She reached out and laid her hand atop Wade's.

"Wade, we made a mistake last night. It's not something we can undo, but we can make sure it doesn't happen again."

Wade looked up at her. "Oh, God, Claudia. Please don't say that."

"I just did."

"But I want to be with you. I'm willing to give up everything for that. I truly am."

Wade locked his eyes onto mine. I could see the hope draining out of them. He looked as tired as I'd ever seen him, like a linebacker late in a losing cause, hunched over on the sidelines with a cape around his shoulders.

"I gave it a helluva shot," he said, staring into the ashtray. "Two years, clean and sober. And it doesn't ever start to feel like you made the right choice."

He batted his eyes and sucked at his lips as though he'd just tasted something bitter. For a moment, I thought he might cry. I didn't think I could take that again, seeing two men bawl within twenty-four hours of each other. But then he got hold of himself. He took a deep breath, his hands already beginning to shake beneath the bedsheet.

"I'm gonna get my things," he told Claudia. "I'm gonna get my things and go on home."

36

We found the Sandbar Deluxe right away, down near the end of the strip, sandwiched between a go-cart track and a Hardee's. The motel was a two-story job, with aqua paint on the room doors that had faded to gray and a section of the second-floor railing patched with a pair of two-by-fours. Even the palm tree planted out front was stooped and sickly.

Dewey, Cash, and I walked inside the tiny office. The window unit blasted out a wall of cold air while *The Joker's Wild* played on a TV behind the counter. I could hear Jack Barry making his usual, almost-but-not-quite call: "Joker!—Joker!—*aaaand* a double."

The clerk manning the counter didn't bother to greet us. He wore a dark mustache and a Faster Horses, Stronger Whiskey, Looser Women ball cap. An unlit Tiparillo was clamped in his teeth, Eastwood style. He was bent over a titty magazine, reading the foldout model's bio. When I stepped to the counter, I could see that her turnoffs included "dishonest people" and "poor hygiene."

I asked the clerk if he had a Nick Fulmer on the register, but the guy never even looked up from his magazine. He simply jerked his thumb back over his shoulder.

"Check the pool," he said. "I think he's out there trying to sober up Eddie."

We walked around back and—sure enough—Nick was perched at the edge of the swimming pool in his jeans and BSA T-shirt. He stood over a large fellow in a black button-up shirt. The big guy was down in the water, draped back across the pool's steps. His head rested on the ledge, a pelt of black hair fanned out across the cement behind it.

Nick squatted and splashed water on the guy's face. "Goddammit, Eddie. Get your ass in gear. I mean it."

Eddie groaned and rolled his head from side to side. He looked like a hibernating bear slowly coming back to life. He mumbled, *"Déjanos en paz, Mamá.* I'm drunk." Then he closed his eyes and started to snore.

"I'm not your fucking mama," Nick said. "Now come on, Eddie."

I opened the rusty gate to the pool area, and Nick turned around with a start. He squinted into the fading sun. Finally, a grin spread across his face.

"Well, I'll be goddamn. It's the thrillin' threesome."

He and Cash locked paws and slapped each other's shoulders, then I gave Nick a quick hug and pat on the back. Dewey stepped up last. He grabbed hold of Nick and squeezed him tight, lifting his feet right off the pool deck. Nick finally had to tap him on the shoulder so he'd let go.

"How about putting me down, bro. I need to fucking breathe."

Nick asked how the hell we'd found him.

Cash smiled. "Let's just say your name came up on the golf course."

Nick glanced my way, expecting a real explanation. I told him the sorry tale of Chuck Sosebee.

"Chuck's a piece of work. I knew he'd cut a deal if they'd let him."

"Oh, he's been singing like Neil Diamond," Dewey said. "That's why you need to get the hell out of here."

Nick walked over to a chaise lounge and fetched his Winstons from his jacket. He lit one, sat down, and blew out a big cloud of smoke. He pointed at Eddie with the cigarette. The big guy was still sawing logs in the pool.

"Eddie used to be one of Whitlaw's wrestlers," Nick said. "We've been working together since all the shit hit the fan up there with Chuck."

"Doing what?" Dewey asked.

Nick shrugged. "Let's just call it transportation."

Cash's eyes flickered, acknowledging the craziness of the situation. "Does this Whitlaw fool even realize the Feds are getting ready to bust some serious ass?"

"He's feeling some heat," Nick said, "that's for damn sure. The

IRS has been on his ass about the books at his radio stations. The FCC even took away his broadcasting license, so he's gotta sell out. That pretty much fucked my plans."

Nick looked at me and shook his head. I took the opportunity to ask why the hell he was sticking around.

"Me and Eddie are working on some new plans." Nick pointed to his waterlogged pal. "Eddie's got a cousin out in Chula Vista. He owns a par-three course and driving range. We were thinking of cashing out with Whitlaw and heading to California, maybe going in with his cousin and opening a pro shop."

"So, go get your damn money and get the hell out of here," Cash said. "The FBI's planning to make a move on Whitlaw. They're gonna put his ass away for a long time."

Nick cocked his head, puzzled by our urgency. "How the hell do y'all know all of this?"

I told him I'd gotten it straight from the horse's mouth.

"Let me guess," Nick said. "Wade Briggs."

"Actually, it came from higher up. Muskgrave told me."

"Muskgrave? Hell, you can't trust him."

"Maybe not. But I gave him some incentive."

Nick gazed out at the street and the row of taller motels guarding the view of the ocean. He finally stood up and gave the chaise lounge a solid kick, sending it over onto its side.

"There's not a whole lot of time left," I said. "You need to get out of here tonight."

Dewey and Cash voiced their agreement. Nick considered us all for a moment, his eyes full of spite. It appeared that he was sizing us up for a fight. Instead, he gave the chaise another boot, sending it into the pool. Afterward, a warm breeze stood up and seemed to blow all his anger away. He flipped his cigarette into the bushes, pushed his hair back behind his ears, and gave the pink sky a disappointed look.

"All right," he said, "but me and Eddie have gotta get our money from Whitlaw first."

"And what might that entail?" Dewey asked.

Nick gazed down at Eddie. "For starters, he better show up for his match tonight. If he doesn't wrestle, then Whitlaw won't give us a nickel."

We all grabbed hold of Eddie and started to pull. His arms were as big around as my legs, and the skin stretched across them was nut brown and hairless. We grunted and tugged, taking small steps backward. Slowly, like a big trophy fish being hauled onto the deck of a boat, Eddie emerged from the water.

Nick and I sat on the wet concrete, catching our breaths while Dewey and Cash stood over us, marveling at the mass of flesh—at least six feet six inches and 280 pounds worth—that we'd just hauled ashore.

"Hey," Dewey said, "I know him. That's the Blue Lizard."

Nick smiled. "AKA Fast Eddie Del Canto."

"Hey, that's right." Cash grinned and backhanded Dewey's gut. "I saw him on TV, getting his ass whipped by Handsome Harley Malone."

About that time, Eddie opened his eyes. He studied me as though I'd been the one who'd mentioned the ass whipping. Then, he reached up with a hand the size of a catcher's mitt, grabbed the front of my T-shirt, and pulled me down close to his face. He wore the urgent expression of a man struggling to whisper some final words.

"I oughta be making twice as much as that sonuvabitch. Am I right?"

He appeared to be waiting for me to agree with him, but I could not recall having ever seen either him or Handsome Harley Malone in the ring.

Eddie let go of my shirt and sat up. He tucked his hair behind his ears and rolled his neck from side to side. Nick introduced us, and Eddie's jaw relaxed. He smiled and stuck out his hand again. I reluctantly offered my own. I was surprised when Eddie's handshake turned out to be soft, almost bashful.

"Nice to meet you guys," he said.

Nick let out a sigh and set his hand on Eddie's shoulder. "I'm afraid I've got some bad news, buddy."

He laid it all on Eddie. The big man's response was a simple one.

"I need a drink."

37

Nick was planning to talk money with Whitlaw during the wrestling, so we gave him and Eddie a ride to the high school gym where the North Central Florida Wrestling Alliance's Red White and Blue Heroes Caravan was making its weekly stop.

Eddie climbed into the Chevelle wearing the same black slacks and shirt that he'd been soaking in earlier. Much to Nick's dismay, he was also nipping at a half pint of Bacardi.

"Please don't get too drunk to wrestle," Nick said.

"Ain't no sweat," Eddie said. "I wouldn't even go so far as to call it wrestling. It's a fucking travesty, is what it is."

Eddie was sitting in the backseat, between Dewey and Nick. The two of them were pressed up against the door. Eddie was talking about the old days, waving his hands around.

"It was ballet inside a ring. There weren't any of these gimmicks. None of the bullshit that Whitlaw peddles. That man should be collecting golf balls at a fucking driving range. He's an imbecile."

"Eddie, you've got no cartilage in your left knee," Nick said. "You can't bounce around out there like Lynn Swann anymore. You needed a gimmick."

Eddie nodded thoughtfully. He was nothing if not a thoughtful drunk.

"I'm glad this is the end," he said. "Let's just get some money and get the fuck out of here. It's time I made some changes."

"That's a good attitude," Nick said. "Just play it cool tonight, so we can settle up."

Nick reached over and tried to straighten Eddie's shirt. The effort didn't help much. Eddie still looked a wreck, water squishing around in his shoes as he walked through the back door of the gym.

There were a handful of wrestlers in the cramped locker room, dressed in their tights and shiny boots. Two of them sat on a bench sharing a Kool, while another talked on the pay phone about the greyhound races. They all took pause when Eddie walked in. The two with the cigarette made faces like their dinners had not agreed with them. The guy on the phone shook his head like he'd just heard some sad news.

Whitlaw swept into the locker room right behind us. He was short and plump, with the swagger of a little bulldog, and he was wearing a red-white-and-blue warm-up suit. He looked to be about fifty, with puffy circles under his eyes and a glossy black rug atop his head. The piece was one of those pompadour-in-front, floormat-in-the-back jobs. It looked like something he'd stolen off a Jack Lord wax statue.

Whitlaw grabbed Eddie by the shoulders and steered him toward a locker. Then he stumped back over to Nick in a fit of anger. He stood on his tiptoes and got right up in Nick's face.

"What the hell is going on with him? I thought you were looking after his sorry ass."

"I can't watch him every second," Nick said. "Besides, he's upset about something. You know how he gets."

"Yeah, I know too damn well," Whitlaw said. "He just better not pull any shit tonight."

Whitlaw gazed over Nick's shoulder, finally taking notice of me, Cash, and Dewey. He gave us the skunk eye and led Nick over to a private corner of the dressing room, where they began to talk.

We left Nick and Whitlaw alone and walked out to the crowded gym. The locals were on their feet, whistles and catcalls echoing off the cinder-block walls. The smell of popcorn and sweat hung in the air. We stood in back against the wall and waited for Nick while a couple of bruisers flopped around the ring like tunas. Needless to say, we weren't very interested in the turnbuckle mayhem.

"That asshole Whitlaw ain't gonna give them a fucking dime," Dewey said. "He's gonna smell a rat the minute they ask."

Cash agreed. "No offense, Luke, but your brother doesn't have the best instincts for this kind of shit. That's why he's already been to jail twice."

There was no disputing the scouting report. I told them I didn't know how the hell to get Nick out of there before he fucked things up. "Maybe we should just tie him up and throw him in the trunk of the car."

I'd always attributed Nick's legal disasters to other people's short-comings: Bev, Chuck, his bumbling defense attorneys, the guy who'd turned state's witness after Nick's first marijuana bust. I'd never really considered that the one constant in every case, the very straw that stirred each bitter drink, had been Nick himself.

"That's not a bad idea," Cash said. "If you and Dewey can hold him down, I'll hog-tie him. We'll just put his ass in the trunk and drive. Trust me, it's for his own good."

Dewey was on board as well. "We're all gonna end up in jail if we follow him and that drunk wrestler. All that talk about going into business, starting a pro shop . . . Man, Nick's just talking off his head. This shit's gonna end bad."

They left the decision to me. But in the end, I just couldn't sign the dotted line. Maybe I did know what was best for Nick, maybe I had the better instincts, a better sense of when to flee and when to cut bait on a doomed plan. But I couldn't see that any of it had gotten me much of anywhere. At least Nick had the balls to keep throwing shit at the wall, hoping something would stick. And besides, tossing him in the trunk of the car would have been as raw a betrayal as turning him over to Muskgrave. It just wasn't something a brother should do.

"Let's give him a chance," I said. "Maybe he knows what he's doing."

Their grim faces offered little reassurance, but neither of them said a word.

"Of course, maybe we should have a signal," I said. "If he gets us into anything that's looking dicey, I'll flash a sign and we'll put him in the trunk."

Cash agreed. "Don't even worry about a signal. Just say it. It won't matter one way or the other, once we get started. And he damn sure isn't gonna like it any better if we've got some kind of signal."

Nick finally joined us in the gymnasium. His expression made it obvious that things had not gone well with the boss.

"Apparently, Whitlaw knows something's coming down. I think he's getting ready to hightail it out of here."

"Did he tell you that?" I asked.

"No, I heard it from the Masked Stallion. He said Whitlaw's planning to fly his plane to Cabo tomorrow. He's taking a couple of his bodyguards with him but leaving everybody else here to cover their own asses. A lot of folks are planning to hit the road tonight."

"So, what about your money?" Dewey asked. "Is he gonna pay you?"

Nick mimed jerking off. "He said we could talk about it tomorrow."

"All right, then," Cash said. "That pretty much settles things. You gave it a shot, now let's get the fuck out of here."

Nick drew in a deep breath and looked at the floor. "I can still get the money. In fact, I can get it tonight."

"How?" I asked.

"Whitlaw keeps a load at his condo over in Destin. He's got a safe right behind his LeRoy Neiman. He digs into it every time he goes to the dog track."

Dewey rubbed his chin. "I didn't come down here to pull off a damn heist."

"Are you talking about breaking and entering?" I asked.

"Of course not," Nick said. "We'll just walk in there and ask for our money."

"You just asked," Cash said. "The man's answer was *mañana*."

Nick smiled. "I know that. But I didn't have you guys with me when I was asking. There's something to be said for strength in numbers."

"Yeah," I said, "and there's also something to be said for drug dealers with bodyguards."

Nick snorted. "You watch too damn much television. Trust me, Whitlaw's more amateur than you think. It doesn't take a genius to go into this business."

Dewey and Cash eyed me, but I couldn't bring myself to give the signal. Our debate was cut short by the PA system, which was blaring "I Love the Nightlife" through the gymnasium.

The announcer cut in to introduce the next match. The Panhandle Midget Championship Belt was up for grabs, with Little Dick Hoover facing off against Bawlin' Baby Briscoe.

Nick shushed us and pointed to the ring. "This is Eddie's match. You gotta see this."

"Eddie's not a midget," I said.

Nick merely grinned. "Just wait, you'll see."

Little Dick entered the ring first. He wasn't a midget either, just a short guy with a fake handlebar mustache and a wardrobe consisting of black skivvies and knee-high boots. Nick informed me that Little Dick also wrestled in the regular-size matches under the name Smiling Richard Long.

"He's got a pair of boots with lifts in 'em," Nick said. "He's about five-four when he wears those."

I asked Nick where in hell someone might go to buy platform wrestling boots.

"Oh, they're custom-made in Tallahassee. He buys them from the same guy who makes Burt Reynolds's lifts."

Baby Briscoe was shorter and plumper than Little Dick and swaddled in a diaper and blue bonnet. He entered the squared circle clutching a huge nippled milk bottle and a powder blue blanket, both of which were quickly snatched away by Little Dick. Baby Briscoe was brokenhearted over the matter. He burst into tears and started stomping his feet.

The crowd was in full throat over the dispute, everyone on their feet, screaming and waving their fists over their heads. They felt that Baby Briscoe should put a serious ass-beating on Little Dick.

Little Dick ripped the blanket in two right there in the middle of the ring. Baby was on the mat kicking and squalling.

The crowd was giving Little Dick some serious grief. He finally held up his hands to quiet them down. He apologized to the referee and let his shoulders slump in a gesture of regret and pure shame. Then he whipped another goody out of his drawers: a baby rattle. He approached Baby Briscoe, holding out the rattle as a peace offering. The crowd urged Baby not to fall for the trick. A man screamed, "Don't do it, Baby! He's gonna lay your ass out!"

Even amid the chorus of no's, Baby started grinning, seemingly hypnotized by the rattler. He stuck his thumb in his mouth, reached out for the rattle, and—

WHAM. Little Dick sucker-punched him in the gut, stomping his foot against the mat for added effect. That's when the no's turned to boos.

Dewey shuddered at Little Dick's antics. "Damn," he said, "that is some cold shit."

Cash just shook his head and frowned. He looked like he was watching one of those *60 Minutes* stories on child abuse.

Little Dick turned Baby over his knee and spanked him open-hand style. Baby was squalling, and the crowd was chanting something I couldn't quite make out.

I asked Nick what they were yelling.

"They're calling for Mama," Nick said.

"Who's Mama?"

He pointed to the locker room door and smiled. As if on cue, a large male wrestler, wearing a sundress and gray wig, burst through the door with a folding chair in his hands. Even in the Easter-morning getup, there was no mistaking Eddie.

The crowd chanted: "Ma-ma! Ma-ma! Ma-ma!" And Mama did not disappoint them. Eddie jumped into the ring and busted Little Dick's head with the chair. Then, with his pride and joy's nemesis down for the count, he picked up Baby Briscoe and toted him over to the ring mike, whereupon he asked if Baby had anything to tell the fans. Baby leaned into the mike and grinned.

"Baby go poopee."

Joyful bedlam took hold of the gym.

"That was some sick shit," Cash said. "It's no wonder Eddie has to get drunk to do that."

"I'd get drunk, too," Dewey said. "Who'd even think of something like that?"

Nick told them to shut up. "It's just show business, fellas."

38

Nick and I were alone in the motel parking lot, loading his and Eddie's belongings into the trunk of his Fury. Two suitcases, a set of golf clubs, a folding beach chair, and a pawnshop guitar. When you got right down to it, he and Eddie didn't have a whole lot between them.

There was also a photo album among the pile of stuff.

"Hey, I didn't know you brought any of your pictures with you."

Nick looked sort of embarrassed, so I resisted the urge to check out the photos. I handed over the album, and he tucked it into the trunk.

And then I remembered. I hadn't even told Nick about Lyndell. It hadn't even dawned on me since we'd gotten there. And that made me feel all the worse for Lyndell, how easy it was to forget someone.

It was a balmy evening, the breeze heavy with that salty beach smell. Cash, Dewey, and Eddie were still up in the room, checking to see if anything had been left behind. Nick leaned against the Fury and fired up a joint. He took a deep toke and passed it over. I held it for a moment, not sure of how to proceed.

"What about your policy?" I asked.

Nick made a quiet, satisfied groan deep in his throat and blew the smoke out into the night air.

"Fuck the policy," he said. "I know you smoke like a fiend."

I obliged his wishes and had a go at the joint. It had a sharp, ropy taste to it. If Nick was smoking the stuff, I knew it must be high-grade weed.

"There's something I meant to tell you when I got here."

Nick was about to take another toke, but he stopped and lowered the joint from his mouth. "Is Claudia okay?"

"Sort of," I said. "But it's not about her, really. It's about Lyndell. He died last winter in a car wreck."

Nick turned my way and cocked his head strangely, as if he needed to regard me from a different angle. All he said was "Fuck." His voice was faint, pinched by the smoke.

I felt like I should say something else, but only one thing came to mind. "He wasn't driving. It was somebody else's fault."

Nick wiped his hand across his mouth and blew out a deep breath. He looked like he might throw up. All the while, the joint burned away in his hand.

"Well, why didn't somebody tell us before now?"

I shrugged. "Claudia knew about it. She found out not long after he died, but she didn't say anything."

"Why?"

"I don't know. I couldn't bring myself to ask her."

Nick finally took notice of the joint. He flipped it out into the parking lot. Its tiny orange tip glowed beneath the rear bumper of a Cutlass.

"I just saw him last year," he said. And then he waved his hand through the air. "Ah, fuck, Luke. I went looking for him."

"What are you talking about?"

He was pacing back and forth on the asphalt. "I mean, I didn't bump into him accidentally. I made that shit up. I went looking for him. I called him up, invited myself over. Fuck, I guess I missed him."

"Well, why didn't you tell me that?"

Nick had his hands in his pockets, staring at the ground. "I don't know. I guess I didn't think you'd understand. Claudia was giving me the cold shoulder. Hell, she'd hardly even talk to me. I just wanted to see him again, you know."

"Well, hell yeah, I know."

He asked for the details. I told him everything I knew. I told him about Claudia and Wade as well. He asked about me and Rachel. By the time I'd finished with all of the bad news, Nick had nearly polished off a pack of Winstons. He was leaning against the trunk of the car, smoking and shaking his head.

"Damn," he said, "it sure doesn't take long for things to go to hell."

We both cast our gazes upward. The rest of the gang had just stepped out onto the motel balcony. They were about to shut the door and head downstairs.

"Listen," I told Nick, "why don't we forget this money thing. Maybe you and Eddie should just head on out to California. I've got some cash I was saving for Illinois. I don't need it anymore. It's only about six hundred dollars, but it'll help a little."

"Jesus, I can't take your fucking money."

"But I don't need it anymore. I'd rather you have it, so you can get out of here."

He studied my face, as if there was something different about me that he couldn't quite identify. "You don't think I'm gonna slip out of this one, do you?"

As hard as I tried to fight the impulse, I couldn't help looking away from him. "It's not that I don't—"

"Tell me this," he said. "And be honest. You thought a lot more of me before you moved in, didn't you?"

"It's not that."

Nick sighed. "Then tell me," he said, "what did you learn from living with me? Just tell me one useful thing."

The rest of the crew was milling around the motel snack machine, banging on the glass, trying to get a bag of Chuckles to drop. And I couldn't think of one damn thing that I'd learned from Nick.

"It's all about tempo," I finally said.

Nick laughed a little. "That's good," he said. "That's a good one."

And then he stopped laughing, looking me over again as if to confirm his worst fears. "It ain't very useful, though."

"It has its place," I said.

Nick fired up another Winston, took a long puff, and stared at the street. We could hear the ocean waves crashing on the other side of the tall motels.

"Bev was right," he said, "and I couldn't even see it."

"About what?"

"Our lives," he said. "She used to try to tell me that these were our salad days. And then I'd always tell her that I didn't like salads."

The wind picked up and beat his hair down over his eyes. He stood there with his jaw set like he was trying to convince himself of something. "I was always kicking myself in the ass, wishing I'd done something different with my life. Gone to school, or something like that. I didn't think any of that other shit mattered: you know, dealing and playing in a half-assed band, fighting with Bev every day."

"Well, maybe things are gonna get better when you get to California."

Nick looked up at me, his face a mask of regret. "The joke's on me," he said. "And you know why?"

I waited for his answer.

"It's on me because all of that stuff really does matter. And I miss the shit out of it. I've missed it since the day I left Green Lake. It's like I had a motorcycle wreck and lost my leg or something. I wake up every morning thinking it's still there, and then it's not."

He pushed himself away from the car and stared off across the parking lot. The chain on his belt swung sadly by his side. "I just want to go back home."

He was standing in the breeze now, and I could smell the cigarette smoke and the leather jacket. It was like walking into his house again after he'd left town.

"Poor fuckin' Lyndell," he said.

Dewey, Cash, and Eddie had finally captured the bag of Chuckles. They were walking across the parking lot, looting the bag of candy.

Nick turned and faced me again, scratching his cheek as if he was trying to remember something.

"I think you oughta call that girl," he said. "Even if nothing changes, you oughta call her again."

"And say what?"

Nick shrugged. "You'll know what to say when the time comes."

I found myself wondering what Rachel might be doing that very moment. I could see her shuttling salads out of Yuri's kitchen and then sitting alone in the Peugeot during her break, watching TV later on that sofa in the living room, Brute snoring away beside her. And I'd never felt so far away from where I really wanted to be in my entire life.

39

Whitlaw's condo was perched way up on the nineteenth floor of a beachside high-rise. I double-parked the Chevelle in the turnaround out front, just behind Nick's Fury, and then we all headed upstairs, armed with nothing more than foolishness and Nick's shooting wedge, which he'd stuffed into the back of his jeans.

As soon as we stepped off the elevator, we could hear the music coming from Whitlaw's place. It was one of those Jimmy Buffett rum-and-sand songs.

"All right," Nick said, "y'all just stand behind us looking serious. Let me and Eddie do the talking."

Dewey glanced up and down the hallway uneasily. It appeared that he'd completely lost his already faint appetite for adventure. "You sure you don't need somebody to wait in the car, maybe keep the engine running?"

Nick reached out and massaged Dewey's shoulders. "We're gonna be out of here in ten minutes, bro. I already told you, this guy's no criminal genius. He ain't Cesar Romero."

"What if some shit starts up?" Cash asked. "You flash that pellet gun, and we're all gonna get killed."

"Relax," Nick said, "have some fucking faith. I'm not planning on using the shooting wedge. It's only for persuasion purposes, if it comes to that. I can reason with Whitlaw. We've done a lot of business together."

Nick looked my way, as if to make sure I wasn't going to voice any doubts. I wouldn't have even known where to begin.

The door to Whitlaw's condo was open a crack, so we walked right in, Nick and Eddie leading the pack. The condo's interior stood in sharp contrast to the building's sober and dignified hallway. I suppose Whitlaw's decorating style could best be described as early Hefner, with leather furniture, nude sculptures, and furry white rugs. We found Whitlaw parked on a white leather sofa with a gin and tonic in hand. He'd traded his red-white-and-blue warm-up suit for a solid white model and a matching pair of Gucci loafers, sans hosiery. He'd set off the whole ensemble with a gold medallion that resembled a sundial.

"Hello, Caligula," Dewey muttered.

A blonde-haired girl with a certain stripper aura about her was snuggled up to Whitlaw, nuzzling his jowls, while he peeked down the front of her blouse, chuckling at his good fortune. The LeRoy Neiman painting Nick had mentioned hung right above the love birds' nest. Its canvas was a jumble of color splashes that looked like Secretariat thundering down the backstretch all alone at the Belmont Stakes.

A couple of the wrestlers we'd seen back in Pensacola were also at the condo. One of them was a big guy whose ring name had been Captain Love. The other wrestler in attendance was none other than Little Dick Hoover, minus the mustache.

The wrestlers were dancing across the white carpet with another pair of blonde girls who looked like they probably worked at the same club as Whitlaw's sugar pot. All in all, they were not an intimidating crew, and my confidence in Nick rose just a bit.

Of course, the dancing stopped as soon as we walked in. Whitlaw pushed the girl aside, sat up straight, and slammed his drink down on the glass coffee table. He waved his hand at Captain Love, and the big man walked over to the stereo and mercifully killed the Buffett.

"Have you two got shit between your ears?" Whitlaw asked. "I thought I told you we'd talk tomorrow."

"We've come for our wages." Eddie spoke in a measured and reasonable tone. "It can't wait until tomorrow."

Whitlaw shook his head like his initial anger had been nothing but sawdust caught in his wig. He plucked his drink off the table, playfully jiggled the ice, and stood up. He was smiling, and he appeared very much at ease. It was a posture that left me feeling a bit anxious.

"Why can't it wait, Eddie? What's your big hurry? You planning on going somewhere?"

Nick pointed at Whitlaw. "Maybe we think you're planning on going somewhere."

"Oh, really? And where might I be heading, Mr. Travel Agent?"

"Cabo San Lucas," Nick said. "And I don't think you're planning on coming back."

Whitlaw's smile shriveled. He ran his hand across his chin and studied the five of us. For the first time, he appeared mildly concerned. He took another swallow of his drink. The gin seemed to stoke his agitation.

"Goddamn that little half-assed Delta pilot. You told me he knew what the fuck he was doing."

"We both took a chance," Nick said. "Who else was willing to make those flights? I didn't see people lining up at your door."

Dewey, Cash, and I were parked in our designated spot, directly behind Nick and Eddie and just at the edge of the foyer. I felt Dewey tug on the back of my shirt, so I turned to see what was so important. He gestured toward the walls of the entryway. They were covered with framed photos of Whitlaw standing beside famous country musicians. Hank, Junior. Freddy Fender. Charlie Pride. Loretta. It was like a music hall of fame.

Of course, the photos only served to complement the two guitars propped up on stands beside the wall. They were both acoustic models, one a Gibson autographed by Willie Nelson, the other a Martin signed by the Gambler himself, Kenny Rogers.

Dewey whispered, "He knows everybody in Nashville."

"You know what they say in that commercial," I told him. "A toupee can change your life."

Eddie, Nick, and Whitlaw were still arguing about the money.

"We don't care if you're beating feet out of here," Eddie said. "We don't blame you. All we want is the eight grand you owe us."

"Eight grand?" Whitlaw pretended to be flabbergasted. "Just how do you figure I owe you that much? What about all those pills I give you, Eddie? Do you think I get those for free? You come to me nearly every damn day wanting something. There ain't a doctor in Florida that would give you so much as a Bayer aspirin anymore. Hell, you've done conned all of them once or twice. They know what you are.

"And you," he said to Nick, "you're the one who got me hooked up with Sosebee in the first place. Do you know how much that little shit is gonna cost me?"

Eddie clenched his fist, opened it back up, and ran his fingers through his hair. "Goddamn you. I'm not leaving until I get my money."

Whitlaw flashed his SOB smile again. "Son, I'm doing you a favor by not giving you that money. Hell, it'd be negligent to fill your pockets with that kind of cash. You'd probably be dead by morning, a needle sticking out of your arm in some alley."

Whitlaw scratched his chin in a thoughtful way. "I'd hate to pick up the paper and read that. It'd really break my heart. 'Eddie Del Canto, pro wrestler, found dead in alleyway. Drugs suspected.'" Whitlaw dotted the air with his finger, as though he were following the lines of Eddie's obituary. "'A once-promising talent, Del Canto never lived up to his potential.'"

Whitlaw finally pushed the wrong button. Eddie clenched his fists again and took a step toward the boss. Nick grabbed Eddie by the back of the arm and stopped him.

"Whoa, hoss. Keep your cool."

Captain Love stepped forward and tried to act as peacemaker. He had his hands up in the air—palms open—as though he were approaching a twitchy rottweiler.

"Come on, Eddie. Take it easy. Why don't you let me drive you down to the strip and buy you a beer."

"Fuck off, Ronnie. I quit drinking."

That proclamation could have best been described as breaking news.

Eddie gave Whitlaw the finger, then turned around and lumbered toward the door. Whitlaw smirked as though he knew it was all over, that he'd gotten the best of Eddie and Nick and they were going to walk out of there like a couple of jobbers, with their tails between their legs. All in all, it didn't seem like such a bad ending to me. We all could have imagined a lot worse.

And then Nick pulled out the shooting wedge and leveled it at Whitlaw. The act caught us all by surprise. My heart jumped up and took off like Secretariat.

"Open the fucking safe," Nick said.

Whitlaw somehow managed to flinch and smile at the same time. "What safe? This ain't no goddamn bank."

Nick grabbed the front of Whitlaw's warm-up jacket and leaned into his face. "Open it," he growled.

Whitlaw pushed Nick's hand aside and straightened his jacket. "Get your hands off my damn Tacchini, boy. This is a two-hundred-dollar warm-up suit."

By now, Eddie had turned around to see what was happening. He appeared to be as shocked as the rest of us.

Whitlaw surveyed the situation (Love, Little Dick, and the girls already had their hands in the air) and it drained some of the piss out of him. He decided it was time to negotiate.

"I tell you what I'll do," he said. "I'll write each of you a check for a grand. But that's it. That's as far as my rope stretches."

Nick just laughed. Eddie stepped back up to the front of the room and took his place beside Nick.

"You think we're fucking idiots?" Eddie said. "I haven't taken that many folding chairs to the head."

Nick stuck the muzzle of the BB gun to Whitlaw's temple and bluffed his ass off. "Open the safe, and get the goddamn money, or I'm gonna paint another horsey picture up there on the wall."

Whitlaw slipped off his Guccis, climbed atop the sofa cushions, and swung the Secretariat painting away from the wall. Sure enough, there was a safe right where Nick said there would be one.

"You just dug your own graves," Whitlaw said. "Five of them, to be exact. I don't even know these other three characters, but I'll get you. You can bet your fucking ass on it."

He pulled out stacks of green bills. They were clean, and they looked like little cakes. Dewey found a Burdines shopping bag in a closet. He held it out so that Whitlaw could drop the money into it. Meanwhile, Cash and I walked around the condo jerking the phone cords out of the wall. Cash used the cords to hog-tie the Captain and Little Dick. As for the girls, we told them to get the hell out of there and keep their mouths shut. We gave them two hundred dollars apiece from Whitlaw's stash, and they seemed more than obliged to follow our instructions.

It appeared everything was taken care of. My heart had even slowed to a trot. But then Whitlaw reached into the safe one last time and produced his trump card: a .357 Magnum.

"I couldn't interest y'all in a handgun, could I?" He cackled and then hopped down from the sofa. He slipped his feet back into his Guccis and leveled the gun at Nick's chest. Nick swallowed hard and leveled his shooting wedge at Whitlaw.

Whitlaw was grinning like Mr. Ed. "Well, what do we have here?" he asked.

Nick clenched his jaw like a gunslinger. "I believe they call it a Mexican standoff."

"Quit trying to jerk me off," Whitlaw said. "That's a fucking air pistol."

"The hell it is," Nick said.

Whitlaw snorted. "You fucking half-wit, I've been collecting guns all my life. You don't think I'd know something like that? That's a twenty-two Daisy. You probably paid fifteen dollars for that thing at Western Auto."

"So what if I did?" Nick asked. "I don't think you'd look too good with a glass eye."

Whitlaw laughed. "You couldn't hit a goddamn bull in the ass with that thing, much less my eye. Besides which, if I decide to pull the trigger on this bad boy, I'll blow a hole right through you and take out your fat friend standing there behind you."

When he heard this, Dewey edged closer to me.

"Now quit fucking around and drop it," Whitlaw said, "before I really get pissed."

A helpless feeling washed over me. It was like being in the backseat of a car as it spun out of control, the steering wheel just out of my reach.

"Plan A," Cash whispered. "We should have put his ass in the trunk when we had the chance."

Nick eyed the muzzle of the Magnum, and, ever so slowly, lowered his arm to his side. He looked at the floor and sighed like he'd just dumped an approach shot into the water.

Whitlaw grabbed the shooting wedge and stuffed it into the elastic waist of his pants, then he motioned toward the door with the Magnum.

"All of you," he said, "get your asses over there. Slow and easy, too.

Any of you get cute, and I'll pick off two or three of your buddies before you even know what happened."

Dewey's face had turned whiter than Whitlaw's carpet. Cash, though, looked like he was trying to think his way out of the jam. It was a welcome sight, seeing how my own mind had already kicked itself into high gear.

"Goddammit," Whitlaw said, "this is the last fucking thing I need right now. Why couldn't you two fucking leave well enough alone?"

I'd gathered from my encounter with Dot Knox that it was sometimes best not to answer a question. Obviously, Eddie had not learned the same lesson.

"Why couldn't you not be a greedy prick?" he asked Whitlaw.

"Fuck you," Whitlaw said. "I'll have your goddamn asses dumped in the swamp with the gators. Won't nobody ever find you."

He kept the gun on us, but edged over to the corner of the living room, where Cash had hog-tied the Captain and Dick. He tried to unfasten them with his free hand, but Cash's knots were unyielding.

"Who the fuck did this?" Whitlaw asked.

Cash raised his hand.

"Get your ass over here, Mr. Eagle Scout. Untie these boys."

Cash walked over and surveyed his handiwork. "Can't do it," he told Whitlaw.

"Fuck you," Whitlaw said. "Don't tell me you can't do it. You tied it, you can fucking untie it."

"I need a knife," Cash said.

"Yeah, and I need a fucking blow job. But y'all screwed that up for me, didn't you?"

Cash held up his hands as if they were useless in the matter. The gesture really pissed off Whitlaw. He swung the gun around and aimed it at Cash, flat out turning his back to us.

"I said get down on your goddamn knees and untie those boys. Now you fucking do it, or I'll kill you where you stand. I'll call the sheriff of this county, who hunts in my dove field and happens to be a close, personal friend of mine. I'll tell him you were breaking and entering, and he won't give a good goddamn."

With Whitlaw railing like a maniac, I seized the opportunity. He was about four quick strides away from me. It was a gamble whether I could reach him before he turned back around. But somehow, that felt appropriate. I grabbed the Kenny Rogers guitar, which was perched in its stand beside me, raised it over my shoulder, and made a charge. I had the back of Whitlaw's head in my sights, sizing it up like a high hanging curveball.

Whitlaw was still yelling at Cash, not paying us any attention. Unfortunately, Little Dick gave him the heads-up.

I was still a couple of strides away from Whitlaw, when he spun in his Guccis. "What the hell?" Those were the last words he spoke before pulling the trigger.

I don't remember hearing it, but I saw the flash from the muzzle, like a hiccup of flames. I didn't feel a thing. I kept moving forward. Cash had already reached around from behind Whitlaw and pulled his arm down to his side. I was swooping in for the knockout blow, when the guitar began to feel strange in my hand. At first it felt lopsided, and then hot, as if it were melting, as if Whitlaw's bullet had caught the neck of the instrument and set it afire. First, my hand burned, and then my arm and my shoulder. I took my best swing. I tried to get the good hip rotation, arm extension, and everything behind it. I was thinking short and compact, just like Bob Horner's stroke. But nothing happened. The guitar never came down. Instead, I found myself standing dead still, as if I'd come up against an unforgiving wall. My ears were ringing, and Cash and Whitlaw were still on the floor wrestling. First, Eddie jumped into the fray with Cash, and then Dewey. I still wanted to get in on the action, but I couldn't take a step forward. In fact, my knees had turned to water. My head was pounding and I was nauseous, and the shaggy white carpet was coming up to greet me. I saw Nick's face, and then I was sinking into the lake again, down to the bottom of a brown water cove, the muck pulling at me as I reached out for a pair of hands that were too far away from me, still hoping they might lift me up one more time.

40

The first person I saw was a girl with dark hair.

"Rachel?"

"No, I'm Gail. You stay quiet now. You don't need to be moving around."

My body felt heavy, my pulse lurching as if my veins were filled with hardening cement.

The next face belonged to Cash. But just as I'd lined him up, my eyelids betrayed me.

"Hey, man, can you hear me?"

The best I could manage was a grunt.

"Listen," Cash said, "Whitlaw got a piece of you—in the shoulder. You're at the county hospital. We told them we found you on the road, no ID or nothing. But they're gonna have the cops here soon enough. We gotta get you out of here."

I understood what was required of me. But every time I blinked, I would sink into a sweet and peaceful darkness where it seemed the cops would never find me.

"Unhook the damn IV," Dewey said. "Hell, they've pumped him full of Dilaudid."

My peace was finally broken by a searing pain. It felt like my shoulder had been pierced with a white-hot railroad spike. The pain shot right across my jaw, locking it up so that I could barely utter a profanity. And then I realized that Dewey and Cash had lifted me out of the bed.

"Can you walk?" Cash asked.

"Do I have a fucking choice?"

Dewey braced me against the wall while Cash checked the hallway.

Standing there I began to shiver, soaked in a cold sweat, swelling up with nausea.

"How bad is it?" I asked Dewey.

"Went in one side, came out the other," he said. "Missed all the bones and arteries. You've got the luck of the Cartwrights."

I finally looked down to check myself out. Someone had dressed me in a green hospital gown. My right arm was in a sling, bandaged close to my body. My gear-shifting arm, of all things.

"I don't think I can drive," I told Dewey.

Cash laughed. "I'll take care of that."

"What about Nick?" I asked.

Dewey's expression turned sour. "They got their damn money, and then we tied up Whitlaw and got the hell out of there. Nick wanted to come to the hospital with us, but we threatened to put his ass in the trunk if he didn't get the hell out of town."

"That's good," I said. "You made the right call."

And then Dewey smiled. I couldn't imagine what he might have found so amusing at that particular moment.

"What?"

"The guitar," he said. "We couldn't get you to let go of Kenny Rogers's guitar. Even after your ass had been shot. Man, you were holding on to that thing for dear life. It's still in the car."

The sun had just finished creeping above the treetops when we pulled up to Nick and Dewey's house. Cash and Dewey helped me inside and got me situated on the couch. Cash told me he'd clean the blood out of the Chevelle and drop it off at Lance Hillin's house. After that, he was going to visit a dentist friend of his. He said he'd have the guy come over and take a look at my shoulder.

"A dentist?"

"He can keep the wound clean," Cash said, "give you some pain-killers and antibiotics. And trust me, you're gonna need those fucking painkillers."

I was already in need. Whatever they'd given me in Pensacola had worn off, and now it felt like Willie Stargell had taken a round of BP on my shoulder.

Dewey turned on the TV for me and went back to his bedroom to get some shut-eye. I was wide awake, the pain throbbing in time with my pulse, banging out an angry 4/4 beat. I lay there in my old, familiar spot, with the morning light cutting a line across the room and a man reading the news on the TV screen. They were showing films of people rioting in Iran.

I can't say if it was the pain, or the lingering effects of the drugs they had given me in the hospital, but I had a sudden and strong desire to climb inside a liquor bottle. I pushed myself off the sofa and walked unsteadily to the kitchen, stopping on my way to silence the television. Dewey had a fifth of Wild Turkey under the sink, and I took hold of it with my good hand and carried it back to the living room, passing by the sofa and taking a seat in the recliner.

The place hadn't changed since I'd climbed through the window back in the spring, other than the blue panties being rescued from the television set. The bluesmen still had their spots, as did Dewey's drum kit and Nick's Les Paul. The aluminum foil still rose from the rabbit ears like unwieldy vines. But none of it felt like destiny anymore, at least not my own. I felt sad for Nick, that he'd never get to sit in this spot again and play his guitar, sliding a beer bottle up and down the strings.

Rachel picked up on the fourth ring. Her voice stunned me. It was like I hadn't heard it in years. I couldn't say a word. The heavy ache returned to my shoulder and spread through my whole body. I almost dropped the receiver out of my good hand.

"Hello?" She sounded sleepy, then irritated. "Who is this?"

Finally, she hung up.

I dialed her number again. This time she picked up on the first ring.

"Who the fuck is it?!"

I said her name.

There was a long pause. "Luke? Is that you?"

"It's me," I said.

"Jesus, what's wrong? You sound like shit."

"I've been up all night. I just got back from Florida."

"Florida? What were you doing in Florida?"

"I'm sorry," I told her. "I hope I didn't wake you up. I just had some things I wanted to tell you."

"That's okay." Her irritation had changed to a tone of concern. "You can tell me."

What I'd called to tell her is that I wanted the privilege of running away with her and fucking up her life, because if I didn't do it, somebody else would, and I thought that I could do it in a way that she'd never regret, even after we parted ways. I wanted to tell her that if I was about to die, that if I was floating in a swamp with a bullet in my back and gators on my flanks, my last thought would be of her.

But then I couldn't get any of it to come out. And what I ended up saying was something completely different. "Can I come see you? Right now? I know it's early and all, but I was just thinking about you and . . ."

It all came out too fast, and the desperation got the best of me. I felt the catch in my voice, and I stopped myself before it became something else.

The phone line was silent.

"Luke?" she said. "Are you still there? Are you okay?"

"I'm sorry. I shouldn't have called so early. It's just been a shitty couple of days and . . ."

"Don't apologize," she said. "Of course you can come over. Do I need to come get you? You don't sound like you need to be driving."

"I don't have a license," I said.

"Yeah, I'm aware of that," she said. "Are you at Nick's? I'll come get you."

"And bring some Juicy Fruit," I said. "Don't forget the Juicy Fruit."

"Okay, don't worry. I'll bring some." She sounded afraid. "Luke?"

"Yeah?"

"Hang up so I can come get you."

"Okay."

41

I suppose it broke Mrs. Coyle's heart to walk in from her AA meeting and see me on that couch again, to see me back in her daughter's life. Rachel and I told her that I'd been in a car accident. Considering my history, she never questioned the explanation.

I was sober by then, having slept through the afternoon and right into prime time. Rachel was sitting on the floor with Brute's big dome resting in her lap. She was looking up at me, shaking her head as if I was the sorriest sight imaginable.

"Does it still hurt?" she asked.

"What do you think?"

Rachel sighed. "I think you should be in the fucking hospital."

"I already told you, no hospitals. Cash knows a guy who's gonna look at it."

"But you said he was a dentist."

"So?"

"So, that is—without a doubt—the stupidest thing I've ever heard in my life. You could get an infection and die."

The TV was playing with the volume down low. HBO was showing *Midnight Express* again. Billy Hayes scampered down a dark Turkish street, making his escape.

"I'm still leaving next week," she said.

That got my attention. Somehow, I'd completely lost track of time. It all came back to me. Only a week remained until my second at-bat against Dot Knox.

Rachel sat there with her hair hanging over one eye. I liked the way that she'd duck her head and make it happen. She'd done it a lot when we used to sit in her car talking, making our plans.

The thought of never seeing her again was worse than being shot. "Can I go?"

Her gaze fell. She began to stroke the top of Brute's head. "I don't know. All that stupid shit we planned, none of it will ever happen. You know that, don't you?"

"I know."

"So, what's the point?" she asked.

She looked up again, pushing her hair off her face and tucking it behind an ear. Her eyes were clear and dark, her lips parted to speak. I didn't care if she could make sense of anything or not. I just wanted her to keep talking until the pain went away.

Cash brought his dentist by the apartment the following afternoon. The old man appeared competent enough, although his own teeth were the color of brass. He gave me Percocets (firmly endorsed by Lance Hillin), some antibiotics and antibiotic cream, and then he showed Rachel how to rebandage the wound.

With the examination complete, I lay back down on the sofa. Dr. Gums, as Cash called him, stood up straight and smiled, stroking the gray tuft of hair on his chin.

"You're lucky," he said. "I've seen a lot worse."

"In your dentist office?" I asked.

He chuckled and glanced at Cash as though I'd amused him. And then he headed out the door. Rachel followed him, leaving for her shift at the Holiday Inn.

I asked Cash if he was sure that Dr. Gums was on the up-and-up. Cash was sitting on the arm of the sofa, wearing his Phillies hat and watching an Australian Rules Football match on ESPN.

He pointed to the screen. "Those motherfuckers oughta wear some pads."

"Did you hear my question?"

He dismissed my doubts with a wave of his hand. "I've known Doc since I was a kid. He's a good man."

"Where'd he get his training?"

"Reidsville."

"The prison?"

"Look," Cash said, "it's a good study environment. You think he had any distractions? Hell, no. Plus, he studied some veterinary medicine. That's how he knows about wounds and stuff. The man's damn near a genius. He could treat you *and* that fucking dog if he had to."

Cash eyed Brute with some concern, recalling their initial tussle.

"So what's your plan?" he asked. "You and Miss Tempo."

"Assuming I get my license back, we're going to Illinois."

Cash nodded as if it made enough sense. And then he seemed to remember something.

"I saw Claudia last night."

"Where?"

He appeared to regret having brought up the subject. "The Cove Bar, over at the Holiday Inn. I was meeting some people there."

"What was she doing?" I had to ask him, even though I had a pretty good idea.

Cash took his time, trying to find the appropriate words. "She was being entertained by a gentleman."

"Wade Briggs?"

Cash shook his head. "Younger guy. Way younger."

"Was she drunk?"

"Man, don't put me on the spot like that."

"Just tell me. I don't give a shit."

"That's what you say. But if I tell you she was drinking those Harvey Wallbangers, you're gonna blame my ass for it."

"So, she really was drunk."

Cash shifted his eyes to the TV set. "She and this guy were all over each other," he said. "It was a damn show—for mature adults only."

"Okay, I got the picture."

"See there," he said. "Didn't I say you were gonna get mad?"

I changed the subject, asking if he'd heard anything through the pipeline about Whitlaw's situation with the Feds.

"I called a buddy of mine down in Gulf Shores. He hadn't heard any big news."

"I guess Whitlaw's in Cabo by now."

"Probably drinking tequila with a couple of señoritas," Cash said.

"What about Nick and Eddie? You think they made it to Chula Vista?"

Cash grunted and went back to watching the Australian Rules Football.

"I tell you what I think. I think you're doing the right thing getting the hell out of here."

He didn't have to say any more. I already knew how he felt about people, how you couldn't help them, how they never changed, even though they might vow to do just that when their ass was in a sling. Whitlaw's bullet had enlightened me—there was nothing I could really do for Nick or Claudia. But without their predicaments and perils to consider, it hardly felt like I even existed anymore.

Cash glanced at his watch. "I gotta hit the road. Somebody's coming to take a look at the boat."

"To buy it?"

"No, he ain't that stupid. But I'm hoping he can stop it from leaking."

He walked to the door, stopping to survey the Kenny Rogers guitar, which was propped against the wall. Cash had brought it with him, thinking, for some reason, that I might want it as a souvenir.

"The Gambler didn't know when to fold 'em," Cash said, and then he started laughing.

I pushed myself up so that I could gaze over the back of the sofa. "Go to hell. And why don't you take that thing with you? I don't want it."

Cash looked at me like I'd completely lost my mind. "Man, I'd be embarrassed to have this thing in my house. Besides, you oughta keep it. It's a helluva conversation piece. Still got your blood on it and everything."

He was still laughing when he walked out the door.

42

The Feds finally made a play on Whitlaw's cocaine ring. The story hit the *Gazette* on Saturday, two days before our departure for Illinois. The article said that seven of Whitlaw's top associates had been rounded up, along with 150 kilos of cocaine. Whitlaw, himself, had yet to be found. There were thirty-two total indictments. Two of those named were already under incarceration in Texas, having been picked up a day earlier for traffic violations and marijuana possession. I knew immediately it was Nick and Eddie.

My shoulder still hurt, but I was finally able to walk around without feeling like I might pass out. I'd even come to the table to share the morning doughnuts with Mrs. Coyle. She'd actually gone out and bought them herself.

"What's the matter?" she asked.

She'd just sat down across from me. Before I knew it, I'd told her the truth.

"I think my brother's in jail."

I showed her the front-page article. She read it quickly and then looked back up at me, her face almost desperate, as if the two of us needed to do something about it.

"It's all right," I told her. "It was bound to happen."

We sat there a moment longer. I managed to take a few halfhearted bites off my glazed doughnut.

"So, when are you two leaving?" she asked.

"Rachel hasn't said anything to you?"

Mrs. Coyle stared down at the table.

"Monday," I said. "But she was planning to go, anyway—even if I hadn't come back."

She took a sip of coffee. "It's okay. I don't blame you."

"Rachel doesn't hate you," I said.

Our first stop was Claudia's house. Rachel waited in the car. I still had my key, so I let myself in through the carport door, stepping inside the sunny kitchen. I was carrying the Kenny Rogers guitar in my good hand.

Claudia walked in from the living room, wearing the same blue suit she'd worn for my court date with Dot Knox. She had her hair pulled back, lipstick on her mouth, hurrying through like she was running late.

"You going to court for something?"

She poured some coffee at the counter, took a sip, and made a face. That's when I realized she was hungover.

"I got a job at the bank."

"Teller?"

"Junior teller."

"What does that mean?"

"It means I've gotta be detail-oriented, good with customers, and excellent in math."

She made it sound as if those were unreasonable demands. And then she looked up long enough to notice my bad wing.

"My God, what happened?"

"I fell down."

There was some truth to the explanation, but I was quick to change the subject before she could press for details.

"Did you hear about Nick?"

She set the cup on the counter and frowned. "Wade told me."

"Did he know any details?"

"He said they'd probably be extradited to Florida. It doesn't look good."

She pointed at my sling again. "Please tell me you're not involved in this."

I shook my head, and then I held up the guitar.

"What's that?"

"Nick wanted me to give it to you."

"Did he steal it?"

"No, he didn't steal it."

She reached out and touched the neck, turning it toward her. "Pretty nice," she said. "A Martin."

I showed her the Kenny Rogers autograph. "I know you're not fond of the Gambler. I thought maybe you could rub that off with some paint thinner."

Claudia smiled and propped the instrument against the kitchen table. "That was sweet of you," she said. "I mean, sweet of Nick, too."

She asked if I wanted some breakfast, though all she had in the cabinets was an old box of Raisin Bran that Charlie had left behind.

"I can't stay. I've got somebody waiting on me."

She looked disappointed. "That's okay. Maybe you can stop by later. Bank closes at noon today."

I explained that I probably wouldn't be doing that. I told her that Rachel and I were leaving for Illinois in a couple of days.

"So, it's been six months already?"

"Yeah, it went by pretty fast."

"I told you it would."

She ducked her head and peeked out the window at Rachel's car.

"Is that what you're driving?"

"Yeah, I just hope it lasts for six hundred miles."

Claudia smiled. "Sure doesn't look like a Lyndell Fulmer car."

We stood there for a moment, unsure of ourselves. Finally, she reached out and patted my shoulder.

"I've been wanting to tell you something," she said. "I should have told you before now."

"It's okay," I said. "You don't have to say it, if it's too hard."

She gave me this curious look. "If what's too hard?"

"What you're going to tell me," I said. "It doesn't really matter, anyway."

"All I wanted to tell you," she said, "is that I'm happy with the way you've grown up since last spring. You've become the kind of person I always hoped you'd be. Loyal and kind and independent."

She stopped herself and smiled a little. "It's just good knowing that

I don't have to worry about you. And it hasn't been any of my doing, either. It was all yours. You went out and grew up, and I'm happy about that."

She walked back over to the sink, reached up and switched on the radio. I didn't have any idea what to say. But that was all right. For once, I didn't feel like I had to say a word.

43

There was no mistaking Speedy Brown's voice, even as it advanced from behind me at the gas tanks. I was filling Rachel's car at the Amoco when he walked up and squeezed my shoulder.

"How's my little puppy dog?"

I turned around and shook his hand. He was wearing a brand-new Crimson Tide baseball cap.

"Hey, when did you get out?"

Speedy clucked his tongue. "Three-seventeen P.M., day before yesterday."

He asked if Cash and I were going racing later that evening. I told him Cash was taking a break from the track.

"That's too bad. I like racing against him. He's a good driver. Chicken shit, but good."

Speedy squinted as if reading a transcript of what he'd just said. "Don't tell him I said that."

I made no promises. Instead, I gave him an update on Brute, how he'd settled down a little and had gone after only a couple of people since Rachel had adopted him. One of the incidents had actually been my own fault for leaving the apartment door open. Brute went after a guy who was walking through the parking lot with a sackful of Krystals. The man had to take refuge atop a conversion van.

"So, when did you get shot?" Speedy asked.

He was the first person to actually figure out the circumstances of my injury before I could spin a web of deceit.

"How'd you know I got shot?"

"That's just the way they wrap 'em up," he said. "I've seen enough of 'em."

Speedy was looking for work and asked if I'd had a sniff of any opportunities. Seeing how he liked cars and was also quite the conversationalist, I told him I might know of a position for which he was perfectly qualified.

"You mind wearing a beeper?"

"Fuck, no," he said. "I'd wear a codpiece, if I had to."

I leaned into the car window and borrowed a pen from Rachel, then I wrote Lance Hillin's phone number on the inside of a matchbook. I handed it to Speedy and told him he might want to lose the Bama hat before he met the T-Bone King.

I asked Rachel if she wanted to get out of the car to witness the great floating turd that was Cash's houseboat.

"I'll take my chances on living to see it another day," she said.

She lay back in the driver's seat and turned up the stereo. She had a Television cassette in the deck—that croaky singer of theirs warbling over a reggae beat. She leaned her head against the side window and stared out the windshield, her thoughts obviously far away.

Cash and Dewey were sitting on the rear deck of the *Register,* drinking Michelob and wearing jackets to fend off the wind. Teddy P. was playing on Cash's boom box.

"It's the Gambler," Dewey said.

He and Cash laughed like he'd actually said something original. They were sharing a joint. I did the only natural thing, which was to flip them off.

I tried to be careful with my step, but soon realized the boat deck was completely dry. That wasn't the only noticeable improvement aboard the vessel. Fresh plywood framed the cabin, and a shiny black Evinrude was latched to the back side. Last, but not least, the fishy smell had been greatly reduced, if not quite squelched.

"Not bad," I said. "You planning on keeping it?"

"Fuck, no," Cash said. "I'm keeping my costs down. Spit and shine, and then I'm selling in the spring. The man at the marina thinks I can take a two-grand turnaround on it."

He passed the joint to Dewey, who took a toke and offered it up to me. I declined the opportunity, having decided to go without for a while.

"I got this shit from your buddy at the Holiday Inn," Dewey said.

"Who, Stan?"

"Yeah, we had to find somebody new with Nick gone."

He sounded apologetic, though I understood the situation.

"It ain't half bad," Cash said.

"Must've been grown near some water," Dewey said.

The wind kicked up and jangled a bell hanging from a little sailboat. The green water lapped at the shore nearby.

Dewey asked how I'd gotten to the marina.

"In the passenger seat," I told him.

Cash craned his neck to peer over the side of the boat. "Who's that waiting for you? Miss Tempo?"

He and Dewey started giggling. I'd quickly come to learn that it wasn't much fun being around stoned people when I wasn't stoned as well.

I asked Dewey if he'd remembered to bring Nick's camera. I'd stashed it back in Nick's closet after taking care of business with Muskgrave. Dewey reached up under the beach chair and pulled out a paper sack. The Nikon lay wrapped in the soft, crinkled paper.

"What'd you want it for, anyway? You got a shoot tonight in Muskgrave's boudoir?"

"Nah, I just thought I might start taking some pictures. Maybe I'll send y'all some from Illinois."

I lifted the camera to my eye and told them to smile. Instead of saying "cheese," Dewey said "gonorrhea." The shutter clicked, but there was no film in the camera. It would have been a good shot, too.

Cash passed along the number of his bondsman friend in Skokie, Illinois. He told me to give the man a call when I was ready to get started in the business. I wasn't just yet, but I figured it was a good idea to leave the door open.

"And try to stay in touch," Dewey said. "Give us a call."

I told him I would, though I knew that my promise was as useless as that empty camera. I felt certain that we'd all forget each other soon enough. I would have bet a bag of Stan's weed on it.

44

The defroster wasn't doing its job, so I wiped the fog off the windshield with my sleeve. I was waiting for Rachel, sitting in the Peugeot in front of her mother's apartment building, its white brick shaded a bruised gray in the rainy morning light.

I'd been the one to send her back upstairs to wake her mother and tell her good-bye, clutching the car keys in my hand and refusing to hand them over until she relented. She hadn't been too happy about it. She even threatened to punch me in the shoulder. And now I had this feeling she wasn't coming back down.

I reached over to lay on the horn but caught myself and decided against it. Our driving directions, scribbled on a paper napkin, were taped to the dash. The tape was starting to give way, curling back from the fake Italian leather. I just sat there in the passenger seat and watched it. The car engine idled. The rain fell softly. Nothing moved. And all our plans had changed.

The thing is, she hadn't even known the route to Champaign in the first place. For all her talking and planning, she'd hardly even considered the actual getting-there part of it. I had to call Cash the night before and ask him to plot us a course on his road atlas. Rachel was sitting on the sofa not saying a word, just staring off at the pictureless wall.

My meeting with Dot Knox was set to begin in eight minutes. I already had our suitcases in the trunk, those and a thirteen-inch RCA that I'd bought with some of my Lance Hillin money. Brute was sawing logs atop an army blanket that I had spread across the backseat. He was primed for nine hours of car captivity, courtesy of Sominex-laced Ken-L Ration.

I could have never been mad at her for changing her mind. That's not to say a good bit of hope hadn't sunk right down into the bottoms of my new Fayva dress shoes. And despite everything, this was still a situation that called for action. I understood that much very clearly. And so I opened the car door, walked around, and took charge of the driver's seat. One way or the other, I was going to get my goddamn license back.

I ditched the shoulder sling, eased out of the apartment complex, and hit the main road. My shoulder throbbed when I changed gears, but it still felt good to do it again. It felt good to be in control. I pushed that little car's motor like I'd pushed it the night the helicopter was behind us. The wipers squeaked and the defroster fan hummed. The big lake was hidden in the fog.

I parked on the street, across from the Justice Building's lot, so that no one would see that I had driven myself there. Brute raised his head, looked around the car, and whimpered. I reached back and patted his head.

"It's all right, big boy. I'll take you home soon as I'm done here. We'll go get us some Krystals."

Stepping out of the car in my new suit and tie, I felt my heart slow down a bit. And then, gazing up at the sky, I spotted an airliner among the gunmetal clouds, a mere speck on a far-flung trajectory. The clouds were moving east, the tiny airplane west, and the rain was falling from the sky at an angle. I had no idea where I was going to land at the end of the day, where I might sleep or what I was going to drive when I got there. My shoulder was hurting, and my suit was wet, and despite my best efforts, I was still late for my court date with Dot Knox. But for an instant, all of that stuff reassured me. It all felt like a miracle, everything that had brought me here.

And then a car passed on the street, an older Valiant moving fast through the rain, leaving a spray in its wake. The brake lights shone, and then the Plymouth turned and disappeared at the intersection. I never got a look at the person, or people, inside the car. It could have been a man sipping whiskey on his way to work, or a woman rushing home from a rendezvous with her lover. For all I knew, it might have been a grown-up and a little kid, one of them driving and the other leaning back, talking with his eyes closed: "If you remember one thing, let it be this . . ."

What I remembered was slinging that Chevelle around the curves on Green Lake Road, tires squealing and spitting up loose dirt from the shoulder of the road. As the pavement straightened, I dropped the Muncie down into fourth, punched the accelerator, and let the wheel unwind. The speed pushed my head back into all of that space between me and the seat. I held on tight to the wheel. It felt like a hurricane was trying to blow me into the backseat. The engine was screaming, piercing right through my heart.

Lyndell stopped playing piano on the dashboard long enough to applaud me. "That's the Fulmer touch," he declared. "That's smooth as glass. Goose-shit smooth. Johnnie Walker Black smooth."

He laughed a little and slapped at my shoulder in a gentle way. "Hey, how about this one?"

I took my eyes off the road to give him my full attention.

Lyndell was grinning. "Smoother than Charlie Rich in a silk suit."

We both started laughing. We were hurtling through the dark with trees and water all around, laughing like a couple of lunatics. Lyndell reached over, grabbed my arm, and squeezed it. Then he leaned in like he was going to tell me a secret.